secret of the rose

D0115075

WEST FARGO PUBLIC LIBRARY
109 3RD STREET EAST
WEST FARGO, ND 58078

WITHDRAWN

secret of the rose

The ELEVENTH HOUR

MICHAEL PHILLIPS

Tyndale House Publishers, Inc., Carol Stream, Illinois

Visit Tyndale's exciting Web site at www.tyndale.com

TYNDALE and Tyndale's quill logo are registered trademarks of Tyndale House Publishers, Inc.

The Eleventh Hour

Copyright © 1993 by Michael Phillips. All rights reserved.

Cover photograph of woman © by Taxi/Getty Images. All rights reserved.

Cover photograph of mountain range © by Photodisc. All rights reserved.

Cover photographs of flag, yellow roses, single red rose, pink roses and the estate © by Photos.com. All rights reserved.

Author photograph by John Ward.

Floor plans of German mansion and map of Europe copyright © 1993 by Hugh Claycombe. All rights reserved.

Black and white illustration of German mansion copyright © 1993 by Michael Hackett. All rights reserved.

Cover designed by Jennifer Lund

Published in association with the literary agency of Alive Communications, Inc., 7680 Goddard Street, Suite 200, Colorado Springs, CO 80920.

Scripture quotations are taken from the *Holy Bible*, King James Version.

The Scripture quotations contained in chapter 57 are taken from *The New English Bible*, copyright © 1970, Oxford University Press, Cambridge University Press.

This novel is a work of fiction. Names, characters, places, and incidents are either the product of the author's imagination or are used fictitiously. Any resemblance to actual events, locales, organization, or persons living or dead is entirely coincidental and beyond the intent of either the author or publisher.

Library of Congress Cataloging-in-Publication Data

Phillips, Michael R., date.
  p. cm. — (Secret of the rose ; 1)
  The eleventh hour / Michael Phillips.
  ISBN-13: 978-0-8423-3932-2
  ISBN-10: 0-8423-3932-9
  ISBN-13: 978-1-4143-0787-9 (pbk.)
  ISBN-10: 1-4143-0787-X (pbk.)
  1. Germany—History—1933-1945—Fiction. 2. Fathers and daughters—Germany—Fiction. I. Title. II. Series: Phillips, Michael R., date. Secret of the rose ; 1.
PS3566.H492E44   1993   93-4858
813'.54—dc20   CIP

Printed in the United States of America

11 10 09 08 07 06
7 6 5 4 3 2 1

CONTENTS

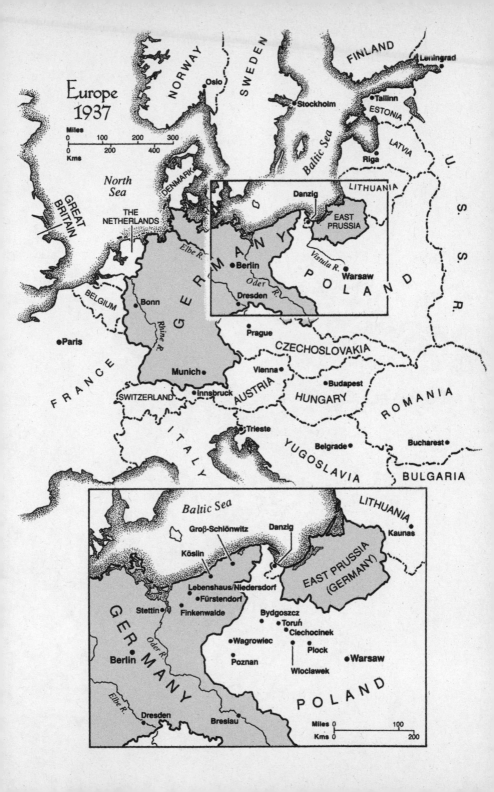

Europe
1937

Miles
0   100   200   300

Kms
0   200   400

NORWAY

SWEDEN

FINLAND

Leningrad

Oslo

Stockholm

Tallinn
ESTONIA

Baltic Sea

LATVIA

Riga

North
Sea

DENMARK

LITHUANIA

Danzig

EAST
PRUSSIA

GREAT
BRITAIN

THE
NETHERLANDS

G
E
R
M
A
N
Y

Elbe R.

Berlin

Oder R.

Vistula R.

Warsaw

POLAND

BELGIUM

Bonn

Rhine R.

Dresden

Paris

Prague

CZECHOSLOVAKIA

U.
S.
S.
R.

FRANCE

Munich

Vienna

AUSTRIA

HUNGARY

Budapest

ROMANIA

SWITZERLAND

Innsbruck

ITALY

Trieste

YUGOSLAVIA

Belgrade

Bucharest

BULGARIA

Baltic Sea

Groß-Schlönwitz

Danzig

LITHUANIA

Kaunas

Köslin

EAST PRUSSIA
(GERMANY)

Lebenshaus/Niedersdorf

Fürstendorf

Stettin

Finkenwalde

Bydgoszcz

Toruń

Ciechocinek

G
E
R
M
A
N
Y

Oder R.

Berlin

Wagrowiec

Plock

Poznan

Wloclawek

Warsaw

Elbe R.

Dresden

Breslau

POLAND

Miles 0   100

Kms 0   200

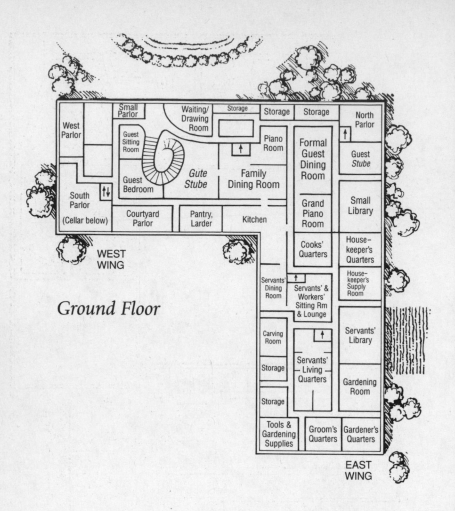

West Wing

- West Parlor
- Small Parlor
- Guest Sitting Room
- Waiting/Drawing Room
- Storage
- Storage
- Storage
- North Parlor
- Piano Room
- Guest *Stube*
- *Gute Stube*
- Guest Bedroom
- Family Dining Room
- Formal Guest Dining Room
- South Parlor (Cellar below)
- Courtyard Parlor
- Pantry, Larder
- Kitchen
- Grand Piano Room
- Small Library
- Cooks' Quarters
- House-keeper's Quarters
- House-keeper's Supply Room

Ground Floor

- Servants' Dining Room
- Servants' & Workers' Sitting Rm & Lounge
- Servants' Library
- Carving Room
- Servants' Living Quarters
- Gardening Room
- Storage
- Storage
- Tools & Gardening Supplies
- Groom's Quarters
- Gardener's Quarters

East Wing

Lebenshaus

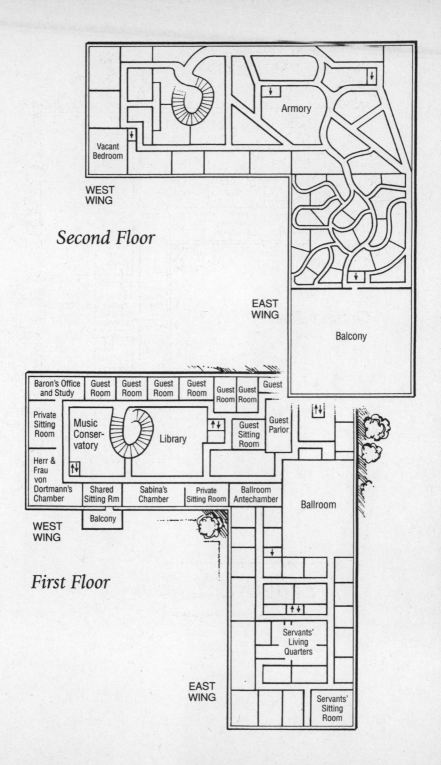

◦◦◦

Introduction

Nobody but an author could understand quite how a book takes you over and, in a sense, "writes itself."

You've all heard that phrase, I'm sure. You probably have mixed reactions to it. One of my editors, quite some time ago, in response to my attempt to explain the phenomenon, replied, "That's a little spooky, Mike . . . you don't want readers to hear you talking like *that!*"

Well, certainly, no book really does *write itself.*

It's a lot of hard work and takes a long time, and of course the author has to put in his fair share of the process and know what he's about.

Yet there really does exist a mysterious dynamic in it all. Once you set some foundational momentum in motion, characters actually do sometimes pull you along almost as if they were setting the pace and direction. Your only job is to follow where they lead!

My wife, Judy (who is intrinsically involved with me in the development of nearly every book bearing my name), and I, along with our friend Judith Pella, were all three aware of that process throughout the writing of *Robbie Taggart.* Robbie himself proved such a captivating fellow that we quite literally followed him all over the globe, waiting—and maybe here's where it gets spooky—to see what would happen to him next.

In the writing of the Stonewycke books, the two main characters, Maggie and Ian, did not even exist in the three of our minds when we began. They wandered into the story sort of accidentally, and then proceeded to take the whole thing over. Before long they were setting the course for the entire rest of the series!

Characters do that. Plots and situations and relationships do that too. There can be stories that quite literally compel themselves to be told.

The Secret of the Rose is such a story.

⤳⤲

We love roses. I gave Judy yellow roses before we were married, and we have been exchanging them ever since.

The other day, in the dead of winter, Judy picked a stray red bud that didn't seem to know the season for blooms was past off one of the bushes in our yard. The leaves were a little small, sort of a brownish green, not the lush and brilliant shapes and textures of spring. Though nicely formed, the flower itself was stinted of size, and it seemed clear this specimen would never mature to full stature. It was a "wintry" rose.

Judy clipped it with about twelve straight inches of stem, put it in a slender vase, and set it on the bathroom counter.

Something about it, however, was unique. This was no ordinary rose.

Perhaps its charm was heightened by the tiny bud-shape, which would never open into full-petaled array. Perhaps it was the strong odor of red which, in spite of the petals being tightly folded, warmed by coming inside the house, began to spread its perfume out through the bathroom and beyond. Perhaps it was the symbolism of its brave flowering in the midst of the two weeks we had just had of driving rains and frigid, fierce winds.

How did it come to find life in the midst of all that? Yet there it was, sticking up its proud, tall head—let the rain and wind do their worst.

Every time she passed the bathroom Judy could not help glancing in. There stood the small red fragrant winter rose . . . calling her . . . beckoning her to inquire into its mystery.

It was only a flower, you might say. Do you really think there's all that to read into it?

I suppose all writers have a healthy dose of poet and mystic in them. Judy and I are always looking at everyday occurrences from such allegorical and significative angles.

If it seems a little odd, you'll have to forgive us. We've been married over twenty years and still give each other roses. I suppose we're hopeless romantics. But then . . . maybe that's why I write books!

In any case, we had, during this time, been talking about and brainstorming several new book and plot ideas. Two mornings later Judy called at my office and told me about the rose she had picked.

"I can't help thinking there's a story here," she said. "Can't you just see a book called *The Rose?* It's so simple, yet full of . . . I don't know—don't you feel the mystique in it?"

"Yeah, yeah . . . right," I replied. I was busy on something else at the time. End of discussion.

Half an hour later the phone rang again. Essentially we repeated the same conversation all over again. My wife was being the romantic at that stage, not me!

Again the phone rang.

"I'm sorry," laughed Judy. "I don't mean to sound like a broken record, but I think there's something here. There's a *story* behind this rose, I'm sure of it! A mystery, a love story . . . something! Picture this scene. . . ."

By this time I was ready to listen.

Actually, in the meantime, somewhere between the second and third call, the same compelling sense of a story had begun slowly to come over me too. So now when Judy called, I found pictures and feelings and thoughts rising spontaneously out of my own awakened poetic side as well. Suddenly in my mind was the image of a man, lonely from loss, sitting in a rocking chair, holding the fragrant dead leaves of a treasured rose potpourri—

Before I could finish telling what I had envisioned, Judy was telling me of—

Well, you will read all about it soon enough!

We finished our conversation. A few minutes later Judy showed up at my office door with the red rose in hand, in a vase for my desk. She sat down and, after we both admired it a while, we began to talk once more.

Literally within a matter of minutes, we both knew that this was a story that *had* to be told, a story that compelled itself onto the page, a story that was bigger than we were. Perhaps you'll agree with my editor's comment of years ago and think all this sounds a little strange. Another editor once told me that authors were known to be somewhat of a peculiar breed, so maybe all this is in keeping with that!

But in all seriousness I say that there was a strong sense of truth about the whole (may I call it this?) revelation. It became extremely *real*, as if a *true* piece of history were being "revealed" to us, a story that our little wintry rose knew all about, because it knew the universal story of roses everywhere and was determined to tell us.

So it raised up its persistent head in the midst of the storm, and it beckoned to us. "Let me tell you of some of my brother and sister roses," it said. "They are dead now, but their hearts are preserved, and some of their petals have been crushed, so that in death they might live on. For the aroma and bouquet of a rose never dies. If but one has smelled of its glory and sighed, or smiled, or thought of a loved one, that rose has been lifted into realms of the eternal. For those who love them, even the petals have fragrance. In the hope of giving such pleasure they expend their perfumes abroad over all the lands of the earth.

"In the heart of the rose is contained the tale of love universal. For what other purpose have roses been created than to assist in the telling of that saga and to offer faint, fragrant glimpses of that greater creating Love out of which are born and in which dwell all the loves of the universe? The reminders of its sachet can be bittersweet as well as jubilant, however. Love is no respecter of feelings. And that is why I, a winter's rose, with a touch of sadness in my shriveled leaves, have come to lead you into *this* particular tale.

"I came out of the ground, not to tell you the story of the rose, but so that you might smell my sweet balm and behold the creating Love by beholding me. And, gazing into my wintry face, that you might seek and discover that story I would tell you if I could but speak of my brother and sister roses, who lived across the sea, in a time now gone and of the men and women who loved them."

So I sat down at my typewriter the next day to see if I could discover the beginning strands of the mysteries our rose may have been thinking about.

But first of all, before I even began, I paused to write these few thoughts of introduction to those of you who may someday read my words.

I nearly always wait until a book is completed before attempting to add any particular word I might have to its readers. On this occasion, however, I felt it might be appropriate to share my thoughts before the quest begins.

You see, at this moment in time, I know little more than *you* do about what may lie past the next turning of the page. I'm full of excitement and wide-eyed anticipation to find out. But I literally do not know where this story will lead, once we open the door and look back to a time, not so far behind us really, but an era in the world's history that will never come again—and that none of us will ever forget.

I do know that the tale will make itself known. The book will not write itself, but I have the sense its truths *will* tell themselves. This is not *my* story at all, but rather an account of the universal experience we each become part of every time we put a rose to our nostrils and breathe in deeply of the mysteries and secrets God placed within it.

Michael Phillips
Eureka, California

WEST FARGO PUBLIC
LIBRARY

Prologue
1961

A man sat quietly rocking in a plain oak chair.

The hair on his head shone brown and full in the sun's fading afternoon light and revealed only the beginning signs of grey. In all other respects, however, he appeared old, though his face could not readily be seen. His shoulders slumped with the sagging invisible weight of despondency.

The back-and-forth movement of the chair, slow and melancholy as it was, seemed to originate in some ethereal region having no connection whatever to his own limbs. Indeed, both arms and legs appeared to hang lifeless from the rest of his frame and, had they been so inclined, did not look as though they would contain even the modicum of strength necessary to give the wooden pendulum upon which he sat the rhythmic movement it now somehow exhibited.

He wore the aspect of one altogether dead to life, both the life around him and, if there chanced to be any left, that within him as well.

The only sign that he in fact was alive, besides the slow creaking motion of the oak runners over the boards of the floor, was a slight movement of the fingers that lay in his lap, though what they held could not immediately be seen.

Around him, the Bavarian mountainside was idyllic, peaceful, and still, just the consoling balm his soul needed after the tragedy.

The green of the forests, the snow that yet covered parts of the ground, the bells tinkling their random carols from around thick bovine necks, an occasional hiking yodeler who could be heard, and glimpses far to the south of the towering peaks of purest white—all these added their own soothings to his spirit and reminded him of letters from long ago, even as those who cared for him watched over the healing of his wound and leg.

Even if he did walk again, however, what did it matter, he thought. What would anything ever mean again . . . without *her* to share it with?

Life had been so good, so rich, so full of joy! He had never imagined it was possible to know such happiness!

Then so suddenly and cruelly had the evil hand of fate snatched it all away!

So it seemed, at least, in his more disconsolate moments, though deep inside he tried to convince himself otherwise. He did not believe in fate any more than she had, though during these days of darkness, it was very difficult not to slip back into old patterns of thought.

He knew what she would say, that all things turned out good in the end. That this catastrophe could ever be called good he would never accept. That it might *work for good* he occasionally allowed himself to contemplate, though such was an idea equally strenuous to lay hold of.

Yet he knew that is exactly what *she* would say. For the sake of her memory he would do his best to hang on to that truth.

Her memory—it was all he had left.

The sound of her voice in his ear . . . the musical ringing of her laughter . . . images of her teeth and lips and smile . . .

Her memory . . . and these few dried leaves in the container she had given him. What a treasure they had been to share! Now these too seemed lifeless and old, the aroma of their once-cheery perfume now turned pungent and melancholy.

He could no more keep himself from the bittersweet nostalgia than he could bring her back. Though the smell seared his heart with hot iron, it was the odor . . . of *her*.

He raised the box to his face, lifted the lid, and leaned forward to place his nostrils over the opening of the small container.

He breathed deeply the ancient fragrance of many years. He had done so a hundred times before this and would a hundred times again. For in the aroma were many secrets, and his was the only heart that knew them.

He set the small box back in his lap, a lonely tear now falling from his eye, and, continuing to rock, he let his mind drift back many years to the first day he had seen the beautiful face of the one with whom he had discovered the mystery of love.

PART I

The Mystery of the Garden—
Summer 1937

❧ 1 ❧
Among the Elite

A more distinctively old-world setting it would have been difficult to imagine.

To one side of the expansive lawn, a string quartet was playing the "Menuetto" from Mozart's *Serenade in G*.

Waiters attired in fashionable suits made their way inconspicuously among the guests. Silver trays were held aloft by the deft fingers of catering experience, and were laden with truffles and single bites of bread topped with a multitude of colored things and glasses of white and red wine from the Mosel Valley. Many other delicacies adorned various tables spread throughout the garden.

The silently moving waiters were by no means overdressed for the occasion. Most of the men wore tails and black ties, the women long gowns. The occasion had been long awaited. Everyone who was anyone in Berlin was here. Even the Führer was expected, someone had said, though he had not yet made his appearance.

The only men not sporting expensive tails were those in uniform, and more members of the *Wehrmacht* and *Luftwaffe* were indeed on hand than the dozen or two foreign diplomats present were altogether comfortable with. That Germany was rapidly becoming a military power again was certainly no secret, and the look in the faces behind the uniforms was not one to engender a feeling of security concerning the development.

Three or four there were, too, whose eyes revealed an intensity and devotion to their cause which, not many years hence, would produce such panic as to hold an entire nation of their countrymen in terror. Only a year before, the Gestapo had been combined with the SS under the command of Heinrich Himmler. Though the name of the secret police was by now well enough known, the cruel connotations of dread at the very hearing of the word were still in the embryonic stage.

The bright smiles and laughter and setting of cultured serenity that on this day surrounded Gestapo and military officers, as well as the most wealthy and influential from every walk of life in Germany, belied the ominous rumbling of world events as they approached from an ever-shrinking distance. This was Berlin, the eye of the hurricane whence all the windy tumult originated but where none of it could yet be felt. Here were the elite of society, those caught up, though they yet knew it not, in determining the direction history would march, changing the world for all time.

How could they know the facade of ebullience and good cheer for what it was?

They were part of the charade; how could they then recognize its hollow ring? The distant kettledrums of history were beating a faintly discernible cadence, though few of the Berliners in attendance that afternoon were aware of it. All the others—enjoying the quartet's rendition of *Eine Kleine Nachtmusik* and the tinkling of champagne glasses, the laughter of gaiety and the faces full of smiles—basked in the self-satisfying glow of importance, feeling the flush all the more after two or three glasses of the expensive wines Otto von Dortmann had brought in for the occasion.

The host, at the moment, was engaged in the perfunctory process of welcoming one with whom he bore a striking resemblance yet whom he seemed altogether nonchalant to see.

"So, Heinrich," Otto was saying, "Your field hands are, ah, able to carry on without you."

"Of course," answered the other with an imperceptible smile. "As well, I'm certain, as your bank without you."

"Ah, but farming and banking are too different to be compared, wouldn't you agree?"

"You are right, Otto, which is why I am content to be a farmer."

Otto forced a smile. "Well, Heinrich, I am glad your fields and cows could spare you long enough to come to the city. . . . But, now, if you'll excuse me, I need to greet my other guests."

Heinrich nodded and watched Otto walk away.

The tight smile was still spread across Otto's face. To him it had been an awkward exchange despite its brevity. In truth, he did not like it known that Heinrich was his brother. But the state of the family finances demanded that he show him at least the respect of an occasional invitation to such affairs.

The man with whom he had been speaking watched him leave with what almost looked like a twinge of compassionate sadness in his eye. Gradually the sounds of the string quartet and tinkling glasses intruded once more into his hearing.

The "country brother" of the host, however, as Otto referred to him in his absence, Baron Heinrich von Dortmann, was aware of a different strain of music that day than that which emanated from the two violins, the viola, and the cello. And it sent shivers up his spine. As it also did to the few foreign diplomats who were in attendance.

"Ah, Herr Baron, es freut mich sehr Ihnen noch einmal zu sehen," said a man to Heinrich in flawless German.

"The pleasure is all mine, Mr. McCallum," returned Dortmann. "You must let me return your favor and speak to you in *your* native tongue!"

"Favor granted then," replied the other as the two men shook hands.

"And let me add that it is a pleasure to see you once again as well. How are things in the embassy?"

A brief cloud passed over the American's countenance, though it lasted but a moment. "These are . . . uh, difficult and . . . occasionally troublesome times, Herr von Dortmann," he replied, casting an unconscious glance at one of the prominently placed Nazi flags that stood at each side of the entryway into the house as twin reminders of the times. "But then the life of a diplomat in a foreign capital is always one fraught with the unexpected and the perilous, you know!" he added.

He attempted a laugh. It was not as light in tone as that of the society ladies all around them. His laugh and the glance at the flag that preceded it were not lost on the brother of the host.

"I think I know what you mean," said Dortmann. "Please, Mr. Ambassador, you do not have to guard your words with me. I am not a Nazi, and I have few sympathies with them."

"Then in a setting such as this, Herr von Dortmann," said the other, keeping his voice low, "it seems that prudence would suggest that you do not advertise the fact."

"I'm sure you are right. I am learning that I must choose my words carefully."

The other did not speak. In truth, Thaddeus McCallum was not the ambassador, but the assistant ambassador to Germany from the United States, and he was one who knew well when to hold his tongue. His wife was dead. He had lived in Berlin with his one son for the past four years.

"Ah, here's my son—Matthew," he said, turning and drawing in a nice-looking young man of seventeen who was sauntering toward the conversation, several items from one of the food trays in hand. "Matthew, I'd like you to meet Herr von Dortmann."

"It is nice to meet you, sir," said the young man, offering his available hand.

"The pleasure is mine, young McCallum," replied Dortmann. "You seem to be raising another young diplomat to follow in your footsteps," he added to the boy's father with a smile. "My daughter—" he said, glancing around, "my daughter is here someplace. She's about your age, I would think, Matthew—oh yes, there she is with her uncle. Neither of you go away—I'd like you both to meet her."

Dortmann turned and hastily bumped his way through Otto's well-dressed and highly placed guests. Matthew busied himself with the contents of his hands, while his father shook hands with several nearby acquaintances, including the German ambassador to Washington, who was home for a month.

In a minute or two, the baron returned with a young lady on his arm who was nearly the prettiest girl Matthew had ever seen.

"Mr. McCallum . . . Matthew," said Dortmann, beaming with pleasure and obvious pride, "may I present my daughter, Sabina."

"Fräulein von Dortmann," began the assistant ambassador. *"Ich bin—"*

The baron interrupted with a laugh.

"My daughter speaks better English than I do, Mr. McCallum," he said. "And if I know her, she will be excited for an opportunity to use it!"

"Forgive me."

"Think nothing of it," replied Sabina with a musical laugh.

Her English was perfect, just as her father had noted, but yet held a delicate and charming Germanic accent.

"Miss von Dortmann, I am Thaddeus McCallum."

"I am pleased to meet you," she said, extending her hand.

"And this is my son, Matthew."

The two young people shook hands. Neither said a word. Their eyes locked for the briefest of instants, then both looked away.

It had been enough.

They had seen inside, and each knew it.

Before the moment had a chance to prolong itself to the point of becoming awkward, however, the little party of four suddenly became five.

"I say, McCallum," sounded a thickly embroidered and punctilious English accent, "jolly good show these blooming Nazis put on if they stop their *Zeig Heil*s long enough."

"A first-class shindig all right, Worchester," replied the American, laughing. "But you'd better watch what you say—the baron here speaks better English than you do!"

∽ 2 ∼
Conversation on the Lawn

As the diplomat introduced the baron to Lord Percival Worchester, Britain's new special envoy to Berlin, the two teenagers began talking between themselves.

The young man, Matthew McCallum, was of medium build, well-proportioned of physique, though not large or bulky. A healthy crop of light brown hair was just sufficiently windblown and scattered to indicate that he was not overly preoccupied with appearance, though his light grey suit, navy tie, and polished black wing tips fit in admirably with the high-society surroundings of the festive Berlin garden party. Five-nine or so in height, his lean, seventeen-year-old face gave hints of a dawning sophistication, both in the ways of the world and in knowledge and insight into people and relationships, yet it retained enough of the eagerness of youth to reveal a hunger to learn—the most hopeful sign to be looked for in any face—and to promise another inch or two in growth as well. There was surely an athleticism in the muscles and limbs of his frame, though if physical activities had been among his pursuits, they had likely been of an individual variety. He carried neither the muscular heft nor overall height or size to have shown himself imposing on a football field, and the determination revealed by his high cheekbones and the set of his triangular jaw spoke of an intensity to push himself toward his own goals rather than the fierceness necessary to triumph on the field of the game. In his eyes glowed a passion, yet unknown even to himself, for the pursuit of individual rather than group excellence. A straight Roman nose below deep-set light grey eyes gave further corroboration that beneath them was housed the intellect of a thinker whose faculties still awaited their full awakening. That here stood an individual of fiber there could be little doubt, though it would take the cauldron of life's fires to purify and strengthen the mettle. And only by his own sacrifice would it be transformed into the shining gold of selflessness and eternal character.

All this, however, yet lay dormant in the youthful and still developing countenance of Matthew McCallum, as the niece of the host took in the face and overall bearing of the young man to whom she had just been introduced.

"How long have you been in Berlin?" Sabina asked him.

"Four years. It's just my father and me," replied Matthew.

"Your mother?"

"She died eight years ago."

"I'm sorry. That must make it hard for you."

"I suppose so. It was hard when I was young, but my father and I are good friends."

"I am very close to my father as well," said Sabina, "so perhaps I understand."

A brief silence followed. It gave Matthew the opportunity to take in the young lady he had suddenly found himself alone with. From the moment his eyes had first beheld her approaching with her father, he could hardly imagine a more thorough picture of German beauty. The girl was positively stunning!

Yet within seconds, he began to realize the shallowness of his reaction. There was a quality to this young lady, something in the way she carried herself, about her smile, her laugh, her voice, the attentive manner in which he could tell she was probing beyond surface appearances. When their eyes met, he had seen past mere looks. In that moment he knew he had touched something deeper and more personal, though he could not put his finger on what exactly it was.

"I saw you with those others over there," said Matthew, after a moment. "Are they friends of yours?"

"My cousin Brigitte is one of them. I was speaking with her."

"Do you want to join them again?" said Matthew. "I won't mind if you—"

"Not for a minute!" interrupted Sabina with a merry laugh. "The son of the American ambassador is far more interesting than my cousin and her companions. I could not have been more delighted that my father rescued me from their company."

"Son of the *assistant* ambassador," corrected Matthew.

"No matter. You could be the son of Berlin's garbage minister and I would still find you more interesting!"

As they spoke, Sabina glanced over at Brigitte, dressed in a gown designed for a much more mature woman, trying to look older than she was, blinking her long lashes and flirting with the men around her, one of whom she knew to be a friend of Herr Himmler's nephew. A look of mixed pity and annoyance came over her face, and a small unbidden sigh escaped her lips. Matthew was puzzled by the look on her face, but intrigued to know more of what was behind those lovely eyes.

On his part, Matthew found himself noting the face of the man dressed in plain clothes rather than Sabina's cousin. He judged him between twenty-eight and thirty, maybe thirty-one. He wore a look Matthew had already seen many times in the German countenance, especially in young men—a look that reminded him of steel. Rigid, frozen, emotionless. Not even the smile on his face, which gave all the signs that he was beguiled by the girl's attentions, could erase the cold heart of stone which one sensed lay beneath it all. Somehow, Matthew thought, the Nazi programme seemed to remove or desensitize the human hearts of those who embraced it.

As they stood for a second or two observing the scene,

suddenly it dawned on Matthew what his subconscious mind had been trying to figure out about Sabina.

That was the difference he had seen in her almost the first instant!

Every girl he'd ever known—American or German—who was even halfway attractive seemed so preoccupied with and cognizant of it and behaved as though trying to impress the fact upon those around her. You could see it instantly, in everything about their carriage—from tone of voice to body language to a dozen tiny mannerisms—whether outright flirtatious or not. But Sabina, as pretty as she was, seemed utterly oblivious to her looks and completely unconcerned about what others might think of her.

"I'm surprised you're here talking with *me*," Sabina said after a moment. "As you can see, every other young man at the party is in a circle around my cousin."

"Maybe I've got different tastes than the rest of them."

"Well, I'll take that as a compliment. I like you already!"

This girl is certainly one to speak her mind! thought Matthew. Most Germans did nothing but talk about the weather the first time you met them. Getting personal with a stranger, or expressing personal thoughts or feelings, was not something Europeans did. Yet here was someone speaking openly and frankly almost immediately.

"Would you . . . uh, like to go get something to eat?" he asked, trying to say something to divert the conversation away from himself.

"Sure, that would be nice," she answered.

They made their way toward one of the nearby tables. Matthew picked up another two or three of the miniature sandwiches and a glass of fruit juice, Sabina a glass of sparkling water. They walked casually across the expansive lawn. A small goldfish pond lay in front of them. Most of the other guests remained clustered around the patio of the summerhouse and refreshment tables.

"Are you and your cousin friends?" asked Matthew, curious to find out more about this young lady. This was not the kind of girl you fell in love with, but the kind of person you simply found yourself wanting to *know!*

"No more than any two cousins, I suppose," replied Sabina. "We have known one another all our life, and we played dolls together when we were young. But close . . . I would not say that."

"How are you and she related?"

"My father and her father, my uncle Otto, are brothers. They both grew up where we live in the country, but Uncle Otto preferred the fast pace of the city. Brigitte is just the same. She loves the city and crowds, parties and bright lights, ballrooms and fancy dresses."

"And you, what do you love?" asked Matthew.

"I am almost embarrassed to tell you."

"Why?"

"I don't know. There's no good reason. It's just that so few people our age understand."

"People like your cousin Brigitte?"

"Yes," laughed Sabina. "She *doesn't* understand."

"Well, try me, and see if perhaps I can."

"All right then, I will. Let me see . . . I love the country. I love wide open spaces where I can be alone."

"Already you sound much different from your cousin!"

"You do not think I sound too countryish and old-fashioned?"

"Of course not."

"Do you like the country?"

"Yes, but we've lived in the city so long I can hardly remember what it's like," replied Matthew.

"Oh, I wish I could show you my papa's estate!"

"Tell me about it," he said, smiling with pleasure at her obvious excitement.

"I love it so much."

"Why?"

"There is so much to do."

"For instance?"

"Oh, riding by horseback through the fields and woods, or all the way to the sea sometimes—do you know the Baltic?"

"My father took me to see it once," replied Matthew. As he listened, he continued to observe Sabina's sparkling eyes as she spoke about her enjoyment of the out-of-doors. She was so full of life and enthusiasm!

"I relish walking along the seashore and listening to the waves on the sand and the sounds of gulls—oh, and have you gone to the Alps?" she went on.

"No, we haven't been that far south."

"Oh, but you must go!" exclaimed Sabina. "There's simply no place on earth like Interlaken and the region of the Berner Oberland and Luzern and hiking in the mountains near the Jungfrau! Once we were walking from Wengen around the Lauberhorn to Grindelwald. We hiked up over Wengernalp and to Klein Schneidegg. And then from out of the clearest blue sky came a dreadful thunderstorm. Within moments we were positively drenched! Then the sun came back out again, and by the time we were halfway down the other side to Grindelwald we were dry again—oh, but listen to me! I am going on and on, and you probably aren't interested in the least! It's one of my worst faults. I always talk far too much!"

"Please, don't say that," laughed Matthew. "I would love nothing more than to hear about the whole adventure from start to finish."

"You're probably just saying that so that I won't feel foolish," Sabina said, smiling, "but I appreciate it all the same."

"I promise, I meant every word."

"Thank you. You're very kind. But truly, I do love the Alps. I think it is the single place on earth most like what heaven must be like."

"Heaven?"

"Yes, don't you wonder what it will be like?"

"I suppose I never thought much about it."

"But aren't you a Christian? I thought all Americans were Christians. How can a Christian not think about heaven?"

"You mean, do I believe in God? I suppose so."

"You *suppose* so? Don't you know?"

"I guess I do. It never really mattered before."

"Don't you and your father talk about such things?"

"You mean like God and heaven?"

"Yes. My father and I talk about God all the time."

"My father's too practical for all that. All he has time for is politics and diplomacy."

"My father is practical too. But perhaps in a different way. He's the most levelheaded man I know, though I think Brigitte and Uncle Otto consider him a country provincial. I don't think they care enough about us even to despise us. I'm sure they all chuckle amongst themselves whenever we leave after a visit."

"Do you really think so?"

"The rest of the family considers us odd. But Papa and Mama and I don't mind. We love our life in the country, whatever they may think of it."

They had reached the small fishpond and now sat down on the garden bench beside it.

"So tell me more about your life in the country, as you call it," said Matthew.

"We have milk cows—Papa loves the cows—and lots of horses—do you ride?"

"Not much."

"Oh, but you must do more of it then. There's no better way to see the country than on horseback!"

"It's not so easy to do when you're stuck in the middle of Berlin. What else?"

"Fields and fields of wheat and rye and barley—oh, and the most fabulous garden in all of Germany. I wish I could take you through it right now. It's nothing like these potted and cut flowers of Uncle Otto's."

"He's got lots of nice plump goldfish," said Matthew with fun in his tone.

"You're right. And this pond is larger than any of the small ponds in our garden. But I'll trade goldfish for trees and hedges anytime. It's a *real* garden . . . people get lost in it!"

"Lost? Are you kidding?" laughed Matthew.

"No, it's enormous. I tell you, people lose their direction and can't find their way back to the house!"

"I would like to see it. That sounds like a challenge I'd enjoy taking."

"Are you fond of flowers and plants?" asked Sabina.

"No more than anything else. They're OK, I suppose."

"Oh, I love them . . . especially roses. Papa's rose garden sits right in the center and is the best part of the whole Spring Garden."

"I don't know much about roses, though they're pretty and smell nice."

The look on Sabina's face was almost one of shock. "That's all you have to say about them!" she replied.

As she spoke, her hands and eyes, even her feet were in constant animation accompanying her words. *Does she ever sit still?* he wondered.

"They are the most magnificent of all the flowers," she went on. "The more you know of roses, the more you cannot help loving them. And the more you know of roses, the more you discover . . . well, about life and God . . . and everything. They are one of the most special things God has made in all his creation."

They fell silent and found themselves staring at the slow-moving orange fish in the pond in front of them. It was the first lengthy break in the conversation.

Matthew found himself positively enchanted with this vivacious young German. She was so alive, it could not help but be contagious. He felt that he was being exposed to a whole new world by her way of viewing things, things he realized he had never thought much about before.

Unconsciously he began tossing crumbs from the unfinished piece of bread in his hand into the pond, then watched as the fish swam up to nibble at them.

"Are you interested in politics and current affairs?" Sabina asked after a minute or two.

"Yes, actually I am," replied Matthew. "That's what *my* father talks about. But you're not, are you?"

"Why do you say that?"

"Girls rarely are."

"You're not lumping me in with everyone else, are you?" laughed Sabina.

"How could I! No, you're about as different as they come."

"How am I supposed to take that?" she said with mock affront.

"Entirely as a compliment, I promise. But are you?"

"Am I what?"

"Interested in politics and the world?"

"A little. Not near so much as you, I would think, with what your father does. Are you going to follow his footsteps when you're older?"

"I'd like to go into politics, maybe even run for office some-day. Or maybe I'll be a diplomat like my father, who knows? But I do want to work for my government in some way."

"You must really like it."

"You talk about loving the sea, the mountains, the out-of-doors. I love the thrill of events, everything happening right in front of you, being part of them while they're going on, watching important decisions being made. It's stimulating and exciting!"

"You must know a lot of important men back in your country."

"I don't know, I've never thought about it. I did meet FDR after my father's appointment."

"FDR. What does that mean?"

"FDR—Franklin Delano Roosevelt. He's our president."

"You've actually *met* him?"

"Not such a big deal. You could probably meet your president too."

"Hitler? I'm not sure I'd want to. Papa has met him. He said he shivered when they shook hands."

Suddenly a voice sounded behind them.

"Why, Sabina, *dear*—why haven't you introduced me to your friend?"

They both turned, then rose from the bench.

"Hello, Brigitte," said Sabina in a gracious tone, speaking in their native language. "This is Matthew McCallum. He's from the United States."

"I'm happy to meet you," said Matthew, also in German, standing up.

Brigitte held out her hand daintily, apparently expecting Matthew to kiss it. Matthew took it briefly, ignoring the girl's coquettish smile and attempt to catch his eyes, then let it go without raising it to his mouth.

"Wouldn't you like to join us, Mr. McCallum?" said Brigitte in a throaty tone, still working her smile and eyes to maximum effect. "My friends and I were just talking about what foreign men find attractive in German women. I'm sure Sabina is boring you with all her plebeian talk of life on the farm. Besides, we need the opinion of a handsome American like you, who can tell us what *you* find desirable in us."

With her final words she smiled him such a voluptuous invitation to pursue further intimacy as few men could resist.

"*Danke*, Fräulein von Dortmann," Matthew replied. "I doubt I would be much help to you."

"Ple-e-ase," she said in a drawn-out, pouty tone, puckering her lips.

"I am quite content with the conversation I have at present."

"Sabina hasn't been boring you with her talk about gardens and animals, has she?"

"Not at all. I haven't been bored in the least."

"Do you not find European women attractive, Mr. McCallum?" Brigitte asked in an oily voice.

"Probably not for the reasons you and your friends are discussing."

"I would so like to hear what you think. Perhaps you and I could—"

"I really must decline, Fräulein," said Matthew. "Your cousin and I were not through with our conversation. I'm afraid you'll have to excuse us." He gave her a diplomatic smile.

He motioned his head toward Sabina and led her across the lawn and around the fishpond, leaving Brigitte incredulous where she stood staring after them.

"Pushy, isn't she?" said Matthew with a chuckle as soon as they were out of earshot.

"She'll never forgive you," said Sabina.

"I'll survive," he added.

"No, I mean it. She can carry a grudge longer than anyone I know. Believe me, she'll find some way to get back at you. She does *not* like to be made to look foolish."

"She doesn't need my help for that!"

Sabina could not help laughing.

"Sometimes I can hardly stand what she makes me feel inside. I know she's my cousin and that I must be nice to her. Oh, but she tries my patience and goodwill when she acts like that! It doesn't matter who or what it is, if she sees me enjoying something, she always tries to take it away from me. It's been like that since we were little girls."

"You have nothing to worry about on my account, let me tell you. I would rather spend a minute in conversation with you about life on the farm, as she put it, than an hour with her and her friends!"

"Just promise me you'll watch yourself if you have occasion to run into her again."

Matthew laughed lightheartedly.

"Promise me," repeated Sabina. "You don't know her like I do."

"All right, I promise," said Matthew, still chuckling and glancing toward her. As he did his foot tripped over one of the large stones bordering the pond.

He stumbled, losing his balance, and fell toward the water. Sabina quickly reached out to help him.

He grabbed for her outstretched hands, trying to steady himself, but only succeeded in causing her to lose her balance on the uneven footing as well.

He toppled over sideways, half a glass of juice splattering over his suit as it left his hand, and fell with a splash into the water, his clumsy descent coming to a stop when one knee and one hand were resting a foot underwater on the bottom of the fishpond, with his other arm and leg straddled precariously over the edge on the lawn.

Sabina struggled to keep on her feet, though one of them plunged into the water before she then fell backwards onto the lawn, plopping unceremoniously onto her back, one wet shoe still dangling over the edge of the pond.

"Good grief, I can't believe I did that!" muttered Matthew in disgust.

"Are you all right?" said Sabina, sitting up, then rising. Seeing the position he was stuck in, she began to laugh.

She stepped into the pond, stooped down as best she could manage while trying to hold her long dress out of the water, took hold of one of Matthew's arms, still laughing, and helped him crawl out of the water. In another moment they were both lying on the grass. Half of his suit was soaking wet.

"I really can't believe it!" he repeated. "I don't usually do things like that!"

Sabina was laughing hysterically, though trying to keep from making too much noise. In another few seconds Matthew had joined her.

"Won't your cousin love this?" said Matthew sardonically. "Maybe I can sneak out of here!"

"Too late!" said Sabina, trying to stop laughing. "You made too much noise. Everyone heard the splash!"

Matthew glanced toward the rest of the party. All the guests, from the topmost levels of German society, had stopped what they were doing and were now staring directly at the two of them lying on the grass with the water of the fishpond all over them.

For a moment there was silence as all beheld the scene, then he saw Brigitte begin to titter, then laugh outright. All those in her small coterie followed suit, and within a minute most of the other guests were likewise enjoying the unexpected entertainment. Only the fellow Brigitte had earlier been talking to did not seem to enter heartily into the joke. The hint of a smile played upon his lips, but it was not a smile of humor, only chilly tolerance for the boorish amusements of those beneath him.

When word began to circulate that the fop was an American, the joke gained even more favor, and the expression of merriment continued for some time.

Matthew buried his face on the close-clipped green lawn in humiliated mortification.

"Good grief!" was all Sabina heard him mutter to himself.

∽ 3 ∾

Baron Heinrich von Dortmann

An excursion to Berlin, whatever the occasion, put Sabina's father through a wide range of inner emotions.

Driving into the capital city was usually accompanied by a certain churning of discomfort in the pit of his stomach. The anticipation of his time in the hectic metropolis was normally less than enthusiastic.

Making the trip with his daughter helped relax his uneasiness, but now, even with Sabina at his side, the return trip to his country estate turned the baron pensive.

The contrast between the noise and pace of the city and the wide-spaced serenity of the German countryside struck a deep coinciding chord in his own soul and caused him to reflect upon the diverging pathways of life, and upon the one he personally had chosen.

Visiting his brother, especially in a social setting such as yesterday's, accentuated the contrast and always deepened his thoughtful reflections.

The result of his mental wanderings was always the same—a great thankfulness for his life as it was and a pleasure to be returning home.

The baron cast his gaze widely about on both sides of the deserted country road as he and Sabina rode in a comfortable silence.

No one would call it the world's most beautiful land, this Pomeranian plain south of the Baltic.

It was mostly flat and uninteresting, without snowcapped peaks of fairy tales, or dense forests of legends, or even a mighty river about which a single song had been written.

No Schwarzwald, no Danube, no Alps here beckoned visitors.

The coastline, which bordered the holdings of his ancestors along the sea, boasted none of the towering majestic cliffs he had read about in England and Scotland. Trees had once grown plentifully here, and numerous wooded regions were still scattered about the landscape. But the trees that grew on his land were too thin and sparse for any self-respecting gnome of the Black Forest to look twice at. Even the great river Oder could not rightly be given a Prussian or Pomeranian heritage, though its flow was not many kilometers to the west of his land.

There was little to draw a man here . . . but earth—good earth, rich, black earth, earth to grow things, earth that the rains and the warm winds accompanying the ocean currents made green in the spring, full of hope and promise, earth that turned the shoots and stalks gold in the summer, and earth that brought forth of its abundant bounty to feed hungry mouths in the fall.

This was earth rich of soil, imbued with the mystery of life.

WEST FARGO PUBLIC
LIBRARY

It was earth, too, in which he had discovered that flowers and a multitude of ornamental trees and a variety of shrubs and other pretty growing things could flourish. When given care, their roots pulled the rich nutrients from the soil, transforming the rain and sunlight and black dirt into the most exquisite shapes and colors and fragrances his eyes and nose ever beheld.

With every passing year, the simple blossoms and buds and foliage of his garden revealed to the inner eyes of his being more and more of life's mysteries, and more about the Maker of suns and earths and roses and men and women all together.

The countries and kingdoms of his ancestors were forgotten now. In their place, everyone said these days, was the greatest nation the earth had ever known, an illustrious empire destined to fulfill the dreams and ambitions of the mightiest people ever to march across its face.

He was one of those people.

Yet in his heart beat anxious forebodings. The world was changing. Rapidly . . . too rapidly. Empires were rising both to the east and to the west of him. Empires whose greedy grasp, he feared, would one day trample across this verdant plain upon which his eyes rested whenever he climbed to the roof of his country home and gazed around him.

He prayed it would not be so. Yet he could not quiet the tremors in his breast.

∽∾೮ᨆ∾

Baron Heinrich von Dortmann, of distant Prussian and more recent Pomeranian descent, came from a long line in one of the great landowning families of north-central Europe. The ancient kingdoms of Poland, Prussia, and Pomerania had all vied for control of this region between the mouth of the Oder and the Gulf of Danzig, stretching southward to the latitudinal flow of the Warta and longitudinal flow of the Vistula rivers. Each had in its turn, over the preceding half millennium, controlled and laid claim to the right of sovereignty.

They had ruled the land, but the scions of the Dortmann name had not themselves been ruled. The counts and barons and viscounts among them had walked comfortably in the corridors of power, mixing and intermingling with kings and queens. As the rulers had shifted back and forth over the centuries, the fortunes of the family von Dortmann had risen steadily. Its men combined financial cunning with the integrity of their pedigree, to great profit and influence in the northern Germanic, Polish, and Prussian kingdoms. By the mid-nineteenth century there were merchants and bankers, politicians and generals among them. And, of course, those who continued to work the land and bring forth its wealth into the interest-bearing Dortmann granaries in Berlin, Vienna, and Hamburg.

The Poles, the Prussians, and the Pomeranians had all by now disappeared from this land. They had been swallowed into a new race. Only the Poles were left, but they had been squeezed eastward. No one outside these regions would probably even know the name *Prussia* before many more years.

But all the world knew of *Germany*. Knew of it, and trembled.

He had a cousin, the leading shipbuilder in all of Danzig; his brother, one of the most respected financiers in Berlin; and an uncle, a merchant and importer, who sailed his cousin's ships to the far reaches of the world's ports. But Heinrich von Dortmann had always been content with the land itself.

His father and grandfather before him had wielded extensive holdings northeast of Berlin, and he had himself found all he needed to offer satisfaction in life at the family estate a hundred and forty kilometers from the great city. He had traveled widely in Europe but had never left the continent, was well read and spoke three European languages, was content to allow his brother to monitor his finances and assets, and was viewed among many in the family as something of an unambitious anomaly in the Dortmann lineage.

No one would have dared call him a simpleton, for, though soft-spoken, he was clearly a wise and knowledgeable man of undisputed character and integrity. And the millions of reichsmarks alongside his name on the ledgers of the Reichsbank would give credibility even to a fool.

Heinrich von Dortmann was certainly no fool. There was, however, a definite naïveté present in his carriage that uncle and brother alluded to with occasional hushed tones and significant glances. He was urbane enough, sophisticated when he wanted to be, the perfect gentlemanly Prussian country squire, with enough of a business head on his shoulders to have made a handsome profit for the family coffers even during the bleak years of the early thirties. He had been to the *Universität* and then spent time on the best farms in Europe, learning all he could to keep the estate competitive.

But he had such odd notions. He was given to making the most peculiar statements, usually about the metaphysics and spiritual dimension of the world, as he called it. His brother declared himself unable to make heads or tails of most of Heinrich's religious hogwash. But he put up with it as one might a child's foolishness because Heinrich, as the elder in their branch of the line, held a controlling, though silent, share in certain of the family's affairs which it was in brother Otto's best interest not to have looked into too closely.

Of more concern were Heinrich's lofty notions of magnanimity toward all men, whom he guilelessly called his "brothers." When he was a child such ridiculous ideas had been a nuisance to the family, but relatively harmless. Every now and then a neighboring urchin, son of a field hand or poor immigrant, would be found in the kitchen munching on a piece of bread or cake. Their mother almost seemed to encourage such goings-on, and Otto had been content to overlook it even when it passed into adulthood. The occasional odd bank draft to those less fortunate did nothing to jeopardize either the family's fortune or its standing. He overlooked his brother's eccentricities as the effect of living too long in the country with nothing surrounding him but fields and silence, animals and fresh air.

New times were coming, however, and these days even the standing of centuries-old names of repute must be bolstered by prudent and cautious behavior. There were those toward whom it could be most *imprudent* to show benevolence, no matter how large one's heart. Even a word unfitly spoken could prove costly. Invisible ears were everywhere.

His brother and uncle, therefore, were concerned for Heinrich, not to mention themselves, and sought ways to moderate the unwary expressions of his tongue and the ill-advised chivalry of his hand. If they weren't careful, he could get them all into trouble.

❧ 4 ❧
The Opportunist

Baron von Dortmann's were not the only thoughts revolving about his banker brother. Even as he and his daughter made their way back to the country estate that was their home, another who had likewise attended Otto's garden party revolved the events of the previous afternoon in his sinister mind.

The young agent of the Gestapo whose dispassionate and hard-featured face had been noted by Assistant Ambassador McCallum's son now found himself reflecting not on the beautiful daughter of the party's host who had done her best to charm him, but rather on her father.

Emil Korsch indeed looked the part of the prototypical Gestapo agent. Matthew had been correct in his assessment. What he could not see, however, were the frozen fires that boiled beneath the surface of the rigid stare and smileless lips. Unlike most Nazis, Korsch's loyalties were not to the Reich, but only to himself.

He had been fortunate to learn about the gathering and then to wrangle himself an invitation. He knew well enough that in certain circles of high society the Gestapo were not always entirely welcome. And notwithstanding his association with Himmler's nephew, Korsch knew that he did not yet have the status within the organization to go wherever he wanted without asking permission.

That would change, he thought to himself.

He had listened attentively yesterday afternoon, and had logged away every name, every introduction, every bit of idle talk and chatter and conversation.

None of it was idle to him. Every piece of information you possessed these days could spell opportunity. Especially in high circles like those!

The banker's daughter was a charmer, it was true. But Korsch was more interested in the money in his bank. In normal times, money spelled influence and power. These days, however, just the reverse could be true, and power could be translated into money!

These were heady days, filled with potential fortune if fate was with you. There were winners and losers in this treacherous game of power.

These days the losers lost their lives. Putsches and purges had characterized the Nazi method since the beginnings of national socialism, morbidly out-of-step with the advance of modernism and the technological twentieth century. The *Reichstag* fire in '33 and the bloody purge of June '34 left no further doubt as to the consequences of finding oneself on the wrong side of the ever-fluid and lethal fence of the Führer's favor. How could he not be reminded of the cruel czarist regimes from the dark history of his own ancestors?

On the other hand, the winners stood to gain even more! The world would soon be at their fingertips. Power over all of Europe, perhaps over all the world, would proceed from a very select circle. Those who managed to keep their feet would become members of the world's most exclusive fraternity.

That fraternity of power would sit right here, in Berlin, and he intended to be one of its members!

Without knowing why, Korsch found his thoughts moving away from Otto von Dortmann and to his brother, the country baron. He'd overheard someone mention him at the party and had said to himself that he should meet him.

Suddenly he realized he had forgotten all about it for the rest of the afternoon, and now the opportunity had slipped away.

༚ 5 ༚

The Estate von Dortmann

The approach to the Dortmann estate, known as *Lebenshaus*, wound through a tree-lined drive from the west. The trees were mostly birch, with a few larches between, both of which grew naturally here. They had been planted several generations earlier as a close-set border to the narrow drive and had reached considerable height.

Automobiles now, of course, made the drive, though they had to creep up the hill at barely greater speed than had a team of four pulling an elegant carriage in the last century. The way was extremely narrow, without room for two cars to pass for a distance of about four hundred meters. Yet because of the beauty and tradition of the drive, neither of the last two barons had even thought of widening it.

Born in 1894, Heinrich von Dortmann had known of automobiles for as long as he could remember. His own father had been one of the first German nobles to own one, an imported Rolls-Royce from England with a side-valve engine, known as the Silver Ghost. To this he had added a German-made Duesenberg, and was the envy of many men for many kilometers. Yet somehow the younger Dortmann had never quite accustomed himself to the advance of the modern age. He still resisted the idea of paving the drive, used his own auto only when necessity demanded, and continued to travel anywhere up to ten kilometers by horseback.

Not only was his garden renowned, so were his stables. He and his wife and daughter were all accomplished and at home in the saddle. Besides a full-time gardener, a full-time groom was also on his permanent staff at *Lebenshaus*.

He often contemplated that he would have been better suited to life in a different age. *The era of the kaisers would have done nicely*, he thought to himself, *sometime during the last century, before the Great War engulfed all Europe.*

There were moments his fantasies carried him back and he almost imagined that *Lebenshaus* was of another time when life moved at a slower pace and things were simpler than they seemed insistent to become these days. The drive back here from the city always represented more to him than the shift from urban noise to rural simplicity. He felt as though he were traveling backward in time as well.

If he could not halt the tempo of the world, at least he could make his own home a refuge, which the name he had given the estate signified. He and his family did not have to keep up with the frenetic beat of Berlin's drums. Nor did they have to let unpleasant events sweep them into their train. He was determined to maintain the serenity of this place and to offer it to whoever likewise sought retreat from the pace of this hurried and impersonal century.

As the baron and his daughter drove home, he recalled Sabina's enthusiasm when they had talked about going to Berlin.

He had been pondering the future then too as he made his way slowly along the pathway between well-trimmed hedges and ornamentally pruned shrubs and flowering trees of the large *Frühlingsgarten* bordering his home. He stooped down to work the soil around a couple of his roses, but his thoughts were on the upcoming trip into the city.

It was good land, he thought . . . *his* land.

But for how much longer?

Resting upon one knee, he plunged his hand into the rich brown loam he had been cultivating, then raised his hand with fingers spread open, letting the dirt sift through them and fall back to the ground, relishing the very color and texture and smell of the soil of his garden.

Truly, though there was great wealth he could call his own, the plants he grew—and all they signified—were among his most prized possessions. He clipped two flowers from nearby rosebushes, a red and a white for wife and daughter, then rose from his knee.

He paused after a few steps and glanced around with pleasure down the slope toward the pinewood off to the south, seeing the stream flowing out of it, winding toward the hill of the estate before heading off westward to join the great river, and the rich fields in the distance in all other directions. Whatever became of it, this was good land, and he was blessed to have been given such an abundant heritage.

All at once, from around a bend in the path, his daughter came running toward him.

"Papa, Papa!" she had cried. "I've been looking for you."

"And you have found me, Sabina!" he replied with a smile. "Here—I cut this flower just for you."

"Thank you, Papa," she said, holding it close to her nose. "Why were you looking for me?"

"Did you mean what you said earlier, that I could go with you to Uncle Otto's garden party in Berlin?"

"Of course I did. What does your mama say?"

"That if I am with you, she would have no fear to send me even to Russia."

"Even I would be afraid to go there," laughed her father. "Though I try to see good in everyone, I do not find the Bolsheviks an appealing lot. In any case, we are not going there, but to Berlin."

"Oh, I'm so excited! When do we leave, Papa?"

"With the rising of the sun tomorrow morning."

That had been two days ago. Now they had returned, and were making their way between the trees along the snakelike boulevard up the hill. They crested at length what might have been termed its low rolling summit. Emerging from the birch-lined avenue, the baron steered his 1934 Mercedes around a wide, graveled circle toward the front of the estate. In the middle of the entryway sat a stone fountain far more ornate than his tastes were comfortable with.

The great stone horse, out of whose mouth gushed a steady flow of water pumped up from the stream below, rose precariously on his two rear legs with a look of ferocity in his eyes that was no doubt intended to warn any intruder of sinister motive to consider his moves with caution. Such a sentinel was altogether out of place in this serene country setting, the baron would think to himself every time he had occasion to lay eyes upon it.

He had viewed the immobile equine watchdog every day since he was a lad, and to his knowledge it had never scared, inspired, or otherwise moved man, woman, or child with any emotion other than complete disinterest. Every time a winter's storm struck, he walked out his front door the morning after its passing, secretly hoping to find the thing blown over and broken beyond repair. He could never have brought himself to demolish it intentionally. But he would much rather plant roses at the center of the circular drive, and he prayed a violent wind from the north might assist him toward that end.

Thus far, however, the brave, silent, ugly creature had withstood every blast with which it had been assailed for a hundred years and still stood rearing and spewing water toward all who dared approach the estate von Dortmann.

The baron parked the car in front. He would put it in the garage later. They were both anxious to see their wife and mother.

Leaving the granite steed behind them, they now approached
the front doors of the house—a sprawling complex comprised
of two wings set in an L-shape, both three floors in height, one
of which boasted an ornate tower that could be seen for a great
distance from anywhere in the low-lying plain. From the
outside, the composition appeared altogether drab and color-
less, offering no hint of the palatial mansion that existed
behind its walls of stone.

Had the construction been taller instead of spread out, more
ornate around the windows and archways, and the setting
along the Rhine or in one of Scotland's rugged highland glens
the baron read of with such keen enthusiasm, they would have
called it a castle.

As it was, set in the Baltic plain of Pomerania, they only
called it *Lebenshaus*.

The unassuming architecture, however, took nothing away
from the magnificence of the entire aspect of the place. The hills
here were not of great height, rising occasionally only a handful
of meters above the Baltic and the valley of the Oder to the
west. That slight undulation of the plain upon whose gently
rising crest the Dortmann estate sat was probably some
hundred meters above the sea itself, and rose half that in a wide
circular slope out of the farmland that lay surrounding it and
spread out in all directions.

The location, upon what more accurately would be called the
plateau of a huge knoll, had probably been chosen for defensive
rather than agricultural purposes five hundred years earlier,
which accounted for the fact that, unlike most farms in
Germany, the barns were separate rather than attached to the
main structure. The first house had been built, and on that hill it
had been added to, torn down, partially burned, abandoned for
a time, and rebuilt another three or four times.

Many there were who would have wished it torn down for
good and rebuilt elsewhere than at the top of the knoll. Those
feudal serfs of old and hired laborers of modern date who farmed
the fields and tilled the soil for the generations of barons and
landed proprietors cursed the slow uphill trudge back to the
house at the end of every day's weary labor.

Yet there the center of the estate remained, century upon century, and still stood proudly to this day.

Baron von Dortmann and his daughter entered the front doors on the plain west face of the front of the house, which sat in an approximate north-south line. The adjacent wing, invisible from their approach, stretched behind it on the north side, partially enclosing in the back an expansive courtyard, protected thus from north and westerly winds. As a result the courtyard was pleasant through most of the middle of the year. When the winds came from the direction of the Russian motherland, however, there was nothing for it but to endure them or remain inside. Today was one of the warm days, and here they found the baron's wife, Marion, and each greeted her with a kiss.

⌒⌒⌒

From the level grassy courtyard, in the middle of which sat a centerpiece more to the baron's liking and of his own design— a small pond encircled by a few of his favorite rose bushes— steps led downward in two directions, toward the Spring Garden to the south and east. A large ancient oak grew picturesquely opposite the point where the two wings of the house joined, down the hill ten meters or so from the southeast corner of the courtyard. Under its spreading wings sat an ancient stone bench.

Scattered at uneven intervals toward the east were a half dozen or so additional buildings of both stone and wood construction, the various enclosures necessary for their farming commerce— barns, stables, pens, granaries, and equipment storage facilities. These spread down the eastern and northeastern slope from the plateau, the most recently built grain house all the way down on the plain itself amidst the fields of growing corn. An abundance of trees was scattered among them, all planted by either the present baron or his father, both of whom had an eye for aesthetic beauty and desired to see the environment of their trade as pleasant as possible.

Baron von Dortmann and his family occupied the lavishly appointed west wing. The east wing housed the household and farm staff and laborers, the latter comprising no more these days than ten or twelve men year-round, with local day workers added during harvesttime.

With the baron's eye for beauty came a keen sense of efficiency. He always kept up on the latest technological developments, and the yearly advent of new and more advanced machinery had steadily reduced the number of men and horses required since the previous century, so well over half the east wing now sat vacant. Many rooms were empty, others had been converted to storage uses, and two or three of those nearest the joining of the two wings were kept maintained for guest use, although the main west wing also boasted at least a dozen guest rooms of its own. All of the workers lived on either the ground or the first floor. The entire second floor of the east wing was silent as a tomb.

Food preparation and serving facilities were located on the ground floor, the kitchen at the junction of the two wings, family dining room off it to the west, servants' and laborers' dining room off it to the east. A large vegetable garden sat part-way down the slope to the north, spreading around the north-east corner itself.

Around the uppermost circumference of the house ran a parapet wall with battlement about a meter high, leading on the far northeast corner to a flat rooftop balcony. Whether this clever bit of architectural design had been intended to watch for approaching enemies, or so that the yeoman could keep a visual eye on his workers and foremen in the expansive fields stretching out below, might have been a question worthy of inquiry had not any hope of an answer been long since lost in the mists of antiquity.

In either case, on a clear day one could see for many kilometers from this rooftop vantage point toward Poznan to the southeast, toward Berlin to the southwest, and even, on the clearest of days, could one imagine faint glimpses of the Baltic fifteen or twenty kilometers due north.

The rooftop had always been one of the baron's favorite places on the whole estate. Surveying the countryside from this high perch had always given Baron von Dortmann much pleasure. But these days it was with a skeptical eye that he gazed out, watching Berlin with the inner eyes of his thoughts, wondering what would come next. He also took in the countryside in the direction of Poland and Prussia, where they stretched out along the eastern horizon, well aware that *Lebenshaus* sat squarely in the middle of a growing conflict between the new forces ruling Germany and the ancient kingdom of Bismarck. Standing here these days, therefore, brought more sighs than smiles, and a strange feeling of unrest in his heart.

From the balcony the entire courtyard was visible directly below, and beyond that, the baron's other favorite refuge, the place that seemed connected to his very soul: the garden.

∿ 6 ᖆ

Silent Witness

The infiltration of snooping eyes throughout every corner of this land was still two or three years in the future.

The Führer and his inner circle were grooming and training those who would enforce their cruelty, and would, as time went on, root out all hints of subversion to the Nazi cause. But their presence had not yet fully been felt, nor had fear of the plain-clothes secret police gripped every citizen of the nation as it was soon destined to do.

Even now, however, eyes and ears had become more watchful at all levels of society. This was no time to be careless. One had to choose one's words, one's friends, even one's thoughts with prudence.

Booted feet treaded their way through a dense wood. Theirs was not the heavy tramp of storm troopers, and could indeed have been those of a hunter, or merely of a walker out for a leisurely morning's wilderness stroll.

They were none of these, however.

The owner of the feet that made their way through the brush and trees was bent on an entirely different mission, of an intensely personal kind. Though he was several kilometers from any other human being, the clandestine nature of his quest caused him to choose his steps with care. He would not make any more noise than necessary, just in case someone should be around.

The hour was early. Even in a land where half the energetic population arose with the sun, it was unlikely he would encounter a soul out here. Hares or an occasional deer, perhaps. But he was safe from anyone observing *him*. His were the only eyes, on this morning, that would be furtively on the lookout—and they would be watching *another*.

He knew they had been gone, they were supposed to have been back yesterday afternoon. He had to know.

He had been keeping his eye on the place on and off for some time. He knew it almost as well as his own home. He couldn't see behind the doors and walls and windows, of course, from such a distant vantage point, and so the exterior and grounds had to do.

On he walked, up the gradual incline, the trees thinning now and his way becoming easier.

In another fifteen minutes he reached his destination, climbed to the top, sat down, then put the binoculars he had been carrying to his eyes and scanned the lowlands spread out before him. He focused the eyepieces on the huge house on the knoll. He could see everything clearly. Now all he had to do was wait—all day if necessary.

The workers were already out in the fields. But they did not interest him. Slowly he moved the binoculars about, focusing especially on the two windows on the far left, though not quite to the corner, about midway up the great structure. He could see nothing inside.

He sat quietly, in the stillness of the surrounding forest, and waited. Sometimes they came out early, but at other times the fulfillment of his purpose required great patience. He was in no hurry. He had all day.

Several hours passed. There was considerable activity about, but not of the sort for which he had arisen before dawn and made this long walk. Still he kept the binoculars to his eyes, slowly panning back and forth for his quarry.

Suddenly he saw a door open, the door to the roof. His heart began to pound!

There she was! Carrying a book as always.

She sat down, resting her back against the battlement. If only the binoculars were powerful enough to see what she was reading!

He watched for twenty or so minutes. She sat motionless, unaware of the silent witness to her morning's activity.

She glanced up, seeming to ponder a passage she had just read, then rose and quickly left the rooftop perch.

Still he watched, waiting.

Five minutes later the object of his observation emerged, this time from a door on the ground floor, and, still carrying the book, walked across the courtyard, then disappeared under the arch and into the depths of the huge garden. He tried to follow her movements, but the growth was too thick, and for a minute or two she was lost to his sight.

Still searching to recover her trail, he noticed some movement up by the house out of the corner of his eye. Quickly he turned his magnified eyes back up to his right.

There was the baron. Here was perhaps the kingpin to his entire scheme! He deserved careful attention as well.

The baron had just come from the house and likewise now leisurely crossed the grassy courtyard, following nearly in the exact footsteps of his daughter.

The baron is taller, the watcher thought to himself. He would be able to follow his movements more easily.

∞ 7 ∞

Der Frühlingsgarten

South of Baron von Dortmann's house, and comprising nearly a full hectare, sat the spacious green lawns, hedges, and circuitous pathways through what the elder Dortmann had called his *Frühlingsgarten*, or Spring Garden, and which his son, the present baron, after his extensive schooling, had made the envy of every horticulturist between the estate and Berlin.

It was situated on the south slope leading down across the stream and toward the pinewood beyond the shallow valley. The baron had terraced and interlaced the entire space with so many varieties of plants and such a maze of paths and walkways and little stairways and bridges and hedges and overarching arbors and twists and turns and dead-end courtyards of specialty plants or flowers, that one quickly forgot, from within its depths, that it was not built on level ground.

Nor could anyone but the baron, his wife, Marion, and their daughter, Sabina, keep their bearings once within the labyrinth of its depths. More than one visitor had declared themselves altogether lost and unable to find the direction toward the house again until rescued by their host.

A disconcerting adventure, somewhere between the prized dawn redwood the baron's uncle had brought back from China and the arbor of dwarfed flowering plums sixty feet up the eastern slope, had caused one bewildered visitor later to insist that the baron change the name on the stone archway leading from the courtyard above down into the botanical depths below, to *Geheimnisgarten*, or Mysterious Garden.

"My garden does indeed contain many mysteries," the baron had laughed with great delight, "but not of the kind to which you refer. No, I think it shall remain the Garden of Spring, and I will let those so inclined discover its deeper mysteries for themselves."

Had one been able to see across the entirety of the garden in any single direction, keeping one's bearings might have been tolerably possible. As the baron had designed it, however, his walkways and miniature courtyards and arbors and diminutive gardens within the larger garden—indeed every component of the whole—were surrounded by hedges a full two meters high. Only a giant could see over them. He desired to maintain an enclosed sense of privacy and singularity of botanical focus whatever one's horticultural tastes. This he had certainly achieved, bewildering and losing many guests in the process. The slope down the hill from the house, facing south as it did, maximized available light the year round, allowing the baron to grow even a handful of tropical species.

From the courtyard at the rear of the manor house, the large garden opened and, from under the great stone arch, spread all the way down the slope, crossing the stream at the bottom of the valley, the windings of which the baron had made extensive use of by contriving a number of miniature falls and tiny lakes, birdbaths and fishponds, until it left the garden at its western corner to continue its journey across the plain.

From a vantage point on the courtyard above, or better yet,

from high atop the rooftop balcony—to which the baron often first took guests to offer them an aerial visual tour before plunging into the depths of the place—it was possible to send one's eyes scanning over the hedge tops and theoretically achieve a mental lay of the intricacies of the garden's complex plotting scheme. Once on the level of the earth, however, and surrounded by a hundred twists and turns of the high-growing, vision-limiting fences, any prior sense of navigational equilibrium vanished altogether.

On this day, Baron von Dortmann found his daughter where he often found her, at the very heart of *Der Frühlingsgarten:* in the rose garden itself.

It was a warm morning. She sat on one of the oak benches he had had built for the place, a book in her lap, quietly reading.

He had made his approach from above and now stood a moment beholding the tranquil scene before making himself known to her.

She had her mother's deep blue eyes, that much was clear, and the blond Teutonic mane to go with them—the latter inherited from her pure Aryan father—a combination that had bewitched men of Celtic stock for thousands of years before the baron had fallen in love with Marion for other reasons entirely.

There were those who said she had inherited the baron's laugh.

He didn't believe it.

That she *could* laugh there was no doubt. And when they laughed together, as they often did, he would not deny a certain similarity. But when his daughter's lips opened wide, her white teeth sparkling, the musical timbre of her melodic voice rang with a gaiety of merriment all its own. He could take no share in it.

Sabina was sixteen now, and though nearly full grown, she was in her own right in so many ways still his little girl, so innocent, so full of the playful love of life untainted by the sobering realities of adulthood. She was poised on the beguiling threshold of maturity, one moment delighting as she did at seven over some wondrous childhood discovery, the next a fleeting look coming into her eyes that spoke of the dawning stature of her own approaching womanhood.

He could not help occasional pangs stabbing his father's

heart as he realized how brief were the remaining moments of innocence he would be able to share with her.

How many hours they had spent right here, in the rose garden, with one another. She had helped him plant fifty or more of the very plants they had enjoyed so much together through the years. He had held her in his lap here, walked through the rows bouncing her on his shoulder while explaining his enthusiasm for some new imported variety he had just received. He had read stories to her here, dried her tears, and given her many things from out of his own heart.

This was a tranquil world all its own. He came here to be alone, to think, to pray. This was his closet, his place of quiet retreat. So much of his own faith, his own deepest self, he had given to his daughter among these very trees and shrubs and hedges.

Baron Heinrich von Dortmann was a man who cut a striking physical swath across whatever path he walked, a near-perfect specimen of that Teutonic excellence so revered during these times. Standing 188 centimeters, or just over six feet two inches, he was imposing not by mere size, but in nearly all of his features. Conspicuously handsome, by looks he seemed more suited to the corporate boardroom or even the *Reichstag*. Inwardly, however, he was never happier than when dressed in the garb of a workingman, with well-worn boots on his feet, and with his hands covered with the rich black dirt of the earth he loved.

A thick and plentiful crop of hair, light in his youth, had now darkened considerably and had begun to grey. It came down to his ears, but was so thick as to defy a regular part anywhere on his head, a characteristic reinforced by the fact that he rarely wore a hat and was so often outside in the wind and weather. Though the supply of thatch was abundant, it did leave room for a wide rectangular forehead, full of expression, though the lines that could frequently be seen on it were not the troughs of worry. Below it, medium-thick eyebrows—retaining memories of the blond hair of his youth—moved about in curious expressiveness, highlighting the eyes they so perfectly framed.

The entire structure of the face was rectangular, well proportioned with strong, angular lines. High, full cheekbones accentuated slightly indented, well-sculptured cheeks, which flowed downward, with but the tiniest hints of jowl fat, into a wide, sturdy jaw, squared just enough at the chin to provide the perfect complementing frame to the whole with the hairline above.

The lips were slightly thin, but given added expressiveness by the protruding Germanic lingual effect of exaggerated vowel shapes, with movements and twists about them that varied with every distinct word, and which took on curious modifications, subtly affecting the baron's entire looks, when he spoke in different tongues.

The voice that came resonating from his throat was a smooth, even silky baritone, neither particularly deep nor loud, yet resonant and commanding, as if it came from a *Meistersinger* holding an abundance of sound in check. The timbre, though not forceful or commanding by volume, confirmed instantly the reservoirs of dynamism existing beneath the surface. It was a voice one *listened* to, even when it spoke in a whisper. It carried authority by its sheer puissance. An unmistakable dynamic of power existed below the surface that was apparent without the shallow pretence of oratory and volume to which lesser men—like the one presently in command of the nation—had to resort in order to mask insecurity and cowardice.

The overall effect of the man's carriage was unmistakable. A more classic replica of the exquisitely crafted Teuton it would have been difficult to imagine.

It was, however, none of these features of physique that made the baron stand out among his peers, but rather the stature of inner life he exuded, chiefly notable in the eyes as he looked upon others of his kind. Not so dark a blue as his wife's, the baron's were pale, and shone out with a constant sparkle of enthusiasm for living, a peace and contentment with his lot, and a deep and abiding love for all living things. They were eyes that had taught themselves long ago to look *inside,* and never to satisfy themselves with the surface of what their gaze chanced to fall upon.

Heinrich von Dortmann was a man indeed cut from a different cloth than his contemporaries of the German Reich. His sole goal in life was the very antithesis of all that Reich and its promulgators stood for. In spite of his title and the very *Germanness* of his name and lineage and ancestry, his was a birthright extending into other soil altogether than the Teutonic and Celtic from which the name *Dortmann* derived its heritage. His roots went farther south and eastward, into regions on the opposite shores of the Mediterranean. His *true* birthright was not one of parental blood, but had become his after the manner of the third chapter of the fourth Gospel. For he knew that he was one of God's children, one of those privileged Gentiles spoken of by Peter and Paul who had been grafted into the royal lineage of David. He was, if not actually by familial stock, yet a Hebrew by faith and therefore no less a son and descendent of Abraham.

In this day and in this place, however, maintaining such sentiments was nowise healthy or prudent. Baron Heinrich von Dortmann was not a man ruled by fear. Yet he did fear for those he loved, especially for his wife and daughter. What kind of world would Sabina face? Would the tranquility of the childhood she had known throughout the 1920s continue, or would bitter tears mar that smile of innocence? Would he be able to—

He stopped himself. He could not ask such questions. They served no purpose. He could not predict the future, and his hopefulness that all might yet turn out well was not completely dead.

He sighed deeply, brushed away the momentary melancholy that had swept over him, and strode forward into the rose garden.

∾∾

Though he would not have understood a word of it, the silent watcher brooded bitterly that he could not eavesdrop on the baron's conversation with his daughter with his ears as well as with his eyes.

∾ 8 ∾

The Mystery of the Garden

Sabina glanced up and smiled at her father.

"Hello, Papa," she said simply.

"You look deep in thought, my daughter," replied the baron. "What have you been reading?"

"The Asher translation you gave me of the Scotsman."

"Ah yes. Our friend Herr Asher in Berlin does Germans a valuable service with his translations. How do you find the Scot?"

"It is like no book I have ever read, Papa. I would dearly love to try to see if I could read it in the original."

"I will see what Herr Buchmann can locate for us in his shop. It may be difficult. Foreign publications, especially of the sort of the Scotsman, are not so well thought of in some circles these days. But I will see what can be done, Sabina. I have a number of the English editions in the library, though I'm afraid this is not one of them."

"Thank you, Papa."

"What have you just been reading?"

Sabina found her father's eyes and held them just a moment; then her lips parted in a knowing smile.

"I think I have discovered why you gave me *this* particular one of his books to read," she said coyly.

"Do you insinuate I may have had some ulterior motive?" rejoined the baron, with an innocent expression but one that hinted of slyness around the edges of his smile.

"Papa, you knew very well I would find this passage."

"I can't imagine what you are talking about."

"The day you handed me the book you went on and on about our *Frühlingsgarten,* and then about gardens in general. You told me the older the garden the better you liked it. I know you have not forgotten."

The baron smiled. "Perhaps I do recall the conversation," he said.

"I asked you why. You said because sometimes things were buried in older gardens lying dormant under the soil, awaiting a new time to show themselves to the eyes of men and women again. I said you made it sound as though the soil and the seeds and bulbs and roots could think for themselves and decide such things."

"And I replied that my comment had primarily to do with truths rather than plants."

"But then, since we were on the subject of gardens," added Sabina, "you went on to say that though the things in the soil could not *think*, they were yet expressions of God's mind, which never stops thinking of creative ways to reveal itself to those who can see it. You said that when God made seeds and soil and plants and trees, he put his own life within them that can never die and is always awaiting just the right opportunity to spring to life and flower again."

The baron chuckled to himself. His daughter had bested him at his own clever game!

"You seem to recall the conversation with particular vividness," he said.

"I remember everything you tell me about the garden, and growing things, Papa." Her voice was earnest.

"I am glad, my daughter. All living things have much to tell us of their Maker."

"Many of which you have told me."

"Mysteries, truths hidden from all but the most diligent and seeking of eyes."

"Why is it so, Papa? Why would God not want everyone to know all they can about him?"

"He does, Sabina."

"Why, then, are there so many mysteries? Why are so many things hard to understand?"

"For the same reason that some of a garden's most spectacular wonders are hidden under the ground for all but a short time of the year, and even then are truly revealed only to those who love them."

"I do not understand you, Papa."

The baron walked a few steps, dug a knife out of his pocket, then clipped a stalk from a nearby bush that boasted a bright orange rose, well opened and lush, at its tip. He brought it back and handed it to his daughter as he sat down on the bench beside her.

"Tell me, Sabina," he said, "is this a spectacular flower?"

"Yes, of course—it's beautiful."

"Do you think all of your uncle Otto's friends in Berlin, at his garden party, do you think they would admire a rose such as this?"

"Yes. They were admiring all the flowers that were in bloom, and all the cut flowers in vases about the grounds too."

"Do you think they admired them for the same reasons you and I do, or only for the bright colors and pleasant aroma?"

"How do you mean? Do we not love them for their colors and smell too?"

"Of course. But most of all for the deeper truths they have to tell us . . . their mysteries . . . their secrets . . . the glimpses they give us of eternal things."

"Perhaps you are right. I doubt any of the people at Uncle Otto's party were thinking of all *that* when they saw his flowers."

"People see on different levels, Sabina. There are different kinds of eyes. There are inner eyes and outer eyes. That is why our Lord spoke of people seeing and hearing, but not perceiving. Some people see but don't *see*. They hear but don't *hear*. All your life I have been trying to train you to truly *see*, and that is why I brought you here so often when you were young, so that you would learn to love the earth and what the Father brings out of it."

"In God's growing things are contained more mysteries and lessons than we will ever know," said his daughter. "You have told me so many times."

The baron rose to his feet and walked some distance to a barren spot in one of the rows where the ground had been cultivated and several holes dug for the planting of some new roses. He knelt down, scooped up a handful of earth, then returned to his daughter and sat down.

"What do you see here in my hand, Sabina?"

"Soil."

"Do you see color, do you smell the perfume of the rose?"

She shook her head.

"Perhaps the beauty of the rose is indeed embodied in the flower you hold in your hand," he went on. "But the *life*, the *mystery*—they are contained in mine! Now that I have clipped it, that beautiful orange blossom has already begun to die. As long as its roots extend deep into the earth, the plant lives and thrives and continues to bear this most wonderful profusion of color. But take it out of the soil, and instantly the life is gone."

He paused, staring down at his hand.

"Look at it," he said at length. "What do you see? Nothing but dirt, most would say. Place it on a woman's dress, or upon the floor of our drawing room, or upon a plate at our dinner table, and we would stare aghast."

Sabina could not help laughing at the images her father had conjured up in her mind.

"It is even an object of scorn and ridicule. We purge it from our homes and our clothes, and before we eat of the vegetables of your mother's garden, we carefully wash off all traces of residue of the ground. Curious, is it not, that this low, despised commodity we call *dirt* should be the transmitter of very life itself to everything that grows on the face of God's earth?"

"I've never thought of that before."

"God often hides life in the most out-of-the-way, hidden places, even in those things, such as this filthy black soil, that are looked upon with contempt."

They sat a moment in silence. Then Herr von Dortmann rose, threw the handful of earth back into the hole whence it had come, and said, "Come, Sabina—there's something else I want to show you."

She rose, took his arm, and followed him, out of the garden, along the pathway leading down the hill, and toward the fields, now ripening under the blazing summer's sun.

They walked a short distance amongst the grasses of wheat, then rye. He clipped several heads of each, as she had seen him do dozens of times every year, at each stage of the grain's development, then led her along the dirt road, around the eastward slope of the knoll, toward the cow barns and animal pens. They made a stop at the chicken shed, where the baron found an egg that had been missed that morning by the kitchen helpers. It was forty minutes later before they were again seated at the bench in the rose garden, both breathing freely and flushed from the heat and the exertion of the climb back up the hill.

Sabina knew her father well. She knew now was the time for her to be silent and wait. Many things were revolving in his mind, and he would tell her when he was ready. If she became impatient, the thoughts now brewing within him might not reach fruition and she might never be privileged to hear them. She loved to see this process at work, and loved him a little more deeply every time she was thus able to drink of his wisdom.

She sat, regaining her breath, and waited.

The baron sat, also silent, peacefully, even reverently rubbing the kernels of wheat and rye between his hands and fingers, until in his palm rested a dozen or two tiny pieces of the green grain.

"In another month it will be golden and ready for the sickle," he mused at length.

He tossed them about in his hand a moment, then put all but one in his pocket. That one he handed to Sabina.

"The mystery of life itself is in that one tiny grain. Do you know where, Sabina?"

"Inside, in the germ."

"Yes, where men's eyes cannot see it."

He took it back, then carefully split it apart with the nail of his finger. "There, you see—the white pulp of the germ!"

He beheld it a moment, then tossed it in his mouth and ground it between his teeth.

"Oh, Papa!" laughed Sabina, "you love everything that grows, don't you?"

"I am curious to find God's life wherever it exists in everything!"

From his other pocket the baron pulled the egg he had carefully stored there after they had passed the henhouse on their walk. This he now handed to his daughter.

"And where is the life here?" he said.

"In the yolk. You taught me that years ago."

He laughed. "Do you tire of my lessons, Sabina?"

"Never, Papa!"

"So then, what do all three have in common—the egg, the kernel of wheat, and the dirt?"

"They all contain life."

"*Hidden* life!" rejoined the baron. "Life that is invisible except to those eyes that search for it—and therein lies the mystery!"

"But why, Papa?" asked Sabina. "I still do not see why it should be so."

"Ah yes. The question of the ages, Sabina. I had not forgotten that you had asked it. That is the reason I took you on our little

walk to find the wheat and the egg, as my way of getting around
to an answer."

He fell silent, then glanced slowly around at all the beauty of
the garden around them.

"God's ways are often curious, and full of mystery," he said.
"Why is it that he always seems to *hide* truth? There are many
things about our Father I do not understand, Sabina, and that is
one of them!

"Yet it is one of God's ways to enclose truths within mysterious outer shells that seem different from what they contain.
Who would ever guess the color and texture of a yolk from
looking at the hard shell of an egg? Who can fathom what
enables the root of a rose to draw the nourishment from
common dirt so as to make such a thing of beauty?

"I can give you no answer, Sabina.

"It will always remain a mystery to me. Somehow, though, I
recognize another principle at work in it, that throughout all
aspects of his work, God reveals truth only to those who truly
seek it. There is a screening process at work in all things, a
process separating truth-seekers from self-seekers, just as the
machines my men and I use separate the wheat from the chaff
at harvesttime. Truth-seekers discover layer upon layer of truth
as they progress through life; self-seekers become only increasingly blind to truth in their ever-increasing self-preoccupation.

"Therefore, God encloses the deepest truths in husks, so that
truth-seekers who hungrily want to discover and know his
ways, whatever the cost, will dig and search and pray and seek
and ask—until light dawns in their hearts.

"Why that is the process, I do not know. But it *is* the process.
We must look past the husks and shells, deep into the heart of
all things. And it is another truth of God's, that the greater the
truth, the more obscure he makes it, so that the finding of it
must be all the greater a quest. We must peel away the husks,
break open the shells, dig deeper beyond the surface into the
rich soils hidden from view—and there find the life of God in
all things!"

"Is that the mystery of the garden you are always telling me
about?"

The baron laughed. *"The* mystery? No, my child. It is but one of a thousand mysteries!"

"You are sounding more and more like the Scotsman, Papa."

Herr von Dortmann laughed again. But unexpectedly in the midst of this delightful conversation with his daughter, a stray thought drifted across his mind like a cloud, and the baron found himself thinking about his brother Otto. The smile on his face faded, and he grew more thoughtful.

∽ 9 ∾
Inner Storms

A hard, persistent rain pelted against the grimy panes of glass.

The warm summer storm had blown in quickly early in the morning from somewhere over the Baltic and had been pounding the north of Germany relentlessly all day. The farmers would no doubt be glad, but it had turned the streets and sidewalks of Berlin into concrete streambeds. Now with night falling, still it showed no sign of letting up.

Emil Korsch stood and stared out into the blackness. He was no philosopher, yet somehow rain always turned him pensive, as one of his temperament was capable of becoming.

The times are perilous just like the slick streets of Berlin, he thought to himself. Perilous, yet fraught with opportunity! It was a risky enterprise, more dangerous for one such as he than any of his colleagues realized. Should one of his enemies discover his secret and leak it upward to the man he would see an hour from now, he would himself become one of the nameless victims of some future SS purge. But he was not ready to spill his blood yet. He was a survivor. He had not climbed as high as he had without considerable cunning of his own.

Korsch turned from the window, returned to his desk, and sat down to review the papers in front of him. He possessed dossiers on Americans, Germans, Russians, and a whole range of influential individuals from all walks of life—information he had been accumulating for his own personal use when the time came for him to make his move to the next-higher echelon within the clandestine hierarchy of the secret police force. Yesterday's summons from Himmler, *Reichsführer* of the SS, was the indication that that moment had at last arrived.

If he could show himself well in Himmler's estimation, well, advancements came as quickly as declines in these heady days when national socialism was on such a rapid rise. He just had to watch his own flank, to make sure nobody delved too deeply into *his* past.

Loyalty these days was not a dependable commodity. The winds of fortune shifted more rapidly in Berlin than those of the weather. And storm clouds were not so readily visible on those horizons as the ones which had blown in from the north twelve hours ago.

Once more he busied himself with the documents before him, seeing if there was anything he might have missed that would prove useful in the ensuing interview.

He had amassed papers on Nazi party members in high and low places, on leading Jews, on foreigners in Germany, on diplomatic higher-ups, on church leaders, and especially on financiers and industrialists whose fortunes he would tap if the opportunity ever presented itself. He was not above blackmail and extortion. If he could do his job, and pad his own coffers in the meantime, well, no one ever said national socialism did not offer its more enterprising adherents advantages for personal advancement and gain.

Forty minutes later Korsch exited the building, pulling his hat and leather coat tightly to him against the slashing rain, got into his car, and began the fateful drive toward what he hoped would be a fortuitous meeting with the man most people recognized as the second most powerful personage in all of Germany.

As he drove, he reflected on the road that had brought him here, so near at last to the very pinnacle of power.

Born in Moscow as Vaslav Korskayev, he had emigrated to Poland with his parents when he was five, and to Germany two years thereafter, just before the outbreak of the Great War. The painful years of his childhood had taught him two things: to hate, and to form no lasting allegiances except to himself.

The natural antipathy between Germans and Russians first of all caused him to hate himself—to hate his mother tongue, to hate his accent, to hate his name, to hate the heritage of his Russian blood. Everywhere he went he was reviled and treated with contempt, made fun of, laughed at, and used by bullying German youths as an object of scorn and derision. He tried hard to fit in, to be like the other children, to speak the new language correctly. But he was different, and they made sure he knew he was an outcast and would never be "one of them."

Very soon, as a result, he learned to hate the German people as well. He hated them for their arrogance, for their Aryan pride, for the puffed-up superiority they felt over all other peoples and races. But he learned too that to survive he had to pretend to become one of them, to play the game. He vowed that by the time he was twenty he would speak more flawless German than any native Austrian or Bavarian. He would beat them at their own game. He would have his revenge, though he had to achieve it silently. He would disguise himself as the consummate German and have the last laugh on them all.

After the war, he changed his name to Emil Korsch, became a German citizen, and, after his parents' death, in the confused political climate of the early twenties, managed to secure forged identity papers that transformed him into a native German, born and raised right here in Berlin. He was aware of the revolution in his motherland, but was so torn with twisted and confused loyalties that he never took seriously the idea of returning to Bolshevik Russia and became a German Fascist instead, joining the Oberland group and eventually becoming one of the brownshirted Nazi SS agents.

By the time of Hitler's ascendency in 1933, Emil was twenty-seven and climbing up the Nazi ladder in earnest. The many hatreds he had been nourishing for two decades served him well, for was not hatred the fuel upon which the Fascist machine ran? In temperament he could not have been better suited for recruitment by the Gestapo when it was formed out of the Prussian Secret Police that same year. The following year, when Himmler and Göring ordered the Blood Purge, he had been one of those who had helped carry it out. If the truth were known, he had rather enjoyed killing the SA and Catholic leaders and others with whom the Führer had had old scores to settle. He learned, as time went on, to hate the Jews, the Christians, the wealthy. He hated the Americans and the British—and the Germans along with them.

As he grew more entrenched in fascism, however, he began to find himself curiously drawn toward the roots of his past and desirous of knowing more about the revolution that had swept his Russian homeland. Though bolshevism and fascism were avowedly the bitterest of enemies, and though Germans and Russians hated one another passionately, he found within himself a curious mixture of the psyches of both personalities. In a complex schizophrenia of mingled communism and fascism, he secretly took to reading Marx, even Lenin, and found himself drawn to their Communist ideals. To his other hatreds was now added the Communist enmity toward elitism in all forms, the aristocracy and the ancient land barons in both Germany and Russia.

To this extent he adopted the ideals of 1917 even in the carrying out of his self-promoting agenda as an agent of the SS—that all the old power groups would one day fall, and a new elite would take their place. The landowning elite, the Jewish business elite, the powerful Christian church, and the former powerful controlling interests of government—all would one day be toppled, and Hitler seemed to be the one most likely to emerge as head of the new order. Therefore, he would follow the Nazi train where it led. A Russian-born German, member of the Nazi party and elite secret police, with Communist leanings—Emil Korsch was an enigma in every fiber of his psychologically contorted being.

He had learned through the years to mask the inner storms of his personal furies. In today's political atmosphere it wouldn't do to show one's emotions. No one would have guessed from looking at him the vendettas upon which he was bent.

His hatred toward Christians was as intense as Hitler's toward Jews. While Hitler's was ideological and racist, Korsch's was born out of personal experience. The Germans who had persecuted his father and mother and had been so cruel to him had not been Jews but Lutherans, good German Christians every one, and he had had nothing but antipathy toward the hypocrisy of the National German Church ever since. Christians, he found, were the most prejudiced of the lot against those who were different from themselves. Who was it but millions of so-called German Christians that had voted Hitler into power, and who had now turned so viciously against the Jews?

He had, over the years, kept files, adding to them continually, and as soon as the Pastor's Emergency League had been formed in 1933, he had begun watching its leaders more closely, convinced that the information would be useful in time. When the Confessing Church was formed by an anti-Nazi faction, he had immediately begun attempts to quietly infiltrate the new movement. While Hitler and Himmler were focusing on the Jewish problem, he had seen a vast potential for his own advancement in becoming an expert on "the Christian threat" to fascism.

He had also known early that the Americans were as great a threat to the Nazi future as the British or French. They all had their ideals of freedom and religion and the self-righteous pride in their democratic form of government. So he had been accumulating useful information there too.

In all these areas, while he had played the loyal lackey to those above him, he had slowly and carefully been developing his own network of underlings, finding and recruiting young zealots whom he might teach to do his bidding.

But it was time to put all these thoughts and plans on hold. He had arrived. The moment of his destiny had come.

He could not keep his heart from pounding a little more rapidly than usual as he walked up, hesitated only a moment, then knocked on the closed door.

∽ 10 ∽

Low Advancement

"Ah, Herr Korsch," said Himmler, glancing up as the other entered after his summons. "I am glad to see you again." The head of the SS did not rise from his desk or offer his hand.

"The pleasure is mine, Herr *Reichsführer*," replied Korsch, clicking his heels together, shooting his right arm out stiffly in salute, and then walking crisply to the desk and standing before it at attention.

"My nephew speaks very highly of you, Korsch."

"I am honored."

"He says you will be one of my top Gestapo agents one day, and that I would do well to find a role for you of higher standing."

Korsch said nothing.

"Indeed, I have been looking over your file," Himmler went on, "and I find it an admirable one, full of meritorious achievements on behalf of the Reich."

The interview between the thirty-one-year-old Gestapo agent and the man who was ultimately his boss, Heinrich Himmler, the chief policeman for the Third Reich and head of the SS and Gestapo, who was a mere six years his senior, could not have been more in keeping with the climate of the times. In a regime which deified the Aryan ideal of manhood, these two, like their leader, seemed to exemplify almost the precise opposite.

Himmler was a small man, in all ways—short of height, thin of personal attributes, unappealing and uninteresting. His round face, soft high-pitched voice, thin-rimmed spectacles, and timid, hesitant carriage were not such as to convey leadership or authority. Added to this, a certain fussy, fastidious formality gave a stilted quality to his demeanor and seemed to qualify him more for some dusty professorial post than for running a country. He did possess, however, the single attribute most necessary to the Nazi cause: a heart of frozen stone.

What but being something less than human could allow such cruelties of prejudice and ambition so thoroughly to possess the vessel where love was intended to reside? A disciple unto fanaticism of the theory of race superiority, Himmler hated Jews, blacks, Asians, Russians, Serbs, and Arabs. He had already masterminded the June 1934 Blood Purge of the German military and government, and had more recently been secretly drawing up plans in his demented mind for the imprisonment and eventual extermination of Jews and Slavs. He would, of course, perform certain hideous "experiments" on the subjects first, in the interest of science and race purification, much as he had done at the small chicken farm he had operated before joining the Nazi movement.

In truth, Himmler was a perfect reflection of his Führer.

Physically and intellectually limited, relationally unfit for intimacy, emotionally, morally, and spiritually bankrupt, Adolf
Hitler was drawn to others as dwarfed in character as himself,
and by the sheer compulsion of fear and brutality they had
succeeded in enslaving an entire nation to carry out their evil
bidding. He had gathered around himself an influential
clique—including Himmler, Hermann Göring, and Martin
Bormann—known as the Midnight Club. The name could not
have been more suitably chosen, for indeed, rather than usher-
ing in the glorious thousand-year Reich they dreamed of, under
their demonic leadership Germany was swiftly careening
toward the blackest midnight of its long and colorful history.

The ideal of German superiority could not have been more
absent from the very leaders who preached it. The man of true
stature, content in the personhood of his own being, walks the
low road in peace and finds no necessity to exalt himself or
demean those who are different. Only inferiority insists on puff-
ing itself up. Too many proclamations and protestations to the
contrary reveal the very flaws the words so vainly try to conceal.
The mantra of nazism—that German pride, prowess, might, and
dominance must reassert themselves—was transparently motivated at deep levels by the private personal anguish of those who
forwarded it most vehemently, of knowing that they themselves
were unfit specimens of the Celtic lineage.

Never had the integrity of the German temperament sunk
lower than during this heinous hour when national socialism
was allowed to run unchecked across the map of a once-proud
land.

And now Himmler, in his turn, like his leader, sought out
those whom he could gather into his *own* little club of blackness.

"As I understand it," Himmler went on, looking down at the
papers before him, "you possess a particular disdain for Christians, and for the church in general."

"That is true, Herr *Reichsführer.*"

"Are you an atheist, Herr Korsch?" As he said the word,
Himmler glanced up and eyed the man standing before him
beadily but with utterly blank expression. He was clearly testing
him.

"My loyalties are to the Führer and to the Reich, *mein Reichsführer*," answered Korsch.

Himmler continued to stare into his face, the dim light of the bulb overhead reflecting off the uncurved glass of his spectacles, preventing Korsch from seeing the thin eyes boring into him. Apparently satisfied, after a moment Himmler looked down, then spoke again.

"I am glad to hear it," he said. "As you know, our beloved Führer is a staunch churchman and a firm believer in God. His faith in the Almighty is at the root of all national socialism stands for and is attempting to achieve."

He paused, eying Korsch once more. But the young Nazi had become as skilled in hiding his reactions as the *Reichsführer*, and said nothing.

"The church, however," Himmler went on, "has become tainted with an element which does not realize the benefits of our cause to the religion of Germany. There is a minority of church leaders, as you are no doubt aware, that has become increasingly disloyal to the Führer."

"I am familiar with them, *mein Reichsführer*."

"And in your opinion, Herr Korsch, what should be done about them?" Another question of testing had come.

"They must be purged from the church, *mein Reichsführer*."

An imperceptible twitch played momentarily at the edge of the SS chief's lips, then disappeared. His nephew had been right—this young agent showed promise.

"How would you suggest it be done?"

"Discreetly at first."

"And if that failed?"

"Then stronger measures would be called for."

"You said *purged*—only from the church?"

"And from the Reich, if they continued to oppose us."

"What kind of stronger measures, Herr Korsch?"

"A ban on their activities and teachings, oaths of allegiance. If they refused to comply, imprisonment."

"We have imposed such restrictions already."

"With but limited success, if you'll forgive me, Herr *Reichsführer*."

Himmler glanced up at the young man sharply. "And you

think you could perhaps achieve better results?" he said with a hint of cool sarcasm in his voice.

"If you will forgive me again, sir, yes, I do believe so."

"How?"

"I have files and contacts. With the might of the Gestapo and the SS behind me, it is my conviction this disloyalty could be stopped."

A pause followed. Himmler shuffled through several of the papers in the file in front of him, took one, glanced up and down it briefly, then said, "I understand you speak fluent Russian, Herr Korsch."

"Yes, sir."

"How did you come by it?"

"I grew up in the east, *mein Reichsführer,* near Poland. Many Russian immigrants lived nearby."

"And you merely . . . picked it up?" queried Himmler skeptically.

"I have a penchant for languages, sir."

"And you are *fond* of Russia, are you, Korsch?"

"No, sir," replied Korsch just a trifle too quickly, though the Gestapo chief did not seem to notice. "I hate Russia, *mein Reichsführer.*"

"So does our beloved Führer," rejoined Himmler. "Then why have you kept up with the Russian tongue?"

"I thought it might prove useful for our cause one day, *mein Reichsführer.*"

"So it might, Korsch. Have you made use of it?"

"I have some contacts at the embassy that I employ from time to time."

Himmler took in the information with more interest than he allowed to show. "I may have need of a Gestapo agent I can trust," he said. "There continue to be, shall we say, *negotiations* with the Bolsheviks. It may be that I shall need a spy who could pass for one of them. Do you think you could pass for a Russian, Korsch?"

"I believe I could, sir."

"And you would be willing?"

"My service to the Reich is yours to command, *mein Reichsführer.*"

"Have you worked with the Russians before?"

"I have a lackey planted in the embassy, sir."

"You seem to be a resourceful young man, Korsch."

"One does not advance in the SS without being able to prove oneself."

"Is advancement your goal?"

"My goal is to serve the Reich."

A long pause followed. Korsch stood motionless. Himmler continued to stare at his desk, thinking.

"Can you kill, Korsch?" he asked at length, unaware of Korsch's role in the '34 purge.

"I can, sir."

"With your own hands?"

"If necessary, sir."

"Have you?"

"I have."

Again there was a brief silence. By now it was late. The city was quiet. There were no other sounds in the building.

"I am going to appoint you as my special assistant to deal with the Christian problem, Herr Korsch," said Himmler at length. "You will report directly to me. Gather what help you need. Recruit your own assistants, as long as they are loyal, intensely loyal—to me, to the Reich, and of course, to our beloved Führer. Do you understand?"

"Yes, Herr *Reichsführer.*"

"You will have a year to deal with this disloyalty."

"I will not disappoint you."

"Of course you won't. Meanwhile, continue to infiltrate the Russian and American delegations in Berlin. I may want to make use of your contacts there as well."

"Yes, sir."

Himmler looked down and began fiddling with another file. Korsch continued to stand at stiff attention. After a moment Himmler glanced up, showing a hint of surprise to see the young Gestapo agent still before him.

"That is all, Korsch," he said curtly.

"Yes, sir," said the other, saluting again with his arm; then, spinning on his heels, he strode briskly from the room.

PART II

The Mystery of the Kingdom—
Midsummer 1937

Guests in the Country

The invitation could not have come at a better time, Thaddeus McCallum said to himself.

Ever since the open announcement of German rearmament in 1935, the position of those in the U.S. Embassy in Berlin had become more and more ticklish and full of hidden and unspoken pressures. The official American posture of neutrality kept them walking on diplomatic tightropes among the French, British, and Germans—daily more difficult in light of Hitler's increased aggression.

The Rhineland coup last year, McCallum feared, had only been the beginning, and the French impotence to mount the slightest resistance against the *Wehrmacht* in defense of the demilitarized status imposed by Versailles upon the Rhineland did not bode well for stopping Germany's expansions elsewhere. Hitler's designs on his native Austria were well documented. The *Anschluss* was a key Nazi objective. McCallum feared the dominoes would begin falling any time, and once that happened there would be no stopping them.

He read over the letter again.

His friend the baron must have been reading his mind. There was nothing he wanted more right now than to get out of the city. To spend a weekend at the Dortmann estate would be a welcome respite.

Matthew was certain not to object. He had hardly stopped talking about the girl since meeting her at the garden party. And few who had been in attendance had stopped talking about his untimely exit!

"Listen to this, Matt," said McCallum that evening, glancing across the dinner table at his son. "I received this letter today."

He read it aloud.

"What do you think?"

"I don't know whether I'd be able to face her again after making such a fool of myself!"

"She thought it was great sport. She was as wet and messed up as you, and she didn't seem to mind in the least having everyone laugh at her."

"She wasn't the one who fell in the pond!"

"Well, from what I could tell, the baron's daughter doesn't seem the type to hold such a faux pas against you."

Matthew nodded. "Yeah, you're right, now that I think about it. She really is quite a girl. You know, Dad, she opened up more quickly and personally than any German I've met since we've been here."

"Her father's the same. Absolutely personable from the minute I met him. They're a couple of unusual natives, that's for sure. What do you say? I'm ready for a few relaxing days in the country."

"Sounds good to me. When did they want us to come?"

"This weekend. We'll go Friday afternoon, and come home on Sunday."

∽∾ೀ∽

Four days later, Matthew and Thaddeus McCallum found themselves pulling off the country road they had been following, and pursuing the course up through the birch entryway to the hilltop estate of Baron Heinrich von Dortmann.

Emerging at the top, they beheld the rearing watery sentinel with suitable detachment and stopped in front of the house. Baron von Dortmann, who had been expecting them, did not wait for anyone else to answer their ring at the door, but burst out personally to greet them with boisterously warm and enthusiastic handshakes and smiles of welcome as they climbed out of their car.

He grabbed up their two bags himself and led them inside.

Half an hour later, after the McCallums had been shown to their rooms, the three Dortmanns greeted their guests again in the ground-floor guest sitting room.

"I would like you to meet my wife, Mr. McCallum," said the baron in his native tongue. "She does not speak your language, so you will be able to use your German. Marion von Dortmann . . . Thaddeus McCallum and his son, Matthew."

"Welcome to our home," said the baron's wife, shaking hands with father and son. "My husband has told me about you both."

"Frau von Dortmann," said McCallum.

"I hope he did not tell you too much about me," said Matthew, casting a sheepish glance toward Sabina.

"I'm afraid I do know about the incident of the fishpond," Frau von Dortmann said with a smile.

Matthew groaned.

"But not to worry. You are among friends. Please, sit down," she added. "Heidi will be bringing us coffee and tea and cake momentarily."

"I tell you, McCallum," said the baron, as the five seated themselves in the overstuffed leather chairs and couches around the large and well-appointed parlor, "my wife and her maids and cooks keep us so well provided for with food it is a wonder we are not all fat beyond belief!"

"In the German tradition, is it not?" said the American. "At least I have found it so during my years here."

"Indeed," laughed the baron. "We ate lightly this noon in anticipation of your coming. We will dine this evening at six, in the *American* tradition. Tomorrow, we shall dine at one, after the *German* custom."

"It is you who should be the diplomat, Baron von Dortmann," interjected Matthew.

"We try to make our guests feel comfortable and at home," added their hostess.

"Do you have guests frequently?" asked McCallum.

"I do not know if *frequently* is the word, but certainly regularly," answered Frau von Dortmann. "Yes, we have all kinds of guests here—personal friends, acquaintances, sometimes people we do not even know."

"I know about German hospitality, but that seems curious even—"

He was interrupted by the entrance of two maids carrying trays—one containing pots of coffee and tea, the other containing several delicate cakes, a torte with several layers of cream and chocolate filling, and a smaller fruit-topped sponge cake.

They set them down on an oak sideboard and proceeded to serve the hosts and their guests.

It was Baron von Dortmann who resumed the thread of the conversation a minute or two later.

"Perhaps you noticed the words in old script above the door of the house when you entered," he said.

"Yes, I did, though to be honest I did not pause to be thorough in my attempted interpretation. Tell me again what they said."

"The inscription reads *Ein Landhaus Für Leben Und Zurückgezogenheit*," answered the baron.

"All but the last is clear enough."

"Literally it would be translated: A country house for life and seclusion and solitude. I suppose the nearest English word to incorporate all that into it would be *A Retreat*, or perhaps *A Country Hideaway*, but translating such subtleties from one tongue to another is always difficult. So over the years our estate has simply come to be known as *Lebenshaus*, or House of Life. Technically it's inaccurate German. It ought to be *Haus des Lebens*. But I wanted a single-word name, and since we are a multilingual family, I decided to take a liberty with my mother tongue."

"I think I gather the meaning. Sort of a spa for the soul, you might call it."

"Exactly! I like that, McCallum—a spa for the soul! Most well put!" The baron laughed heartily.

"What does it all mean?" asked Matthew. "You've explained the words, but not the *whys* behind them."

"This is a perceptive young man you have here, Herr McCallum," said Frau von Dortmann. "He knows just the right questions to ask."

"I too am curious about the meaning of the inscription," said Thaddeus. "The meaning *behind* the meaning."

"I brought up the inscription in answer to your question about our guests," said the baron. "As you can see, we are a small family who has been blessed with an enormous home, capable of housing twenty families. Even with our servants and farm laborers, which are not nearly so numerous as in former times, much of this grand edifice sits vacant."

The baron paused, took a drink of coffee and a bite of the cake which sat on a small plate in his lap, then went on.

"For a number of years, we have found ourselves blessed with frequent visitors and guests. Some from the neighborhood, some from the larger cities, others from far away. How it began has puzzled even Marion and me. But almost from the moment we were married—what is it now, *Liebchen*, twenty-one years?"

"*Ja*, Heinrich," his wife said, smiling at him, "*einundzwanzig.*"

"During nearly all that time we have found people coming to our estate here in the country. At first they were mostly friends of ours, then friends of those friends, until gradually, I suppose, word quietly spread that there was a place in the country to which anyone might go for a day or two of peace and solitude. It is nothing we sought, or seek even now. But we have been blessed by it and now consider the guest rooms of *Lebenshaus* as important as our own chambers. We always keep several made up, aired, and ready for occupancy at a moment's notice."

"Very interesting. What do people do when they come?"

"There's no set agenda, if that is what you mean. Sometimes we talk, sometimes they keep to themselves. The grounds have a calming and soothing effect. Many have commented or written to us afterwards that they have been forever changed by their time here. Some come especially to see the garden."

"Yes, I have heard of your garden."

"Whatever their reasons, whoever may come has always been welcome at *Lebenshaus*, and though in this life I may perhaps wear a title of some ancient significance, when guests are here, I consider myself their servant. We are here, and our estate is here, dedicated to *life*, Thaddeus . . . life—in whatever manner God chooses to give it, and however much, to those who come."

The room grew silent, as each considered the implications of the baron's words.

The rest of the day passed quickly, not without a tour of the grounds and a preliminary stroll through the garden. The hour was late before they retired, the baron more pleased than ever at his two new friends who had, before the afternoon gave way to evening, passed well beyond the threshold of mere acquaintance.

～ 12 ～
A Morning in the Garden

"I knew I would find you here, Papa!"

"Sabina," exclaimed the baron, turning his head around with a startled expression. "What brings you out so early?"

"The sunrise does not only beckon men, you know, Papa. Sometimes it calls to me too."

The baron laughed. "Of course I know. It is the most wonderful time of any day. How anyone can sleep through it I will never understand, though all are made differently. So . . . how *did* you know I was here?"

"Where else would you be?"

"Ah, you indeed know me well!"

"Also, I followed the smell of your coffee," Sabina added with a smile.

Baron von Dortmann glanced down at the cup he held in his hand and chuckled. The strong Swedish brew was indeed aromatic, though he doubted sufficient to lead his daughter this far from the kitchen. He breathed in deeply, though it was not with the fragrance of coffee that he filled his lungs.

"There is nothing like the wet, dewy air of the morning," he said, "before the heat of the day has taken away the reminders of darkness and dampness and the coolness of the night. Is your mama up and about?"

"She is in the kitchen with Heidi and Carola."

"And our guests?"

"I have not seen them, Papa. I am afraid they are sleeping through the best part of the day."

"We shall forgive them this once," laughed her father. "They had the journey yesterday, and it will take them at least one night to shake off the shackles of the city. And we did keep them up late last night! But tomorrow we shall have them here with us before the cockcrow! They must share the wonders of the garden at sunrise as well as at midday, would you not agree?"

"Without a doubt, Papa! We shall be here even before Heiko has begun milking the cows!"

The baron took a sip of coffee from his cup, while Sabina slowly sauntered along the pathway through the rows of roses.

She continued to walk about, making a large circle, and at length arrived back at where her father still sat.

"Do you wish to be alone, Papa?"

He smiled, then took her hand where she stood beside him. "I would never wish to be anywhere other than with you . . . *or* here . . . *or* with your mother," he added, giving her a wink.

"You were doing more than admiring roses when I came, were you not?"

The baron smiled, then nodded.

"It is always my custom to pray for whomever the Father sends us. He has given us a great deal, such abundant blessings. I would not feel capable or worthy to steward them without his guidance. His purposes here have to do with far more than the harvesting of mere grain. The fields of God are growing a different crop to harvest."

"You were praying for Matthew and his father?"

"I was holding them before the Father's heart and asking him to make their time here of value to them—in the ways that matter . . . in the ways of the Father."

"I awoke early thinking of them too, Papa."

"They are not here by coincidence. Even though I wrote to invite them, all God's ways are purposeful. I am always seeking to fall in with those purposes, though I am slow to comprehend them sometimes."

"You always seem to know God's purposes, Papa."

"Wait until you are my age, my child. Then you will see, as I do, how little you know, how feeble is your trust, and how great is your selfishness."

He sighed. "I may look to you as a man of some faith because I have been walking along this pathway with God for many years. And perhaps I know enough of his truths to pass them on to you. Ah, but my daughter, there are moments I feel so frail and weak, as if I am yet such an infant."

"I can hardly believe I am hearing you talk so, Papa," said Sabina, almost alarmed.

"You will understand one day, my child. One day you shall understand."

They parted. Sabina continued on down the hill into a deeper part of the garden. The baron sat where he was.

Forty minutes later, father and daughter, together again, his arm around her shoulder, silently emerged from the garden through the stone arch and walked up the steps onto the courtyard. The baron held the long stem of a single red rose in his hand. They walked across the trim lawn and into the house, where by now the kitchen was abuzz with the morning's activity.

Greeting the servants with the enthusiasm for which German farm communities are renowned, the baron walked across the kitchen to his wife, kissed her, handed her the rose, then bent and whispered a few words in her ear.

In sole response, her lips parted in a simple smile.

The baron then left the room to see if his guests were yet ready to be given morning's greetings.

"What did Papa say to you, Mama?" asked Sabina, approaching her mother.

"The same thing he tells me every morning," replied her mother.

"But what is it, Mama?"

"He was telling me the secret of the rose."

∽ 13 ∾

Woods and Countryside

About ten-thirty that same morning, Sabina led Matthew through the courtyard at the back of the house, down the hill toward the stables.

They had agreed upon a ride of an hour or two before luncheon, and now as they walked, suitably attired—she in a maroon riding habit, he with riding breeches and boots which his host had provided for him—she explained the differences in personality between the two horses he would have to choose between. Schmidt, the groom, was standing by to saddle the selection of their guest. He already had Sabina's favorite ready for the morning's romp.

Twenty minutes later, they set off from the stable, she on the dark Morgan, he on the light-grey Belgian. Sabina led at an easy walk down the pathway bordering the garden's perimeter on the outside, toward the south, crossing the creek by a narrow wooden bridge not far from the point where it twisted its way under the hedge and into the depths of *Der Frühlingsgarten* and on toward the pinewood.

"Have you recovered from your fall in my uncle Otto's pond?" Sabina asked as they rode along.

"I was hoping you wouldn't bring that up!"

"It wasn't really so bad, was it?"

"Humiliating is the word for it! I hated to do that to my father, around all those important people."

"I thought it was fun!"

"You didn't mind what your cousin thought to see you traipsing back to the house, your dress all wet and me soaking and dripping all over, everyone laughing?"

"Who cares what she thought?" laughed Sabina. "I still think it was fun!"

"I'll let you keep your opinion, but it's a day I'd rather forget!"

They rode on, across the grass on the other side of the creek, until the dirt roadway entered the pinewood. Soon they were enclosed within its shadows. A quietness came over them, and they rode for a good while to no sound other than the steady *clomp, clomp, clomp* of their horses' feet along the hard-packed dirt.

"Don't you just love the smell!" sighed Sabina at length.

Matthew breathed in deeply, and nodded a smile of consenting satisfaction. "There's nothing quite like a pine forest," he said, "especially on a warm sunny day. I've always thought that there must be some special ingredient in the pine itself—in the needles or the bark or something—that is particularly responsive to the rays of the sun and its warmth. There is an odor released on a warm day that is like nothing in all the world."

"Why Matthew," exclaimed Sabina, "you are a lover of nature too! You let me think I was the only outdoorsman."

"I never said such a thing."

"You let me think it, all my going on and on about the Alps and our garden!"

"Well I haven't been to the Alps, or to the seashore very often. But I *do* love forests!"

"Are there forests where you come from?"

"Are there ever!" answered Matthew. "Why this little thing, as wonderful as it smells, would hardly even qualify to be called a forest where I live. At least where we used to live."

"Where is that?"

"It's a state called Montana."

"Hmm . . . I've heard of New York and California, but not Montana. Is it very beautiful?"

"Beautiful is hardly the word to describe it! It's so huge and open. There are no Alps, but there are mountains we call the Rockies. And huge open plains where deer and elk and even buffalo roam free."

"And forests?"

"Forests like none you've ever seen! Forests of pine and fir and spruce—each with smells and undergrowth and wildlife all their own."

"How big is the state you call Montana?"

"It is as big as your whole Germany!"

"One little state, as big as Germany!"

"Can you imagine the forests now?"

"Perhaps a little."

"Imagine a forest stretching from here to Berlin and down to Poznan, without a break in it, without a town, without even a village, and then a little clearing for two or three towns, and then another forest equally large on the other side. That is how big the forests are in Montana."

They fell silent for a moment.

"Do you hate my little pinewood, then?" asked Sabina.

"No," laughed Matthew. "It's the closest to Montana I've been in four years. There is something different about it too, that I can't quite put my finger on, something I find appealing, but I don't know quite what it is."

"Different?"

"I think it's how the trees are more spread out. It isn't as dense. You can see right through. It's a more friendly-feeling kind of woods, perhaps that's it."

"You should see the Black Forest down near Bavaria. That's not a friendly forest!"

"Maybe what I notice here is peculiar to the north, then. I like it. It seems that this is a wood you could walk and walk in, and even get lost in, without feeling that you were *really* lost—do you know what I mean?"

"Perhaps not, but let me show you one of my favorite spots among the pines."

Sabina galloped off ahead and Matthew did his best to follow, but she was nearly out of sight ahead of him when suddenly she pulled up and dismounted.

Matthew caught up, stopped, and joined her on the ground. They tied the reins of their mounts to branches, then she led off through the trees.

They walked over the springy, grassy, needle-strewn floor amongst pines whose trunks were no more than nine inches or a foot in diameter. Now that their horses were not with them, the only sounds came from their own feet breaking dead bits of debris and pine twigs as they went.

Gradually the trees became more tightly packed. Still Sabina bore straight ahead. Branches began clustering more and more densely around them until, following single file behind her, Matthew found himself so buried in the branches and greenery of close-growing pines that he had to hold his hands to his face for protection and could not see more than a foot or two in any direction. On they walked, Sabina fearlessly stomping through the heavy growth, he following blindly, until all at once they emerged into a grassy clearing.

Matthew glanced around in amazement.

"Was that dense enough for you?" laughed Sabina.

"I couldn't tell *where* you were leading me! Yes, you could sure get lost in a place like that in no time—but what is this?"

"A clearing, a meadow."

"But it's . . . it's so perfectly sheltered, so hidden away, but tucked right in the middle of the forest."

How could either of the two young people have realized the prophetic import of the words that had just fallen from

Matthew's lips? Indeed, this idyllic time they now shared was as a season of leisure, reminiscent of a pace of life quickly vanishing in the gathering urgency of the twentieth century. This sheltered life would all too soon be shattered, and both would look back on those precious days with longing remembrances.

He continued to gaze about. Indeed, they stood at the edge of a circular clearing of only some forty or fifty feet across, bordered all the way around by dense-clustered pines so tight that they quite literally formed a wall around the meadow. Yet the meadow was so flat and clean that not a shrub or stump was to be seen—only lush green forest grass, thick and still wet from the morning's dew.

"Our forests may not be so huge, but they have their own unusual qualities too. There are many such little meadows scattered all throughout them. But from the outside, you would never dream they were here because you cannot see through the thick growth that surrounds them."

"It's wonderful . . . so protected and quiet," he said, slowly walking to the center of the grass, then stopping and turning in a complete circle as he took in every inch of the place. "You can see nothing but the grass under your feet, the wall of trees, and the blue of the sky straight above us. It's a private little world! How did you find it?"

"I've played and ridden and walked in these woods since I was four or five," she replied. "I know almost every inch of them."

"Do you come here often?" asked Matthew.

"I have several favorite meadows such as this. They are favorite places for the deer, which we have in abundance."

"It's so absolutely isolated and peaceful—I just love it!"

"But come—there's something else I want to show you."

Sabina led the way to the edge of the meadow, plunging without hesitation straight through the encircling wall of pines. Once again Matthew found himself scratching and scraping and walking blindly through branches and leaves and brush until the trees began to thin and gradually they were walking again through the spacious and open wood. In another moment or two they arrived at the spot where they had left their horses.

Matthew glanced back the way they had come. "I'd never

dream it was there," he said. "Your eyes think they're looking through a wood that just goes on and on, and you can't see so much as a hint of what's hidden right there in the middle of it."

"We have to ride farther," said Sabina, mounting her Morgan.

Matthew climbed onto the back of the Belgian and followed. He did not fully comprehend their direction, but the course they now pursued was drawing a wide semicircular arc through the wood toward the southeast, gradually moving up a sloping rise in the terrain. After about fifteen minutes, though still in the heart of the wood, they had reached the crest of a wooded hill that, at a distance of a kilometer or two, was about half the height of the bare knoll upon which sat the house and buildings of the Dortmann estate.

"What's that?" asked Matthew, pointing ahead into the trees at a small wooden structure.

"It's a hunting box."

"It looks like a tree house to me, without the tree."

"You build them *in* the trees?"

"Sure, I've never seen one freestanding like that."

"Shall we climb it?" said Sabina, scrambling off her horse and dashing toward the wooden ladder which led up to the small enclosure.

Matthew was right behind her, and in two or three minutes they were comfortably seated inside, though the quarters were cramped.

"What a view!" exclaimed Matthew, gazing out above the tops of the trees that fell off below them in all directions. "I hadn't realized we were climbing, but from up here you can see the top of the forest all around, and out across the fields in the distance."

"Why do you think I brought you here?" laughed Sabina. "This is one of the most spectacular views for many kilometers. The wood is full of hunting boxes, but this is the one I like to climb best."

"I know why! You can see all over the valley out there, the fields off to the right, and there's your father's estate straight ahead of us. I hadn't noticed before, but there seems to be a village straight off in the distance."

"Yes. Niedersdorf."

"And is that another estate between your father's and the village?"

"Not so large as Papa's, yet sizable. That is Count von Schmundt's villa." As she said the name, a chill came into Sabina's voice.

"You don't like the count, from the sound of it?"

"It's more than just not liking him, though, come to think of it, I probably don't like him much. But let's don't talk about that now. I'm having too pleasant a time today. Let's enjoy the view."

"I'm sorry I asked," said Matthew, then turned his gaze once again to the Dortmann property. "It's almost like looking at the whole countryside from an airplane, or a picture of it."

"You see, there's the *Frühlingsgarten* sloping down to the left below our house, and the stables to the right. And there, on the far rooftop, is the balcony."

"This is great," said Matthew. "Being up high like this gives you such a feeling of the whole area."

"I love high places," agreed Sabina.

"Like Alps?" suggested Matthew.

"And the rooftops of houses, and hunting boxes in the middle of the woods."

It was quiet for several long minutes as they continued to gaze at the nearby forest, the valley beyond, the fields, and the knoll and the estate.

"We probably should go," said Sabina. "It's getting close to dinnertime. If they are not already waiting for us, they will be by the time we are back. We still have some ride ahead of us!"

❧ 14 ❧

House of Intrigue

"Your home amazes me, Baron," said Thaddeus McCallum as they sat around the table in the dining room finishing their midday meal. "You have shown me all around outside. I have beheld it from many angles, front and back. There are windows everywhere that reveal what must be a host of rooms and passageways. Yet I cannot account for but the tiniest fraction of it from what I have seen on the inside."

The baron laughed.

"It is an enormous old place. I even forget myself what some of its out-of-the-way corners are like. I don't doubt there are rooms I haven't laid eyes on since I was a boy."

"How many rooms does it contain?"

"I don't know, now that you mention it. I used to know—do you recall the number, Marion?"

"Isn't it something around a hundred and twenty, Heinrich?" replied his wife.

"That sounds close to the number."

"It is like a castle!" exclaimed Matthew. "Over a hundred rooms—I can't imagine a house so big!"

"I think it is more than that, Mama," said Sabina.

"You could be right," added the baron. "Just our ancient, but comfortable, country cottage."

"Like no cottage I have ever been in," laughed McCallum. "It must have been some undertaking to install electricity and plumbing."

The baron laughed. "You cannot imagine! Ten bathrooms, all told, on the three floors, and electricity in every room—yes, it was a feat of engineering genius!"

"Would you like to see more of it?" asked Sabina.

"Would we ever!" replied both the younger and older Americans almost in unison.

"Then we'll take you all around it!" rejoined Sabina enthusiastically. "You may have larger forests, Matthew, but we Europeans have larger houses! Can we, Papa?"

"By all means. It will be the perfect exercise to stimulate body and mind after lunch."

"After that ride this morning, I don't think my body will need any exercise," said Matthew. "But why our minds? How will *they* be stimulated?"

"Why, in keeping us from getting lost, my boy!" answered the baron. "This is no ordinary house. There are turns and twists and passageways and secret chambers and false walls and hidden staircases innumerable!"

"And dungeons!" put in Sabina.

"Only in old Eppie's fantasies," rejoined her father.

"Who's old Eppie?" Matthew asked.

"Our oldest servant," replied the baron. "She is what I believe you Americans would call 'retired' now. She's eighty-five if she's a day, though no one knows her age for certain, and she certainly doesn't want to think of herself as retired."

"She's still here? You still take care of her?"

"Certainly. She's part of our family. She served my father before me, and her mother served my grandfather."

"She was born in the middle of the nineteenth century," added Marion. "Germany was not even a nation then. She is from a different time, there is no doubt about that."

"You'll excuse me from the tour, won't you, dear?" said Marion. "I need to tend to the kitchen."

The baron kissed his wife, then led the way from the dining room, located on the ground floor, almost in the middle of the west wing of the house, just off the kitchen. He continued through the adjoining parlor and turned left into the wide corridor on its opposite side, arriving at length at the wide entry just inside the main front doors.

"This is the proper place to begin," he said. "There are four separate stairways connecting the three floors—"

"Six, Papa," said Sabina.

"I was saving the other two for a surprise," said the baron with a smile. "Let me say there are four known stairways, and two that are, shall we say—well, you shall see!"

He turned and led them up the great, wide, circular oak staircase, which made the single round of a giant corkscrew in arriving at the next level up, or the first floor. There he paused.

"The grand staircase, as we call it, and the other stairways are the only points of reference from one floor to the next. As you have probably already noticed, there is no correspondence of rooms or corridors. Each floor seems to have been designed not only independently, but with altogether different architectural motifs in mind. The corridors on the ground floor are wide and spacious, as are the rooms, designed, it would seem, in this west wing to accommodate guests, for entertaining and dining and the like. But on the first floor, where we are now, the hallways are narrower and the rooms smaller, strictly utilitarian, bedrooms and various sitting rooms mostly. Even in the east wing, which has traditionally been the servants' and workers' quarters, there is this same distinction."

"The stairway continues up, though I haven't ventured a look beyond here. So there is obviously one more floor above us, is there not?" asked McCallum.

"Yes, and the second floor is different from either of the others."

"Much different!" chimed in Sabina.

"How?" asked Matthew.

"It's a maze of twisting hallways and small rooms. The hidden passageways I told you about—they're all on the second floor. Most of it is a puzzle to me yet. It was either designed by someone with a very unusual sense of humor—or a drunk, as my father used to comment about it. Most of it is vacant now, though, as I have told you, we do keep several of the guest rooms near the grand staircase made up and they see a fair amount of use.

"Your rooms, of course, are just to our right here, looking out the front of the house to the west. Let me take you now around the perimeter of this west wing."

He led away from the landing of the stairway toward the southernmost side of the wing, then left, paralleling the southern wall, and left again, and into a long, straight corridor extending all the way the length of the house toward the north face. Along the way they passed, on both sides, numerous doors.

"On our left here is the music conservatory, and to the right these are all bedrooms and sitting rooms," said the baron as they walked. "Our family quarters are here."

With his right hand he indicated the rooms they were passing on their right.

"Marion and I occupy the corner room, from which we are able to see down into the courtyard and across into the garden. And then," he continued as they made their way down the hall, "we come to Sabina's room here. She looks straight down onto the courtyard, but is only able to see a portion of the garden. The room just above us, on the corner of the second floor, is vacant, but she insists she would rather remain where she is—

she doesn't want to be too far from us, is that it, Sabina?" he said good-naturedly.

"Yes, Papa—or too far from the library!" laughed his daughter.

"Ah yes, the library," said the baron. "Let's go in—it's just here on our left."

He opened the tall door across from Sabina's chambers and walked into the expansive library. Both Thaddeus and Matthew gazed around them with wonder as the baron led them slowly through such a maze of ceiling-high shelves and bookcases as neither had imagined could exist in such an out-of-the-way place.

"It's remarkable, Baron!" said the American. "I've never seen such an extensive private collection of books. What do you have—there must be, I would think, twenty or thirty thousand volumes here!"

"Actually, it's closer to fifty thousand," returned the baron.

They continued to wander randomly through the rows and rows of tall shelves. The smells of dust and mold, leather and paper, all combined to produce olfactory sensations known and loved by those who haunted libraries and old bookstores. Such individuals, Sabina and Baron von Dortmann among their number, enjoyed nothing more than to bury their nose among the pages and between the boards of the books giving off such subtle odors of age.

It was not merely the smell that drew family and visitors to this place, however, but the collected ideas of the ages that resided on its shelves. As the Wisdom of Proverbs called aloud in the streets to those who would listen, here Wisdom was calling silently from the secret chambers of many minds, living and dead, inviting all who could hear her voice to partake and sample of her intellectual, literary, poetic, theological, and historical wares. Here were authors and nations, epics and ideas, philosophies and stories and poems and journals and histories. Here were friends of the spirit, sojourners who had traveled similar pathways in years gone by, inviting companionship by their mere presence, but making no claim upon the attention until the mood was right.

"This is truly remarkable, Baron," said Thaddeus in scarcely more than a whisper. "It must be worth a fortune. Many of the volumes, it is easy to see, are of ancient date and, unless I am mistaken, extremely rare."

"It is not for their rarity nor their monetary value that they are a treasure to us, but for what they contain. To be truthful, the vast majority of these volumes are from my father's and grandfather's time and, though worth a great deal, do not consume much of my time or interest. But the works of those authors with whom I have discovered a camaraderie of spirit, I would not part with for a million reichsmarks, pounds, or dollars."

"Are they mostly in German?"

"The older ones, yes. But we in this household enjoy a wider diet than only what fruit has been grown in our own linguistic garden. We have a fair amount in Spanish and French, and of course the Greek classics, in their originals and in translations into the various European tongues. And nearly all the great English literature from the sixteenth to the nineteenth century is represented. That is Sabina's passion. She hopes to continue her studies in English literature, perhaps at one of the British universities. And then we have many of your famous American authors. Sabina and I read English fluently and relish the great British writers—Burns, Shakespeare, Scott, Tennyson, Dickens, Wordsworth. Actually, my favorite of all is a nineteenth-century Scotsman. I have a complete set of his works right over here."

The baron led the way to a prominent bookcase set apart from the rest, which boasted an array of leather-backed volumes of great variety of thickness.

"MacDhonuill . . . hmm, I've never heard of him," remarked McCallum, gazing back and forth along the spines of the books.

"Very few people have these days," said the baron. "I'm afraid his reputation has fallen on some hard times in this century. But one would think, with the similarity of names, that you would be familiar with his work."

"Ah, Baron, you betray your lack of knowledge. *Mc* denotes Irish roots, *Mac* Scottish."

Baron von Dortmann smiled. "I might counter by reminding you that they are the same roots if you dig deep enough into the soil of your common past, the very word *Scot* originally being the name of those who came across the North Channel from *Scotia,* as Ireland was then called."

"Touché, Baron! You do me one better at my own history! Still, I must confess my ignorance of your favorite author."

"You are forgiven. Perhaps when you leave, I shall lend you one of his books so that you might sample to see if his style suits you."

"I'd be delighted."

"He's not for everyone, but I find his books meat indeed."

"Do you read them in English?"

"Usually, although nearly all have been translated into German, and we have a few of those as well."

"What does he write?"

"Sermons, poems, fairy tales, essays, but mostly novels."

"Stories? What—romance, adventure?"

"Everything in one—romance, mystery, characterization— like no stories you have ever read. You'll see when I give you one. But shall we continue on? We've come all the way through."

Indeed, as they talked, they had slowly worked their way through to the west wall of the library, the front entrance to it, through whose wide double doors the baron now led.

"Why, we're right back where we started," said McCallum. "Here are our rooms, Matt," he added to his son.

"I thought you said we were going to get lost, Herr von Dortmann," said Matthew.

The baron laughed. "Give us a chance, my boy! We've only completed one small rectangle around the south side."

"May I lead the way to the ballroom, Papa?" said Sabina.

"Lead on!"

They turned right, and Sabina led past the several guest rooms on their left along two turns in the hallway. She stopped at an intersection where the corridor split off to the right.

"This stairway here," she said, indicating the narrow staircase at the joining of the two corridors, "goes both up and down, and if you follow this hallway to the right, it leads back to where we were a minute ago at my room and the back door of the library. But I want to show you the ballroom. It's straight ahead."

So saying, she continued on, around a couple more turns and branches of the corridor, arriving at length at two massive and ornate wood-paneled doors.

"Here we are—Papa, do you have the key?"

The baron stepped forward and pulled from his pocket a large ring with an assortment of old and interestingly shaped keys. One of these he put to the lock, and the next moment the doors swung wide.

The room they entered was nearly square, easily the largest single room in the entire house, some thirty meters from end to end in both directions. The floor was of polished oak, perfect for dancing. On the walls hung an assortment of large portraits of family members as well as Prussian and Pomeranian royalty and several large tapestries, and one wall was almost completely taken up with a painted mural of obvious historical scenes. The huge place was nearly empty, though chairs were scattered about the edges.

"Do you ever use it?" asked Matthew, his voice echoing off the walls and ceiling. "I mean for balls and dances and that kind of thing?"

"Occasionally, though not often. My grandfather was more given to that sort of thing. Apparently all through the nineteenth century most of Europe's royalty visited this room at one time or another. They say the czar has been here, several kings of England, Bismarck, and of course Kaiser Wilhelm was a frequent guest. He and my great-grandfather were close friends. I've even heard that King Ludwig of Bavaria visited here—the entire grounds, I mean, not only the ballroom—when he was designing his three castles in the south."

"And the rest of the time it just sits vacant?" asked Thaddeus.

"I'm afraid so, though we have used it from time to time to put on concerts as well, and every fall, after the harvest, we put on a grand celebration for all our workers and staff, and we do that here. But you're right, most of the year it remains just as you see it now—empty and silent."

He led on through the center of the floor toward a single door on the opposite wall.

"The two wings of the house—" the baron began. But he was interrupted by the sound of the door they had just come through opening behind him, followed by his wife's footsteps running toward them.

"Heinrich, Heinrich, come quickly!" she cried as soon as she came into sight.

"What is it?" he said, hurrying toward her.

"It's Eppie," replied Marion. "She's had a fall and is delirious."

Immediately the baron and Sabina followed Marion back in the direction from which she had come.

"Can the two of you find your way?" he called back to Thaddeus and Matthew.

"We'll try," replied Thaddeus.

"Feel free to explore if you like. If you can find your way back to the library, we'll meet you there."

The next moment the three Dortmanns had disappeared from sight, leaving their two guests alone in the huge, empty ballroom.

ᘛ 15 ᘚ
Prayer for an Aging Saint

When Heinrich, Marion, and Sabina reached Eppie's bedroom, where the fall had taken place, they found Heidi seated on the edge of the bed and the old woman lying comfortably with her eyes closed. Heidi held one of the old woman's frail hands in her palm, and with her other hand she gently stroked the forehead and white hair that rested against the pillow.

Heidi glanced up.

"How severe is it?" asked the baron as they approached.

"I do not think there was a break, Baron," replied the housekeeper, "but she twisted her knee as she fell, and the pain was dreadful. She fainted, and then when she came to she was carrying on so that I couldn't make out a word of it."

"Carrying on about what, Heidi?"

"Oh, you know Eppie," she replied with a smile. "She was

ranting about Bismarck as if he and she were friends, talking about him as if he were still alive, and then she went on and on about Count somebody-or-other trying to get his hands on a treasure."

The baron looked upon the thin form on the bed with an expression of tenderest love. "She is very pale," he sighed.

"She is weak, Baron," said Heidi. "Do you think—"

"No, Heidi, I believe she will be fine. I do not think her time has yet come. Nevertheless, we shall pray."

He walked around to the other side of the bed and laid his hands gently on top of the white head. Her forehead was cool to his touch, and he could sense, even in her sleep, that she was still suffering.

Marion and Sabina likewise approached the bed and laid their hands on Eppie's shoulder and legs.

After several moments of silence, the baron prayed, and the other three joined him silently.

"Oh, Father," he said softly, "we lift our sister, your servant, into your care. We give you thanks for her life, and for the privilege of sharing it with her. We join, as two or three of your children gathered together, to ask you, in the name of your Son, Jesus, to restore her to health, to touch those places of pain in her body with the healing love of your hand. We give her into your hands, our Father. If this is the moment when you would bring her into the home of your bosom, then we bless and give you praise and honor for a life well lived in service to you and to us. If it is your will that Eppie yet remain with us, then restore her to vigor, and may her remaining years accomplish that which you ordain."

The baron paused momentarily.

"And Father," he went on, "give us the grace to serve you with steadfastness and devotion, as Eppie has, all the years of our life."

Whispered *amen*s came from the others around the bedside.

Almost the same instant the baron removed his hands from her head, Eppie's eyes shot open and she struggled to sit up in the bed. Heidi immediately renewed her attempt to soothe her, but old Eppie would have none of it.

Seeing Marion, she glanced back and, finding the baron so

close beside her, calmed slightly, then began to speak in an agitated though weak voice.

"Be on your guard, Baron," she said. "They're all about you!"

"Who, Eppie?" he said, trying with calm voice to reassure her that there was nothing to be anxious about.

"Spies, Baron," she said. "Watchful eyes are upon you, seeking to devour and plunder. There are tunnels, Baron! He would come in through the dungeon and take the treasure and gain power over you!"

"Who are you talking about, Eppie, the enemy?"

"Yes . . . yes, of course—the enemy. He is *your* enemy, Baron!"

"He is the enemy of all of us, Eppie. All of God's people must be vigilant and watchful."

"Not *him*, Baron! Oh, how will you see the danger? You must understand! I've seen his eyes . . . he means you ill, Baron . . . he means ill!" she said, then fell back on the bed with moanings that grew increasingly more inarticulate and devoid of meaning to any of the three listeners.

Still Heidi held her hand while the baron softly stroked her hair. In another two or three minutes she was again asleep.

Ten minutes more they sat with the old servant, until they judged her sleeping more peacefully.

"I will remain with her," said Heidi.

"Come get me if she awakens again," said Marion. "In the meantime, I will prepare some broth."

The three family members left the small chamber. The baron and Sabina sought the library, while Marion went downstairs to the kitchen.

∽ 16 ∽
The Tour Continues

The baron and Sabina found Matthew and his father in the library. Thaddeus was seated, thumbing through a German translation of American history he had located, while Matthew was prowling the bookshelves reading what he could of the titles on the spines.

"Is everything under control?" asked Thaddeus, rising.

"Yes," replied the baron. "Old Eppie, whom I was telling you about, is having a sore time of it. But she is sleeping comfortably now."

"Does that mean we can finish our tour of the house?" asked Matthew.

"Are you sure you're not bored with it?" laughed the baron.

"Are you kidding?" rejoined Matthew. "This is great! Besides, while Dad was in here, I snooped around down at the end of the hall where you left me."

"And what did you find?"

"I went down a narrow stairway, off there somewhere around a few corners from the ballroom. Then I came to a wall where I'm sure there's a secret doorway to somewhere, and I want to know where it goes."

"Ah-ha," laughed the baron. "So you've been doing a little detective work on your own! Why didn't you open it?"

"I didn't know how. It wasn't a doorway, just a suspicious-looking part of the wall."

The baron laughed again. "Well, shall we continue then? Where were we?"

"You had just started to tell us about the two wings."

"Ah yes! Well, the house is divided into what we call the west and the east wings," the baron explained, leading the way out of the library and back into the ballroom. "They were built, as far as we are able to tell from what drawings remain from centuries past, at different times, or at least in their present form that is true. There seems to be a common foundation, and yet the many changes that were made over the years blur exactly how and in what order the construction was carried out. When we get to the second floor, you will immediately see evidence all about that its design is far different from either of the other two floors, leading me to the conclusion that the remodeling of its interior was carried out by a different one of my ancestors than these bottom two floors. In any event, the two wings were built so as to minimize contact between the two. In former days, the distinction between the nobles of aristocratic families such as ours and their servants was greater and of more consequence than it is to us today. Those who work for us now we consider friends, even part of our family to some extent. But it was not always so. Therefore the communication between the two wings was minimal, almost as if they were two separate houses. On this floor, for instance, the only way from the west wing to the east wing is exactly as we have come, through the ballroom. The ground floor originally had no communication whatso- ever, but I had the wall opened up so that the corridor between kitchen and dining rooms extends straight through in both directions. And on the second floor—well, you shall see that presently!" he added with a grin, leading out of the ballroom and into the east wing.

Immediately they found themselves in narrower corridors with numerous doors on each side.

"Here are the servants' rooms," said the baron. "We'll just go off to the right here a bit—most of our people, now that the staff is not so large, have rooms to themselves, and the stairs here—" he indicated the stairway they had just reached open- ing to the right off the hall— "go down to the ground floor into the sitting room and lounge, and near their dining room. But," he added, turning back around, "let's backtrack here and we'll take the east stairs up to the second floor."

So saying, he led them back the way they had come, then right, and, making a large, somewhat rectangular loop through the far eastern end of the wing, arrived at length at the east stair- way, which led in both directions, both up and down.

"And now we come to the *pièce de résistance*, to use a wonder- ful old French phrase," said the baron as they climbed up the narrow, circular stairway. "At the top we will emerge into one of the most delightful spots on the whole estate."

One by one they followed him up the tight stone steps, arriv- ing at the top, making a quick turn, then through a door ahead of them, and suddenly finding themselves greeted by bright sunlight.

"I hadn't realized how dark it was inside!" exclaimed Thaddeus, shielding his eyes.

"You'll be accustomed to it in a minute," said Sabina. "It happens every time, except on a dark cloudy day."

Gradually, they wandered to the edges of the flat stone balcony and stood at the parapet wall gazing out over the flat expanses below them toward the north, east, and south. It was silent for several minutes as Thaddeus and Matthew slowly made their way around the perimeter of the three sides, taking in everything they could see below them.

"It's wonderful," said Thaddeus at length, stopping while his son continued around. "The view is positively stunning. And it's so quiet and peaceful besides. It makes me wish we could stay a week!"

"Why don't you?" rejoined Baron von Dortmann. "The invitation is open-ended."

"Duties press, Baron," sighed McCallum. "Unfortunately, this calm quiet here is not indicative of the state of the rest of Europe."

Now it was the baron's turn to sigh wistfully. "I know you are right," he said, "as much as I try sometimes to dismiss it from my thoughts. Just look at them there," he added, nodding toward the two young people who were standing at the balcony's southeast corner, peering into the distance where Sabina was pointing out the location of the hunting box they had climbed in the woods. "I fear for their future," the baron went on. "I fear for what is coming at the hand of our idolized leader. I fear that this world we now know is passing, Thaddeus—that the serenity of this time is slowly vanishing. I fear especially for such as they—young, carefree, full of life, innocent—"

Suddenly he stopped, shivering involuntarily. Premonitions of gloom came over him more often these days. He shook it off, then gave a little laugh. "Forgive me! Sometimes I grow pensive and begin reflecting to myself."

"Think nothing of it, Baron. I appreciate your candor. It is not so usual to hear a German talk as you do."

"I would hesitate to say such things to another of my kind. There are eyes and ears everywhere."

The baron could not have known how accurate were his words, for even at that moment two eyes focused on him from afar.

"For me to venture such sentiments among my fellow Germans," the baron went on, "at my brother's garden party in Berlin, for instance, would have probably already resulted in a not-so-friendly call by our neighborhood Gestapo within a day or two. I can be candid with you where I would be more tight-lipped elsewhere."

"What would they have done?"

"Probably I would not have been arrested. My position in society might still carry *some* weight, though that is diminishing every day. A new order is rising up very quickly in this country. Be assured in any case, henceforth I would have been watched very carefully."

"When you say *neighborhood* Gestapo, you are being face-tious, are you not?"

"I suppose," laughed the baron. "However, in truth there *are* agents of the SS and the Gestapo everywhere."

"The new order you speak of?"

The baron nodded, and silence fell between them.

After a moment he sighed again, then looked seriously at his guest. "I tell you, Thaddeus," he said. "He is an evil man."

"You mean . . . ?"

"Yes, our beloved Führer. I love this nation of ours. But I am deeply afraid. Watch yourself, and tell your colleagues in the diplomatic circles to do likewise."

"Such should be my counsel to you as well, Baron," replied McCallum with an equally serious tone.

"I do—believe me. Too much is at stake here, for me, for my family, to behave otherwise. If it were just myself, perhaps I would more freely speak my mind. But there are many others to consider."

"Many?"

"More is at stake even than I am at liberty to say. So yes, I heed your counsel, and I walk with wary step and cautious tongue."

Just then Sabina and Matthew bounded toward their fathers. "Quite a spot, isn't it, Dad?" said Matthew.

"You'll get no argument from me there!" replied Thaddeus.

"Can we continue the tour of the house?" asked Sabina enthusiastically. "I want to show you around the second floor!"

"The floor of mystery and intrigue, eh?" said Thaddeus.

"I don't know about that, but twists and turns anyway."

"You found it pretty mysterious when you were a child,

Sabina," laughed the baron. "Don't you remember that time I found you lost and crying, thinking you were never going to see us again?"

"Please don't embarrass me with that story, Papa!" said Sabina, laughing too, but pretending to be hurt. "I was only three or four."

"Actually, you were six."

"Oh, Papa!—Come, Matthew, I'll show you. We'll leave these two to find their way back down as best they can!"

She ran back to the door they had come through, but now turned to the left immediately after they were back inside, walking quickly into the dark passageway.

"Wait," said Matthew. "I can't see a thing! It's too dark."

No sound of his guide replied. Tentatively he continued walking, eyes adjusting to the dim light. But there was no sign of Sabina.

"Sabina," he said. "What are you trying to do, scare me?"

Still she did not reply.

Matthew found himself in a long, gradually curved passageway, narrow and lined on top and bottom and both walls with rough stones. Had he not known he was in the top floor of the house, he would have thought it an underground tunnel. It was especially here on the second floor where the house often seemed bigger from within than it appeared on the outside. When walking through its labyrinthine passageways for the first time, it was more than a house of intrigue, but in a sense, a whole world of mystery.

"Sabina," he called again, continuing slowly on. "Not fair . . . you have an advantage. *Sa-bi-na* . . ."

"*Buh!*" exclaimed Sabina suddenly, jumping out from a corridor opening off to the left just as Matthew reached her.

Even though he had expected exactly what she had done, he still could not help jumping.

"If I learn my way around this place, I'll get even with you for that!" he laughed. Sabina joined him.

"Come on," she said, "follow me."

"Only if you promise to stay with me."

"I promise. No more frights . . . none from me, at least. I can't make promises on behalf of the ghosts."

"Ghosts!"

"Of course!" laughed Sabina. "All ancient houses like this have ghosts—didn't you know? Or don't you have ghosts in America?"

"What kind of ghosts?" Matthew asked, not answering her question.

"I don't know—people who used to live here, old ancestors. I've never seen one. But old Eppie tells tales going back centuries. And not just about ghosts. She tells of hidden passages and murders, and all kinds of spooky things!"

As they had been talking, they had slowly wound their way around through such narrow and curving passageways, with numerous branches opening off in both directions, that Matthew had become utterly lost.

"I have no idea where we are," he said. "If you run ahead of me now, I could never hope to find my way out of this maze. It's more like a dungeon, with these stone walls and low ceilings, than the top floor. If I didn't know better, I'd think we were underground. And I'm still waiting for you to show me that secret door I found."

Sabina laughed. "All in good time."

They continued on.

"The wonderful thing about this part of the house," Sabina said after a minute, "is that it's so unlike all the rest. It is a giant puzzle. And the rooms behind these walls of stone are just as unusual as the rest of the floor—odd shapes, curved walls—it's wonderful."

"Is any of this used?" asked Matthew as they walked.

"Not here in the east wing. There are twenty or more rooms here, but none are occupied or used. The servants are afraid to come up here. But some of the top of the west wing is still in use—and we are almost at the door into it."

They had just emerged from a very narrow hallway out into one somewhat wider and higher. Immediately the voices of the two older men could be heard echoing through the passage from behind them.

"Hurry!" said Sabina, running to her left. "Let's don't let them catch us."

Matthew followed, and moments later they had walked

through an ancient iron-studded wood door that likewise appeared to belong to a dungeon. Sabina closed it carefully behind them.

"We'll hide from them in the armory!" she said, leading on into the west wing.

Here the passages were not nearly so narrow and dungeonlike, and they were somewhat better lit, though still curved and winding this way and that. Matthew hadn't the slightest notion of their location or direction, until his guide led him through yet another door. Suddenly he found himself inside a large room, very oddly shaped and well lit from a skylight in the roof. All around him on the walls hung dozens of varieties of swords, knives, daggers, coats of mail, shields, and guns. In each of the four corners of the room stood a full coat of armor, looking almost human in their metallic silence as they stood watchful guard over these weapons of the centuries.

Matthew stood gaping at the incredible collection. Never had he seen such relics before. But Sabina gave him no leisure to admire them.

"Papa's sure to bring your father in here!" she said. "It's one of his favorite places in the whole house, next to the library. They'll be here any minute—let's hide behind the armor! I'll hide here—you get behind that fellow over there," she said, pointing to the adjacent corner. "He's bigger."

Matthew complied.

Sabina continued to whisper to him for another minute or two until they heard the door begin to open.

"*Shhh . . . !*" she said.

" . . . though I personally consider myself a pacifist," the baron was saying as they entered, "I must confess to a fascination with old weapons. I find it somewhat embarrassing, yet there it is, and I cannot deny it."

The reaction of Matthew's father to the room was much like his son's. "I'm no authority on the subject, Baron," he said, "but I would judge this to be an extraordinary collection worthy of any of the finest museums in Europe."

"I think you are probably right, Thaddeus."

"Is the armory your own doing?"

"Most of the items were here when I was a boy. My father used to bring me here and tell me tales of each sword and whose it had been and in what battles it had been used. No doubt my present interest stems from those long-planted roots of childhood."

"Perfectly understandable."

"My love for history, too, cannot help but be intrigued. My only additions since my father's time are the Scottish swords, the several two-handed claymores here." He led the American toward one of the walls, then stopped in front of it. "This particular giant is said to have been used at the Battle of Culloden, though I have no way to verify that fact. Then there are several dirks and skean-dhus that I am particularly fond—"

"*Buh, Papa!*" exclaimed Sabina, jumping from behind the suit of armor that stood only about two meters from where the two men were engaged in conversation.

"Ah, Sabina, you are always full of merry surprises!" rejoined her father.

Matthew emerged from his hiding place without exclamation, a bit embarrassed to be playing childhood games. Sabina fascinated him, but he found his natural reticence hard to shake loose. When he was with her there seemed no distinction between childhood fun and adult sophistication, and the two blended almost into one.

"Quite a place, eh, Matt!" said his father. "You could get lost in this house."

"I've already been lost once," replied Matthew. "Sabina ran off and left me."

"Only for a minute!" said Sabina.

They all laughed. The baron continued to lead the way around the four walls of the armory, pointing out this and that piece of special interest or historical significance, then led them out of the armory by the door opposite that by which they had entered. All four stayed together for the remainder of the excursion through the labyrinth of the second floor until, some thirty minutes later, they arrived back at the top of the grand circular staircase.

"Well, as you can see, we've come back safe and sound to the

front of the house where things are more orderly and defined
than in the farther reaches of this floor."

"I would not want to be left alone in these passageways we
have come through," said McCallum.

"Especially at night," added Sabina.

They walked around the giant snaillike stairway together.

"And here we are again at the first floor and your own
rooms," said the baron.

"Thank you very much," said the American. "I must say I
have never been in a house quite the equal of yours, Baron."

"Only using not more than half of it, I do sometimes wonder
what good the monstrous thing is. But it may prove of use yet
. . . one never knows."

They paused at the landing.

"Well, that should certainly have worked off a good portion
of our dinner," the baron added. "Why don't the two of you rest
up a bit," he said to Thaddeus and Matthew. "Then later, if you
like, you can join me in the library. I'll have Heidi bring us up
some tea later."

"Sounds good," replied McCallum. "You can show me that
book of the Scotsman's you are going to lend me."

"I'd enjoy nothing better!"

∽ 17 ∾

Old-Fashioned Farm Work

The following day, Sunday, Thaddeus McCallum awoke early.
It was only just light, but he knew further sleep would be
impossible. The country was proving as great a boost to his own
soul as he knew it was for his son. As much as he had always
enjoyed his work, he found himself feeling more energetic and
invigorated than he had in years.

He rose and dressed, determined to have one last walk
around the place in the quiet of the early morning.

He let himself out the front door. It was chilly and still, and
the air felt tingly and fresh, not only to his lungs but to his
spirit. He knew it would warm up quickly once the sun shone

over the land, but for the present the nip of the morning could not have better suited his mood.

He took his way directly out from the house, about halfway down the driveway, then turned left and strode around the southwest incline of the knoll upon which the house sat, arriving at length at the western hedge of *Der Frühlingsgarten*, which he then followed to his right, gradually encircling the entire vast garden by way of its outside perimeter. Encountering the stream, he stopped, thought for a moment, looked about for the narrowest spot, then backed up several paces, got a running start, and leapt over it, laughing as he landed on the other side.

This place made him feel like a child again!

Continuing on his way, he skirted the edge of the pinewood on his right, discovered the bridge back across the stream, took it, and at length found himself drawing near the barns and outbuildings down the eastern slope from *Lebenshaus*. It was still early. There were no other evidences of work in progress. As he neared the largest of the barns, however, he heard the unmistakable *moo* of cows, with an occasional clank of a milking bucket acting as a metallic cymbal in the midst of the otherwise exclusively bovine symphony of sound.

Deciding to poke his head inside for a look, he headed for the open door.

"Good morning, Thaddeus!" he heard a familiar voice call out from somewhere in the darkness.

He took a few tentative steps inside, trying to adjust to the dim light.

"Is that you, Baron?" he asked.

"Yes, come in and meet my ladies."

"You actually supervise the milking, Baron? Personally?"

Thaddeus heard a good-natured roar of laughter from the baron's mouth, then finally saw his host as he stood and walked out from between two cows down the row.

"*Supervise*, Thaddeus?" he said, approaching the American. "Why, I'm the only one here! There's no one else here *to* supervise."

"You're milking the cows yourself?"

"Of course! Although if you're offering, I'll be glad for the help!"

"I don't know a thing about cows, but if—that is, if you need me—I'll do whatever you tell me."

"Great! I'll have you milking like an expert before the hour's up! Here—grab that bucket," he added, pointing to a half-full, narrow-necked container not far from where Thaddeus stood. "Follow me."

Thaddeus did so, and the baron, carrying the bucket he had himself just filled, led him to the far end of the barn.

"But don't you have men who do this for you?" asked McCallum.

"Yes, but I love my ladies and I like to involve myself too. It's too easy to get fat and lazy. I try to get dirt on my hands and manure on my feet at least once a day. Anything I hire a man to do ought to be something I am willing to do myself—and would do myself if I had time. I work alongside my men, in the barn, out in the fields, everywhere. I am a farmer and I enjoy hard work. So, there you have it, Thaddeus: my philosophy of farming!"

"But surely you don't milk the cows alone all the time. It would never give you time for anything else."

"You're right. My men do it every other day, but on Sundays I let them sleep in and I handle all the barn chores myself."

"*All* the barn chores?"

"Not so much, just the milking, taking the ladies out to pasture, and then cleaning out their stalls—making their beds for this evening, as it were."

"But why? Why do you do it once a week alone?"

"To give Heiko and Friedrich a break, and to keep myself involved. I *must* keep involved in all aspects of the farm and its business, otherwise what kind of an owner would I be? I am experimenting with some milking machinery too, and use this opportunity to try out new devices I have either invented myself or borrowed from others. I travel a great deal, trying to learn what others are developing to make the milking process more efficient. I have been to the school of agriculture in Copenhagen. There are many exciting developments."

"You are a remarkable man, Baron."

"Not so remarkable, really. I just love what I do, and so I throw myself into it with everything I can. But first you must take off those shoes of yours. I've an extra pair of rubber boots over there in the corner. Change into them, and then come—sit down here. We've only six or eight more to do, and you will milk Gerta."

Thaddeus changed his shoes, then with a look more of fear than of enthusiasm, approached and sat down on the stool, listened to the baron's instructions as he set a fresh wide bucket under the cow, and watched as he demonstrated. Then he timidly reached out to Gerta's plump udder and took the first teat between his fingers.

"Now, pull and squeeze," said the baron. "That's it, in a firm downward motion."

A tiny, thin line of milk dribbled out and sprayed against Thaddeus's leg. He groaned.

"Not bad for a first effort!" laughed the baron. "Once you get the milk coming in a good flow, *then* you can get your aim perfected so that it goes into the bucket!"

Thaddeus tried again, this time coaxing a little more warm milk from Gerta's full supply, but without much improvement of direction. The toe of his boot was suddenly white and wet.

"*Agh!*" he exclaimed with a laugh. "I don't think I'm cut out for this, Baron!"

"You'll have it in no time. Just keep at it, while I take care of Toni down here."

Gradually the metallic echo in the bucket indicated that Thaddeus was finding his mark, and in another five minutes or so the regular streams from between his fingers were splashing into a rising level of milk instead of merely sounding against the bottom of an empty container.

"I can hear from the sound of it that milk is accumulating, Thaddeus," said the baron, finishing Toni and moving down the line. "You must be doing fine."

"I'm sure Gerta knows she's in the hands of an amateur," rejoined McCallum, "though I do have to admit it's not so bad. I've never done anything like this in my life!"

Within the hour, Thaddeus was moving from teat to teat, then from cow to cow down the row, not exactly as if he had been doing it for years, but with far less faintheartedness than when he first sat down next to Gerta's imposing girth. As he did, he heard the baron fiddling with suction cups and rubber tubing, moving back and forth between the cows and an electric pump which apparently operated the device.

At length they met one another at adjacent cows. The baron turned off the milking device, finished up his cow by hand, and announced, "We've done it, Thaddeus. You were a big help!"

"I don't know about that. I only did four cows."

"You gave me the chance to work on my machine a little more."

"Well, I'm glad for that."

"What do you think?"

"Actually, it's wonderful fun," said Thaddeus. "Why didn't anyone ever tell me how dull the three-piece-suit life was?"

"This can get tedious too," replied the baron. "Somebody has to be here twice a day, 365 days a year. There are no vacations if you have dairy cows."

"I'm sure that's true. But there's something so wholesome about it all, interacting with the ground, the dirt, with these animals who know nothing but the most basic needs of life. I can see why you love what you do and why you want to be part of it with your men."

The baron's farm, like even the smaller ones of the region, did not exclusively produce any one crop or commodity, but with variety insured against the massive failure of a single product or a devastating drop in price. In addition to his herd of dairy cows, he raised a nearly equal number of bulls, which he sold for beef; grew rye, wheat, summer and winter barley, sugar beets, corn, oats, and potatoes; and raised three dozen or so pigs.

Once the milking was completed, they carried the full containers to the back of a flatbed wagon to be pulled by tractor to the loading platform out beside the main road, where they would be picked up and taken into the processing plant in Niedersdorf. But now the faithful milk givers had to get on with their vital business for the day—ten hours of contented grazing, from which tomorrow's milk, and next winter's fertilizer over barren fields, and the following summer's wheat would all result.

"Stand over there," the baron instructed Thaddeus as he

swung open one of the large doors at the barn's end. "They all know the way to the field, but there are always one or two ornery ones that will try something if you let them. They're particularly feisty on Sundays because they know I'm alone."

"What do I do then?" asked Thaddeus, the uncertainty suddenly showing again in his voice.

"I'll go on ahead. The lead cows will follow me and all the others will come along. All you have to do is follow the last one out of the barn to make sure they keep going. Some of them are so slow that if you don't make them move, they'll just stop and lie down in the path!"

"But what if they won't go, what do I do?"

"Just yell at them, give them a swat on the rump."

"What if they get upset, or if they run at me or something?"

The baron laughed. "You're not afraid, are you, Thaddeus? Of a little old cow?"

"They're not so little!"

"Well, you just have to show them who's boss. Get a run at them, yell at them, swat them. And don't ever let them know you're timid."

"That's easy for you to say!"

The baron laughed again. *"Hast du angst?"*

"Yes, I have angst!"

"Then bluff your way, Thaddeus. Believe me, these ladies are just big, three-hundred-kilo marshmallows when it comes to courage. But watch out, here they come! Stand over there, and I'll lead them out into the field."

Thaddeus hurried over to the point Heinrich had indicated, while the baron called out for the lead cows to follow him, speaking to them by name. They did so, and gradually the barn emptied and the black-and-white holsteins stretched out and made their way single file along the path behind their master. Nothing, it appeared, could have induced them to greater speed even if fire had rained down from the sky behind them, though every once in a while Thaddeus let out with a timid yell of exhortation. Out in front the baron glanced back every few seconds, smiling inwardly, asking himself whether the cows understood the timorous English of the man whose voice carried the weight of a nation in diplomatic circles, yet who was now in fear and trembling to speak with authority to a few dumb beasts. It was not a question he resolved before reaching the gate to the field where today's breakfast and lunch was awaiting the huge, slow mammals now hungry from their ten-minute trek along the country road.

"Here we are," he shouted back, walking off to the side of the entrance while the cows, one by one, filed into the field and immediately set off in search of fresh green grass left over from the day before. In another minute or two he was closing the gate behind the last of them.

"That wasn't so bad, was it?" he asked.

"No," admitted Thaddeus, smiling. "Kind of fun, actually. You've got to realize, every bit of this is new to me. I feel like a kid again."

"I know," replied the baron. "Did you have any trouble?"

"One of the slow ones tried to wander off onto that other lane back there. But I did what you said and just yelled at it and ran a few steps to block its way."

"Scared?"

"To death! I was sure it would turn and charge me and tram-ple and gore me like the bulls do in Spain!"

"And?"

"The second it saw me, it jumped back in line like you said it would, just like a big baby."

"I told you, all you have to do is show them who's boss!"

"I'll try to remember. If only we could control certain unruly world leaders as easily," he added wistfully.

German and American walked slowly back to the barn the way they had come.

"Do you want the full bovine experience?" the baron asked.

"You mean there's more!"

"The best part is yet to come."

"Which is?"

"Now we've got to clean out the *Kuhstall*—as I said before, make the ladies' beds for this evening."

"Is it scary?" asked Thaddeus.

"Not a bit—only a little messy."

Reentering the vacated barn, Thaddeus noted that it suddenly seemed very quiet with the occupants no longer at home. Heinrich grabbed two pitchforks leaning against the wall and tossed one of them to his guest with a smile. He then walked to the far end and scooped up a large forkful of wet, brown manure mixed with straw and hoisted it with some effort onto the wide flat handcart standing in readiness for just this purpose.

With an unceremonious *splat*, it fell onto the cart, spraying tiny missiles of manure in all directions, including one moist projectile onto Thaddeus's shirt as he stood by observing the process.

"*Ugh!*" he cried, leaping back.

"Excuse me!" laughed the baron. "Hazards of the trade. But now it's your turn. You have to take up that pitchfork like a man! I want to see what kind of stuff you Americans are made of!"

Another *splat* from the baron's fork landed squarely on top of the first, and he sent wet prongs eagerly after a third.

With even more timidity than he had shown with the cows, Thaddeus dug his fork into the brown, gooey mess at his feet, looking more like a child fiddling with some detestable portion of vegetables on his plate than he did a farmhand. At length a small forkful of the recycled grass from Heinrich's field landed softly on the cart.

"Good!" exclaimed the baron triumphantly. "You'll get used to it, just like herding the cows. You'll soon be enjoying it!"

"Enjoying it!"

"Smell and all . . . I guarantee it. You'll get back to Berlin, and within a week you will be longing for my barn and its ladies. This is the ultimate in touching the true meaning of nature, as you were speaking of earlier. It's the organic completion of the rounds of life—from grass to the cow, to make milk and manure. The milk feeds children and makes cheese for me to enjoy. The manure we pile up outside until time to load it onto a wagon and spread it on the bare fields after harvest. Then it will nourish next year's grain to make bread to feed the children's parents and to eat with the cheese. It's wonderful! We're standing in the middle of the complete cycle of the growing process."

"If you say so," said Thaddeus, looking down at his boots

buried in the ugly mire. He reached down and gathered up another load, a little larger this time, and emptied it onto the cart.

"To be truthful, I cannot imagine how one such as my brother Otto could content himself to have to do with nothing but money and investments. Money is such a dead thing. This manure has more *life* than all the money in all the banks of Germany. Can gold make bread? No, but this manure can!"

The two worked their way down the series of open stalls, gradually piling the cart higher and higher. When the mound had at last reached its limit, the baron set down his pitchfork and wheeled the cart outside to dump it where a huge pile already awaited the end of the harvest for distribution.

"Three or four more loads," he said, reentering the barn, "and we'll have the ladies' beds all nice and fresh!"

With increasing gusto Thaddeus plunged his fork into the organic dung, hardly taking notice of the brown splotches steadily accumulating on his trousers and shirt.

"We'll have those things washed for you before you leave," said the baron. Even as the words were leaving his mouth, he burst out with a great laugh.

"What?" said Thaddeus.

"You just smeared a big brown smudge across your face from the back of your hand! I'm sorry. I couldn't help laughing."

Thaddeus glanced down at his hand and saw the offending stain.

"What would my colleagues at the embassy say if they could see this!"

"They would be too busy holding their noses. They probably wouldn't see the true man beneath the grime."

Twenty minutes later, after five bales of fresh, clean, yellow straw had been tossed down from the hayloft above and spread out across the floor of the stalls for the evening's comfort of the inhabitants, baron and diplomat leaned their pitchforks back against the wall and left the barn.

"Thank you, Baron," said Thaddeus as they walked slowly up the hill to the house together. "Every day around here is full of new experiences—for both me and my son. I am very grateful."

The baron smiled. *"Unusual* experiences, is that what you mean?"

"I haven't felt more alive since coming to Germany. Cows and manure and green fields of grass . . . sleeping in a house hundreds of years old . . . wearing another man's boots . . . a cobweb-filled hayloft . . . the smells of farm life . . . fields full of golden grain awaiting the harvest—I just can't tell you how it all goes down into my soul. I wish Matthew could spend a week here."

"We'd be happy to have him."

"Perhaps the time will come," said Thaddeus.

∽ 18 ∽

Change of Plans

That same afternoon, when dinner was over, Sabina agreed to take Matthew on one more ride prior to his departure with his father for the city.

She had hoped they would have time to ride all the way to the sea and back, but such an adventure would have taken far too long. She satisfied herself, therefore, with a jaunt eastward, along the roads and trails through her father's farmland and endless fields of growing, ripening grain.

They rode eastward for about an hour, then turned to make their way back to *Lebenshaus.*

Meanwhile, Baron von Dortmann and Thaddeus McCallum sat chatting together in the rose garden.

"Have you recovered from your morning of *unusual experiences?*" asked the baron.

"I think so," laughed Thaddeus.

"Quite a boy, that son of yours, Thaddeus," said the baron. "I've grown fond of him already."

"I would say the same thing of your daughter."

"What's it been like for him, being raised by a busy father and spending his teen years in a foreign country?"

"I'm afraid it hasn't been altogether easy on him. And you're

right, I have been busy, perhaps busier than I ought to have
been."

"You occupy a position of importance."

"Perhaps. But the time goes so fast, you know. Suddenly
they're practically grown. I haven't spent near the time with
him I should have."

"He doesn't seem to have suffered. He and you have what
appears to be a good and communicating relationship, and he
strikes me as a well-integrated young man."

"He is," replied Thaddeus. "I feel very fortunate, especially in
that he takes so well to my job and our surroundings. I think he
likes being part of the diplomatic world."

The two fathers continued to chat, while on another part of
the grounds, their son and daughter had turned the horses back
toward the house.

$$\sim\!\infty\!\sim$$

When they were about a kilometer from the estate, suddenly
Sabina broke into a gallop.

"Race you back!" she called out over her shoulder.

Matthew did his best to urge his horse into a run, but he was
no match for her. As his steed bounded over the uneven terrain,
it was all he could do to remain in the saddle, hanging on for
dear life.

Within two minutes Sabina was flying over the stream and
reining her mount in at the foot of the road leading up the
knoll to the stables. She stopped and turned in the saddle to
watch Matthew's approach.

She saw instantly that her challenge had been foolish. The
horse, caught up in the excitement, tore across the ground, and
Sabina could tell that Matthew was far from secure on its back.

"Rein him in!" she cried.

Even if Matthew heard or made the attempt, there was no
visible slowing of the mighty creature. Already the Belgian was
gathering itself to leap over the stream. Fearing the worst,
Sabina immediately dug in her heels and chased toward them,
hoping to intercept horse and rider before the situation grew
any more dangerous.

But it was too late. Into the air they both flew.

The jump itself was accomplished with reasonable success. But as the roan landed, the jarring of its four hooves was too much for its rider. Matthew wobbled from side to side and then, unable to right himself, toppled at last onto the hard-packed dirt, falling awkwardly with his legs bent beneath him and landing in a heap on the ground.

Sabina was off her horse and running toward him the same instant. She reached him to find him grimacing in what was obvious pain and holding the lower part of his left leg. "Well, if I don't wind up on the ground every time I'm with you!" he groaned, trying to laugh. But his face was white as a sheet.

"I'll bring Papa," she said, trying to sound calm but sensing the injury to be a serious one.

Matthew nodded but said nothing. In truth, the pain was so intense that his eyes had begun to water, and he would rather be alone.

Sabina remounted her horse, then sped up the hill, jumped off at the stables, and sprinted the rest of the way on foot, calling out as she went. Her father heard her, and before she was halfway across the courtyard to the house, the two men emerged at a run from the garden. The next minute all three were running down the hill to the site of the accident.

The baron reached Matthew first and knelt down. A hasty examination removed any doubt that the doctor would have to be summoned. He stood, and as Thaddeus knelt down beside his son and spoke softly to him, the baron gave his daughter instructions.

"Sabina," he said, "go quickly and telephone Herr Abrahams in the village." After a moment's reflection he added, lowering his voice, "Tell him to bring what he might need to set a bone."

"Oh, Papa!" cried Sabina, bringing her hands to her cheeks in terror.

"He will be fine," said the baron, "but if there is a break, it needs to be set quickly. Now go."

Next the baron went for Schmidt and a flat cart, while Thaddeus remained with his son. A few minutes later the cart rumbled down the hill behind a sturdy old plough horse. They carefully eased Matthew onto it, taking precautions not to bend or move his leg. The pain from any movement, however, was sufficient to insure its protection. Schmidt slowly turned the ambulance-horse and led him up the wide winding pathway to the house, while the baron and Thaddeus walked along on either side of Matthew. Presently Sabina came running back down from the house and met the slow ambulance train.

"Does it hurt terribly, son?" asked the baron.

"I would say it hurts about as bad as anything I've felt before," replied Matthew, attempting a laugh.

"It won't last, I can assure you of that. We'll give you something for the pain as soon as we have you settled, and you couldn't do better than Doctor Abrahams, even in Berlin."

They reached the top and stopped. Being the larger of the two men, the baron stepped forward.

"I think it best, Thaddeus, if I carry him in myself. Two of us might make awkward work of it. If you don't mind, run ahead to the kitchen door there. Tell Heidi to find Marion and tell her to make a place ready in the courtyard parlor."

So saying, the baron stooped down and lifted Matthew up in his arms as if he were no more than three years old.

"Hang on, my boy!" he said, then walked toward the east stairs leading up to the courtyard. Already Thaddeus was out of sight ahead of them.

Within ten minutes they had Matthew tolerably comfortable on a wide divan in the ground-floor parlor looking out upon the courtyard. His shoes and socks were off. His father sat at his side, holding an ice pack to the injury. By the time they heard the doctor's car on the gravel of the front drive, the ice had sufficiently numbed the leg so as to reduce the pain and prevent serious swelling. Some color was beginning to return to Matthew's pale cheeks.

"Thank you for coming so quickly, Aaron," said the baron, greeting his friend with a shake of the hand.

He led Herr Abrahams to the divan. Thaddeus rose and stepped aside.

"Ice . . . excellent," said the doctor, glancing at the leg, then beginning to probe with his fingers.

"Tell me what you feel, boy," he said, not realizing the baron's guests were Americans.

"Ow! That hurts!" exclaimed Matthew, forgetting to speak German. Watching from the side, Sabina winced involuntarily even as he cried out.

"I don't think a translation will be necessary," said Thaddeus.

The doctor continued to probe, encountering a tender spot every so often, which he knew instantly from Matthew's exclamations.

After a minute or two he stopped, then rose and spoke to the baron.

He pronounced the fibula broken just above the ankle, probably in only one spot, though perhaps two. He would set it in a plaster cast immediately.

"Can he travel?" the baron asked.

The doctor's face clouded. Once the cast was dry, it would be possible, he told him, though the likelihood of a completely successful recovery would be greatly increased if he remained where he was for no less than three days. After that the danger would be greatly reduced.

"I'd feel better about it, just to make sure there are no compensating injuries, either higher on the leg, or even in the other leg, if he could remain in bed a day or two," concluded the doctor.

"I've got to get back to Berlin tonight," said McCallum seriously. "I have a meeting with the Austrians and French in the morning."

"We'll be happy to look after Matthew," said the baron. "Why don't we keep him for the week? Your wish from earlier in the day would seem to have become an imperative. Either you can come back next weekend, or we'll bring him into the city."

Thaddeus thought for a moment, then looked at Matthew. "What do you think, Matt?"

"That would be all right with me," Matthew replied. "Whatever you and the baron think best."

"Well, this is a sudden change of plans," sighed Thaddeus, still pondering the options. "I suppose it is for the best. And I did speak of it, didn't I?" He paused, then said, "OK, tell the doctor to proceed, and I guess we'll take his advice and your offer."

"Good," rejoined the baron. "It's the safest way, and it will be a pleasure to have Matthew with us a while longer."

"There's only one condition," added Thaddeus.

"What's that?" said the baron.

"That as soon as he is able you get *him* into the barn with you. I want my son to meet your ladies too!"

The baron laughed heartily. "I'll do my best!"

The doctor picked up his bag and walked toward the door of the room. The baron followed him, the smile quickly disappearing from his countenance as they spoke for a moment in hushed tones. The doctor then exited the house to gather what he needed from his car to cast the leg.

∽ 19 ∾

A Visitor

Sabina sat reading on the balcony of the first-floor sitting room. Her mother entered and approached from behind.

"Gustav is here calling, Sabina," she said.

"For me?"

"Who else, dear?" replied Frau von Dortmann, smiling.

"Oh, Mama, must I?" groaned Sabina. "He is so tedious."

Marion did not reply.

Sabina sighed, set aside her book, and followed her downstairs. Her mother left her and she went to the front door alone, where a young man stood waiting outside.

"Hello, Gustav," said Sabina.

The boy's face brightened as he greeted her. "Hello, Sabina," he said. "Mother asked if you would like to come for dinner?"

"Today?"

He nodded.

"I'm afraid I cannot, Gustav. Give your mother my regards."

"Your mother seemed to think you would like to come," he replied, with the faintest hint of a whine.

"We have a guest. It really would not be right for me to leave."

"Guest?" repeated Gustav, though he well knew visitors had been at the estate.

"Yes, an American boy. He was here with his father and broke his ankle in a riding accident."

Gustav stiffened slightly, but did his best not to show it. "A *young* boy?"

"A young man, I should have said."

"How young?"

"About your age. I believe he is seventeen."

"I am eighteen, Sabina," said Gustav, not altogether successful in camouflaging his annoyance.

"Of course. I'd forgotten about your birthday."

"You were at my party."

"I remember now."

"How could you forget? You danced with me most of the evening."

"Forgive me. It just slipped my mind, that's all."

"Slipped your mind! It was the biggest social event Niedersdorf has seen in years. Your cousin said it was the equal of any party in Berlin."

"I was wrong. I'm sorry I forgot about your birthday. Now, I have apologized twice. What do you want from me, Gustav?" said Sabina, at last becoming exasperated.

"You might accept my mother's invitation to dinner. She is beginning to think you do not like her."

"That is ridiculous, Gustav. I have a suspicion you're just saying that to get back at me. I don't think your mother has said anything of the kind."

Gustav did not reply immediately, shifting awkwardly on his feet. "At least, then, would you like to go for a ride?" he asked after a moment. "I have my new automobile."

"I don't think so. I do not think it would be right for me to leave my guest like that."

"*Your* guest?"

"*Our* guest, then."

"Then shall we at least take a walk in your father's garden before I return home?" said Gustav, doing his best to moderate his vexation and put a pleasant tone over his tense features.

"I don't think so, Gustav. I'm afraid I'm not in the right mood for a walk."

"You used to take me to the garden all the time. We played there nearly every day when we were children. You used to tell me the name of every plant, every tree, every exotic shrub your father had imported. Surely you have not forgotten."

Sabina said nothing.

"Have things really changed so much that you do not even want to go into the garden with me? I'm sure your mother would be as disappointed as mine to hear of it, Sabina."

"I'm sorry, Gustav. We'll walk in the garden the next time you come. I promise. But I just cannot today. Give your mother my best. Good day."

Sabina turned and reentered the house, leaving Gustav at the base of the steps, standing as still as the rearing horse behind him.

And with similar expression in his eyes.

ᔆ 20 ᔆ
The Invalid

Sabina von Dortmann and the son of her father's nearest neighbor, Count Ernst von Schmundt, had virtually grown up together, both children of parents with vast holdings in the northeast of the ever-expanding German Reich. There had been other children in the farming village of Niedersdorf, of course, but none with similar aristocratic blood extending back to the proud old days at the height of the Prussian kingdom. It was natural, therefore, that the two had seen a good deal of one another, had played with each other, and had been nearly as familiar with each other's lands as their own.

Childhood affections, however, had, on the young lady's part, waned in recent times, exerting a gradual strain on the relationship between the parents as well.

Gustav von Schmundt drove his car back down the drive, then made a right turn. As he drove, faster than was wise on the narrow country road, he turned several resolutions over in his mind, determining at length to talk to his mother. It was not exactly the most manly tack to take, but he couldn't take any chances even if it meant stooping that low. First, however, he had a matter in the village to attend to. When he came to the entrance of his father's estate after some two kilometers, he continued straight ahead, arriving after not more than another three minutes in the small town of Niedersdorf. He drove about halfway through, turned left, and pulled up in front of a *Wirtshaus*.

∽ა⌒ა

Sabina found tending Matthew much more to her liking than trying to keep up a conversation with the son of the count. As soon as she reentered the house she went straight to the room where he was convalescing. As her annoyed visitor was speeding northward, she greeted the son of the American assistant ambassador.

"How are you feeling this morning?" she asked.

"Still foolish, but not in pain."

"Why foolish?" laughed Sabina.

"Because I keep falling and tripping over myself around you. What is it anyway? I tell you, I never used to be so accident-prone!"

"You have nothing to feel foolish about. People are injured riding horses all the time. Two years ago a man was killed in Niedersdorf by his horse."

"How?"

"He was being careless and overconfident. He forgot what powerful and sometimes temperamental creatures horses can be. All of a sudden he was on the ground and one of the beast's hooves crushed in his skull. He was dead instantly. It was dreadful."

"Are you saying I ought to consider myself fortunate to have only a broken leg?"

"Perhaps I was hinting in that direction," admitted Sabina with a smile. "And look at the other side of it. You are able to remain here in the country for a longer stay."

"What good does my lying in this bed accomplish?"

"The doctor is coming back this afternoon," said Sabina. "I heard my father talking to him on the telephone. If the cast is sound and your leg safe, I'm sure he will let you get out of bed. And Papa asked him to bring a wheelchair with him."

"A wheelchair! Oh no!"

"I'll be able to wheel you for walks outside."

"A wheelchair!" groaned Matthew again.

"Perhaps you will be able to walk about on crutches too."

"Good grief! You're talking about me as if I was a full-fledged invalid!"

"You are!" laughed Sabina. "Now you just have to relax, let us take care of you . . . and enjoy it! Here, I will read to you from my book."

She sat down in a chair near the bed and picked up the volume she had left there the evening before.

"What's it called?" asked Matthew.

"*Der Geheimnisvolle Raum,*" she answered. "It's all about a huge castle in England. There are adventures and romance and ghosts and secrets and mysteries!"

"Are you sure it's not about *your* house?" said Matthew.

"Ours is a mere shack compared to the castle in this book!" laughed Sabina. "Listen." She flipped through some pages to where she had been reading, found her place, then read, " 'To fulfill the very necessities of our being we must be God's children. Then only is our creation fulfilled—then only shall we be what we were made for.' "

"I thought it was a mystery about a castle!"

"It is, but with many little truths about God sprinkled in too. I just love how he mixes it all in together."

"Well, I need some excitement. I'm already tired of this bed. Read me something scary!"

"All right!" laughed Sabina. "I'll see if I can find something—wait a minute!" she said.

She turned back through what she had already read, then settled on a passage and began. Thus they passed most of the morning.

True to his word, within a few hours Doctor Abrahams arrived, bringing the wheelchair with him.

"You may take him outside if you like, but keep him in the

chair," he said to Sabina. "Tomorrow perhaps, if he feels no pain to stand on the leg, he may try to get around with the crutches. But do not let him be too active."

Sabina nodded, and the doctor turned to leave the room. He paused at the door and spoke in a low voice to Marion.

"Is Heinrich here?" he asked.

"He's gone down to Finkenwalde for two days," replied his wife.

"Hmm . . . " intoned Abrahams with a grave expression.

"Is something wrong?"

"I don't know, Marion. There are developments, that much I will say, although if he is at the seminary no doubt he will soon be aware of them."

"I do not want to bring danger on my husband or daughter. What should I do, Aaron?"

"I think I know Heinrich well enough by now. He would rather face whatever comes *with* you than be safe *without* you."

"I know, of course you are right. It is only that I fear for them."

"These are fearful times for us all."

"There is nothing I need do now?"

Again the doctor thought for a moment. "Ring me when Heinrich returns. I will need to check the boy's leg anyway. But the three of us have serious matters to discuss."

∽ 21 ∽
The Mothers

As Doctor Abrahams returned to the village, a speeding auto passed him, dangerously close to the center line. The doctor swerved slightly, then continued on into the village.

Behind him, Gustav braked hard, then turned left and drove into the estate bearing his father's name.

He found his mother in her parlor.

"Mother," he began, "Sabina refused your invitation."

"Was she busy, dear?"

"Not in the least," he answered, crossing the room to where

she sat. "She just said she didn't want to come. She wouldn't go for a ride with me either."

"Gustav," said his mother, a serious look coming over her face as her son drew close, "have you been drinking? You seem very upset."

"I had a beer in the village."

"What were you doing there?"

"I had to see some friends. And yes, Mother, I am upset," he went on quickly, changing the subject. "Sabina sometimes treats me like I am a stranger. She never invites me to the garden anymore, and whenever we go riding—and half my invitations she turns down—I feel she is merely putting up with me. I just don't know what to do, Mother. She does not behave at all with the courtesy she should show the man who will soon be her husband."

If young Gustav rather overplayed the severity of Sabina's ill-treatment of him—in truth, she was always as cordial as she could make herself be toward one with whom she had less and less in common with every passing year and had on this day spoken more boldly to him than ever before—he excused himself on the grounds that the situation had grown intolerable, and he saw nothing for it but to coax his mother toward intervention on his behalf. She desired the match as much as he did, and he well knew how she would respond.

Ingrid von Schmundt listened to her son with sympathy. He had been well skilled in getting his way with her almost from birth, a tactic she was as unaware of today as she had been when he was two.

She was a woman still of considerable beauty, though in her late thirties, it had already, as is its way, begun to betray her. A life of ease had added more than a few centimeters to thighs, buttocks, midsection, and breasts, and her pure silky black hair, once able to command second glances from any man young or old, now had more grey than she enjoyed seeing in the mirror during her ever-more-lengthy morning toilette. She had instructed her *Friseur* to try one of the new products that promised an end to the grey, but it had given a subtle greenish hue to the rest of her coiffure, insuring second glances again, but this time for the wrong reasons. She scrubbed her hair fiercely every day for months until the hideous effect was gone and resolved thereafter to put up with the grey as best she could, though she hated every new strand that revealed itself. The steady increase of her weight would have been more easily combatted, though the determination of will necessary for success involved a strength of character that had not been required of her early in life and thus was almost entirely absent now.

She and Count von Schmundt had had one of the region's storybook romances during the Great War. They had courted before the outbreak of hostilities. He had gone off with great fanfare, had distinguished himself on a number of occasions, and had returned as a hero; and the wedding had been the largest social event of the decade. Their son was born the next year, and through the peaceful, prosperous, rebuilding years of the twenties and the Weimar Republic, the Schmundt villa outside Niedersdorf was the scene of countless parties and balls, attracting society's elite all the way from Berlin.

The following years were the high point of Ingrid's life. Unfortunately, the economic collapse and depression struck her husband—whose reckless speculations made him a wealthy man by 1926—with greater severity than it did their neighbor, the more cautious husband of her best friend.

It did not ruin him, but the count took to occasional drinking, left home for longer and longer periods of time, and made friends in the infant national socialist movement; and their life of ease and luxury had to be drastically curtailed. With little inner strength to fall back on, his wife's interest in life slowly began to deteriorate. She poured herself into her son, far more than was good for either of them, lavishing upon him every advantage, every gift, every luxury she saw slipping through the fingers of her own vanishing youth, doting upon him as he grew, spoiling him with every fleeting reminder of privilege she could.

"I will speak with her mother, Gustav," said the countess at length. "Perhaps I shall invite her for *Kaffee trinken* tomorrow afternoon."

Gustav nodded, then made his exit before the conversation could come back round to his activities in the village.

The following day, at three-thirty in the afternoon, the

baron's wife arrived at the estate of her friend. The two women met in the private parlor of the hostess and were soon nibbling on cakes, drinking coffee, and visiting freely, first about the weather, then about flowers. It took some time for the subject of the children to be brought up.

The two women had been best friends for some time. They had married within a year of each other, to neighboring noblemen, then given birth to their firstborn within two years of one another. And as the years went by, and neither had more children, and the two youngsters played and romped and laughed and cried together, how could it have been otherwise than that the two friends would find themselves speaking upon occasion of a potential marriage? Such could not have been more perfect and fitting, especially in Ingrid's eyes, and as the years slowly progressed, the onetime daydreaming of two young mothers and friends became more and more considered, on the one of the two estates, a *fait accompli*.

All the while as her own fortunes declined, Countess Ingrid von Schmundt cherished an ever-more-fervent desire after her son's success and reputation and standing, the foundation of which lay in the joining of the vast estates and the union of two respected aristocratic names. The joint holdings would be formidable, one of the largest estates in all the northeast of Germany. Her son would be respected throughout the land, and she would remain at his side. He would one day occupy a powerful role in the new German order. If the limelight was not directed upon her as it once had been, she would be content to share in its glow. For would not all recognize her as the societal matriarch of the Schmundt name, and look to *her* as the far more capable mistress of the empire, rather than the lightheaded and naive daughter of that simpleton of a baron?

For her own convenience, the count's wife assumed her friend felt exactly as she, though the two women spoke less and less of it as time went by, for very different reasons on each side.

In recent years Marion had known a distance was creeping between them. Not a distance of antagonism or conflict, but of gradually diverging directions of purpose. Such was no doubt inevitable, for had they not married men as different as night and day? How could the two wives not be influenced by the path of each of their husbands? And on a more profound level, did not the man each one chose speak as forcefully as her *own* character concerning the kind of woman she was at the core?

The selection of a spouse, though integrity or flaw of character may not reveal itself to the world for years, surely indicates as much wisdom—or lack of it—on either side of a marriage as do the attributes of character a man or woman appears to possess in his or her own right. Husbands or wives were not islands unto themselves. A spouse is a mirror into one's own soul. Wise men and women recognize wisdom and seek it. Fools are content to join themselves with those of like persuasions. The consequences are enjoyed, or suffered, by each in his turn—with greater blessings, or greater ills, as the years slip quickly by.

Such were the divergent consequential fates of the two former companions of the heart, and present friends of convenience—the wives of Baron Heinrich von Dortmann and Count Ernst von Schmundt.

The one woman had been impressed with worldly acclaim, honors, and reputation. The other had chosen a quiet, thoughtful man considered something of a dullard by the peers of his society. While the count and countess were hosting parties and amassing a fortune that was the envy of the entire region, the baron next door was tending a ridiculous garden and collecting books and opening his home to strangers and passersby—even peasants, Ingrid had heard!

She loved Marion, though she hadn't understood at the time, nor had she understood since, what she saw in the man. That she had married a fool was obvious enough. Yet he did have a daughter who would one day inherit the estate, and that in itself was enough to make up for every innocent notion the man himself might possess.

Neither woman knew that it had been the baron himself who had rescued the count from complete financial disaster. Dortmann had gone to Schmundt in private at the height of his troubles with a secret offer of 425,000 marks, exactly the amount necessary to clear the debt off his property, which was only days from foreclosure. The only requirement, the baron told his neighbor, was that no one should know the source of the funds. Schmundt agreed, took the cashier's draft with stoically

Germanic humility—as much meekness, that is, as the German temperament is capable of summoning—thanked him with a simple though heartfelt *danke*, and the gift had never been mentioned between them again. Nor did the count, when his fortunes were again on the rise and he found himself flush with reichsmarks, once offer to repay the baron so much as a pfennig. In his heart of hearts, in fact, the count secretly resented what he thought was the baron's holier-than-thou interference and vowed, if Dortmann ever found *himself* in dire straits, to instruct his own solicitor to buy the estate out from under him.

As Marion sat listening to her friend chatter on about one meaningless nonentity after another, her heart grew quietly heavy. In truth, the count's wife seemed to have stopped growing in the most important ways that define personhood and individuality. She had become steadily more self-absorbed, taking to her shallow romances and magazines and fussing about her clothes and the state of her home. The count was often in Berlin, Gustav was nearly a man, and the poor lady was left with no companion at her side other than the disposition of her own being. She was finding, sadly, more to her friend's dismay than her own, that she did not possess enough sustenance of brain and heart to keep herself well occupied.

Marion found the friendship they had shared as young people fading more and more into memory. As it did, she gave more and more thought to the airy castles they had built on behalf of their son and daughter and realized what a mistake it had been ever to allow talk of it to go so far. When Countess von Schmundt, therefore, brought up the subject, it was already not far from Marion's mind.

"Do you not think, Marion," she said after a brief silence had fallen between them, "that it is time we begin making plans?"

"Plans, Ingrid—what kind of plans?"

"Why, for the wedding, of course. My Gustav is eighteen."

"Yes, and my Sabina is only sixteen. I wouldn't think of her marrying so young."

"But time is passing quickly. It is not too soon to be thinking of these things."

"You speak as if it were completely decided."

"Isn't it? I thought we—"

"Ingrid, that was years ago," the baron's wife answered, feeling a sense of grieving pity in her heart.

"Marion, I do not understand," said the count's wife in a tone of injury. "You haven't . . . changed your mind?"

For a fleeting moment, Marion's heart nearly broke within her. The very tone of her friend's voice betrayed not mere surprise or even hurt, but the stultifying trauma of being mortally wounded by her best friend.

"Please, Ingrid," said Marion tenderly, "it was only daydreaming. We only said *what if* to one another, there were no *plans*." Her voice was quiet and tender, hurting for her friend.

"You weren't serious, Marion?" said the countess, still trying to absorb the blow. Suddenly she looked so much older than Marion ever remembered seeing her. The fleshy jowls of her cheeks sagged below her dark, drooping eyes, and Marion could scarcely hold back the tears. How could they have become so different, almost without her noticing?

"Perhaps I was seriously daydreaming," she said, "but not serious as to a firm commitment. The children were so young then. Such is a decision neither you nor I can make for either Gustav or Sabina."

"But my Gustav is in love with Sabina."

"In love, Ingrid?"

"Surely you must have known. He visits her frequently."

Marion nodded. "Yes. Yes, he does. They have been friends for years, but—"

"He will be heartbroken when I tell him what you have said."

"There is nothing so heartbreaking to tell him, only that I think it best that the young people decide for themselves. Surely, Ingrid, even Gustav would not want a marriage forced upon him."

"Forced," repeated the countess, a sudden hint of vexation replacing the injury of her tone. "Is that what you think I have been trying to do, *force* my dear son on your daughter?"

"No, please, Ingrid, that is not what I meant."

"I would not *force* Gustav to marry. Any young lady would be honored to be his bride." Her voice rose as her feeling of affront grew. "But if your daughter does not think my son good enough for the likes—"

"Oh, Ingrid, no. It's not like that at all," pleaded Marion. "Both Sabina and I think Gustav is a fine young man."

"Just not good enough to marry," snapped the countess peevishly. "Don't condescend to me, Marion," she added, pulling herself up in a huff.

Marion kept her peace, looking down at her lap.

"Does your *husband* feel as you do?" asked the countess, curtly, emphasizing the word with obvious intent.

"I have not spoken to him about it," replied Marion softly.

"Then I suggest you do. Perhaps he will talk some sense into you, though that is no doubt too much to expect from him."

Still Marion remained silent, heartbroken herself, although for reasons neither the countess nor her son could have fathomed.

"Will you speak to him?"

"I don't know, Ingrid, I—"

"I want to know if you will speak to him. I insist you do."

"All right. I will speak to my husband," replied Marion softly.

Her hostess sat back with the vaunted dignity of temporary victory spreading over her countenance.

"I suppose I ought to go," said Marion at length, glancing up and attempting a smile. "Thank you, Ingrid, for the coffee and cakes. I am—I am so very sorry for this misunderstanding. I pray you can find it in your heart to forgive me for my part in it."

Countess von Schmundt said nothing, merely gave a hinting nod of acknowledgment.

Marion rose, then left by the front door. The countess watched her go from the vantage point of her overstuffed chair. She then sat forward and helped herself to another one of the cakes, which she proceeded to eat in the silence of her own thoughts.

ᴄ⌀ 22 ᴄ⌀

Infiltrating the Brotherhood

There were some things best handled by oneself.

He could have sent someone else up to Stettin and then out to this little country village. But if this was truly the center of the anti-Nazi sect of the church, as the report had indicated, then he wanted to see it for himself. He had the power to order it shut down with a snap of his fingers. But he had to be sure this location was not a mere diversion, and that if he did take action it would have permanent and far-reaching results.

It was still too soon to arrest church leaders and pastors en masse, despite his boast to Himmler that he would not hesitate to do so. A few, perhaps, might be in order, as an example. But there were plenty of ways to bring the hypocrites to their knees. And if the measures he had in mind failed to work before the year he'd been given was out, then more arrests would surely follow.

The face which stared out of the car window was remarkable chiefly for its eyes. Their vision, from years of experience, had trained themselves to see not merely what *was*, but what *could be*. They were eyes that sought opportunity. As a result they always bore a slight squint, revealing lines around their edges, not of age, for the Gestapo agent was yet merely in his early thirties, but of craftiness and guile. They were eyes which had grown skilled in masking the true thoughts and intent of their owner, an essential requirement in the rarefied atmosphere of Nazi leadership, where deceit and backstabbing were the oxygen and hydrogen so necessary for survival.

The face was rather a thin one, though the nose was wide and thick. Sunken, pockmarked cheeks fell toward a square jaw, angular and sharp at the chin but growing less pronounced as the jawbones retreated back toward the ears. The mouth was wide and the lips full, though the teeth, which rarely revealed themselves, were narrow and yellowed.

A shrewd student of anthropology would have detected the unmistakable signs of Slavic and Russian lineage. But in the circles he frequented, perceptions as well as loyalties tended to be blind. So long as his skin was white, and he saluted the swastika and kept *Heil Hitler!* ready on his tongue, the primal idiosyncrasies of his face would never be questioned.

Hair of pure black showed signs of wanting to thin, and, well oiled, was combed back from the high forehead and lay greasy and straight against his scalp. A fuller mane, or even a mustache, might have helped, for in truth the overall appearance was not an appealing one. But Emil Korsch had ceased being concerned about his looks or what people thought of him years ago. His objectives were bent in altogether different directions.

Again he scrutinized the several buildings across the field from where he sat in his parked car, paying special attention to the Mercedes. The large automobile, though not of new make, was enough out-of-place among all the others to make him wonder if its owner was part of the little community. He had been curious about it ever since his arrival a few minutes ago and had determined to have a closer look as soon as it was dark.

But he was too far away to keep a good eye on the place and see what was going on. He needed a closer vantage point.

A farmhouse sat adjacent to the buildings. He had seen a woman come out and hang laundry on the line, so it could not be part of the compound.

He would take up a position there.

He started his car and drove cautiously forward, parking around the side of the farmhouse, out of sight from the other direction. He got out and approached the back door. He had seen the woman go back inside. There didn't seem to be a man around, and he saw no other automobile.

He walked inside without a knock.

The woman stood in the kitchen, a basket of laundry in her hands. She looked up, her face filling first with confusion, then greeting.

"*Guten—*" she began.

"Silence, Frau!" barked Korsch in a low voice.

"Who are you?" she said, angry now, and not one to be intimidated.

"Gestapo," he answered, walking around the room and looking about.

"What do you want?"

"I need your house," he said, peering out the windows, then proceeding to walk into an adjacent room.

"My house is not available. Now get out. We have nothing to do with your kind."

He spun around and approached, leveling upon her a sneer of evil cunning.

"Perhaps you would like that fact reported," he hissed. "I could arrange a raid by the SS for your treason."

She stared back with a look equally venomous as his own. These were not days when strangers readily made friends in Germany, as it had been in the old days.

"Please," she said, "just go away, and do your dirty work someplace else."

"Dirty work, you ugly old hag!" he shouted. "The Gestapo goes where it likes!" he added, suddenly raising his arm and striking her a vicious blow across the cheek with the back of his hand.

She screamed out in pain, staggered back, and tripped on a chair and fell.

Korsch did not even pause to watch, but was already making his way about the small house again. From another room a baby began to cry.

"Make the baby shut up or it will get the same!" he hissed.

The poor woman struggled to her feet, doing her best to keep from crying, and ran into the other room.

Korsch found a suitable vantage point in one of the bedrooms, returned to the kitchen, where he grabbed what food he could find, then returned to the window he had chosen and took up his vigil.

For an hour or two he sat. He did not see the woman again. Still there was little activity to be seen about the place next door.

When dusk was well advanced, he rose and left the farmhouse by the back door, and walked toward the row of parked cars.

Something told him he had stumbled into a mystery it behooved him to get to the bottom of. He would not arouse undue suspicion if he could avoid it. But he had to get the number of that license plate. Some of his more impertinent colleagues in the Gestapo would have marched straight to the front door with their bluster and threats and demanded the information point-blank. If they did not receive it, intimidation and arrest might well follow.

Sometimes such tactics were necessary. But he liked to keep stealth and secrecy on his side. He would make his move with lightning speed when the time was right. But he did not like to tip his hand too soon.

When he had covered about half the distance, suddenly the door of the school building opened. Two men emerged.

Immediately he turned around and began to saunter nonchalantly back the way he had come. In another moment, he heard a car door open, then slam shut two or three seconds later.

An engine roared. He knew it was the Mercedes.

He quickened his pace, hid behind the wall of the farmhouse, then watched as the Mercedes backed up, pulled out, and came straight toward him. Keeping out of sight, he was just able to make out the plate as the car passed. He ran for his car, got in, grabbed his notebook, wrote down the number, waited another minute or two, then turned his own key, pulled the car into gear, and sped off.

He had seen all he needed to see.

He would order the raid. In the meantime, he would find out who was the visitor in the Mercedes.

Meanwhile, in pain and paralyzed with fear, the poor woman inside remained crouching in the corner of her daughter's bedroom for another hour, when her husband returned home from Stettin to find the entire house dark, silent, and the back door wide open.

∽ 23 ∾
Husband and Wife

Baron von Dortmann and his wife sat together in the sitting room adjacent to their bedroom. The evening was well advanced and most of the servants had retired. They had said good night to Sabina an hour earlier.

"Are there any developments at Finkenwalde?" Marion asked. Her husband had only returned from the seminary two or three hours earlier.

"Dietrich fears the Nazis are closing in."

"Is there danger? Their lives are not being threatened?"

"No, nothing so serious. But the seminary is still not sanc-

tioned since the leaders of the Confessing Church asked
Dietrich to direct it two years ago. It is independent, and it
serves as a continual slap in the face of the requirements the
national socialists have imposed on the university seminarians.
It is probably only a matter of time before they move to do
something."

"What can they do?"

"The Nazis *can* do anything they want, it seems," sighed
Heinrich mordantly. "What they *will* do is another question.
They dismissed Karl Barth from Bonn University. They
outlawed the training centers of the Confessing Church. They
have Nazi-ized the National Protestant Church. They have
outlawed Jewish businesses, forbidden Jewish/Aryan
marriages, canceled Jewish citizenship—"

He stopped abruptly. The words hit too close to home, but
neither made comment.

"They can and will do anything, it seems," the baron continued after a moment, "to rid Germany of all but a hollow, shallow, empty religion that worships our so-called Führer rather
than God."

The room was silent a minute, as the implications of the
baron's words settled over them.

"I must learn to control the passion I feel over it," said Heinrich,
chastising himself. "I should not say such things. But I fear for
Dietrich. He is far more outspoken. I honestly do not think he
even fears death. He has been flying in the Nazis' face for years,
making many enemies with his bold pro-Jewish sentiments
and his pronouncements to the church to awaken from its
complacency."

"What is it you told me he said to you recently?"

"I know what you're thinking of. He said, 'When Christ calls
a man, he bids him come and die.'"

"Yes, that's it."

"He said it again yesterday. It is one of the cornerstones of
this series of teachings he is giving on discipleship. He is putting together a book from his lectures too. Listen—I was so
struck with something he said yesterday that I wrote it down."

As the baron spoke, he rose and walked to where he had laid
his coat upon his return. From the inside vest pocket he pulled

a single sheet of paper. He unfolded it as he walked slowly back and resumed his chair.

"Whenever Dietrich speaks, it all mixes so powerfully together—discipleship, the call of Christ to die, and what he calls cheap and costly grace. Here's what I wrote down."

He looked at the paper in front of him a moment, then read to his wife:

Cheap grace means grace alone does everything, and so everything can remain as it was before. Let the Christian live like the rest of the world, let him model himself on the world's standards. Cheap grace is the preaching of forgiveness without requiring repentance.

Costly grace is the treasure hidden in the field. It is the kingly rule of Christ. Costly grace is the gospel which must be sought again and again, the gift which must be asked for, the door at which a man must knock.

Such grace is costly because it calls us to follow, and it is grace because it calls us to follow Jesus Christ. It is costly because it costs a man his life, and it is grace because it gives a man the only true life. Above all it is costly because it cost God the life of his Son.

"I understand why you were taken by it," said Marion, after a lengthy pause.

"He is a remarkable man. I derive great strength from my association with him."

"Aaron was here yesterday," said his wife, after a brief silence. "He asked you to call when you returned."

"Did he say why?"

"He said there had been developments—I assumed he meant in the village."

"He did not say what?"

"No. He said you would probably know of them from Finkenwalde. Perhaps it is what you were telling me of earlier."

The baron's grave expression gave evidence that subjects of more immediate political import than discipleship and costly grace had been raised during his two days at Finkenwalde. The time at the seminary had only increased his conviction that frightful times were coming to them all, but he would not burden his wife with the purport of it all now. He knew she would face it soon enough, and he would protect her from all he could.

"I was at Ingrid's this afternoon," said Marion after they sat a few minutes, both alone with their own thoughts. "She is pressing me about the children. She made me promise I would talk to you."

"What about?"

"They are intent on the two marrying."

"But that was just a notion—from years ago."

"I told her that. She doesn't see it that way."

"Have you spoken to Sabina?" asked the baron.

"Enough to know that this is no time to rush a decision regarding her future."

"Is she favorably disposed toward the young man?"

"They have been good friends for years, Heinrich. At the moment—well, their friendship seems strained. But the question is have *we* altered our enthusiasm for the marriage—that is what Ingrid is pressing me to know. She feels that we will sway Sabina favorably."

"My enthusiasm has not *altered*," said Heinrich. "I have *never* felt any enthusiasm for the union. It was you and Ingrid who used to talk of it when they were children. I thought nothing of it. I would never make such a commitment until we had a good chance to find out what kind of man the boy turned out to be. It was idle talk as far as I was concerned, nothing more."

"I'm afraid I have been guilty of conveying to Ingrid more certainty in our position than either we or Sabina feel," replied Marion with a sigh. "I now see the folly of allowing such idle words. Ingrid, and apparently Gustav as well, consider it a foregone conclusion."

"What do you think now?"

"Ingrid has changed, Heinrich. It was a sad exchange. I feel so badly for her. She has nothing to live for but Gustav."

"Are you saying you *have* changed your opinion on the matter?"

"I never did really take it seriously. It was just dreamy talk when the children were young. They are not about the same business in life that we are, Heinrich. Unless that changes . . . " Her voice trailed off. Her husband knew well enough what she meant.

"I know what you mean," replied the baron, sighing now in his turn. "I am worried too for Ernst."

"Have you and the count spoken of it together?"

"Ernst and I have spoken together about very little of anything," answered Heinrich. "I haven't spent more than ten minutes, I don't think, with him in the last two years. His head is being turned, I fear, by the elitist circles in Berlin in which he moves. He will probably be asked to join the government in some capacity before long. To answer your question, however, in years past whenever the children came up in conversation between us, it was more in the way of chuckling lightly at the feminine whims of their mothers—no offense meant," he added with a smile.

"None taken," returned Marion, though without a smile on her lips. "What ought we to do, Heinrich?"

"I don't see that there is anything we can or should do. Events of this kind, as all kinds, must take their course. God will reveal his will in time. Sabina is young yet. And Gustav is not yet a man. We must see what becomes of them both. Both we and Sabina, I fear, will face more ominous decisions, perhaps even crises, than this if events continue on their present course."

A long silence fell between them. By now it was quite late. The house was silent, and the night nearly black.

∽ 24 ∾

Noises and Dungeons

Thursday morning, where he lay sleeping in the guest room into which they had moved him across the hall from the courtyard parlor, Matthew was awakened by an irregular tapping noise. As he came to himself, he realized he had been hearing it for some time. Even before consciousness fully returned, the sound had intruded into his dreams and then had eventually led to his waking.

He sat up as best he could in bed and glanced around.

It was still early, six or six-thirty he guessed, though he could hear the sounds of servants and laborers outside making ready to begin the day's work.

It was a dull, thudding sound, very faint. At first it sounded like some distant kind of old-fashioned machinery, probably wooden, coming from a great ways away across the fields. Yet as Matthew came more and more to himself, he realized it wasn't far away at all, but close—very close by.

He strained to hear. It even sounded like . . . yes, he was sure now. It was coming from somewhere in the room!

Slowly he rose to a sitting position, reached for his crutches and got to his feet. He put on the robe lying on the couch nearby, and hobbled with the *thump, thump, thump* of his plastered foot across the floor. Immediately, as the sound of his cast echoed in the quiet morning, the other noise ceased.

Matthew opened the door and glanced up and down the hallway. Not another soul was to be seen, nor was there so much as a sound.

Puzzled, he reentered the room, lay down for a while longer, and read for some time from a newsmagazine, until the manservant who had been helping him came to assist him in getting dressed and then took him down to the family dining room for breakfast.

The rest of the morning passed much as had the two previous days. Sabina visited him several times and read to him, and they talked about many things. After lunch she left him alone again in his room and eventually, after reading for a while, he dozed off.

Again he was awakened by the strange sound.

This time his brain came alert instantly. He sat up in his bed and listened. It was probably two o'clock in the afternoon, so there was none of the early morning eeriness to it, but otherwise it sounded exactly as it had earlier.

It seemed to be coming from one of the walls opposite him.

Matthew determined to make no sound this time. He stole from the bed as carefully as he could, then, with his crutches under his shoulders, made his way noiselessly across the floor toward the tapping noise. He took each step with care, setting his casted foot gently down on the hardwood beneath him.

He approached the corner of the room opposite his bed. It was the shortest wall in the odd-shaped room, out of which a large quarter circle seemed to have been sliced to make way for the great staircase on the other side. Just as he reached the wall, his cast bumped one of the chairs sitting nearby. Instantly the room was quiet. He heard nothing more of the sound the rest of the day.

A few minutes later a knock came at the door.

Still contemplating the strange sound, Matthew gave a start. Then realizing someone was there, he called out for the person to enter.

Sabina opened the door and came in, an unusual twinkle in her eyes. "Doctor Abrahams has arrived," she said merrily. "Papa's talking with him, but he'll be here in a minute."

The doctor pronounced Matthew's leg and cast sufficiently sound to walk freely about with the help of a single crutch under his left shoulder, if he didn't want to use them both.

"I don't have to be easy on it anymore?"

"No, my boy. It's well set and there's nothing you can do to hurt it now—the cast will see to that. I'm certain too that it has caused you no additional problems."

It was awkward work at first, learning to get up and down stairs and over the uneven terrain outside, but after being cooped up several days he was anxious to try out his newfound freedom. He and Sabina spent most of the rest of the afternoon outside, either in the courtyard, in the garden, or walking down the path past the oak tree and down to the stream below. By the end of the day he was moving about with tolerable ease, although he had tired himself out.

That evening at dinner he brought up the strange noise he had heard. Everyone looked puzzled and professed no insight as to what could be the cause.

"Any old house like this has its share of mice, even rats sometimes, Matthew," said Herr von Dortmann.

"I've heard mice in walls, sir," replied Matthew. "But this was different—a tapping sound. *Something* was knocking against the inside of the wall, I'm sure of it."

"Maybe Matthew's found the secret dungeon, Papa!" said Sabina excitedly.

The baron laughed.

"Secret dungeon!" exclaimed Matthew.

"An old wives' tale, Matthew," said Marion, "nothing more. And nothing you'll hear anything about from *this* wife!"

"Is there really a dungeon?"

"To hear old Eppie tell it," laughed Marion.

"There's supposed to be one somewhere underneath this floor," said Sabina.

"And is there?"

"If there is," rejoined the baron, "it's been lost to time, and the legend has been added to over the years by the likes of Eppie. Nobody's ever seen hide nor hair of it, including Eppie herself, although she insists it's here and that ghosts still wander out of it from time to time."

"You should hear her tales, Matthew!" said Sabina.

"I would love to. This place is getting more and more intriguing all the time!"

"We'll go visit her tomorrow! May we, Mama?"

"It's all right with me," replied Marion. "Just be watchful you don't excite her too much. She's still not altogether over the effects of her fall."

"We'll be careful. Do you want to, Matthew?"

"I can't wait!"

∽ 25 ∾
The Hidden Passageway

As he lay down in bed that night, all Matthew could think of was the dungeon he had heard about, said to be full of treasure and ghosts, that no one had ever seen but that a mysterious servant just short of a century in years swore was hidden somewhere beneath the house, with all its past locked away and shrouded in ancient legend.

He laughed to himself.

It could not be more perfect, he thought. An old house like this, an old woman, probably with fewer than half her wits left about her, telling of ghosts and treasures and dungeons. This was the stuff of old mystery tales, yet here *he* was lying down to sleep in just such a house! Somewhere above him, old Eppie was lying in her bed too. *What dreams and memories and tales must be going through her brain!*

Slowly Matthew drifted into semiconsciousness. Images filtered into his sleep-fogged brain. An old lady with white hair shooting out in all directions was walking down a dark and musty passageway. Underfoot the ground was damp. The way was so narrow as to allow but one person to follow another in single file, and the stone enclosure of walls rounded up into a curved ceiling scarcely higher than his own head. The old lady walked with noiseless step. She stood erect, though the wrinkles on her face spoke of centuries, not mere years.

Uttering not a peep, Matthew followed, not sure whether she was aware of his presence and not wanting to call attention to his being only a step behind her. The passage was dark, the only light coming from a candle the old woman carried in her hand. He had to stay close for fear of being lost in the dark. Though she was walking, the candle's flame moved not so much as a flicker.

Matthew realized neither he nor she was moving along the passageway in the body at all, but only in some ethereal, dreamlike state. He leaned to one side and attempted to blow at the candle over her shoulder. Still the flame burned straight upward without so much as a flicker.

Suddenly the truth dawned on him—she was a ghost!

Now he realized . . . he could see the candle right through her body . . . and the passageway beyond!

He tried to stop, but his feet would not obey. Still he followed her down the passage.

He would go back to his room, he thought to himself. He tried to turn. He could not. Fear swept through him. He opened his mouth to scream. He could not move his lips. All was silent.

Paralyzed now with fear, he felt himself trembling, breaking out all over with perspiration, still following. Though he was behind her, he suddenly realized all along the way he had been able to see her face. In the darkness of the passageway, her eyes burned with a glow of passion almost the equal of the candle.

As they went, occasionally her free hand would lift from her transparent body, pointing to some door or turn of the passage-way. Her lips moved, but he heard nothing. He knew she was telling him secrets and mysteries and legends of this place, but he heard nothing, only saw into their depths by the fire in her eyes.

She turned and they entered a dead-end corridor. Ahead only a few steps more, he could see a stone wall blocking their way. She stopped. There was a door on their right. Without his will-ing them to do so, his feet stopped too, a step or two behind her.

She turned, and now for the first time she looked straight into his eyes, speaking rapidly. No sound met his ears. But he knew they had arrived at the hidden dungeon, and that she was telling him everything they would find inside. The glow in her eyes burned even more brightly with visions of the past.

She turned again toward the door, lifted her hand, and began to knock.

Why was she knocking? Why didn't they just go in? Was she waiting for someone to open the door?

Who could be inside? he thought in heightened dread. *Who but another ghost!*

She continued to knock . . . *tap* . . . *tap* . . . *tap*, her knuckles rapped against the door. It was of stone, yet the sound was as one made by wood.

Tap . . . *tap* . . . *tap* . . .

Suddenly Matthew bolted awake and shot upright in his bed, breathing heavily, heart pounding, wet with sweat.

How long he had been asleep he had no idea.

The tapping on the wall of his room had returned. It was clearly coming from the corner where he had heard it that same morning, louder now.

He sat staring, not tempted this time to rise in exploration. The vision of the ancient lady's ghost still fluttered around the edges of his consciousness, and he would remain in the bed right where he was. He did not want to encounter her again, somewhere in the middle of his room!

Slowly he lay back down, pulling the large featherbed cover-ing up over his head.

The tapping continued for about five minutes, then suddenly

stopped. Matthew drifted back into an uneasy sleep, but was haunted all night with the sense of aimless wandering down long, dark, subterranean corridors of earth and stone.

∽⌇∾

When he awoke the morning was well advanced. There were no windows in the room, but he knew he had slept longer than usual. He turned on the light. A quick look at his watch revealed that he was right. It was eight-fifteen.

What day was it? Oh yes, Friday, he said to himself. His father would be here later.

He rose and dressed by himself, thankful that no mysterious noises in the wall had awakened him this time. He opened the door and began making his way down toward the dining room, trying to shake off the effects of the night.

He found Sabina and her mother waiting for him, though they had finished with their breakfast.

"*Guten morgen*, Matthew," said the baron's wife. "*Hast du gut geschlafen?*"

"I had a long sleep, Frau von Dortmann," replied Matthew, shaking his head, "but not so sound a one."

"Is the bed not agreeable to you?"

"No, the bed is fine. It was the ghosts that kept me awake."

The sound of laughter broke out behind him. Matthew turned to see the baron walk into the room. To all appearances he looked like a field hand.

"The mysterious sounds in your walls and our talk about old Eppie last night after dinner, eh?" he said, still laughing.

"I suppose so."

The baron sat down and poured himself a cup of coffee. He looked to have been working already several hours. "The rye is coming along nicely," he said to his wife. "With all this warm weather we've been having, it could be ready in a couple more weeks."

Heidi brought Matthew some fresh slices of rye bread, meats, cheeses, and tea.

"Ready for what?" asked Matthew, helping himself and buttering a piece of bread.

"Ready for harvest, my boy," answered the baron.

"Oh, I wish you could be here for it," said Sabina. "It's my favorite time of the year."

"We can hardly keep her out of the fields," laughed Marion. "Ever since she could walk, when the harvest came she followed the workers and wagons around from dawn to dusk."

"Back in those days, so much of it was done by hand," said the baron. "But every year there are such advances and so many ingenious new kinds of equipment, it becomes easier and easier."

"And Papa buys every new machine the moment he learns of it, don't you, Papa?"

"I try," the baron said, smiling at his daughter. "We have such a great amount of grain to harvest, I'm always looking for ways to make the process more efficient. So much of the harvest, as I said, had to be carried out by hand in earlier times, in my father's day, for instance. There might have been fifty or more workers on the estate during the summer months. But now, with the *Mähdrescher* and other equipment, it is so much smoother and faster. We can do the same work with fifteen or twenty, in a fraction of the time."

"What is that, a *Mähd*—"

The baron laughed. "A *Mähdrescher*—it's what you call a 'combine,' a combination harvesting machine and thresher. It was invented in your United States, in California if I'm not mistaken. It has changed the entire harvesting process."

"Papa's got the only one in the region," said Sabina proudly. "If he finishes our harvest in time, he helps some of the other farmers to get in their grain too."

"It's a big, clanking, tractor-driven contraption," said the baron, "really quite interesting to watch. I still find myself fascinated with it."

"What does it do?"

"It cuts the tall stalks of grass, then separates the grain from its heads, holding it in a compartment inside, and then spews the stalks of grass back onto the ground to be gathered and baled and used for the animals."

"I'd love to see it work."

"Maybe you can come back for one of our harvests sometime."

"And the straw-baling machine too!" said Sabina. "That's what I like best—stacking the bales and bringing them into the barn for the cattle."

"What did my wife tell you, Matthew?" laughed the baron. "Once the harvest gets underway, Sabina's there for every hour of it. She's getting to be as good as any two of my men!"

"Oh, Papa!"

"Unfortunately your father will be here later this afternoon. We'll hate to see you go," said the baron.

"You've all been so nice to me. I've enjoyed myself in spite of the broken leg."

"And in spite of ghosts in the night?"

Now Matthew laughed. "Yeah. In fact, are you still going to take me to visit the old servant woman," he asked, turning to Sabina, "so that I can hear the real tales instead of my own dreams?"

"We're not going to be able to, Matthew," said Sabina. "Eppie had a bad night. She woke this morning saying she'd been out for a long walk and was too tired to move."

Matthew shuddered involuntarily, but tried to keep his composure.

"Whatever the cause," added the baron, "she was in a weak and excitable state this morning. Doctor Abrahams is with her now and has prescribed a sedative. Eppie is prone to fits when her mind wanders. At such times we have to watch her closely."

"That is too bad. I'm sorry to hear it."

"You'll have to visit us again!"

"Yes, do!" added Sabina. "You simply have to hear the stories from old Eppie's own lips."

"Well, if I can't meet Eppie, I will at least have one more good tour around your garden before I go," said Matthew. "I want to know it well enough so that I could not get lost."

"It is entirely at your disposal," rejoined the baron. "Nothing could please me more!"

Sabina rose. "Of course, you can go to the garden anytime you want to, Matthew. But I have some things to do this morning, so if you'd like I'll go for a walk with you right after lunch."

"Great!" he replied, and Sabina walked from the room.

Forty minutes later, Matthew hobbled back down the corridor toward the courtyard parlor and the room where he was staying. He went inside, sat down, and began to read.

The moment he opened the book, the strange wall tapping sounded, louder than it had ever been before.

This time he was going to find it!

He jumped to his feet and strode as quickly as he was able to the narrow portion of wall from which it sounded. He expected the sound to cease, but instead it grew even louder as he approached.

He leaned his ear to the wall. It was very clear now. It was coming from right behind the wall where he stood.

"Hey!" he called, curious to see if whatever it was would respond to his voice. If it was a rat or other animal, that would scare it off.

Instead he heard the muffled sound of giggling. The tapping stopped.

Before he had the chance to contemplate the meaning of the new sound, suddenly beside him a wardrobe began to move.

Matthew jumped back. But almost before his heart had a chance to climb up into his throat, out from behind it stepped Sabina, laughing now in earnest.

"You!" he exclaimed. "Have you been the mysterious noise-maker all this time?"

She continued to laugh, nodding her head.

"But . . . I don't understand," he said. "Were you . . . did you sneak in and get behind—"

He never finished the sentence. As he spoke, Sabina took hold of his arm and pulled him forward. Behind the wardrobe that had swung out into the room, Matthew now beheld a doorless hole in the wall, opening into a dark corridor behind it.

"I thought you said you had things to do!" said Matthew, now entering into the joke that had been played on him.

"I did—hiding from you! Come on," she said, still pulling his arm and leading him inside.

The passage was very narrow, and after a landing no wider than could be stood upon, where lay a thick stick of wood, a tight, stone, circular staircase led down into blackness.

"This is what I was knocking with against your wall," said Sabina, picking up the piece of wood. "Just let me get my candle here." She stooped down and picked up a candle, whose odor Matthew suddenly realized he had smelled. "I blew it out just before I shoved open the wardrobe," she said. "I'll light it and show you how I got here."

She pulled a match from her pocket, struck it, and lit the candle, then proceeded to carefully wind her way down the stairs, with Matthew following awkwardly close behind her.

"You told me there were hidden staircases," said Matthew. "But this is unbelievable! This is really hidden, behind a moving wardrobe no less!"

"A house of intrigue, as Papa told you and your father last weekend!"

They spiraled down the corkscrew. Matthew was carrying his crutch, but it was of little use on this stairway. He braced himself on Sabina's shoulder for support as they descended. In less than a minute Matthew found himself standing on the dirt floor of an underground passageway extending in a straight line into blackness in both directions, wide enough for two persons to pass if their shoulders touched. It was silent as a tomb and in fact reminded him of just that, and the only light came from the flickering of the candle in Sabina's hand.

"Where *are* we?" asked Matthew, unconscious of the hush in his tone.

"Under the house."

"So there really is a dungeon?" said Matthew. "You weren't all just pulling my leg last night?"

"No, silly," laughed Sabina. Her laugh echoed cheerily up and down the silent length of the corridor. "This is no dungeon, just a long passageway leading from one end of the house to the other. Follow me—I'll show you."

So saying, she led the way, holding the candle in front of her, while Matthew followed behind her. As they went, it was with an eerie and disquieting sense of déjà vu that he recognized his dream from the night before, though with relief he noticed that the candle danced about from the movement, and that Sabina was *not* transparent to his eyes.

"It leads from the cellar under the south parlor, straight

under the hallway upstairs, to the north end of the house under the small library."

"What's it for?" asked Matthew.

"Nobody knows exactly. Papa thinks it may have been an icehouse one day, or that there was an underground spring or well down here that supplied the house with water. As you can see, the dirt is damp underfoot."

Matthew glanced down. Indeed, it was damp, unusual for such a high-placed house, especially in the middle of summer.

"Papa thinks there was a small springhouse somewhere along where we are now, from which they gathered water, but that was walled up after the wells and pumps were installed outside. He thinks that's where the talk about a secret room or dungeon came from. Look, here—"

Sabina stopped and held the candle down to the ground.

"You see, there's a lot of seepage. Papa's knocked about all over the walls here trying to find a room that might have been used for the water supply, but he's discovered nothing, except that it stays wet here all year round. There's a little room at the other end, just under the small library, and then a stairway up into the hallway between it and the guest *Stube*. Another of the legends of the house is that there was once a secret passage from the basement here to the outside. Papa's sure it runs under the foundation from the room we're going to, out to the north of the house by the vegetable garden. The ground slopes off there rapidly and he says it would be perfect for such a tunnel. But he's been over every inch of the room and the slope outside and has found nothing. So it's probably just like the dungeon legend."

As they went, Matthew kept expecting a second passageway to turn off at right angles to the one they were walking along, as in his dream. But the corridor was long and straight, without sign of door or hall or room on either side, leading eventually to the small room Sabina had described. At the far corner, a stairway much like the one they had descended rose from the dirt floor out of sight.

They stopped and looked around the empty cubicle.

"Not much here," said Matthew. "Maybe this is the dungeon."

"Perhaps," replied Sabina. "Papa thinks this was the

icehouse, with some kind of a tunnel leading outside through which they brought the ice to store in the winter."

"What's it used for now?"

"Nothing. None of this down here is used for anything. No one ever comes down here but me. I used to play down here, though it was scary when I was alone. All the servants are afraid of the place. I think they're more convinced they're going to stumble onto ghosts or dead bodies than buried treasure!"

"It does sort of resemble the catacombs, you know. Show me these stairs over here," he added, moving toward the corner.

Sabina handed him the candle.

"Go on up," she said. "I'll be right behind you. Give me your crutch, and if you fall, I'll catch you."

Tentatively Matthew limped his way up, good foot first, pulling his cast up behind him, arriving at the top where solid walls met him in all three directions.

"It's a dead end," he said back down to Sabina, his voice echoing through the circular tunnel.

"No it's not, silly," she laughed. "You just have to know which stone to pull out."

"What are you talking about?"

"One of the walls is a door. Its latch is recessed into the wall, with a stone cut to exactly fill the hole. You just have to pull out the stone and push down on the latch . . . like this—"

As she spoke, Sabina scampered up the stairs, stretched her arm around Matthew's waist, and pulled a loose stone from the wall. Matthew saw the hidden latch immediately, reached in, pushed it down, and instantly a doorway opened away from him. He stepped forward and found himself at the end of the hall beside the guest *Stube*, back on the ground floor.

Sabina followed him, shutting the door behind them. As he heard it thud, Matthew turned around to see a solid wall.

"This is where I was the other day! I was right—there was a hidden door!"

"You said you wanted to know the mystery of it."

"You sure found a roundabout way to show me—all that tapping on the wall."

Sabina laughed. "I thought it would be more fun to show you the secret door from the inside!"

"It's completely invisible," Matthew said. "No one would ever know it was there!"

"No one's supposed to," laughed Sabina.

"Can you open it from this side too?"

"*If* you know how," she answered with a sly smile.

"I want to know."

"Close your eyes."

"That's not fair!"

"It's my house," she laughed.

"Your father's," he corrected.

"Well, almost mine—close your eyes."

This time Matthew obeyed. The next second he heard the door open again. He opened his eyes, and there was the stairwell open to them once more.

"Take me back through," he said. "This is great!"

Matthew had not had such fun in years. It was not only the excitement of hidden chambers or secrets, but that Sabina's playfulness was injecting his otherwise serious existence with such fun.

"I want to see the whole passage from one end to the other!" he said.

"I'll lead down," said Sabina, "so you don't fall. Here . . . pull the door closed behind you . . . now, hang on . . . ."

Down they went again, retracing their steps, until once more they were standing in the empty room under the small library, which Sabina called the icehouse.

Slowly Matthew walked around its perimeter.

"It's almost like a cave," he said. "Except for the stones along this one wall here," he added. "They're arranged like shelves, with these indentations going into the wall here at even intervals. What are these containers here for?"

"I don't know, just old pieces of pottery and flowerpots. They've been here as long as I can remember."

"It almost looks like a gardening supplies room," said Matthew, "which would be another reason for the tunnel leading outside from here. Isn't the vegetable garden just on the other side of this wall?"

"Yes."

"Maybe it's not so mysterious after all."

He completed his round of the room, then they again entered the long passageway and began the walk southward again.

All of a sudden Sabina blew out the candle.

"Hey, what are you doing!" exclaimed Matthew. "It's pitch black!"

Sabina did not answer.

"You're not going to scare me again, are you, like you did on the top floor?" said Matthew into the darkness. "I'm even more defenseless now, with my bum leg!"

All was silent.

Then began to echo through the passageway an eerie sound. "*Ooow . . . ooow . . .*" wailed Sabina in the most ghostly voice she could put on. The effect was spoiled, however, the moment she broke into laughter.

"Some ghost you make!" said Matthew. "Now come on, get that candle lit again."

"You're not very adventurous. Wouldn't you rather grope your way back in the dark?"

"No. I don't trust you."

Sabina laughed. Matthew heard the sound of a match striking, and suddenly the narrow catacomb exploded into light. Sabina lit the candle, then continued walking.

"Here's the stairway up to your room," she said as they passed it on the right. "And then as we continue about another six or seven meters . . . here we are!"

Matthew saw that they had reached the end of the passageway.

"What now?"

"Another hidden-latched doorway," she replied, reaching into a tiny hole in the wall ahead of her. The click of a latch releasing sounded, and the stone door swung on invisible iron hinges. They entered the cellar, and Sabina closed the door behind them.

"Papa also says possibly there were originally two cellars, joined by this passageway, but that for some reason the one at the far end ceased to be used, while this one, more useful and accessible to the kitchen because of the larger rectangular stairway, continued in everyday use. Anyway, you've now been over every inch of the house, and I'm hungry. It must be almost time for lunch!"

Sabina made for the stairs, leaping up them two at a time, while Matthew followed, with crutch and cast, more slowly.

∽∾∽

Two hours later, after lunch and a pleasant conversation with Herr and Frau von Dortmann, Matthew wandered outside alone and sat down on a bench in the courtyard.

It slowly began to dawn on him that these were his final hours in this place. A quiet began to descend upon him, and he found himself filled with many questions about these people he had been with for a week. It wasn't merely the adventurous and interesting nature of their home. There was something unique about these people as well. Certainly they were different from the usual aristocrats he had met. But come to think of it, they were different from *any* family he had ever known. He found himself wondering what the difference was.

His thoughts were interrupted by Sabina, standing in front of him. She had stolen up quietly, and he had not heard her approach.

"You look deep in thought," she said.

"I suppose I was," Matthew said, smiling.

"What about?"

"Oh, I don't know," sighed Matthew, "about—well, about all of you, I suppose, and this place. It's so different here, so peaceful. And—*you* are different too. I don't mean just you, but your father and mother too."

"Good different or bad different?"

"Oh, good different!"

"Whew!"

They were silent a few moments.

"Anything you'd want to talk about?" asked Sabina.

"I don't know—maybe. It's just that there's nothing specific that I'm thinking, just . . . like I said, that there's something different here."

"And you want to know what it is?" said Sabina.

"I don't know, maybe that's it. I don't want to leave here puzzled about something that was right in front of my nose."

"Feel like a walk?" asked Sabina.

"Sure."

"Then let's go down into the garden."

After their playful excursion through the cellar of the house, this afternoon's stroll was much different in tone—quieter and more thoughtful.

Two playful children had scampered through the hidden passageway pretending dangerous mysteries and adventures. Now two young adults, in their own ways seeking meaning both to life and to this new friendship suddenly forming between them, found themselves walking side by side, saying little, but each full of many thoughts. The day was a warm one, and they walked slowly down the hill, Sabina steadying him as they descended the stairs.

At length they passed under the stone arch and into *Der Frühlingsgarten.*

∽ 26 ∾
Mystery of the Kingdom

Baron von Dortmann found his daughter and their new young friend an hour later in the rose garden.

An inner prompting had led him here, and the moment he saw the looks on their two faces, he knew why the urging of the Spirit had come to him.

They sat silent, obviously deep in thought.

The baron sensed he had walked into the midst of an important conversation. The very air tingled with a stillness he recognized immediately as the presence of God. Gliding across the ground softly, as if the garden itself were a chapel, which in truth it was, he took a seat nearby and prayerfully waited.

Several minutes passed.

It was Sabina who broke the holy hush.

"I was just telling Matthew," she said softly, "what our faith in God means to us, Papa."

"Ah," he murmured with a smile, "I wish I had heard what you told him."

"Why, Papa? You know well enough what I would say."

"It is always uplifting to hear it from another's lips. And every time we talk of the things of God, it seems some new truth is revealed."

Both were quiet again. Time was plentiful for such things. Discussions of this nature could not be rushed.

It is not often in life that the intercourse between two or three individuals results in such harmony of spirit, that every word is received with the meaning it was intended to carry. Such requires an abandonment of personal motive and a humble hunger for truth rarely seen.

In most discussions, each person possesses an agenda of ideas and perspectives, which he seeks to interject into discourse at every potential opening the conversation affords. His object in dialog is to introduce as many of his own points of view as possible, then to maintain and bolster them, while countering his neighbor's. Most, no doubt, originally adopt their views because of elements of truth once seen in them. But the rest of their life they proceed to wall up every door and window in their mind where *more* truth might enter.

Unusual as it is, therefore, on this particular afternoon, here *were* three individuals intent only on probing honestly and with no motive but the truth into the deep meanings of life. With such a point of beginning, the conversation did not take long to settle into the right channels.

"I've just never heard the kinds of things Sabina's been telling me, Herr von Dortmann," said Matthew at length.

"What kinds of things?" asked the baron.

"About how you make God a part of all you do and think. She mentioned some of it when we were talking in Berlin, but I guess it didn't really sink in. But being here with your family, and talking to you and seeing how you live, I guess I'm beginning to see how seriously you take your religion. I've never known people quite like you before."

A smile parted the baron's lips at the word *religion*, but he made no comment.

"Well then," he said, "if how we view God is new to you, how are *you* accustomed to thinking of him?"

"I suppose I *haven't* thought of him much. I don't know, just sort of out there, I guess, looking down on the world from . . ."

He hesitated.

"From heaven?" suggested the baron.

"Yeah, I guess," answered Matthew.

"Wherever that is?" added the baron inquisitively.

Matthew nodded.

"But not having much actually to do with the daily goings-on of life?"

"Yes, I guess that's it. That's why it's so different—and if you'll forgive me for saying so, sir, it's almost *peculiar* to listen to Sabina talk as if . . . as if God is actually a member of your family, and is just walking around beside you all the time."

"What do you think of a notion like that?"

"Do you really want me to tell you?" asked Matthew hesitantly.

"Of course. Nothing you can say will offend me."

"Well, sir, it seems kind of spooky—maybe a little fearsome. I'm not sure I altogether like the sound of it."

The baron laughed heartily.

"A very common response, Matthew, my boy," he said, still chuckling. "Why don't you like the sound of it?"

"I don't know, I never thought of it before. I suppose because I'd be afraid, if it was true, that he'd be always watching to see if I did something wrong."

"To punish you if you did?"

"Yeah—I suppose."

"But if God stayed up in heaven and wasn't around up close, and you did something wrong—then what? Would he be any more pleased?"

"No, I guess he wouldn't."

"But you wouldn't be quite as afraid of stepping out of line because he'd be far away and probably wouldn't bother you?"

"I've never reasoned to myself like that, but to hear you say it, I suppose that's something like what I've thought."

"Well, Matthew," said the baron tenderly, "without knowing it, you've stumbled into the misunderstanding nearly everyone in the world has about God."

"And what's that?" he asked.

"The misunderstanding of who God is."

"Who God . . . *is?*"

"Very, very few people have the slightest inkling of what God's character is really like. That's where your reaction came from, by thinking of God as different from who he really is."

"What *is* God's character like?" asked Matthew. "How can anybody know him so well?"

"What you've asked, Matthew, is *the* most important question in all of life. It is *the* universal question. Finding the answer to those five simple words you just spoke is the only thing life is really about. But I'm not even going to answer you."

"What? Why not?"

"*I'm going to do something even better,*" said the baron. "I'm going to show you the pathway on which to find the answer."

Matthew continued to look earnestly into his face, and the baron continued.

"There is no *single,* specific answer to the question, *What is God like,* Matthew, like a box full of ideas, or a list of characteristics, or a set of principles that I can recite off to you. There's no *list* of God's attributes. The answer to your question, as I said, is a *pathway,* not a list. Do you understand what I mean?"

"No, sir, I'm afraid I don't."

"The answer, Matthew, is a journey, a path you travel along, a process of ongoing and continual discovery. That's why I said I would rather show you the pathway than try to give you an answer. Because the full *answer* is something you can only discover for yourself. *If* you are in earnest about wanting to know what God's character is like, *this* pathway *is* a lifetime journey *you* must embark on. *No one can do it for you.*"

"You say it's a process of discovery. What exactly do you mean? Discovery of what?"

"Discovery of the character of God. The quest is to discover nothing less than who God is. The reason I use the word *discovery* is because, in a manner of speaking, it's a mystery."

"A mystery? You've lost me again."

The baron laughed lightly.

"The attributes of God's being are both plainly visible *and* hidden from our earthly eyes at the same time. That's why I call

God's character a mystery. There are mysteries in knowing God, just as Sabina and I are fond of talking about the mysteries in this garden of ours. Aren't we, Sabina?"

"You help me see some new garden mystery almost every time we talk here, Papa."

"There are millions and millions of clues, Matthew," the baron added, "but most people never see them. That's what walking down the pathway is all about: seeking the clues, learning to spot them, discovering how to see into and behind everything, learning to see into the hidden meanings of life and the universe—all to discover God's presence in and through it all!

"It's marvelous, Matthew, like no other life I can imagine. The quest to discover who God is never stops. The pathway has no pot of gold at its end where you someday find a single answer. The pathway goes forever, every step adding more and more to the discovery, adding more and more fullness to our capacity to recognize and know who God is and what his purpose is."

A long silence followed. The baron had clearly given the young American many new things to ponder.

Herr von Dortmann rose after a few moments and stretched, then walked about the rose garden.

"Do you feel like a little exercise?" he said. "Can you hobble about, or would you rather stay here?"

"I have been sitting a long time." Matthew rose as well. "I think I can make it around, if you go slow."

"Fine, then let's walk as we talk."

So saying, the baron led the way out of the rose garden and began down the hill, choosing the most level paths, while Matthew and Sabina followed him.

∾ 27 ∾
A Father to Call Father

They walked a good while before the baron resumed the discussion, chatting occasionally about this or that in the garden, both the baron and Sabina showing Matthew their favorite trees and shrubs and flowers and other plants.

At length he picked up the threads of their previous dialog.

"Would you like to know one of the first important discoveries there is about God?" asked the baron.

"Yes, sir," replied Matthew.

"If you are in earnest about this pathway of discovering what God's character is like, this is the beginning point, the foundation. I tell you, my boy, lay hold of this, and the discovery will be such an adventure that your life will never be the same again!

"Matthew, do you remember saying, right when we began, how you noticed that we take God seriously in everything?"

"Yes, sir."

"Well, now I'm going to try to tell you why."

A pause followed.

"Who is master of this estate, Matthew?" he asked after a moment.

"You are, Herr von Dortmann."

"What have you learned during your time here?"

"In what way?"

"Would you say that you have learned more about the grounds and our farming operations, or perhaps about this garden of ours and its many varieties of plants, or maybe you have learned about the history of this region of Germany once known as Pomerania? Are those the kinds of things you have learned during your stay with us?"

Matthew thought a moment.

"Now that you mention it, I don't suppose I know much about any of those things."

"Have you learned anything during this past week?"

"Oh yes, of course!"

"What?"

"Well, you and Sabina have told me a lot about God."

"That's true. But can you say you really *know* them to be true yet? Haven't you been mostly just listening?"

"I suppose you're right."

"Then what are some things that you have *really* learned about this week? What is something you can say you really *do* know far more about than when you arrived? If it's not the farming or the history or the garden or God—what is it you've learned most about?"

He gave Matthew a long time to think. At last a smile broke over his face.

"I think I see what you're getting at!" he said.

"What?"

"The answer . . . is *you*. I've learned about you people—you and Sabina and your wife, all of you—your whole family."

"Exactly!" exclaimed the baron. "You have come to know us. And when you leave here, that will be the thing you will take away that you didn't possess before—you will be on intimate terms with some people whom you didn't even know existed before, people I hope you will consider friends for the rest of your life. And you don't merely know us, I venture to say— wouldn't you agree that you know quite a bit about us, about the people we are, about how we think and relate to one another, about what kind of family we are, about how this whole estate functions?"

"Yes—certainly."

"How have you come to know us, Matthew?"

"By watching and listening to you, I guess."

"Observing what we do, how we conduct ourselves, listening to what we say, learning how we think?"

Matthew nodded.

"And by talking to us, asking us questions, that kind of thing?"

"All of it," said Matthew. "It has all helped me to get to know you."

"In other words, you came to an estate in the country. That estate had an owner, who happens to be me. There was a family who lived here, grounds, a garden, workers going about the labor of the place—all kinds of things are involved in making *Lebenshaus* what it is. And as you have been silently watching and listening to it all, you have been drawn into the life of the place and have gradually learned a great deal about how the whole estate functions. But who have you learned *most* about in all of that?"

Again Matthew thought for a while.

"I suppose it would be you, sir," he said.

"Right again, Matthew! Everything you see about the estate, even the relationships, this garden we're walking through—it's all a reflection of me, isn't it? Even Sabina, as you've gotten to know her, is a reflection of me, her father."

"I understand what you're saying."

"And if you were intent on doing so, you could study your surroundings here, watching everything extremely carefully, listening to how everyone talks and so on, and you would be able to find out much more about me, wouldn't you think?"

"Yes, sir."

"Do you think you would discover me to be a good man, a kind and generous man, an unselfish man—a loving man?"

"I have already found you to be those things."

The baron smiled. He found it uncomfortable to use such adjectives to describe himself, but knew under the circumstances that it was the quickest way to illustrate his point. He knew himself deeply enough to know many of the places where the opposites of those qualities dwelt in his fallen human character as well.

"Or do you think I am a man who goes around waiting for someone to pick a flower out of my rose garden so I can throw him in the hidden dungeon up there in the house that old Eppie talks about?"

Matthew laughed. "I can't imagine you being anything but delighted if people were enjoying your roses—even if they plucked every one!"

"You are getting to know me very well already. Now, here's what I've been pointing toward, Matthew. The whole world is *God's* home, *God's* estate—just like this is mine. In the same way that you have discovered my character from being here, watching and listening and asking and conversing and living with us, you can discover God's character too! And that is the most exciting prospect life has to offer!"

"How do you do that?"

"By entering into life on his estate, his kingdom, just like you have here entered into mine. And then by watching and observing and listening and asking, and getting to know what the owner of *that* estate is like, as you have gotten to know me here. You see, everything in life mirrors and reflects deeper principles in God's kingdom. This estate here is a tiny little reflection of God's whole world. My relationship as Sabina's father is a tiny little reflection of God's fatherhood over us all. If I had time to tell you, Matthew, in this garden itself are a thousand reflections of God's character and being—all the little clues of discovery I was talking about earlier. He made every inch of the world, every plant, every thorn on every one of my rosebushes to go along with the flowers. He made you and me and Marion and Sabina and your father. Everything—*everything* in the world reflects something about God's personality—*if* we have eyes to see all the hidden mysteries of meaning!

"The most important mystery of all is this: *God is our Father.* He's a Father whose great desire is not to punish us for doing wrong, but who wants to reveal himself to us, his children. His desire for his kingdom is just like mine for this estate. He wants us to know him, as a loving and kind and generous and giving Father who positively delights in his children. He wants to walk and visit and fellowship and converse with us in a growing friendship of love— exactly as we relate as we're getting to know one another. He wants us to pick *all* the flowers that grow in his garden!

"He's approachable, Matthew, not far away. He does not want us to think of him merely as the awful, powerful, almighty Sovereign of the universe, Creator of the heavens, destroyer of sin. Do you see the difference? There are thousands of aspects and attributes to his character. But what he wants us to call him is *Father.* He wants us to go to him so he can wrap his arms around us and speak to us tenderly and lovingly as his children."

"I've never heard God talked about like that."

"Now we're to the point where I can answer that question of yours from a while ago—why we delight in God's being so close to us, why we take him so seriously in all we do, why for us it is wonderful to realize God is beside us every moment rather than fearsome, and why we are not afraid of him, but rather delight in being in his presence every moment.

"The reason is not hard to find. God is a *good* Father, whose delight is in revealing himself, not an evil father intent only on punishing us. He is a Father anxious to give that goodness to his creatures, anxious to smile with them, anxious to speak tenderly to them, anxious to hold them and protect them in his arms. *That's* the kind of Father we have. Sabina," he said, glancing over at his daughter, "who would you most rather sit with in the rose garden?"

"With you, Papa. Or Mama. Best of all, both of you."

"Why me?"

"Because you are my father and I love you."

"And do I love you?"

"Of course, Papa. How could you do otherwise, you are always so full of love."

"Thank you, my child. Alas, not as full of love as I pray someday to be. But I do love you. And you see, Matthew," he said, addressing Matthew again, "such is exactly the kind of Father-friendship we have with God."

They walked a while in silence. By now they had slowly wound their way to the bottommost part of the garden on the flat, and gradually now they began walking around and up again on the other side.

"Tell him about Jesus, Papa," said Sabina after some moments.

"Ah, yes."

They continued on.

"What do you know about Jesus, Matthew?" the baron asked.

"I don't know . . . I guess the same things everybody knows."

"Why did he come to earth?"

Matthew thought a moment.

"To die, I guess."

"Why to die?"

"To save the world from its sins?"

"You sound like you are asking me," said the baron. "Your tone is uncertain."

"I guess I don't know what answer you mean."

"But you think he came to save us from our sins?"

"That's what they taught us in Sunday school—when I used to go, that is."

"Well, that is why most people think Jesus came."

"And you don't?"

"No, I don't. Jesus *did* die, and he *did* save us from our sins. Such was an intrinsic part of God's purpose. But that is not primarily why he came."

"Why then?"

The baron was thoughtful a minute, thinking of the best way to convey his meaning.

"Picture this, Matthew," he said. "Imagine that you had to come here, to this estate, and you knew you had to spend a week here. But you had heard that the owner of the estate was a giant ogre intent on killing any trespassers. Now if you *had* to come, you might think of bringing with you a good giant, someone powerful enough to keep the ogre from killing you, to stay with you at all times, and to protect you. Wouldn't you say that was prudent of you to do?"

Matthew nodded.

"And that, sadly, is exactly how most people view Jesus' mission to earth, acting the part of the good giant, protecting us from the ogre waiting to kill us. That is how most people view the Atonement and why Jesus died on the cross. They see Jesus as saving us from God as much as from our sins. They see Jesus as protecting us *from* God. They say, 'God is love,' but deep in their heart they are afraid of him like they would be of an ogre, and they take refuge in Jesus as the protecting good giant. Now, do you see what's wrong with that?"

"That God couldn't be both loving and an ogre at the same time."

"Exactly! Now, picture a different situation. Imagine that you had to come here and had heard of the ogre, but imagine that when you arrived at the gate, you were met by someone who told you that the rumors were all wrong, and that the owner of the estate was really good and loving and kind, in fact the most wonderful being imaginable. This guide took you in hand, showed you all about the estate, and finally introduced you to the owner, who turned out to be exactly as he said. Do you see my point?"

"I think so."

"Jesus came to show us his Father, to tell us about him, to reveal his nature to us, to show us all the wrong things we had thought about him all this time. Jesus didn't come primarily to save us from the punishment for our sins at the hand of an avenging God. Jesus came to say, 'Your sins are going to result in your death. But your Father loves you so much that he has sent me to take you to him. And he alone, your tender and loving Father, can save you from them. Come, take my hand, let me show you your wonderful and loving Father.'

"*That* was Jesus' purpose in coming to earth! To reveal God's personality and character to us and to lead us into a friendship with our Father, so that Jesus and the Father *together* might help us to be saved from our sins."

They had nearly reached the top of the garden now, and they walked out and through the arch in silence.

"Everything you say about God is so different from what I've always heard and thought," said Matthew as they slowly walked toward the steps.

"Because most people have never realized the most basic truth in all the universe—I mean truly apprehended what a huge truth it is, the truth that is the foundation of the kingdom of God . . . that God really is just what the Bible says of him—he is *love*. It is just too good to be true. People cannot bring themselves to believe that the Father really is *good*. Yet if God is God, how could he be other than good?"

They reached the courtyard and slowly walked across the lawn to the door of the house.

"Thank you, Herr von Dortmann," said Matthew. "I've never had such an interesting conversation with anyone in my whole life. I won't forget what you've said."

"It's a pathway, Matthew," the baron added, "a lifelong pathway of continuous discovery."

⤮

Little did seventeen-year-old Matthew McCallum realize how prophetic his words were. For in after years, this day in the garden of *Lebenshaus* and this conversation with Baron von Dortmann would always come back to him as the time—though he had no foreshadowing inkling of it at this moment—when he first began walking through the door into the house and presence of his Father.

After their remarkable conversation in the garden, the three went inside the house. Thaddeus McCallum was in the courtyard parlor, where he had been visiting with Frau von Dortmann since his arrival about half an hour before.

He remained the rest of the day and spent the night, and midway through the next morning, he and Matthew returned to Berlin.

PART III

The Mystery of the Fellowship— Fall 1937

Finkenwalde

Baron von Dortmann always enjoyed the drive down through the countryside to Finkenwalde. He only wished the circumstances of these times were more pleasant so that he would be free to enjoy his friend's lectures on the Sermon on the Mount and the book he was compiling from them. Dietrich was a fearless man.

The seminary had first begun at Zingsthof on the Baltic, but had quickly moved south to its present location at an abandoned private school in Finkenwalde near Stettin. Several hastily built houses in addition now housed his friend and the twenty-five or so young vicars and clergymen and ministerial candidates under his tutelage.

The place was a bold experiment not only in independent non-Nazi training for ministry, but also in community living. For those who were part of it and their few visitors and friends, such as the baron, it was a haven of peacefulness, spiritual growth, freedom, and deepening relationships of practical unity among believers committed to a common cause.

The days were taken up with community prayer, individual study and meditation, communal work and service, and Bonhoeffer's teaching and training lectures. There was also recreation and fun and a regular musical diet of Negro spirituals, which Dietrich had fallen in love with in America in 1930 and had brought back to Germany with him. Many were the evenings when the strains of "Swing Low, Sweet Chariot" could be heard through the night air, still being hummed softly by the baritone voices of the men as they walked from meeting hall back to individual houses, apartments, and rooms. The low tones of these men of God, forced to live out their convictions in hiding, bore eerie resemblance to the struggle of the black slaves who had sought their own brand of freedom in another time, on a continent far from this.

It was at such times that Heinrich von Dortmann most

longed to be a full part of the community. A tugging came to his heart when, with the sounds of Dietrich's passionate and eloquent teaching still in his ears, and the soft strains of some spiritual melody still ringing through the night, he climbed into his Mercedes to begin the thirty-six-kilometer drive north back to *Lebenshaus*.

Yet he knew the eternal story of his friends' lives could not be his, nor his theirs. Each had to walk according to the drumbeats the Father's destiny had laid out for him to follow.

He had been blessed with the most wonderful wife and daughter ever a man could have, and with house and property equally capable of ministry as the seminary. It had not been his calling to serve in the clergy. Thus he would serve as God's minister in the quiet ways afforded him and in the lives sent to him, gaining strength and the sustenance of spiritual friendship along the way by communion with his brothers at Finkenwalde.

He had first heard the name Dietrich Bonhoeffer four years earlier, in 1933. Quite by accident, Dortmann had stumbled onto the lecture broadcast over Berlin radio in which the fiery young pastor had taken the German public harshly to task for desiring a "leader" who was almost certain to become a "misleader" as long as he allowed himself to be made an idol of the masses. Hitler's true threat was already clear to the baron, and he found his heart immediately in tune with this one who was courageous enough to address the nation so boldly. It was not surprising that the broadcast was cut off before it was finished.

He made a point of finding out more about the man, continued to follow Bonhoeffer's movements, and read articles from his pen. He met him for the first time when he traveled to Ulm in 1934 to participate, with five thousand other pastors and German laymen, in the formation of the "Confessing Church."

The breakaway church was a reluctant response to the decision by the National German Evangelical Church to endorse allegiance to the Führer's anti-Jewish policy. The National Church had become so infected with national socialism that brown Nazi uniforms were even worn, and those of non-Aryan extraction were forbidden to hold official positions. As the

Reich Church became more and more pro-Nazi, it became of
necessity more and more compromising, racist, and political,
with the state viewed on almost an equal plane with the church
as God's agent.

Under the leadership of Bonhoeffer and others, therefore,
the Confessing Church was formed and thereafter assumed an
active role in denouncing the Nazi programme. Its goal was not
to overthrow the Nazi regime but rather to preserve the scriptural truth and integrity of the church. It was a risky and
unproven path of spiritual, political, and personal resistance.
Hitler declared the Confessing Church illegal the following
year.

Though he followed the events with keen interest, lending
support in whatever quiet ways he could, Baron von Dortmann
was not a churchman and knew his calling lay in other areas.
He could not have been more delighted, therefore, to learn of
the forming of the seminary at Finkenwalde, less than an hour's
drive from his own home. And during the past two years, he
and Bonhoeffer, who was twelve years his junior, had become
deep friends of the spirit.

He pulled into the small compound of buildings, stopped
his engine, and got out. He strode toward the largest of the
structures, the original abandoned school, which was now
being put to educational uses of a far loftier nature than had
been originally intended, and walked inside.

He found Dietrich in his room, at his desk, pen in hand.

"Ah, my friend," said the young pastor, rising and greeting
the baron with outstretched hand as the latter walked through
the open door. "It is good to see you again." Bonhoeffer
motioned him to a chair. "Please sit. I'm just finishing notes for
Nachfolge."

"Has it not already been delivered to the printer?"

"Yes, but I cannot keep from finding bits to change and add
and tamper with. The life of a writer is a constant frustration,
Heinrich," he added with a laugh.

"You will have to let your manuscript be at some point or no
one will ever read the book," rejoined the baron.

"Of course you are right. The printers will impose it upon me
if I cannot impose it upon myself. But discipleship is such a vast

topic of such vital importance to God's followers that I cannot stop myself from thinking of things I must add. With every lecture I give to the young men here, I find principles coming out of my mouth that are new. I am learning as much as they!"

"It is a sign of a growing Christian. I should think you would be worried if it were otherwise!"

"What is a blessing to a Christian is a curse to a writer!"

Both men laughed heartily.

"What are you teaching on tonight?" asked the baron.

"I was hoping perhaps I could convince you to address the men, my friend," said Bonhoeffer.

"You don't think I would drive all this way to hear myself!" exclaimed Dortmann. "I have my own little flock to tend, and my own gardens to cultivate, spiritual and temporal. When I come here, it is I who am the learner, the listener, the hungry, the seeking. Especially today. We have been working from sunup to sundown getting in our wheat and rye. Every muscle in my body aches and I have blisters upon blisters on every finger. I have come to rest my weary body, as well as refresh my soul. No, I will drink from *your* storehouse."

"You can't blame me for trying!"

The baron laughed.

"To answer your question, then," Bonhoeffer said, "I am planning to discuss a few passages from Matthew 10."

ᑫᓬ 29 ᑫᓬ
Private Scheme

It was more than he could reasonably have hoped for!

Emil Korsch stared down at the report on his desk. He never dreamed following the license plate would turn over a stone this size! To link the illegal seminary to the brother of one of Berlin's most influential bankers—how could such a plum have fallen so easily into his lap!

And he was the only one who knew!

Not Himmler, not Göring, not even Hitler himself! Otto von Dortmann, wealthy aristocrat and financier, friend of the

Führer, they said—and now *he* held the power to bring him down.

It wasn't quite as choice a tidbit, he admitted to himself, as if he had learned that Jewish blood flowed through the man's veins. But it still might prove sufficient to induce the million-aire to pay handsomely for his silence.

It was just what he had been looking for, a way to put this climate of fear to use in lining his own pockets. What good was power if it didn't yield something to stash away in a Swiss bank account?

Emil Korsch was more than Russian, more than German, more than Nazi. He was above all an opportunist. And here was opportunity of grand proportion staring him right in the face!

It would be good, however, if he could find out more, if he could strengthen the links. He needed to know for certain if there was indeed a connection between the fellow and the ille-gal Christian church or if there were some other explanation. His position was not so secure that he could afford a major blunder. He had to walk with some degree of caution until Himmler saw that he could be trusted completely.

He sat back in his chair, still staring at the paper in front of him. The raid on the seminary was set. He had to make sure the fellow wasn't accidently brought into that net or his blackmail scheme would be thwarted. On the other hand, he had to keep close tabs, to make sure his charges were accurate and well justi-fied.

He ruminated on the implications a few moments longer, then sat forward, picked up his phone, and spoke into it. Then he sat back waiting.

A moment or two later his call was answered.

"Yes . . . very well, yes . . . right! Say, do we have anyone up north of here, across the river . . . the farming country on the other side of Stettin?"

He listened attentively while the voice on the other end spoke.

"No . . . doesn't have to be Gestapo—though of course if we do have someone—"

Another wait while he listened.

"Of course . . . I understand, I didn't expect there would be . . .

in Stettin, you say—right . . . yes . . . but out in the country—how about any party loyalists? . . . yes, I'll wait."

A long pause followed. Korsch leaned back and lifted his feet onto his desk. Two or three minutes passed. The look on his face presently indicated that the voice on the other end of the phone had returned with an answer to his question.

"I see . . . attached to the *Luftwaffe*, you say . . . Niedersdorf? Yes—good . . . hmm . . . Schmundt, you say . . . yes—seems to me I have heard of him. Loyal?"

He listened a moment, mind spinning rapidly with the information he had just heard. It was the very same village!

"Family?"

A brief pause.

"A son? How old . . . hmm . . . that's interesting—anything on the boy's affiliations? . . . hmm . . . yes, a very good age—yes . . . right—yes, thank you . . . you've been very helpful."

Emil Korsch hung up the phone, pondering the new wealth of information. This little nest he'd stumbled into had all sorts of interesting twists and turns! He'd send someone up to Niedersdorf right away and see if contact could subtly be made with the count's son. For reasons of the Dortmann girl, this young Schmundt might be just the angle he was looking for. It would be best if he didn't get involved personally himself just yet. If the young fellow proved suitable, he would step in when the time was right.

In the meantime, he saw no reason to delay on the matter of the banker. It was time to pay Herr Otto von Dortmann a private visit.

∽ 30 ∽
A Most Difficult Question

Not many days after Matthew's departure, Sabina received a letter from him. After reading it, she sought her father.

"Well, what does Matthew have to say?" he asked when she told him that he'd written. "How is his leg?"

"He says he feels good, but the cast must remain on a while

longer," Sabina replied. "But what I wanted to ask you about, Papa, was what to say to him."

"About what?"

"He is very interested in what you talked to him about in the garden and has asked some very difficult questions."

"Good!" the baron replied enthusiastically. "Questions are the beginning of wisdom and knowledge. I'm glad to hear it."

"But I don't know how to answer him."

"What does he ask?"

"May I read it to you?" Sabina asked.

"Of course."

Sabina glanced down at the stationery she was holding and began reading. " 'Ever since I spoke with you and your father about God when I was there,'" she read, "'I haven't been able to get this one thing out of my mind. If God is so full of goodness and love, and if he is the kind of wonderful Father your father described, then why is the world as bad off as it is? Why are there wars? Why do people hate and kill? It seems that if God made the world and made men and women, then he either ought to have made them so they would be better or else make them behave better. It just doesn't seem to make much sense to me. I like everything your father said about God being a loving father, and that part of it makes more sense than anything I've ever heard about God. But if he loves us so much, then why does so much badness exist?'"

Sabina looked up at her father.

"It is a very difficult question," he said with a pensive nod. "That is probably the question that most keeps people from a belief in God. So, Sabina, what are you going to tell him?"

"I don't know, Papa. I was hoping you would help me."

"But he wrote to you. I think he wants to know what you think, not what I would say."

"I was wishing you would tell me what to say."

"I think you know the answer already. It's inside you."

"Maybe so," replied Sabina. "Maybe it's in my heart some-where, but I don't think it's gotten to my head yet."

The baron smiled and added, "Well, then, perhaps I will give you a hint."

"Yes, Papa?"

"I think it has something to do with falling off of horses and why there are so many different colors of roses."

Sabina thought hard for a few moments. "I'm afraid I still don't understand."

The baron stood up, a smile on his face. "You will," he said. "You will." And with that he slowly walked away, leaving Sabina to ponder his words.

~~~

Later that evening, an hour before bedtime, Sabina sat down at her writing desk and began to write a reply to Matthew:

Lieber Matthew!

I am so happy to hear that your leg is better. I'm certain the cast is a great nuisance, and I know the itching can be terrible, but Papa says that if you are patient and allow the leg to heal fully, it will be as strong as it was before.

I was curious to know if your leg has kept you from activities and so has caused you to spend more time in thought? I wonder because your letter was filled with such deep and hard thoughts. And you ask such difficult questions! (I think you are quite different, Matthew McCallum, than when you first came to visit us!)

Well, I cannot say I understand all of it, or even most of what you ask, but I will tell you what I think. I have thought about this a lot since I first read your letter. I think perhaps I have always thought those thoughts at different times, like when bad things happen or when an animal dies, but I've never spoken them aloud. Maybe I've been afraid to.

I think you are asking about something that must be the hardest thing of all about God to understand. Why didn't God make everything good and perfect and full of love, just like himself? Sometimes I wish so hard that would be so.

Well, it confuses me as much as it confuses you. Papa wouldn't tell me the answer, or rather, he said I already knew the answer, but I am not so sure. I wish you could just be here, and we both could talk with him! He can make everything seem so sensible. But maybe he would then tell the two of us the same riddle he told me. So, in any case, it seems that you'll have to put up with my attempt at explaining things I don't even understand!

One thing I have believed for a long time is that God made everything good. I simply cannot make myself think that God would create bad things, or even bad people. I believe that it all got started with the devil, who refused to obey God. And from the devil, the whole world has gotten infected. So when you ask the question, "Why does God allow wrong in the world?" my answer is that really he doesn't. I think he created people to be good, but that somehow however good we try to be, we fall short and wind up doing bad things.

But it was your other question that I had the most trouble with: Why doesn't God make people behave better? Why doesn't he just make us all be good? Why doesn't he just keep us away from doing bad things or things that hurt us? I have often thought that everything would be so much better if that were so.

This is what I have spent so much time thinking about today. Papa gave me a hint toward the answer. He said it had to do with the many different colors of roses and also something to do with you falling off your horse! It made no sense to me for the longest time.

But I started thinking of the garden—oh, Matthew, you should see the late bloomers now! I thought of the many different varieties of roses. Why did God make so many different kinds and colors? Wouldn't one kind of rose be enough for him? But no, he made dozens and dozens of roses, all different colors and varieties. And I began to think that he makes people like that too. People are like roses. We come in different sizes and shades and colors, and we have different personalities. Why would God make us so very different?

And then I understood something new: God likes that we are different. That's why he made us this way! He likes you because you are Matthew and not like anyone else. He likes me because I am unique too. And my papa and my mama and everyone—we are all different and special! He likes our differences, and he doesn't want us all to be the same or do the same things even.

I think that's what Papa had in mind when he gave me the hint about the roses. But it took me a while longer to understand what you falling off your horse had to do with God and the bad things in the world.

But it finally did come to me. Matthew, your falling off the horse was a terrible thing. Maybe not as terrible as some things that are going on in the world today, but it was a bad thing even so, and it hurt you. So why did God let that happen? Why did God let you be hurt? He could have kept you from climbing onto the Belgian. He could have kept the two of us from riding horses at all. He could have made us stay inside where it was safe.

*But if he did that—don't you see?—then he isn't letting us be us! He would be controlling us like little puppets. He doesn't want that. Just as he likes different varieties of roses, he likes people to be different too—people who make their own **choices** about what they do and who they are!*

*That was the specific word that came to my mind. Matthew, I really think that's it! **Choice**. God loves people for being unique the way he created them, and along with that goes our **choosing** to be the kind of people we want to be. Of course, that means he has to allow us to choose wrong things if we really must, or else we wouldn't really be free to choose. (And do you know what I am thinking now? I think God is sitting there really hoping that we will choose him.)*

So maybe God allowed you and me to choose to go riding, and for you to ride the Belgian, and with it the danger of it, and the hurt that comes from it, like other hurts that happen just from living in the world.

Oh, I don't know! This is so much to think about. (My head hurts, and I think it's overcrowded with new thoughts!) I'm afraid I must finish this letter and go to bed. Please write again soon and tell me what you think about these ideas!

Sabina

P.S. I still wish God had kept you from falling off the horse!

∽ 31 ∽

A Fateful Call

It was but two weeks later when the phone rang at the Dortmann estate. Heidi knocked on the door to the baron's study.

"Yes, Heidi?" he said, opening the door.

"You are wanted on the telephone, sir," she said.

The baron followed her to the stairs and they descended together. "Do you know who it is?" he asked.

"It's Pastor Bonhoeffer. His voice is urgent, sir."

"Thank you, Heidi," said the baron, entering the *Gute Stube*, or family sitting room, where the telephone was located.

He picked up the receiver.

"*Ja . . . tag, Dietrich,*" he said then listened a moment.

"*Ja, ja, ich verstehe . . . hmm . . . ja . . . nicht gut . . . daβ ist unge-heuer . . .*" he said, continuing alternately to listen, punctuating the other's words with brief exclamations and comments of his own.

At last there was a lengthy silence. The baron's face was clouded with serious thought.

"You must bring them here, Dietrich," he said at length.

Another pause. He listened.

"What does community among believers then mean? . . . No, it is the best way. . . ."

A pause followed while he listened.

"I am not worried about the danger," he said. "We will pray for protection. I know the angels are busy these days, but we are told there are hosts of them."

He fell to listening once more.

The silence in the room was broken by the sound of the door opening. Herr von Dortmann glanced up to see his wife enter. He motioned her toward him. Marion knew instantly from his expression that the call carried an evil omen.

"Dietrich, I tell you to come, and bring your small flock along. You will be safe here. You know that is what *Lebenshaus* means. We will pray together. Then you can decide what he wants you to do next. . . ."

A pause.

"Retreat, solitude . . . and safety—if I do not have such to offer my brothers and friends, what good is my life? For what other purpose has our Lord placed me here?"

Another pause.

"Yes . . . yes, I am certain, my brother. Come . . . yes, quickly . . . tonight if you can. You will be safe here."

He hung up the phone and sighed deeply, then looked into

his wife's eyes. The look that passed between them carried more ominous meaning than either dared voice.

"I am afraid it has begun, my darling," said the baron. "The Gestapo stormed Finkenwalde this morning. The seminary has been closed. Dietrich fears for his young students. You heard most of what I said."

"They are coming?" asked Marion.

"Yes."

"How many?"

"I do not know."

"I will tell Heidi and Sabina to begin preparing the guest rooms, and Carola to make more bread and to begin baking some cakes."

She turned to leave. The baron stopped her.

"Marion," he said. The very sound of his voice sent a tingle of foreboding up Frau von Dortmann's spine.

She turned. His face bore a look of dignity and decisiveness she had never seen in all their years of marriage.

"Leave the guest rooms on the first floor as they are. Tell Sabina and Heidi to begin airing out and taking linen to the rooms behind the armory."

∽ 32 ∽

Bonhoeffer at *Lebenshaus*

A grey dusk had settled over the land when four automobiles crept up the winding drive and stopped in single file around the silent stone sentinel who guarded the entrance to *Ein Landhaus Für Leben Und Zurückgezogenheit*.

Sixteen young men slowly climbed out on both sides of the cars and stood waiting, while a seventeenth, a few years older, in his early thirties, short of stature, with wide oval face, plain round spectacles and thinning hair, crunched his way across the gravel to the front door. He never had a chance to knock.

The door opened.

He and his companions were expected.

The baron beckoned them inside. The visitor signaled

behind him, and the sixteen followed him, still without a word, toward the great stone house. Not until they were well inside the drawing room did any of the anxious newcomers utter a sound.

"You made it without incident?" asked Baron von Dortmann.

Bonhoeffer nodded. "It was not my impression they wanted to follow us or arrest us," he said, "only disband the seminary, which they certainly succeeded in accomplishing."

"What happened exactly?"

"A car rolled in, followed by a truck. Almost before the two Gestapo agents were out of the car, the truck emptied of a dozen or more SS troopers, who immediately began running toward all the buildings, rousting the men from their quarters. The two agents served me papers of termination and eviction. I asked how long we would have. They said, 'The order is immediate, Herr Bonhoeffer. You have no time for anything but to evacuate the premises!' The men were already being dragged from their rooms and the chapel, some at gunpoint. Within minutes doors were boarded up, every book any of us owned was put in a big crate, which they took with them, and we were ordered to leave immediately."

"Were you able to save anything?" asked the baron, incredulous at the sudden turn of events.

"A few personal belongings, but not much. The Nazis hate books and took every one. Especially do they hate religious books. They find the world of truth dreadfully threatening."

"Your manuscript notes?"

"Unfortunately, they ransacked my office, too, and made off with everything. All my work of the last month is gone."

"Dietrich!" exclaimed the baron. "I am so sorry."

Bonhoeffer smiled a wry grin. "I have known for years that to resist them meant danger. It would appear it has finally come."

"But your book—"

"Not to worry, my friend. It is being printed even as we speak. The Nazis will never silence the voices of truth entirely. My recent notes were only a few modifications."

The door opened. Marion and Heidi and Carola entered with trays of tea, sliced bread, and some cakes.

"Ah, ever the hostess, aren't you, Marion!" exclaimed Bonhoeffer. "We are fleeing for our lives, and you serve us cake!"

"Even martyrs and refugees must eat," rejoined Frau von Dortmann.

"Thankfully we are neither yet. But we will partake of what your hand offers as from our dear sister in the Lord."

As the women poured tea and served the men, the baron and Bonhoeffer sidled to the corner of the room and continued to speak in low tones.

"Are you, in truth, fleeing for your lives?" Dortmann asked his younger friend.

"It may come to that in time," replied Bonhoeffer, "but I doubt it is so serious at the moment. Many threats and angry words—you know the Gestapo. But I do not think those young men in the SS uniforms were anxious to use their guns on men of the church."

"There could be arrests."

"That is true. I see fear in some of the younger faces."

"And you?"

"I fear no prison. But the men are my charge, so I must do what I can to keep them safe until we decide what to do. That's why I called you."

"I'm glad you did. What will you do?"

Bonhoeffer sighed. "For myself, try to relocate. The seminary must keep on with its work. Young men must continue to be trained. Even if we have to go further underground, there *must* remain a voice in the German church that does not fear these evil Nazis and the ungodliness they bring even to the official church."

"For yourself, you say?"

"I mean, that is my duty as head of the seminary. I will take as many of the men with me as want to remain, come what may. The others I will send back to their homes. It is certain not to become easier. I fear the hour of night is falling upon our land."

"Whatever I can do to help you, my friend," said the baron, putting his hand on Dietrich's shoulder.

"I think one of the first orders of business would be to conceal the automobiles. The next will be for us to pray together. With the Lord's help we need to determine our next course of action."

"You are welcome to remain with us as long as you like. But, why hide the cars? I thought you were not followed."

"I'm certain we weren't," replied Bonhoeffer. "Still I would rest easier if they were not in plain view. I loathe the thought of bringing danger upon you from curious eyes. They ordered us to disband, and if they chanced to discover more than a dozen of us together for any length of time, I do not think they would be kindly disposed about it."

"Where are the others of the fellowship?"

"Those who had cars of their own, and so chose, are on their way back to their homes. These sixteen—" Bonhoeffer nodded his head toward the others sitting quietly, talking and drinking their tea— "these wanted to remain with me."

The baron thought a moment.

"I suggest, then, that we move the cars—let me see . . . " The baron brought his hand to his mouth and rubbed his chin.

"Yes," he said at length, "I think that would be best—we'll take them around the other side and down to two of the grain barns. I'll get Heiko and Hans to help us, and three or four of your men to drive the cars down. I'll go get my men and we'll begin making space. Enjoy some tea with your men. I'll be back in a few minutes."

The baron disappeared.

He returned some fifteen minutes later and nodded to Bonhoeffer, who spoke a few brief words to his men. They all stood, went back outside to take their few belongings from the cars, and then all except for Bonhoeffer and the three other drivers returned inside. These four drove around the north side of the house, parked one of the cars next to the baron's in the automobile garage, then continued on around the knoll, down the eastern slope, where within thirty minutes the other three cars were safely resting out of sight in two of the now-nearly-empty grain barns.

"Now perhaps we should show you to the rooms we have prepared for you," announced the baron to the small assembly once they had rejoined the others. "They are not the most luxurious of accomodations, to be sure. But under the circumstances, I think we would all rest easier if, during your time with us, whether it be a day or a week, you are concealed as safely out of sight as possible. We do have visitors from time to time, and I would not bring danger upon you unnecessarily."

"We understand, Heinrich, and are grateful," added Bonhoeffer. "These are dangerous times for God's people."

"If you'll get your things and follow me," said the baron.

He led the troop of young pastors and seminarians out of the drawing room and along the ground floor corridor toward the north of the house, around two corners of the hall, until he came to a ninety-degree turn, where he stopped.

"This is the north parlor," he said, indicating the door just behind him. He led them inside. "It is not too far from the kitchen, and Marion and I have decided this is probably the best place to serve you meals. It adjoins a small guest *Stube*— through that door there—and you are welcome to use both rooms freely. You are free to use the whole house, for that matter! I am only thinking of your safety. We *could* use the formal dining room for meals," he added. He paused, again rubbing his chin thoughtfully. "No, it must remain unused and set, just in case . . . yes, the parlor is best," he stated in a firm voice to the others.

"Now," he went on, "you will have ready access to your rooms by this stairway here." He led the way and they followed him up, single file. "Should we have any unexpected visitors, you will be able to climb quickly back up to the second floor, where I do not think anyone will bother you."

Up they went, back and forth up the narrow rectangular staircase, arriving at the first floor.

"There is a sitting room you may use just down the hall here in the corner of this floor," he said, pointing from the landing down the corridor. He then continued upward once more, arriving at length at the landing of the second floor.

"You will see the construction on the top floor to be rather peculiar," he said. "The halls are narrow and the rooms oddly shaped, designed, it would seem, around the principle of curvature rather than right angles as are most buildings. In any event, though the rooms are not often used—we will try to make you as comfortable as possible. There are nine rooms here at this north end of the west wing. Most have either two or three beds, so you may arrange yourselves in any manner you like. Our house is yours. Everything we have is yours."

"We are most appreciative, Heinrich," said Bonhoeffer. Rounds of thanks chimed in from the rest of the men.

"There are only two bathrooms on this floor, and no tub. But you are welcome to any of the bathrooms on the floor below you, and there are two tubs there—one between the guest sitting room and the library, and another next to the ballroom. I'll show you both later. Heidi and my daughter have furnished you with towels and linen. I believe there are enough feather-beds for you all."

"Wonderful, Heinrich . . . *sehr schön!*"

"So, we will leave you for the night. I'm sure you are tired. *Frühstück* at seven-thirty two floors below you. And with that I will say . . . *schlaff gut!*"

"Thank you again!" said Bonhoeffer, shaking the baron's hand, followed in turn by each of the other men.

"*Gute nacht!*" said the baron, then, turning, descended the stairs.

❧ 33 ❧
Curious Proceedings

Dark German beer had flowed freely for several hours.

Echoing through the close quarters of the public room of the only inn in Niedersdorf were the familiar and pleasant sounds of hardworking men relaxing, drinking, and having fun at the end of one more strenuous day at their labors.

Only a few women were present, all in the employ of the *Wirtshaus*, whose nightly job it was to serve as much beer as the men could hold, while smiling, talking, flirting, laughing, and teasing each one in such a way that every man present considered either Hilda, Gretchen, or Klara his own personal barmaid, mistress, and intimate friend.

The knowing smiles, glances, winks, pinches, and whispered intimacies, as well as the fact that to a man nearly everyone present was a nightly customer, gave ample indication that the three good-natured and robust fräuleins had succeeded in their assignments.

In the larger beer cellars and inns of Berlin, a live polka band would have accompanied the festivities and heightened the merriment. But in Niedersdorf the music came from a large radio, which blared the latest lively dance tunes from one corner of the room.

As voices and laughter throughout the place had grown livelier and more raucous, the tones of four men occupying a table in one corner had become more subdued. The contents of the steins in front of them had become warm and flat. They had not been touched in more than thirty minutes. In the glowing orbs of these faces burned a fire whose light originated from an altogether different source than the dull twinkles of inebriation showing from the eyes of the villagers who had come for no other purpose than to make merry with their comrades after the day's work—and to drink as much as their laboring bodies could tolerate while still maintaining consciousness.

One of the men at the table was clearly older than the other three, though he himself was not quite thirty. The black leather overcoat draped over his shoulders was more for effect than for warmth, for though fall was well on the way, the weather was yet mild. He clearly enjoyed the prestige inherent in his calling—and the amenities that went with it. When Korsch had selected him for this secretive recruiting assignment, he had hardly been able to believe his good fortune, and now he was playing the role with these three country lads to the hilt.

He knew his kind were feared. It added to the thrill. What better motivator could there be? Fear drove their cause.

It was either fear or be feared. There was no middle ground these days. Everyone would ultimately wind up on one side of the fence or the other. Those on the topside of the equation of fear would occupy the posts of power and would dominate all those below them.

These words Korsch had driven into the brains of his followers. And just such a demented sermon of intimidation and conquest the black-clad young zealot, one of Korsch's favorites, was now giving these wide-eyed protégés in his turn, whom he would proselytize for the cause. His words fell on eager, hungry ears. For like sought like, and in the economy of national socialism, those natures who frequented the low places of what was intended to be their manhood naturally found one another and banded together. Truly the last had become first. The nation was more and more being controlled by such as these, the roots of whose beings drew nourishment, not from the springs of life planted within them by their Father, but rather from the evil, dark, and most sinister places within their fallen humanity.

"By proving your allegiance at any cost," he was saying, in response to a question posed by one of the others.

"But how?"

"Every situation varies. We are looking for those who are, shall we say, *creative*, and whose loyalties to the Reich are unquestioned."

"What can we do?" asked one, a boy of sixteen or seventeen.

"Information is always useful."

"Information? What kind of information?"

"If I have to tell you that, my young friend, then I fear you will have no future with our agency."

The boy's two companions listened to the exchange intently. One of them, a year or two older than his friend, knew exactly what the agent was talking about.

"He means information about people," he said. "They are looking for informants—am I not right?" he added, glancing now toward the young agent from Berlin.

"You are more shrewd than your friend."

"You mean . . . *Jews?*" asked the younger boy, his eyes widening.

"Keep your voice down, you fool!" snapped the agent with whispered wrath. "Secrecy is our greatest weapon."

A tense silence followed around the table. The sounds of music and gaiety from the other end of the room penetrated once more into their brains, but only momentarily.

The visitor leaned forward, squinted his eyes as he looked intently into each of the three faces, then spoke in a sinister tone barely loud enough for them to hear.

"Jews. Yes, of course," he said. "To discover the evil identity of such traitors to the Reich is always a key part of our intent. And when you bring us such information concerning your fellow villagers, such loyalty is not forgotten."

"But how do we tell you when we find out that someone is a traitor?" asked the eager sixteen-year-old.

"We have ways of passing along information. I will leave you a telephone number. But it is not only Jews we seek. There are other, shall we say, *enemies* of the Reich not as readily apparent."

"What kind of enemies?"

"Subversion comes in many guises."

"Subversion?"

"Those with loose tongues who speak against the Nazi cause, those with other affiliations—Christians, for example, or those with British or American or Russian relatives, or ties of some other kind—the wealthy and powerful are especially interesting to us—aristocrats from old and influential families. My own superior is personally intrigued with such potentially negative affiliations. We are looking for *anything* that dilutes pure loyalty to the Reich and our Führer. . . ."

As the man spoke, Gustav's eyebrows rose imperceptibly, though he did his best not to give himself away. His own private thoughts were moving in many directions.

" . . . anything unusual or out of the ordinary we like to be informed about," the visitor was saying. "One never knows what might be behind it if one digs deeply and persistently enough, which is why I say to keep your eyes and ears open—to *anything*. And get in touch with me if you even *think* I might be interested, do you understand?"

All three nodded.

"Now, one at a time," he said, "I want you to get up and leave. Go home. Do not talk to anyone about what we have discussed, not even your parents. If you are going to work for me, secrecy is the most important element of our plan. If I should find that *you* have been disloyal to *me*, then, well, I'm sure I need say no more."

He cast upon them a glare whose intent was impossible to mistake, then nodded first to the sixteen-year-old, who rose and left, followed several minutes later by the next.

After the small clique had broken up, however, he remained

another thirty minutes, speaking privately and sharing a new stein with the oldest of the three, he whom Korsch had specifically instructed him to draw into their net. He wanted to make sure that when he returned to Berlin tomorrow, the fellow knew when and where to contact him.

∽◌∽

An hour later Gustav climbed into the Mercedes his father had recently bought for him. He had had three or four more beers after the fellow was gone, and two or three glasses of brandy as well. It was late enough, he thought, that his mother would be in bed, and if he snuck in the side door, she would never hear him. His father was not at home.

In the fogginess of his stupor, his brain had difficulty focusing on the road ahead of him, much less organizing itself coherently about any train of ideas. Everything that had been talked about through the evening ran in scattered, random fashion through his consciousness, already blurring with the passage of time and the deepening of his drunkenness.

What would his mother think if she chanced to still be up? . . . What difference did it make, he thought, she was in no better state half the time, the fat old hausfrau, though he couldn't afford to let Sabina see him like this, the conceited little prude . . . that would be the end of everything!

She wouldn't see him . . . she couldn't see him . . . but he could see her! Gustav chuckled, congratulating himself on his sly methods of keeping track of her. *She'll make a fine wife, the little wench . . . someday I'll tell her . . . I'll take her to the very place.* She'd belong to him . . . the whole valley and hill and woods and both estates . . . it would *all* be his! . . . no one would look down on little Gustav then!

Scattered words from the visitor from Berlin filtered back into the midst of his dreams about the future . . . *anything that dilutes loyalty . . . information . . . Christians . . . anything out of the ordinary . . . call me. . . .*

He pulled off the road and toward his father's estate.

Out of the corner of his eye he saw something in the night . . . a glare . . . a flash . . . .

He turned. What were those lights away there, across the fields?

What could it be?

He slowed the car and squinted, trying to focus his eyes, but with little success.

He drove on to the house, stopped, and left his engine idling. He got out . . . the strange lights were still there.

There were . . . yes—whatever was the cause, the lights were coming from across the fields at the baron's house! Still he tried to focus, but his drunken brain could make no meaning of it.

A sudden sense of curiosity, annoyance, and anger filled him.

He jumped back into his car, ground it into gear, and roared out into the fields toward the Dortmann estate across a bumpy dirt tractor path, still glaring into the distance.

They were headlights! The headlights of a car . . . several cars . . . what was going on at the baron's? Why were cars driving around at such an hour and in such strange places?

His alcohol-induced rage rose. He turned off his own head-lights, but even as he did so he thrust down farther on the accel-erator. That would be his estate before long, he thought. He had a right to know what was going on! Whatever had to do with Sabina was his business—how dare they keep such secretive goings-on from him! He always had wondered about the baron. He was up to no good!

Suddenly, with a great bumping and jerking, his car stalled and slammed to a halt, both right tires deep into the ditch on the side of the narrow dirt path.

Hardly taking note, Gustav jumped out. With indignation, he broke forward into a run . . . they had no right to keep secrets from him . . . it was his estate . . . it probably had to do with that American! The baron was probably an American sympathizer! That would be something to uncover . . . this was his chance . . . *anything unusual or out of the ordinary* . . . he had to get in touch with that fellow!

Suddenly the lights in front of him disappeared.

It was dark. Still he continued to run, falling down, getting back up, then tripping and falling again.

At length, exhausted and having covered only about a third

of the distance between the two houses, he stopped—panting, sweating, confused, and drunk—and stood staring.

A light or two appeared on the top floor, but he was too tired and too far gone from the brandy and strong ale to later remember seeing them.

Finally he turned, then staggered back toward his own home—muddy and bewildered by everything he had seen—tracking a huge mess into the house, across the expensive entryway carpet.

The countess *was* still up, though the few mumbled phrases her son uttered interested her far more than the state of his breath. After a few moments, Gustav continued up the stairs into his own room, where he fell asleep, still in his filthy clothes. The following morning he was able to recall nothing but that he had seen strange lights, and that he was supposed to do something about it.

⌘ 34 ⌘

Neighboring Visit

The appearance of her neighbor at the front door bright and early caught Marion von Dortmann completely off guard.

"Why, Ingrid!" she exclaimed hesitantly, still recovering from the surprise. "Good morning . . . what . . . but what a pleasant surprise!"

The expression on Frau Schmundt's face, as she glanced this way and that, indicated that she had called for more than merely morning coffee.

"I understand you have guests, Marion," she said.

"Why, Ingrid . . . whatever gave you that idea?"

"My Gustav said you had visitors," repeated the countess with importunity. "I just thought perhaps I could help." The look of annoyed curiosity on her countenance said that it was something other than being helpful she had really come for.

"I can't imagine—"

It was with great relief that Marion saw her husband come round the corner of the house toward the front door. He wore his work boots and had the sleeves of his shirt rolled up. He carried a large, black, greasy component of tractor engine that he and Hans had been working on. His face was covered with perspiration, for the day was already warm, and his shirt and pants were well coated with dirt from his labors.

"Look who's here, dear!" she said, trying to hide the sigh of relief that accompanied the words. "Ingrid says she heard we had guests," she added nervously.

Heinrich laughed. "I can't think how," he said. "No, only family here. But it is nice to see you, Ingrid! Come in and join us for coffee!"

The baron set the hunk of iron down on the ground, wiped his hands across the front of his trousers without much effect, led the way inside past the two women, who were still standing at the front door, and went to the west parlor.

"Why don't you go tell Carola to bring us coffee and tea, dear," said the baron to his wife. "Countess von Schmundt and I will visit in the parlor until you return."

~~~

Even as his mother was pretending to enjoy the feigned social call with the baron and his wife, Gustav von Schmundt awoke, sprawled across his bed still in his clothes, feeling worse than he looked, and with a dreadful headache. What he wouldn't have given to have slept another ten or twelve hours!

With great difficulty he turned himself over on his back, thought for a few minutes about taking off his clothes and climbing under the featherbed covering he had spent the night on top of, thought better of it, then groped his way to the edge of the bed and tried to stand.

His head exploded with pain as he rose, though the throbbing did serve to bring him fully awake. If his brain wasn't exactly clear, at least its pain sensors were functioning.

He staggered out of his room and somehow managed to make his way downstairs.

He found the kitchen empty. A servant girl entered as he stood there, bewildered and gaping.

"Where is everyone?" he asked, wincing even as he spoke from the echo inside his skull caused by his own voice.

"Your mother is out, *mein Herr*," answered the girl.

"I can see that!" he snapped. "Where is she?"

"I don't know, *mein Herr*."

"Well, get me some coffee then!" Gustav demanded. "And make sure it's strong."

"Yes, *mein Herr*."

"And be quick about it, you young fool," barked Gustav rudely. "Bring it to me on the patio."

The girl disappeared. Such treatment had brought tears to her eyes a year ago just after she had been hired at the Schmundt villa. She was used to it now, however, and took it as a matter of course.

Thirty minutes later, beginning to piece together fragments of what had happened the night before, Gustav left the house, head still splitting but some of the other remaining effects of the alcohol beginning to be moderated by the dark roasted coffee his father imported from France.

He went to the garage and started up his father's old car, which no one used much anymore. Satisfied that it was driveable, he pulled it outside, then, leaving it idling, went to find one of the men around the place, whom he told of the previous night's mishap, giving him orders to haul his car out of the ditch and back to the house.

Then he jumped back into the old automobile and sped off toward the village. He hoped the fellow hadn't left for Berlin yet and might still be at the inn.

◈

Gustav's mother was trying to find a way to excuse herself. She had had all she could stand of Baron von Dortmann's ridiculous pretending to be nice. She knew his game and didn't believe those smiles of his for a second!

"I rarely see Ernst these days, Ingrid," Heinrich was saying. "His business in Berlin must be on a high level."

"A very high level, Baron," answered the countess.

"Is he considering a role in the government? I had heard he was asked."

"His interest is primarily with the *Luftwaffe*. He flew in the Great War, you know."

"Yes, I did know that. A post under Göring, perhaps?"

"You will have to ask him that yourself, Baron von Dortmann."

She stood abruptly. "I must get back home," she said. "That is, Marion," she added, turning to her friend, who was seated next to the baron, "if you're sure you need no help with your visitors."

"No visitors, Frau Schmundt!" said Heinrich, rising quickly and offering her a shake of his hand. "Except yourself, of course!" he added, laughing.

Marion rose and stood beside her husband. "Thank you for coming, Ingrid," she said sincerely. "It was very thoughtful of you. I hope you know you are always welcome here."

The countess said nothing in reply.

The baron led the way out of the parlor, through the corridor, and toward the front door. As they emerged around the corner, two men hastily scampered up the grand stairway and out of sight.

"So you *do* have visitors after all!" said the countess, in a tone of annoyed surprise as she followed them with her gaze.

"Just family, Ingrid," said the baron, continuing toward the door.

"Nonsense, Baron."

"They're brothers of mine, Ingrid."

The baron opened the door.

"Don't lie to me. Those men are perfect strangers. I've never seen either one of them before."

Suddenly the countess was in no hurry to leave. The baron, however, began walking steadily toward her car.

"I tell you the truth, Ingrid: Those two men are my brothers."

"I don't believe you."

"I'm sorry."

"I know all your family, Baron! Whom do you think you're talking to, a fool?"

"Not for a moment, Ingrid," said Heinrich politely, opening

the door and courteously helping the countess inside. "It's just that those two brothers of mine you've never met before."

"I want to meet them, then."

"Now would not be convenient, Ingrid. I'm sorry. Hans is waiting for me, and we must get the tractor operational again."

"When will be convenient?" insisted the countess.

"We shall call you."

She eyed him steadily with a look of high irritation and suspicion, then started the engine.

The baron returned her gaze with a smile and wave, then turned and walked back with Marion toward the house.

The moment they were inside and the door closed behind them, he breathed an enormous sigh of pained relief.

"What have I done, Marion?" he said. "Have I lied to protect the fellowship? I cannot let myself become as unprincipled as those who threaten us!"

"You did not lie, Heinrich."

"The lines are fuzzy and grey for many people, Marion," rejoined the baron wearily. "But I worry when they become grey for *me*."

∾ 35 ∾

Suspicious Inquiry

The roar of two loud cars speeding up the driveway could hardly be disguised. Spewing dust and gravel, they raced to the top and circled around the horse. By the time they braked to a reckless stop, the baron and his wife, with most of the household staff, stood at the door watching the spectacle with amazement.

A cloud of dust still trailing in the air behind them, four black car doors shot open almost simultaneously, while several more men jumped off two motorcycles with sidecars, and within seconds eight Brownshirts stood facing the house, rifles poised, feet planted firmly on the ground, helmeted faces staring expressionless straight ahead.

The two agents in charge, dressed in plain clothes, got out of the automobiles more slowly and now approached the house.

With grave expression, the baron nodded to Marion and the others to remain back, then approached to meet them.

"I am Baron von Dortmann," he said. "What may I do for you gentlemen?"

"We know well enough who you are, Baron," said one of the men rudely. His voice was high-pitched and condescending. "We have come to search your house."

"Search it?" repeated the baron. "For what purpose, might I inquire?"

"You may not inquire," snapped the agent. "But I will tell you anyway. We are looking for traitors to the Reich."

"There are no traitors here, I assure you," said the baron, doing his best to keep calm.

The man smiled a very unpleasant smile. "And," he chuckled, "you expect us to take your word for it? You are really most humorous, Baron."

"I tell you there is no one here. We are but a family—a farming family."

"We know all about your family, Baron von Dortmann," said the man, the smile suddenly disappearing from his face as he cast upon the baron a squinting glare of menace.

"Then you know we are not traitors."

"I do not know that you do not *house* traitors."

"I can assure you—"

The baron was cut off by a wave of the man's hand. "Please, Baron," he said, "your assurances mean nothing to me. I will find out for myself. Are there any Jews here?"

"Jews?"

"You heard me, Baron—Jews!"

The baron swallowed hard and took a deep breath. If ever these small-minded and heartless people could cause hatred to rise up within him, it was at times like this.

"No, I have no Jews on my staff," he said, with great difficulty maintaining his composure.

The man eyed him steadily, staring straight into his eyes. The baron returned the gaze for several long moments. At length the Gestapo agent turned away, then motioned to the eight storm troopers with a nod of his head.

Suddenly six of them shot toward the house, brushing past Marion and the others without regard for courtesy, while one ran around the side to search the garden and grounds and the eighth headed for the barn and outbuildings down the slope to the east. They were all well prepared and knew exactly where to look.

The baron and his people followed the six inside, accompanied by the sound of loud clomping and running from the heavy-booted feet going up the grand stairway and down the halls in all directions. The men seemed unconcerned with the ground floor, but went straight up to the first and second. However they had come by their information, the baron thought to himself, it was remarkably accurate. They knew precisely where to search for signs of any guests.

Fortunately, all the rooms had been cleaned and changed the day the brothers from Finkenwalde had gone, and the baron didn't believe there were any remaining traces of their presence.

Marion clutched her husband's arm, trembling in fear. The servants watched the terrifying violation of their home in mute shock. They had all heard things, but none had witnessed the cruel reality of what the fascism that had taken over their country meant, until this very moment.

"Papa, Papa!" cried Sabina, suddenly bursting through the front door. "There's a man with a gun in the garden, and—"

Suddenly realizing there was more to fear for than only their plants, she stopped dead in her tracks, staring with wide, frightened eyes up to her father.

"It is all right, dear," said the baron calmly to reassure her. "These men are only searching the house for traitors. They will not be with us long."

The two Gestapo agents followed their men up the stairs and disappeared also. Heinrich followed cautiously, while his family and staff, as if huddling behind him for protection, crept up also, listening to harsh and frightening noises and shouts and bangs in the distance coming from all parts of the house.

Five or six minutes later, one of the men bolted in from outside and ran straight up the stairs, where he found the agent in charge. They spoke a moment together, then the man crashed back down past the baron and again ran outside.

The agent approached the baron slowly with an unpleasant look on his face.

"My man tells me one of your barns is nearly empty," he said.

"Yes . . . ," said the baron slowly, not understanding the man's meaning.

"For what purpose?"

"Do you mean why is it empty?"

"That is precisely what I mean. It is large enough . . . to conceal, say, several . . . *automobiles.*"

"It is a storage barn. We are readying it for the potato harvest."

The agent reflected a moment.

"My man said there were fresh tire tracks inside, in the dirt on the floor," he said. "Does that too concern the potatoes, Baron?" he asked with obvious sarcasm.

"I move wagons in and out all the time. Not a day goes by that a tractor or wagon of some kind does not go across that floor."

"Where are these wagons now, Baron?"

"Out in the fields, of course. This is a large farm. I have many wagons out daily, upon any number of hauling errands."

The tense little conversation was suddenly interrupted by the sound of breaking glass and several loud banging noises above them.

Marion gave a little cry and began to run toward the sound. The baron held her back, casting her a barely perceptible look of sternness. To all the others who were standing in varying degrees of fear and anger, he gave a look that said, *Stay calm, we will put things back in order when they leave. No one say a word.*

"Does your search include destruction of private property?" he asked aloud.

The agent smiled, then glanced up to see his men returning. They all shook their heads. He nodded toward the outside. They all descended the stairs loudly and went back outside.

"To answer your question, Baron," said the man in charge, turning with his assistant to return more slowly to the ground floor, "there is no private property. All belongs to the Reich. I suggest you remember it. As to what you heard up there a moment ago—my men sometimes tend to be a little clumsy. Let it just serve to remind you of our visit."

"I am unlikely to forget it," replied the baron, thinking to himself how little good using the top floor had done. If he had to make similar use of his house again, his precautions would have to be more thorough than they had been this time.

"Make sure you don't. And if you hide traitors again, Baron, we will find them. It will be more than the breakage of a few trinkets and lamps then. Believe me, if that happens—it will go the worse for you all. *Heil Hitler!*"

The man turned on his heels and suddenly was gone.

Two minutes later the cars and motorcycles, containing both Gestapo agents and all eight storm troopers, were roaring down the drive, disappearing through the trees.

∾ 36 ∾

Exchange of Letters

D*ear Sabina,*

Finally, my cast is off and I feel like a normal person again. My leg feels like new, and perhaps it is as good as it was before, as your father said. However, I don't believe I will test out his theory, for now anyway, and I think I will stay away from spirited Belgians for the time being!

Your last letter gave me much to think about. I think it indeed was an answer to my question—a good one too—but the kind of answer that keeps getting bigger the more one ponders it. It's like your beloved Lebenshaus—one would never believe how much is contained in it.

When I think of God allowing us to make choices for ourselves, it makes me feel both important and, to be honest, scared. I feel important that God might think so much of me to allow me to choose what I will be and do. But I also feel a little scared by the thought of it because if God allows me to make my own choices, then it seems to me that's a great deal of responsibility.

Matthew

∿◉∿

Lieber Matthew!

I'm so glad you wrote, and to know that your leg is well and your cast off. It must have been so uncomfortable. What did you do when your leg itched inside it?

There have been exciting times here, but Papa says I must not tell about it, for reasons also that I cannot write about. I can say that we had a visit from the Gestapo—yes, right here at Lebenshaus! *They went all around, poking so rudely about with their guns and big black boots, breaking things and being dreadful to Papa. I probably shouldn't say all that, but I don't care—they are so mean!*

Nothing came of it, but Papa was so serious after they left and kept saying over and over, "What is coming to our homeland? What is coming to Germany?" He says it is not good, and that it will not get better. What does your father say, Matthew? Are you in any danger in Berlin? We sometimes hear there are bad things that happen in the city.

But guess what—this is news of a happier note! I will be finished with **Gymnasium** *after the first of the year. Papa and Mama have always talked about sending me to England to study literature at Oxford if that was my desire. I will be seventeen then, but now with all the trouble between our Herr Hitler and Mr. Chamberlain, Papa thinks I should not go until we see how the situation resolves itself. It is a little fearsome for me to think of going so far from home anyway, so I am not exactly saddened by this decision.*

So I am going to go to Switzerland for five months instead! Isn't it exciting? The only drawback is that the moment my Uncle Otto heard of it, he made arrangements for Brigitte to go with me!

Sabina

∿◉∿

Dear Sabina,

What great news about your trip to Switzerland! I'm certain you will be able to survive five months with your cousin.

Life here for me goes on as usual. I have my studies and schooling. I go some of the time to a school for Americans in Germany, and also I have a tutor. I'm afraid I do not share your enthusiasm for English literature. I would rather read mysteries than Jane Eyre and Moby Dick (I have had to read both this year and write papers on them). They are both in my native language, but I am certain you understand them more than I do. Our teacher is always talking about symbolism and themes, but I can't make heads or tails out of it. Mathematics and science are more to my liking.

My father is busier and more tense from the political situation. I can tell that. In our embassy they are walking such a fine line with everything they say in trying to remain officially neutral.

To tell you the truth, I have been thinking more about some of the things we talked about when my father and I were there, than I have about the world's political climate. You asked *me* about my leg and life in Berlin. I have many questions about God. Thinking about him in this new and close-up way, as your father described it, has changed my whole way of looking at everything.

Matthew McCallum

✦

Lieber Matthew!

The cold of winter is just around the corner. Autumn is such a changeable time, beginning so warm and peaceful and fragrant, then turning yellow and gold and beautiful as the leaves die and fall, and sometimes ending with snow and freezing rains.

I love autumn, yet it always brings a certain sadness with it as well. I know growing things need their sleep as well as human creatures. Sleep and rest seem important for all of God's creations. But somehow it is always sad to see Papa put his garden to sleep for the winter. He has been pruning and clipping all week, digging up bulbs, getting all his trees and plants and bushes ready for their long, cold nap. He loves them all so much and takes care of them as if they were his own children, which I suppose they are. Even the way he prunes the rosebushes shows how much he loves them. A few varieties are blooming yet, and he cherishes every blossom he finds from now till year's end. He always leaves a few varieties unpruned, just to see what they might produce even in winter. He says there are always surprises, and he looks for them eagerly even in the bitterest of cold weather.

I was in the garden alone several days ago, and it was the oddest thing!

*You know how much I love the garden, but this time I had an uneasy feel-
ing. It was almost as if I was being watched. It felt like someone was in the
garden with me, so close I could sense that person's presence. I looked
around, but saw no one. Still, the longer I sat there, the more I became
frightened, and finally I just ran into the house. Do you ever get feelings
like that, Matthew? I was afraid to go back to the garden for two days!*

*That has all passed now though, and I am enjoying the last of the
autumn colors in the garden as much as ever.*

God bless you!

Sabina

Dear Sabina,

*I am sorry for not writing back to you sooner. My studies have kept
me busy, and Father's business at the embassy has become more and
more busy. There are always new people to meet, and important
names to remember. I suppose it is exciting in some way, but dinner
conversations get long, and I wish for conversations once again with
you and your father in the garden.*

*Your experience in the garden does sound unusual, but I am glad
for you that the feeling passed. I think with all that's happening in the
world right now, many people feel uneasy. It seems like everyone is
watching everyone else to see what will happen.*

*My father and I will be returning to the United States for
Thanksgiving and Christmas. We leave in eight days. We will spend the
holidays with some of my cousins and aunts and uncles. My father has a
brother and two sisters, and everyone is coming to my grandparents'
home in Montana for Christmas. We still have a home there too, but it is
rented out, so we'll be staying with relatives. I'll see my mother's mother
too, who is still alive. She lives in Philadelphia.*

If we don't hear from each other again, have a great Christmas!

*I wish I could see you before we go, but my father is so tied up with
arrangements and things, and I have a lot of schoolwork to do in preparation for being gone too. Maybe when I get back. When do you leave
for Switzerland? We will be back on the 11th of January.*

Matthew

~∽∾~

Lieber Matthew!

I'm afraid we won't see one another after you get back to Germany—not soon at least. I will by then already be in Switzerland! I hope you get this card. I'm sending it to your address in Berlin.

I think it is wonderful that you are returning to America for a visit. I would like to see your country sometime. Papa and Mama have talked about our family going to England sometime, but now with things the way they are, I don't know when or if that will happen.

This is too small, not even worth counting as a letter. But I mean what the card says, that I hope and pray God makes it a special Christmas season for you and your father!

And that you have an enjoyable stay in the United States!

Sabina

~∽∾~

Dear Sabina,

Your Christmas card was forwarded to me here in Montana. I'm glad the mail is still going through OK. My father is not at all sure how things will be when we return to Berlin.

Our visit here is very busy with seeing people, relatives and old friends. The best of all is the pine forest just outside our town. Remember when I told you about the forests in Montana! This is where I grew up, so these woods and I are old friends. My mother and I were here while I was young and in school. My father traveled a lot and we would join him when I had school vacations.

It is winter here, but there are always things to do. There is a lot of snow on the ground, so this morning I got together with a friend from several years ago, and we went cross-country skiing. We were only gone three or four hours, but I have been completely worn out the rest of the day. My leg is fine, by the way.

The memories here are all good ones for me, except of course my mother dying. But it happened so suddenly that it doesn't change this place for me.

It is different, I think, for my father. The memories are not all so good for him. He feels bad that he was gone so much, and coming back reminds him of her. They were very close, I think, like your parents are. I know he misses her most when he is here. When I see him like this, I remember the talks I had with your father about God. I wonder why God, if he is so loving, would want my father to be sad. I can't see that my mother's dying and my father's sadness has much of anything to do with what you talked about in your letter about free will and all that. But I'm not going to try to figure everything out about God—I don't suppose we could ever do that, could we! I guess you can ask a lot of questions, but eventually it will always come down to whether you believe God is good or not—no matter how much you might not be able to understand. I think I am learning to believe that! At least I hope so! I'm trying to.

My father is going back to Washington, D.C., at the end of the week, but I am going to stay here with my grandparents until the school vacation is over. Some of my school buddies and I have planned a hunting trip on snowshoes. When school starts for them I will join my father in Washington. I won't really have to take up my studies again in earnest until we get back to Berlin, though there are two books and a long paper I am supposed to be working on.

I will be finished with the high school part of my schooling next June, and then will be ready for college or a university. Dad and I have talked about where I should go and what I should do, but we haven't made any decisions yet. I don't even know what field I will study. Maybe politics!

Right now I want to stay with my father and go where he goes. If he stays in Germany, I'll try to go to school there, though he never knows if he might get transferred someplace else. I guess we've become pretty good friends in the last few years, and neither of us is quite ready to split up for nine months of the year.

What your father said about God being like a father is making more sense to me all the time. Sometimes I pull some pretty bone-headed moves, and my dad has to get after me. I always feel pretty stupid and sorry afterwards. But most of the time I want to please him and do what he says and be with him. And he is always completely understanding and forgiving. If God is like that, then that is the kind of God I could believe in.

Matthew

∽ 37 ∽
Fateful Decisions

After leaving *Lebenshaus*, Bonhoeffer and his small band of men split up temporarily, some returning to their homes, others seeking shelter elsewhere until a new seminary could be established.

While Baron Heinrich von Dortmann was engaged with his men harvesting late fall crops of potatoes and sugar beets, and while Marion and her household staff tried to forget the ugly desecration of their home, and while the baron's daughter and the son of the assistant American ambassador exchanged correspondence, the Gestapo proved to be busier than Dortmann's young pastor friend had anticipated. Apparently authorities kept closer tabs on the members of the Finkenwalde community than Bonhoeffer realized. In November a series of arrests were made of many of its former participants, although its leader managed to avoid imprisonment. That same month, Bonhoeffer's book on discipleship, entitled *Nachfolge*, was published. The following month, in December, he established two "collective pastorates" northeast of the Dortmann estate in the little rural villages of Köslin and Groß-Schlönwitz, through which he hoped to continue training young clergymen. For a time these disguised seminaries seemed to elude the eyes of the Gestapo.

It was not until February of the following year that Dortmann saw Bonhoeffer again.

Without warning one stormy day in the middle of the month, he drove into *Lebenshaus* alone, apparently in good health, though clearly weighed down by a burden of some kind.

"It is good to see you again, my friend," he said after he and the baron had greeted one another. "We miss you at our meetings."

"Once you are well established, I will rejoin your community as time permits."

"I'm afraid there will be no community, Heinrich. We are little more than a seminary on the run now. The peaceful days of Finkenwalde are gone forever. We remain but one step ahead of the Gestapo at every turn. You heard of the arrests?"

"Yes. How did you avoid their net?"

"The grace of God, and not being where they thought I was."

"I am happy you are safe," said the baron. "But come in! Why are we standing here in the doorway in the chill! Let me go tell Marion. She will be delighted you are here. We will have tea. Shall I have Carola bring bread? Are you hungry?"

"Wonderful. Yes, I suppose I am. It is good to be back among friends."

"How long do we have you for?" asked the baron, closing the door and leading his friend into the adjacent waiting room.

"Unfortunately, not for long. There are some matters I must discuss with you, in private I'm afraid. Then I must go."

Dortmann's brow clouded.

"I will bring Marion," he said after a brief pause. "We will eat and drink. Then you and I shall go up to my study and talk. I am at your service."

～◦○◦～

An hour later the two men took seats in the baron's southwest corner study on the first floor. A large window looking out over the countryside to the west revealed empty fields in all directions, some showing only the rich black dirt of fallow, others green with a winter's crop of green manure ground cover. A light dusting of white was visible here and there from scattered snow flurries that had been attempting all morning to begin in earnest but which had thus far been unsuccessful.

"We may be snowed in before morning, Dietrich," said the baron as he stood gazing out upon his land. "Perhaps you will be with us for a while after all."

"Then I must be off with as little delay as possible."

"Where are you bound?"

"To my sister's, at Göttingen."

"You have a long drive. You are welcome to stay the night."

"No, no, I really must not," replied Bonhoeffer with urgency in his tone.

"Berlin, then?"

A look of surprise passed over Dietrich's face.

"You did not hear?"

"Hear what?"

"I thought I had called you, perhaps I only meant to—it has been so hectic."

"What have I not heard, Dietrich?" asked the baron seriously, moving now away from the window and taking a chair opposite the one in which his friend sat.

"I was ordered out of the city last month."

"Ordered—by whom?"

"Who else? The Gestapo. I have lived there all my life, but I was forbidden to live or work there any longer." The sadness in his voice was clearly evident.

"Where have you been since?"

"East of here, up in Groß-Schlönwitz."

"And now you are going to Göttingen. What will you do there?"

"For one thing, I think I shall be safe. For a while at least. And my presence will not endanger the work here. Göttingen is far from the power base of Berlin. Perhaps the Nazis will forget about me."

"What are your plans?"

"I want to write about the Finkenwalde experience and Christian community. I shall call it *Gemeinsames Leben*. It is an important work I must complete. After that, I do not know. . . ."

Again his countenance darkened as his voice trailed off.

"You are not telling me all?" said Baron von Dortmann.

"Perhaps I was wrong in coming," said Bonhoeffer, rising and taking a step toward the door. "There is no need for me to endanger you with—"

"Dietrich, Dietrich," interrupted the baron, rising also to his feet and laying a restraining hand on his friend's shoulder. "We have known one another too long for this."

"I have no right to drag you into my troubles."

"What are you saying? You plan to write about community but then withhold your thoughts from me? What does community mean, my friend, if it is not to bear one another's burdens?"

Bonhoeffer resumed his seat and let out a heavy sigh.

"I am sorry," he said. "I only wanted to protect you from . . ." Again the sentence trailed away.

"From what, my friend?" implored the baron with quiet

earnestness. "You need not fear for me. Our Father will keep both of us in his hand."

"Perhaps it is for myself that I fear," sighed Bonhoeffer. "Not for what the Nazis can do to me, but for what they may make me become."

"I do not understand you."

"Ah, Heinrich, these are perilous times. Night is closing upon our beloved land. And I fear it is closing upon the church as well, and—God help me—I simply cannot sit by and watch the clock approach midnight and keep silent."

"You have never kept silent, Dietrich. You have been one of the church's most vocal opponents to the Nazi regime."

"I have spoken, yes. But the time has come for stronger measures. Difficult decisions must be made. That is why I hesitated. I did not want to draw you into a decision I must make within my own conscience."

"What decision? What kind of *stronger measures?*" asked the baron soberly.

The study became deathly silent. Even without the words being spoken, as with one mind both men seemed to apprehend the import of the moment in the future of their friendship and the future of the paths of their individual lives.

Several long minutes of silence passed between them. At last Bonhoeffer spoke.

"I have made contact with the resistance, Heinrich," he said.

"You mean the resistance to overthrow Hitler?"

"Yes—Admiral Wilhelm Canaris."

"But they're . . . it's strictly political, is it not? Aren't they advocates of violence, if necessary, to bring down the government?"

Bonhoeffer nodded.

"When you say you contacted them, what exactly do you mean?"

"I'm considering joining the movement, Heinrich, offering my services."

Now it was the baron's turn to sigh. He leaned back in his overstuffed chair, pondering the implications of his friend's words. Again it was silent.

"I understand now why the decision has weighed heavily upon you," said the baron at length.

"Do you see why I wanted to speak with you about it?"

The baron nodded.

"I have wrestled the matter through in such depth," Dietrich went on. "I have prayed and prayed for years about what should be our response as Christians to the Nazi evil. Still I have no answer. I was on my way to visit Gandhi to study pacifism before being asked to lead the seminary. The very thought of violence is odious to me. And yet my conscience tells me that the Nazi evil against the Jews is of such magnitude that bringing force against it may be necessary. How does a Christian pacifist reply to one such as Adolf Hitler?"

"I don't know, Dietrich. I don't know."

"We cannot sit idly by."

"As I said, you have been anything but idle."

"Yet the darkness deepens, the night surrounds us. Mustn't we do more?"

"My prayers have taken me down the same paths."

"But the time has come when the paths fork. Fateful times and fateful decisions are upon us . . . perhaps dangerous decisions."

"What do you mean by the forks in the road?"

"Some of my fellow churchmen made their choice years ago. They fell in with the evil, accommodated themselves to a religion dictated by the *Reichstag* rather than the Bible. They took their fork in the road. I took another. I spoke out, and I have not been alone. But now comes another fork in the road. Do we resist? Do we exercise passive restraint? Those of us with Jews in our families will not be allowed the luxury of an easy answer."

"You . . . in your family?"

"My brother-in-law has been classified Jewish," replied Bonhoeffer.

"What will they do?" asked Dortmann with heightened interest.

"That is another of my reasons for traveling to Göttingen. I intend, as soon as opportunity affords, to get him and my sister, Sabine, and their two daughters out of the country and to Switzerland."

Baron von Dortmann nodded. "I see . . . yes, you are right. The dangers are great."

"Aiding Jews in any way will very soon be punishable with severity."

The baron nodded. "Such may be required of me one day also," he said. "I have already found myself considering it. There are many Jews in this region. I have many friends, and neither could I stand idly by and watch them hauled away to prison."

"Prison—and worse," added Bonhoeffer.

The baron nodded once more. Both men silently reflected on the personal implications to them both in what they had been discussing.

"Would *you* consider joining the resistance?" asked Bonhoeffer after some time.

The baron did not answer immediately.

"You mean join with you?" he asked at length.

Bonhoeffer nodded. "You are in some ways closer to powerful people in the government than I. Your family name, your contacts—you could be a powerful force for the good of our nation."

The baron took in his friend's words but did not reply. He thought for a moment, then slowly rose from his chair, strolled toward the window and gazed silently out, his back to the room. Still the snow struggled to release its white blanket from the thick clouds above, with here and there a large flake fluttering about in the gusty wind.

When at length the baron spoke, his voice revealed that his brain had considered every angle of the question long before this day.

"There is not a man of conviction and conscience who possesses even an ounce of courage who has not asked himself that question a thousand times in the past two or three years," he sighed, as he turned and paced slowly through the room. "The only ones who have not considered it are either blind or fools, or altogether without the backbone of a man. I make no claim, Dietrich, to much more than an ounce of courage. I pray to our Father that when it is demanded of me I shall indeed have the courage of one of his sons. But I do have convictions, and my conscience is extremely busy these days. And so, yes, I have pondered and prayed over your question many, many times—as I know you have."

"And what answer have you arrived at?"

"Nothing concrete, I'm afraid. I continue to pray. And as I do, I cannot reconcile the example of Jesus to active societal and political involvement—for me, I say, not for you, or anyone else. My conscience only extends around the boundaries of my *own* being, and imposes its constraints upon no one else."

"I understand."

"I recognize," the baron went on, "that our Father has taken us down very different roads, Dietrich. You have been in the public eye, I have not. You have a ministry among many, whereas my flock is here at *Lebenshaus.* I have a family that must be my chief concern."

He paused.

"In answer to your question," he went on after a moment, "I doubt I could join the resistance. I do not necessarily say it is wrong for a Christian to do so. I cannot say that, for I know you did not arrive at your decision without much prayer. But I feel for me to do so would not be God's purpose for me."

"What do you see as his purpose for you in these troubled times, Heinrich?" asked Bonhoeffer.

"I see but through a glass darkly, and I continue to pray for wisdom and guidance and the light of his lamp to go before my feet. There is a work for me to carry out here, I do sense that. I do not think it will have political or national significance such as your involvement in the resistance may. When this time is past, people the world over may recognize your name, but I doubt anyone will have heard of me. Different callings are given us by our Father. Much of the work he needs done is quiet and private and individually personal. Such, at least for now, is the calling I sense to be mine. I feel God may give me to speak to men's spiritual needs in the midst of the darkness, rather than to try to eliminate the cause of that darkness. I will continue to offer safe haven to all those who seek it under our roof."

"That could eventually prove dangerous."

"Danger is coming to us all," rejoined the baron, saying nothing about the Gestapo visit that had already come. "It is not avoiding danger that is our calling, but to find our *own* work in the midst of it, that which God purposes for us to do in service to his people. It may be that I will do what you hope to do for your sister, though what form a network of escape would take I do not know."

"There are already those talking about such things," added Bonhoeffer.

"I am in touch with a few people," said the baron. "The ministry of *Lebenshaus* may be to give life and retreat and seclusion in new ways than we have seen before. To do the Lord's will as he reveals it, that is my only plan and purpose."

"And mine!" rejoined Bonhoeffer. "There is no other plan we can or should have than that."

"May God help us to discern his purpose."

"Amen!"

With one accord the two friends began to pray, committing their way unto the Father of them both, then praying, each in his turn, for the other.

When they opened their eyes fifteen minutes later, both wore solemn expressions.

"I do believe you are right," said Bonhoeffer. "The snow will not hold off much longer. I must be off in hopes of outdistancing it as I head south. I have at least to make my destination for tonight."

The baron led him downstairs.

At the foot of the stairs they stopped and shook hands, then embraced. They held one another tightly for several long seconds, then slowly stepped back. Their eyes were wet.

"Godspeed, my friend Bonhoeffer," said the baron in a husky voice full of emotion. "I will thank my God upon every remembrance of you, and I will never cease praying for you."

"Nor I for you, my friend Dortmann," returned the young pastor. "Godspeed to you too, and his blessing upon this House of Life. May *his* life be transmitted to all who enter here!"

Yet a moment more they stood, holding one another's eyes. Then quickly Bonhoeffer spun around and exited through the main front door. The baron followed him, standing in the open doorway until his car had disappeared from sight down the driveway.

He turned back inside and closed the door behind him.

Somehow sensing the finality of their parting, as well as the import of what was at hand for the world, he retraced his steps back up the stairs, tears now falling freely down his cheeks, and once again sought the privacy of his study.

He strode to the window and saw his friend's car turn onto the main road, then head south into the gathering storm.

He watched it until it disappeared from sight, then turned back into the room, fell to his knees, and once more found himself praying for both himself and his friend, the nation they both loved, and God's people everywhere in it, and asking God to reveal his way as the night closed in around them.

∽ 38 ∽
Irregular Correspondence

Throughout the politically tumultuous year of 1938, Sabina von Dortmann, young German maiden, and Matthew McCallum, son of the American diplomat, continued to maintain a scattered ongoing correspondence with one another.

At first, the letters came to and from Switzerland. Sabina's return home coincided with another trip to the States by Matthew and his father, and so the two young people were unable to see one another when the baron and Marion drove to Berlin to meet their daughter's train.

Every subsequent letter contained promises to write more frequently or mentioned proposed personal visits either to Berlin on the part of Sabina or to Niedersdorf on the part of Matthew. The convenience for the occasion of a visit, however, did not present itself to either of their fathers.

Time, as it has a habit of doing, passed more quickly than either realized, and suddenly the one year gave way to yet another, and all the while the drumroll of world events continued to accelerate.

The two youths were growing as rapidly inside as the matrix of European relationships was shifting all around them. Gradually the tone and content of their correspondence took on more subtleties and deeper patterns of thought, while they continued to discuss and probe between themselves what truth was and where the answers to life's most difficult questions could be found.

Lieber Matthew!

Are you back in Berlin yet?

As you can see from the postmark, I'm in Switzerland. I've been here two weeks. I miss Mama and Papa terribly, but there are wonderful people here too, and my aunt is so nice to me. I think she is trying to be father and mother both to me so that I will not be homesick. Of course Brigitte already knows three or four boys and will probably not miss home once.

Switzerland is not so very different from home in some ways. Of course the land is very different, not nearly so flat as the Pomeranian plain where we live. To think of Switzerland anything like flat is totally comical!

*But the people are similar. The language is the same, although it sounds a lot different. And the people behave much the same too. The main differences come when you travel to small villages and encounter country folk. When I was here before with Papa and Mama we stayed in a small village and rented a cottage. It was such a wonderful time. Papa made a fire and Mama cooked potatoes and we pretended to be peasant farmers. Papa went up on the hill behind the village with one of the farmers and helped him milk his cows. Can you imagine, in the summer here they let their cows roam so much that the farmers have to go out every morning to **find** their cows before they can milk them! I don't know why they don't keep them in a barn like we do.*

Back to now.

Of course my aunt and Brigitte want to do nothing but socialize— and not with the village folk. One of the reasons I was excited to come here is because my uncle, who is dead now, had a wonderful library with some volumes we don't have at home. He spent time in England and I want to improve my English and read lots of English books. But my aunt is not interested in such things, and if I have to go shopping for fabric again, or see the dressmaker for a fitting, or go to another party or tea, I think I will just scream. I hope these first two weeks don't bode for how it will be the whole time! One comes to Switzerland for the Alps and the water and the villages. But I've seen more drawing rooms than snow!

It being winter here, at least I know I am not missing the wild-flowers on the mountains. When spring comes, I can tell you I will get out of the house and up onto the blooming hillsides!

Today I am not going to go with Auntie and Brigitte to the Klupmans' for tea. I begged Auntie if I could stay by the fire and read in her bedroom. Her room is on the second floor and has an enormous window that faces the mountains. I will be alone all afternoon with just my book, the fire, and the mountains.

This is what I came to Switzerland for! Of course Brigitte thinks I am positively a child, but I don't care.

Sabina

∾⌒∾

Dear Sabina,

Yes, we are back in Berlin. Listening to you describe Switzerland, even with all you have to put up with, makes the city seem all the more dreary.

Do you mind if I ask you another question? I've found myself still thinking about this since your letter a while back.

I am doing a lot of thinking about spiritual things, even though I haven't been writing as much as I should. I've taken your father's advice too and have been reading the Gospels in the New Testament, trying to keep moving down the "discovery" path as he calls it, to find out what God is like. I am learning so many things I didn't know before. Reading the Bible from the perspective of Jesus telling us about a loving Father, and learning to quit thinking about God as a mean ogre—it changes everything about what the words of Jesus mean. I'm enjoying it!

I have found another question coming to me though. Isn't one of the main reasons you believe as you do because of your parents, and because they have taught you things about being a Christian? What difference does it make what people believe if they try to live a good life? I'm not asking this in disagreement or anything. It's just that I found myself wondering about it.

Matthew

∼◦⊂∽

Lieber Matthew!

If you pray, Matthew, please pray for my father. I know he's worried and is asking for the Lord to show him what to do.

This may be short, but I want to say just a few words about the question you asked me in your last letter.

*If living a good life was all there was to it, I suppose you would be right, but it isn't. I believe there is such a thing as truth, and so it matters on just the level of falling in with what's true. Whether my parents taught me one thing and somebody else was raised another way, and somebody else another way—none of that changes what is true. So it seems to me the first and most important thing about life ought to be discovering what's **true**.*

That's why it's so good that you're reading the Gospels. That's the first place to find what's true, because Jesus is the most dependable source of truth. Actually, Jesus himself is truth. He said so.

If you're going to find it, and discover what truth is and what God's character is like, that's the best place. I love the Gospels. I wish we had time to talk about them sometime.

I'll write again soon.

Sabina

∼◦⊂∽

Dear Sabina,

Boy, it's been a long time since I wrote. Please forgive me. Writing's not one of the things I do best, but I sure do like to hear from you.

I don't know how much you hear down in Switzerland, but here things are heating up a lot over Czechoslovakia. Dad says it's a dangerous situation. We may be going back to the States again in the summer—I don't know for how long. We've decided that I will come back with him to Berlin and do some independent studying here. I don't want to go to the university in the States while he is here. The world situation being what it is, things could change in a hurry, but for now, those are my plans.

By the way, I read in the Bible the other day where Jesus talks

*about truth. He said, "I am the way, the truth, and the life." I
suppose I had read that before, but it means more now after your
last letter.*

Matthew

❧

Lieber Matthew!
I'll be on the train back north to Germany in just a couple of days.
*It's been a long five months. I've enjoyed Switzerland, but all the
scenery in the world can't make up for relationships, and to tell you
the truth, Auntie and Brigitte just aren't the kind of people you can
talk to about anything of substance. If it wasn't for the letters from
you and Mama and Papa (they both write me every week), I wouldn't
have been able to stand it.*
*Oh, it really hasn't been so bad. I have done a great deal of read-
ing. Auntie finally realized it was simpler to let me read than drag me
to social events. And I have been out on the hillsides a lot. I even
managed to get Brigitte to go with me a few times, and I think she
actually enjoyed it!*

Sabina

❧

Dear Sabina,
How does the time go so fast?
*The Czechoslovakian crisis is accelerating. Dad has been in near-
constant meetings over it. No one knows what is going to happen. I
am worried.*

Matthew

❧

Lieber Matthew!
*Oh, aren't dreadful things happening! Papa and Mama are sick
about the awful violence. Did anything happen near you during the
Krystall-nacht riots? A friend of Mama's in Niedersdorf lost a*

cousin. Can you imagine, Matthew—killed! Papa has been weighed down over it like I've never seen him. I know he's thinking and praying, but he's not saying too much about what he's thinking yet.

I am worried too.

Sabina

PART IV

The Mystery of the Dungeon—1939

Approach to Conflict

In the vacuum created by the collapse of Germany after the First World War and the economic collapse of the Great Depression, the staunch German people turned to a madman to reestablish their hopes, to rebuild their economy, and, at the most fundamental level, to nourish and recultivate the wounded Celtic pride that had been so bitterly stung after the war.

He achieved all these ends by a gradual, then a headlong and unrestrained, restoration of Germany's military might, along with a crazed preaching of Teutonic, Aryan supremacy over all other races and nations of the world. In so doing he found millions of willing and eager ears.

Adolf Hitler joined the fledgling national socialist movement in 1919, just months after its founding, quickly rising in its ranks by his forceful pro-Aryan oratory. Throughout the 1920s the fringe political movement grew, with Hitler more and more in command, and by the collapse of 1929 it was poised to make a run at history.

The Nazis fielded but miniscule contingents in the national elections of the late twenties, looked upon by the general population as a lunatic political party that might as well have been comprised of escaped inmates from some asylum. But they succeeded in electing 107 of their Brownshirts to the *Reichstag* in 1930, over their previous twelve. Suddenly all was changed.

By 1932, with a growing dissatisfaction of the masses toward the leadership of the crumbling Weimar Republic, and with a sense that the emerging nationalism of a new generation of Germans was ready to forcefully, even violently, reassert itself behind him, Hitler prepared himself for the destiny he knew was his.

In January of 1933, President Hindenburg appointed Adolf Hitler—leader of the Nazis, by now the strongest party in Germany—chancellor of the Reich. A year and a half later

Hindenburg was dead. Hitler called for a special election, which he won by a landslide, and by the end of 1934 he was chancellor *and* president and *Der Führer* (or leader) over all of Germany.

Quickly he began a secret program of massive rearmament. In addition the Nazi leader called for a great "cleansing" of impure elements throughout all of German life and society, led and carried out by the secretive elite SS and SA organizations, which, over the years, would come to dominate all of life in Germany. The Nazi police state had begun.

Almost immediately after becoming chancellor, Hitler ordered a boycott of Jewish shops and businesses in Berlin. Gradually Jews were dismissed from political and cultural positions. The notorious Nürnberg Laws were passed in 1935 "for the protection of the racial purity of the state," which totally stripped Jews of political and civic rights.

By the mid-1930s, Hitler's no-longer-secretive war machine had begun to present a clear and present danger to those smaller nations around its borders. The lethargic leadership of Britain and the isolationist feeling in America shared a policy aimed at avoiding war at all costs—a perfect hothouse for Hitler to continue adding to his armaments. The dark cloud of fascism continued its spread across the continent.

Conflict might have been avoidable in 1936, perhaps even as late as 1937, but by 1938, Hitler commanded the flow of events.

In hopes of appeasing the dictator, the British and French throughout this period gave in to Hitler's demands—small at first but steadily increasing—hoping to prevent a confrontation.

But Hitler's objectives had widened since he had taken power. He lusted for control now, not merely of Germany, but of the world. He sought "cleansing," not just within German borders, but throughout Europe.

In March of 1938, Hitler ordered German troops into Austria and took over the government. There was no resistance. Austria had been "annexed" for the Fatherland, and was now a province of Germany.

The first domino had fallen without a shot being fired. Hitler became more convinced than ever that no one would stand up to him. With his military machine in place, and knowing no other nation on earth to be his military equal, he proceeded to make plans to widen the territories of his conquest.

Judaism was not to be the only religion trampled under the hooves of Nazi boots. One month after the Austrian *Anschluss*, an edict was passed ordering all Christian priests and pastors to declare their allegiance to Hitler.

Most took the oath. Others, such as Dietrich Bonhoeffer, cried out against it, doing their best to stir up church leaders and awaken them from their apathy. But their voices cried in the wilderness. The organized German Church became more and more but another arm of the Fascist state. Some men of conscience left for Great Britain or America, trying to make their voices heard on foreign soil. Others remained in Germany. Bonhoeffer himself took his message abroad, but ultimately returned to live out his destiny as God's spokesman on the soil of his homeland.

Hitler now set his sights on Czechoslovakia, where a fifth of the population were ethnic Germans. After a series of humiliating meetings in August and September, culminating with the Munich Agreement, British Prime Minister Neville Chamberlain agreed to carve up the Czech state and give Hitler everything he demanded.

The campaign against the Jews reached new heights in November of 1938, when Heinrich Himmler, then head of the Gestapo under the *Sicherheitsdienst*, carried out a rash of violent acts against the Jewish population of Berlin. SA and SS troops led a huge looting raid of Jewish shops throughout the city. Thirty-six persons were killed. More than 190 synagogues were burned, 76 completely destroyed. Observers and police watched, but did nothing, even as whole Jewish families were herded out of their homes. Whatever innocence the great masses of Germans may have been able to claim in allowing the rise of Nazi cruelty and barbarism was quickly disappearing. The riot, known as "Crystal Night" for the enormous breakage of glass and windows, proved a turning point. Henceforth, the Nazi programme against Jews would be violent, unpredictable, and lawless.

In January of 1939, an order was issued liquidating all Jewish businesses. Jews began to leave Germany in massive numbers. Some 400,000 fled Germany and Austria. Late in that same year, less than 300,000 remained, mostly those either too old to emigrate or those married to non-Jews who wanted to remain in their homeland. The danger, however, had become apparent enough.

Hitler occupied Prague in March of 1939, and every indication told him that he could take the rest of Czechoslovakia without fear of reprisal. Now his greedy eyes of conquest and power began to look eastward toward that ancient land of Prussia and Poland.

He had, however, nearly pushed Great Britain and France too far. Hostilities loomed. Freedom hung in the balance. Paris, London, and Washington—the latter behind the scenes—at last woke to the threat.

As the summer of 1939 opened, they reluctantly but quickly accelerated their belated military preparations to catch up.

∽ 40 ∾
Frustrated Vendetta

Emil Korsch had been through every file on his desk six times. He had exhausted every lead. He had talked to every church leader, both those sympathetic and those unsympathetic to their cause. No one had seen hide nor hair of the underground rabble-rouser and seminary leader.

He had even managed to slip one of his own men into their little ruse of "collective pastorates" up north in the two Pomeranian villages of Köslin and Groß-Schlönwitz. But that lead had gone dry, too. None of the simpletons knew where their leader and founder was. He hadn't actually visited in the flesh for over a year.

He had considered more arrests. But what good would it have done if the young radicals honestly didn't know of his whereabouts? He could have tortured them, even killed them, and still learned nothing!

Besides, those fool Christians were as righteously fearless about their cause as the Nazis! They almost enjoyed torture, it seemed. The more painful you made it, the more they prayed and chanted out their ridiculous Scriptures!

He'd been on the track of their clandestine activities ever since slamming the door shut on Finkenwalde. Despite the arrests that had followed, his sources confirmed that the training centers were still active. Once he had located them, he remained frustrated in that his chief quarry was still not there. He'd decided to let them continue their little game for now. Hopefully the fellow would turn up eventually, and he still had his man in place at Köslin. If not, he would shut them down later and throw the whole lot in prison!

There were rumors that he'd fled the country.

They'd gotten onto his trail last year, but too late to keep him from getting his sister's family to Switzerland. Then the information dried up and the trail turned cold.

Jews! He should have smelled it! Right in the traitor's own family! He was indeed an enemy of the state, and for more reasons than Korsch had first suspected. He'd probably left Germany with them to save his own cowardly skin!

A moment more Korsch stared down at the useless pages in front of him.

Suddenly his arm swept angrily across his desk, sending every paper on it flying. A series of oaths erupted from his lips as he sprang from his chair. The subdued fury at last exploding, he strode back and forth across the room with angry step, face red and eyes flaming.

He hated them! As far as he was concerned, the Jews could stay. If he had his way, they would get rid of the Christians instead. At least the Jews kept their religion to themselves. But the Christians were always bent on their self-righteous mission to evangelize the whole world with their absurd notions!

More than anything he hated to be outsmarted by their self-serving piety!

He would *not* be outsmarted by them! Especially not by this slippery young pastor and teacher and author who had become his nemesis.

He walked back to his desk, picking up the thin volume that

had just come into his possession that morning and which had triggered this latest outburst of passion.

Wherever he was, the fool continued to write!

He opened the book to the first page. *Behold, how good and how pleasant it is for brethren to dwell together in unity*, he read to himself.

The mindless drivel made his stomach sick!

In a sudden motion the book flew across the room, crashing against the opposite wall. With all the restrictions they had in place, how was he able to get such seditious idiocy into print! Himmler and Hitler and all the rest of them were so fanatically obsessed with the Jews, they allowed altogether too much laxity toward these outspoken Christians! When he found him, Korsch vowed to himself, he would not only shut down every teaching facility, he would forbid him to write so much as another word, under penalty of life imprisonment!

Korsch found himself again staring out his window, hands clasped behind his back in a tight grip of spring-coiled wrath.

All at once he spun around and ran back to his desk. Frantically he riffled through the papers again.

He had seen something—a name.

It hadn't registered at first. How could he have been so blind! He hadn't made use of the connection in over a year! The link had almost dropped out of his memory.

Luckily it was still in the file! Why hadn't he noticed it before now? He'd focused so heavily on the money itself he'd almost forgotten the reason for it in the first place. How could he have been so stupid!

Yes, there it was! He picked up the paper, scanned it quickly . . . of course . . . it was perfect. This fellow might do more for him than merely line his account with Swiss francs!

Slowly a cunning smile spread across his thick lips, revealing a thin slit of yellowish-white beneath them.

He grabbed up his coat from where it hung behind him, folded the paper and stuffed it inside, then picked up the phone on his desk and barked into it.

"Order up my car!" he growled. "Yes, immediately!"

∽ 41 ∽
Tightening the Squeeze

"How nice to see you again, *Herr* von Dortmann," said Korsch with a smile as oily as his smoothed-down hair, closing the door of the large office behind him. "The look on your face betrays you, however," he added with a smile.

"I have asked you not to call on me here," replied Otto, doing his best to keep his voice calm. He was highly annoyed, but at the same time fearful of the man's power.

"You are not pleased to see me?" said Korsch with wry sarcasm.

"It is most inopportune for you to be seen here."

"And why is that, my friend?"

"Because . . . people could talk . . . my reputation."

Still Korsch smiled condescendingly as he took a chair and stared across at the rotund banker.

"Are you saying the Gestapo is not highly thought of?" the agent asked, still smiling, but with an edge to his tone reflective of the subdued glint in his eyes.

"Please, don't misunderstand me," said a flustered Otto. "It is only that this is my place of business, and . . . you—you have your own spheres of influence."

Instantly the smile disappeared from Korsch's mouth.

"Everything and everyone is the business of the Gestapo, *Herr* von Dortmann!" he snapped. "I should think you of all people would know that fact well enough by now."

The banker sat silently behind his large mahogany-topped desk. It did not do to anger these people, he knew that. He had had enough interaction with this weasel of a man to realize well enough that compliance was the only appropriate response.

"Forgive me, Herr Korsch," he said, swallowing his pride as he had on how many dozen previous occasions. "Is there some problem with my . . . uh, my debt?"

Korsch smiled to see the powerful financier squirm. It was a common trait of small-minded and even-smaller-hearted men that they enjoyed lording it over those whom society judged their superiors. Of such personalities the Gestapo was almost entirely comprised, and upon their gigantic petty egos the feared arm of the Nazi secret police built its powerful and intimidating reputation.

"No, *mein lieber Freund,*" replied Korsch. "My Swiss account is growing nicely as a result of its monthly payments from your generous bank. I should find myself well provided for when our Reich enters its glorious thousand-year rule."

At last the grin overspread the lips, the yellow teeth revealed themselves in all their grotesque splendor, and Emil Korsch's ugly, scarred face burst out in a mean-spirited laugh.

"Ha! ha! ha! What do you think to hear me talk so, eh, Dortmann! Ha! ha! Does it make your fat rump squirm in your chair, wishing you could get rid of me out of your life? Ha! ha!"

The banker swallowed a dozen outbursts and sat silent.

"Ah, but don't you love the irony of it, Otto," Korsch went on, still chuckling. "I am your protection! You hate me, but I am the only one standing between you and certain downfall and ruin. You *need* me, Otto. Ha! ha!"

Otto von Dortmann well knew the hated Gestapo agent's call on this day had to do with more than the blackmail money he was paying him. Ever since the man's first visit, when he had suggested a financial "arrangement" in order to keep the wrong persons in Berlin's powerful circles from learning of his brother's links with known subversives, Otto had lived in almost daily fear of future demands. It was the Gestapo's way— get their hooks into someone, whether the charges were factual or fallacious, and they would continue to dig deeper.

They were evil! Every one of them. Yet it was impossible to resist them. Their power was unlimited, and—he hated to admit it!—the scum was right. He could snap his fingers and Otto would be ruined!

What could the man want now, thought Otto. *Is he going to ask for more money to continue his silence?* It was already all he could do to disguise the payments he authorized every month. If he had to pay more, he would have no choice but to take it out of his own personal funds. Eventually the man was going to bleed him dry! He would—

Otto's thoughts were interrupted by the slimy tone of Korsch's voice, asking with significant undertones of meaning: "How is your brother, Herr von Dortmann?"

"Uh . . . Heinrich?" said Otto, coming to himself and adjusting his eyes once more to the man sitting in front of his desk.

"Of course," replied Korsch curtly. "He is your only brother, I believe."

"Yes. I do not often see . . . that is, as far as I know he is doing well," said Otto.

"Of course, I'm sure he is," Korsch said. "And you and he never communicate, nor have the slightest connection with one another, is that what you would have me believe?"

"Why, yes, that is exactly the case. Heinrich and I could not be more different—"

He was interrupted by the open hand of Emil Korsch slamming with force down on the front of the desk as he leapt from his chair. With a glare of menace, the Gestapo agent leaned across the desk and stared into Otto's wide eyes.

"What kind of a fool do you take me for, Dortmann?" he asked, seething with anger. "Do you honestly expect me to believe you have no contact with your only brother? I have extensive files on you both. Don't toy with me, Dortmann, or I will bring you down so fast it will make your head spin!"

"I'm sorry, Herr Korsch," Otto said. "I only meant that we do not see one another regularly."

"I know precisely what you meant, Otto," sneered the Gestapo agent. "You meant to save your greasy fat skin! But relax," he added, stepping back and resuming his seat. "I do not intend to ruin you—just yet, at least . . . so long as you prove willing to assist . . . to cooperate with the Reich."

He smiled again, enjoying watching the banker's fleshy cheeks and forehead break out in beads of perspiration at his veiled threats. He had this coward exactly where he wanted him!

Several long seconds of heavy silence ensued.

"A party, a social gathering of some prestige, is being planned next month," said Korsch at length, in a calm and informational tone. "You have no doubt been made aware of the Führer's order that Berlin have a gala time of it this summer, that social and diplomatic circles make merry with gaiety."

The banker nodded. "I have heard it, yes," he said nervously.

"The leaders of the world must see that all is well, that the

Reich is prospering and its people happy, and that its friends and foes alike have nothing to fear."

"I understand, Herr Korsch."

"You would, of course, be more than willing to assist the Reich toward this end, I am certain, would you not, Herr von Dortmann?"

"Of course. Whatever I can do."

"As I said, one such gathering is being planned," said Korsch in a tone of heightened innocence, "in which I am most interested. As it turns out—remarkable coincidence!—the party will be held at the villa of one of our party loyalists out in the country, not far, if I understand it correctly, from where you grew up yourself, Herr von Dortmann."

Otto continued to listen, trusting the man's assumed air of naivete no further than Korsch expected he would. That the location of the gathering was a coincidence he believed not for a second.

"A certain Count von Schmundt and his wife have graciously agreed to host the event," he went on. "Perhaps you know them?"

"The count's estate borders our family's holdings," said Otto, masking his irritation at being treated like a child.

"That *is* astonishing!" exclaimed Korsch, pretending surprise. "So you are neighbors!"

"Yes . . . that is, the count and I knew one another when we were boys."

"Then you will no doubt be receiving an invitation yourself."

"Perhaps."

In truth, Otto had already received his invitation, a fact which Korsch well knew and in fact had arranged himself.

"And your brother will no doubt receive one as well."

"That is likely."

"I would like to meet your brother, Herr von Dortmann."

"I seriously doubt he will attend," said Otto. "He is not given to much socializing."

"I *want* to meet your brother, Herr von Dortmann."

"And you want . . . what do you want me to do?"

"I want you to make certain he is there, *mein lieber* Otto," said Korsch with sarcasm, "and to introduce me to him."

"But what . . . what do you intend to . . . to do to him?"

"I intend your brother no harm, Otto, believe me."

"I tell you, I have nothing to do with my brother's activities," stammered Otto. "He always was the odd one of the family."

"Tut, tut, Otto. I know that. You can trust me."

"But why do you want to meet Heinrich?"

"Relax, neither you nor he has anything to worry about."

∽ 42 ∽
Another Invitation

"Well, Matt, what do you think?" said Thaddeus McCallum, looking across the table at his son. "Shall we go?"

Matthew set down the invitation his father had handed him a few moments earlier.

"Sounds like just another stuffy diplomatic reception, Dad," he replied. "If you don't mind, I think I'd just as soon pass."

"Didn't you see where the party's going to be held?"

"Yeah, some German count's place."

"Look closer."

Matthew picked up the piece of paper again and scanned it.

"Schmundt—should I recognize the name?" he said.

"Probably not. An aristocratic Nazi, from what I understand. Actually, I'm not sure why they're having such an event so far from the city, but it's the location I wanted you to notice."

"Why?"

"The Schmundt villa is just across the way from Baron von Dortmann's. It would give us another chance to visit the baron . . . and his daughter."

Matthew's face brightened. "Why didn't you just say so, Dad? That changes everything. Sure I'll go!"

His father laughed. "I thought you might see it differently in that light!"

"When's the last time you heard from Sabina?"

"I haven't had a letter all summer—I think it was May."

"Have you written her?"

"Actually, no."

"No wonder you haven't heard from her. But a personal visit will be better than ten letters."

"I'll agree with that. What's the occasion, anyway?"

"You know the Germans. They're constantly trying to pretend that nothing in Europe has changed even though their twentieth-century Napoleon has mustered the largest army on the globe and is making menacing moves everywhere. Their way of doing it is to dress up and bring out the wine and string ensembles and talk and laugh and make merry as if all is calm and serene. After the Austrian *Anschluss* last year, there were two or three high-level parties and receptions every weekend!"

"But why? Why did they invite you?"

"To show the world that nothing has changed, that Hitler brings only joy and happiness," answered Thaddeus cynically.

"Are you saying they're hypocrites?"

"You be the judge, Matt. To use an old phrase the Indians used to say about the white man in our country: Nazi speak with forked tongue!"

Matthew laughed.

"If you want my opinion," his father went on, "I have the feeling that all this rash of Nazi goodwill going around this summer means that Hitler is up to something. He's trying to lull us all to sleep."

"Then why do you go?"

"It's all part of the diplomatic game, part of my job. So I brush and mix and talk with the Nazis as if nothing is wrong, listening to them carry on and pretend they're not up to anything and pretending myself that I don't notice what they're up to. It's called diplomacy. But it's all a charade."

∽∾∾

Several days later, the following letter arrived for the baron at the Dortmann estate.

MY DEAR BARON VON DORTMANN,

It has been far too long since we saw one another. I have managed to keep some distant tabs on you through my son's correspondence with your daughter. Alas, the time passes too quickly, and, as you are certainly aware, events have been moving on a very rapid track. This is no time, of course, to enter into a discussion of those events, only to say that I have been extremely busy here at the embassy.

Both Matthew and I would very much like to see you and your family once again. It so happens that all of us here on the ambassador's staff, myself included, have received an invitation to attend a social gathering at the villa of Count Ernst von Schmundt. No doubt you know him and perhaps you will be in attendance as well.

Your having told me about your "House of Life," and your interest in providing a place for solitude and retreat for all who would come, prompts me to inquire as to the suitability of Matthew's and my inviting ourselves for a visit of a day or two. The party is scheduled for the 27th of this month. I realize this is short notice, and if it is inconvenient or overly presumptuous of me, we will make other arrangements.

With kind regards,

THADDEUS MCCALLUM
Assistant United States Ambassador
United States Embassy
Berlin

⚬⚭⚬

"Presumptuous, indeed!" said the baron to himself, rising from his chair the moment he had finished the letter. "I thought you knew me better than that by now, Thaddeus!"

In ten seconds more he was descending the stairs from his study to the *Gute Stube,* and in another four minutes was on the telephone with McCallum himself, confirming the arrangements.

⚬ 43 ⚬
The Party

Countess Ingrid von Schmundt could not have been more beside herself with mingled anxiety and excitement. Such a flurry of emotions had overwhelmed her during the past days, it was a wonder the poor woman had not withered right away before the day of the party even arrived.

As it was, she had managed to hold herself together, to coordinate the servants' preparation of the Grand Hall, and now people had begun to arrive. Alone in her boudoir, she sat before the mirror making sure her hair and dress were perfect.

Everyone from Berlin will be here, she thought, unable to keep the perspiration away. It was her chance to step once again into the limelight she had missed for so long. She had chosen a loose-fitting gown of light blue silk, loose enough, she hoped, to conceal the unwanted centimeters that had added themselves to her person.

When her husband had mentioned being asked to host a summer's event for Berlin's diplomatic circles, she had been completely unable to contain her glee. Even had she known that she was but a pawn in schemes of much larger import, it would nowise have dampened her enthusiasm.

And that it would almost exactly coincide with Gustav's twentieth birthday was all the better! She wanted to put on a grand celebration for her son and invite all the most eligible young women in the entire region. Obsessed with what she judged her neighbor's pomposity, she was determined to demonstrate that she needed the friendship no longer. She would show Marion and that conceited daughter of hers that Gustav was the most eligible young man for a hundred kilometers in any direction!

She wouldn't even invite them! She would let them hear of it! They would come begging for the alliance in the end, that is, if she just didn't decide to find some other more suitable young lady for Gustav to marry!

Marion's daughter was a simpleton anyway, just like her idiot of a father! True, Gustav remained smitten with her, but she had no doubt the wiles of another could turn his head soon enough. And she, for one, was not about to put up with Marion any longer.

Her husband, however, had insisted that the Dortmanns be on hand.

"As little as I am fond of Heinrich," Schmundt had said, "it would not look right."

"I tell you, I can't tolerate the lot of them!" said Ingrid peevishly. "I don't know what I ever saw in Marion!"

"Not to worry, my dear. You and Gustav will be the center of attention. It will be the perfect opportunity to show that vixen of Heinrich's her folly for snubbing you."

"I don't see why we have to invite them, Ernst."

"It would not look right. After all, Otto will be coming."

"And his daughter?"

"I made sure of that."

His wife smiled.

"Are you thinking that perhaps we had our eyes on the wrong Dortmann all this time?" asked the count.

"The idea had occured to me. But I still don't see why the baron and Marion have to come. I tell you, I hate them all."

"Ingrid, dear, they *must* be in attendance. I have been instructed to make sure they are present."

Her husband had said no more, and from his tone Ingrid knew there was nothing more to be said.

She turned her head a third of the way to the left, then in the opposite direction, checking her hair from both sides, making sure it was just right.

If only I can keep all the talk from deteriorating to politics, she thought to herself. Back in the twenties, when everything was so gay, parties and balls were fun and festive. Now everything was world events and politics and armies and Jews and military talk. And they were even told whom they must invite!

She was sick of it! She would make this a day to remember. Marion would think better of her and her son after this. The Schmundt villa would be the talk of Berlin and the highlight of the social season!

Outside in the Grand Hall, while his wife completed her coiffure, Count Ernst von Schmundt busily welcomed his Nazi colleagues from Berlin. Already the drinks had begun to flow and circles of conversation busily discussed everything from the summer's heat in Berlin to the recently concluded Moscow Pact of the previous week.

Two large Nazi flags had been draped from the two opposite walls of the hall, and swastikas were prominent on the arms of many brown military uniforms. The only one of the Führer's innermost circle who was on hand for the occasion, however, was the man whom Hitler would soon make Germany's highest-ranking military officer, *Reichsmarschall* Hermann Göring, who had originally organized the Gestapo out of the Prussian Secret Police several years earlier. He was nearly in his old backyard. Though command of the secret police force had since passed into the hands of Heinrich Himmler, Göring maintained close ties with many of its members and was now talking in confidential tones with Emil Korsch, whom he had heard to be one of the Gestapo's most powerful rising young agents.

"I understand you traveled to Moscow last week?" Göring was saying.

"Herr Himmler requested that I accompany Herr Ribbontrop and the rest of the delegation," replied Korsch. "As his personal liaison."

"Ah," Göring said, nodding knowingly. "In other words, Heinrich wanted someone to keep an eye on things."

Korsch nodded. "To be sure the Gestapo was represented."

Göring smiled. "A shrewd man, our friend Herr Himmler," he said. "And why you, if I may inquire, Herr Korsch?"

"I happen to speak Russian."

"And how did you find Moscow?"

"Unbearable. Between you and me, I can scarcely tolerate Russia or its people."

Meanwhile, at the other end of the hall, Gustav was in his element and already had a small group of fawning young women in a circle about him, one of whom was Brigitte von Dortmann, cousin to the neighbor he planned one day to marry. Brigitte's flirtatious charms, heightened to seasoned perfection from years of practice, were not without their alluring influence upon the emerging ego of Gustav's manhood, though out of the corner of his eye he maintained a watchful vigilance for Sabina's arrival. In the last year Gustav had grown into nearly a man and could have had, in truth, any of the number of eligible young Pomeranian aristocratic daughters whose presence his mother had arranged.

The sting of Sabina's rebuffs, however, had not mixed pleasantly with Gustav's pride, and he had become more determined than ever to possess her. It could hardly be denied that

Sabina was as beautiful as they came, and her feisty, outgoing personality added to the charm. Her cool treatment of him as they had grown older, along with her recent absence in Switzerland, had blinded him to the practicality of how very different they had become.

He had grown up in more ways than mere size and age, and he was through and through a modern German of the Third Reich. He knew what he wanted, and he would have it, whatever it took to obtain it.

What he felt could not be called love. That it was devotion there could be no doubt, but devotion to himself and no other. If it was his desire to make Sabina his bride, then who was she to refuse him? Germany took what it wanted these days—and so would he.

This was going to be a memorable day for more reasons than just his birthday. Gustav had something very special planned!

"Gustav," said Brigitte in an insistent and pouting tone, "I don't believe you heard a word I said!"

"Don't be ridiculous, my sweet," replied Gustav, pulling his gaze away from the door at the far end of the hall. "You have my full attention."

"No I don't . . . who *are* you looking for?"

"Nothing you need trouble your fair head about."

"I insist that you tell me. Is somebody important coming?"

"I was only glancing about to see if your cousin had arrived."

"Oh, *her*," said Brigitte petulantly. "I had enough of her in Switzerland!"

Gustav took another swallow from the glass of wine in his hand, but said nothing.

∽ 44 ∽

Light and Darkness

Thaddeus McCallum and his son arrived some thirty minutes later. A last-minute delay kept them in Berlin longer than expected, and so they had come straight to the Schmundt villa without stopping first at *Lebenshaus*. They had not yet seen the baron or his family. Thaddeus was engaged at the moment with the French foreign minister and a low-level Spanish diplomat, both of whom conversed fluently in English.

"What do you think, Monsieur McCallum?" the Frenchman was saying. "Do you buy the line the Germans are giving us about this pact they made with Russia a few days ago?"

"You mean do I think it signals a new spirit of peace and cooperation by their Führer?" said Thaddeus.

The Frenchman nodded.

"Do you seriously expect me to answer you forthrightly *here?* We're surrounded by Nazis," he added in a low tone.

"Then whisper your answer," said the Frenchman softly.

Thaddeus glanced around hurriedly. "I don't think it signals a thing except more of Hitler's blitz diplomacy," he whispered.

"Do you consider war inevitable, then?" asked the Spaniard.

"I hope it won't come to that," answered Thaddeus. "But I must say, it doesn't look altogether—"

He was interrupted by the sudden arrival of their host.

"Ah, my American and French and Spanish friends!" said Schmundt ebulliently. "I am so glad you could come. And what have you been discussing so quietly amongst yourselves?"

"We have just been congratulating your Führer on his peace negotiations with the Russians."

"A masterstroke," rejoined Schmundt. "He is indeed a great man of peace, something you would do well to communicate to the people in your countries. He is so misunderstood by those who consider him an aggressor. He only wants Germany's historic territories secure so that peace can rule throughout Europe."

"Exactly what we were saying ourselves, Count," added the Frenchman.

As they spoke, Matthew listened with one ear as he gazed about the room. In the two years since he was first in this part of Germany, he had grown at least two inches and filled out in the chest and shoulders. He had become more a man in appearance and bearing though still with a youthful expression of innocence even though he was surrounded daily by such events of import. He now stood five-eleven and, though still on the slender side, showed a well-proportioned musculature that any young man would feel confident to carry. His face had strengthened its lines, and he resembled his father more than ever. In the striking black tuxedo, white linen shirt, and black bow tie, one who did not know him might easily have mistaken him for one of the diplomatic corps himself.

When Baron Heinrich von Dortmann arrived with his wife and daughter, Count von Schmundt greeted them as if they were on the most intimate of terms.

"Heinrich, my friend," he said, shaking his neighbor's hand, "Ingrid and I are so glad you could come! Marion, Sabina," he added, turning his head toward the two women.

"Thank you, Ernst," said the baron warmly, delighted though surprised at the man's gracious demeanor after such a lengthy cool spell between them.

"Breaking away in the middle of your harvest must have been difficult."

"My men are managing just fine without me," laughed the baron.

"Where is Ingrid?" asked Marion, glancing around.

"She will be down presently."

"Have you seen our friend the doctor?" asked the baron.

Schmundt's face immediately clouded.

"Whose friend?" he said coolly.

"What do you mean, Ernst? Our friend—Doctor Abrahams."

"He's not *my* friend, Heinrich, and if you know what's good for you—which I doubt you do—you won't consider him yours any longer either."

"What are you talking about? You did invite him, did you not?"

"Keep your voice down, Heinrich," rejoined the count. "And no, of course I didn't invite him."

"Why not? He has been a friend of your family for years."

"Things have changed, Heinrich. It is time you woke up to that fact."

"But Doctor Abrahams is—"

"Look, Heinrich," interrupted the count, "there are people here from Berlin. Important people. The doctor has had, shall we call it, a *visit* from some of them. It would not be healthy for either of us to associate with him again. It's all changed, Heinrich.

All the past alliances have to be redrawn. I have made my choice, and I suggest you do the same."

He stared intently at his lifelong neighbor with an unmistakable glint of omen in his eyes. Then he attempted a smile, though without much success, and added, "Now, enjoy yourselves, have something to drink—there are plenty of refreshments."

As the count moved off, Marion glanced at Heinrich with an anxious look of worry. He then tried to allay her fears for the doctor with a half-smile. This was not the first time they had been in such circumstances, though in recent years they had made every effort to avoid the social circles most people of their economic standing seemed to thrive upon. Heinrich had not been to a function such as this since the garden party in Berlin at his brother Otto's two years before. Had the occasion been such as to allow it, they would have declined this afternoon's festivities as well, preferring to visit the count and countess privately a day or two later. After the brief interchange with their host, all his reservations about coming swept back over him, and with them a foreboding anxiety about their friend in town.

But Otto had been quite insistent that Heinrich attend. "Influential people will be there. It would not do to be seen as unsupportive of our Führer. They watch those kinds of things, Heinrich. You must learn to keep step with the times."

Heinrich von Dortmann cared not a straw to keep step with the times, as Otto put it. But for his brother's sake, and because it was the first invitation their whole family had had to the Schmundt estate in some time, he had decided to accept. He had been concerned about the count of late and prayed this might indicate a thaw in the chilly relationship that had come to exist between them.

He glanced around as they made their way slowly into the hall.

It's all such a facade, thought Heinrich sadly to himself. The two levels of intercourse were so apparent to a sensitive spiritual nature such as his—the pretended level of gaiety, the chinking sounds of glasses, laughter, string music from the far end of the hall, smiles, light conversation—yet beneath it all he could feel the minor chords resonating, the abundant swastikas everywhere, the talk of politics and careening world events, the crisp clicking of German heels and the robust *Heil Hitler*s that could be heard periodically above the merrymaking din.

This was a show, he thought, full of veneers and undercurrents, everyone with his own agenda to fulfill, all intended to hide what Heinrich knew was a core of corruption and deceit at the heart of his country's leadership. The mood felt like the calm before a storm. Already, though he knew many of the socialites present and would have enjoyed rekindling some of the acquaintances, the baron began to feel the atmosphere stifling.

"First thing tomorrow morning," he whispered to his wife, "I'll drive into town and see if Aaron is all right. But I don't like the sound of it."

"I have been waiting for you, Sabina," said Gustav, approaching briskly in the midst of Heinrich's observations. He held a new full glass of wine in his hand.

"Hello, Gustav," she said politely.

"Come," he said, laying his free hand on her arm and attempting to lead her away. "I have been saving my dancing feet just for you!"

"I only just arrived, Gustav," Sabina objected, glancing at her mother with an imploring expression.

"All the more reason not to delay! Come, Sabina. I have a surprise for you I am saving for later. But now, I want you to dance with me."

From his vantage point with his father, Matthew had seen the Dortmanns arrive. While he stood taking in the changes in Sabina, he watched Gustav walk abruptly away from Brigitte, observed the exchange, and then saw Gustav lead her toward the music at the far end of the hall, where many of the guests were already waltzing to the sounds of Johann Strauss.

He was still staring after them when a voice sounded beside him and a hand laid itself on his arm.

"Perhaps *today* I might be able to interest you in conversation, Mr. McCallum," said Brigitte, flashing him a smile even he could not refuse.

Matthew turned, smiling a somewhat awkward greeting.

"Without my cousin here, *surely* you could find some time for me," she added.

"I honestly didn't mean to be rude."

"Just that you found farm talk more interesting than me," she said, turning on her pout.

Matthew laughed. "I'm sorry, it really wasn't that at all."

They continued to chat lightly, but even as they did, Matthew's eyes were following Sabina's movements with Gustav.

He was surprised to see that she had hardly changed at all.

And yet, as he continued to observe her, he realized she had changed tremendously.

What a fascinating face she had! One moment she looked like the fun-loving child he had ridden with on horseback, the next moment she was a grown woman. The long dress of pale green was highlighted with fresh flowers at her waist and also in her light hair. It was one only a woman of poise and sophistication could wear. At the same time her face was so lively with expression.

Meanwhile, Otto had seen his brother and now approached. The two shook hands and visited amiably for a while.

Seeing Otto with the man he assumed to be his brother, Emil Korsch excused himself from Göring and slowly approached.

"Otto, my friend," he said with a wide smile, "this must be your brother you were telling me about."

"Yes, it is, Herr Korsch," replied Otto, a bit more nervously than he could hide. "Meet Baron Heinrich von Dortmann. Heinrich, may I present Herr . . . uh, Herr Emil Korsch, who is with—"

"I am delighted to make your acquaintance, Baron," said Korsch quickly. "Otto tells me you live just across the way," he added, cocking his head slightly.

"That is correct, Herr Korsch," said Heinrich, in a friendly tone. He didn't need Otto's perspiration and jitters to tell him this was a dangerous man. But his trusting nature always assumed the best about every man or woman he met. Although he saw through the veneer of social situations, he tried to give each individual the benefit of the doubt—even those whose motives he had reason to suspect.

"Was yours the estate I passed as I came along the road?"

"Yes."

"The one with the empty flagpole?"

The baron nodded.

"Are you unsupportive of our Nazi cause," asked Korsch, with a hint of bite in his tone, "that you do not display the black and red of the swastika, Baron?"

Off to the side, Otto was doing his best—with winks and facial gestures—to signal his brother to walk warily and guard his words. Unfortunately he only managed to appear as though something had become stuck in his eye.

"I'm afraid I do have other allegiances, Herr Korsch," replied the baron candidly.

The Gestapo agent did not even attempt to mask his surprise, or the meaning of the knowing look which spread across his face and the deliberate nod which followed it. Otto was beside himself at Heinrich's foolhardy words, terrified that he would say still more, but constrained by fear for his own skin not to interrupt. He stood by, listening in mute horror at the grounds his idiot of a brother was giving the Gestapo to throw them all in prison at will!

"*Other* allegiances?" he repeated with quiet incredulity. "Higher allegiances than to your Reich and your Führer?"

"I'm sorry, Herr Korsch," said Baron von Dortmann, smiling. "I love my country and I am a loyal German. But he is not *my* Führer. I have but one master."

"And who might that be?" queried Korsch with a smile, astonished at the baron's open and frank sedition against the Reich.

"My master is Jesus Christ, Herr Korsch."

Korsch smiled again, this time with the superior air of one speaking condescendingly to a child.

"Come now, Baron," he said, doing his best to swallow his revulsion at the small-minded superiority fanatics such as this espoused, "we are all good Christians here. But we are also good citizens, good Germans. Surely you agree with this one you refer to—I will use the term myself, just for the sake of discussion—this one you call your *master*, who himself said we are to render to Caesar what is Caesar's."

"I do not merely *call* him my master, Herr Korsch. Jesus Christ *is* my master."

As the baron said the name, between his thick lips Emil

Korsch's teeth clenched in hatred and unconsciously both hands, which he held at his side, clenched into fists. He managed to maintain his outward composure, however, sufficiently to continue on with the conversation.

Otto, meanwhile, was on the verge of a coronary at the dreadful turn of the discussion. Korsch was likely to double or triple the fee for his silence! How could Heinrich be such a fool! Couldn't he see that this man had Gestapo written over every inch of his pockmarked face and greasy skin?!

Slowly, by degrees, he began distancing himself from his brother, keeping an eye out for someone whom he might legitimately move across the floor to greet and speak with, leaving Heinrich and Korsch to themselves.

As he glanced nervously about, his eyes fell on Countess von Schmundt as she made her elegant descent down the wide stairway into the Grand Hall. This was the moment she had been waiting for! She swooped down into the room with full ceremonial triumph, to scattered adoration and applause, as her husband strode forward, took her hand, kissed her lightly on the cheek, and then began making renewed rounds of greeting, introduction, and well-wishing.

Marion watched the display with compassion, grief in her heart for what her old friend had allowed herself to become.

After some time had passed, she approached the hostess.

"Hello, Ingrid," said Marion. "You look lovely tonight."

"Thank you, Frau von Dortmann," replied the countess, with noticeable formality, vouchsafing not even so much as a condescending smile.

"Everything looks so nice—the flowers, the decorations—it's very elegant."

"It is very kind of you to notice," rejoined Ingrid, still stiff. "Be sure to partake of the refreshments. The best caterer in Berlin prepared them. Now, if you will please excuse me," she added, "I must see to my other guests. There are many important men and women here from the city."

With a flourish of her dress, she spun around, leaving Marion standing in the middle of the floor alone. Ingrid had intended to snub her, and thought to herself that she'd pulled it off rather well, judging by the look on Marion's face. She smiled smugly

with satisfaction, then floated away toward a group of fashion-
ably attired military wives.

In truth, she had only succeeded in grieving Marion further.
The expression that followed Ingrid was one of pity, not offense.

After a moment or two, Marion returned to where her
husband and the Gestapo agent from Berlin continued to discuss
the implications of spiritual loyalty to God and country.

"Yes," Baron von Dortmann was saying, "I believe with all
my heart in rendering to caesars and Führers alike all that right-
fully belongs to them."

"One might easily interpret your words otherwise, Baron."

"I do my best to be a good citizen. And I think of myself as a
loyal German," rejoined Dortmann. "The allegiance of citizenship is one thing, the allegiance of mastery is another."

"Mastery?"

"The latter is not something that belongs to Caesar, nor that
any human caesar may legitimately and legally require."

"Legally? The ruler of a nation may legally demand whatever
is his will."

"I use the word in its spiritual sense, Herr Korsch. I speak of
universal 'legalities,' as I call them, that are inherent in the created
order of things, by the design and intent of our Maker. I will make
no mere mortal my master. Such complete submission I will give
to none other than him who is my Lord and Savior."

Getting the information he needed was going to be easier
than he had imagined, thought Korsch to himself, fists still
clenched. The imbecile was playing right into his hand! He
could have this man arrested on the spot as a madman! If only
he could keep his own calm long enough to find out the information he had come for.

He took a breath to still the fury such words aroused in him,
then decided he should wait no longer. The time had come to
turn the conversation more toward its point.

"Being so outspoken, then, Baron," said Korsch after a slight
pause, "you undoubtedly are acquainted with another man of
similar persuasion, who has spent a good deal of time in this
region."

He paused, looking directly into the baron's face. He would

use his full powers of discernment to detect whether the
banker's brother was lying to him.

"A certain fellow by the name of *Bonhoeffer*." As he slowly
said the word, one of his eyebrows cocked itself up in menacing
interrogation.

"Dietrich Bonhoeffer?" said the baron.

"Yes, I do believe that's his name," said Korsch with sly innocence.

"Yes, I am acquainted with Dietrich," said the baron.

"You call him by his given name—the two of you are . . .
friends?"

"Yes, I would perhaps say so. Not intimately, but I have
heard him speak a number of times, and I visited him at his
seminary when he was down near Stettin."

"Ah, you must mean at Finkenwalde."

The baron nodded.

"That was an illegal seminary, Baron. Perhaps you were not
aware. It could have been dangerous for you to be seen there. If
that information should fall into the wrong hands . . ."

He let his voice trail off with obvious meaning.

"Hmm, no, I didn't know it was illegal," said the baron. "I
understood it had been closed by the authorities, but that was
all I knew."

At last the baron was growing aware that the man's line of
questioning was purposeful and not altogether of innocent
intent. He feared he had already said too much, and as much as
it went against every fiber of his being, he realized he had to
exercise greater caution. He was not worried for himself, but
there were many others whose safety he needed to think about.

"Have you seen your friend Bonhoeffer recently?" asked
Korsch casually, at last reaching the apex of his intent.

"Actually, no," replied the baron, relieved that the question
was one he could so easily answer with complete honesty.

"When was the last time you saw him?"

"Let me think . . . it was at the time of the closing of
Finkenwalde, and that would be, what?—a little over a year and
a half ago."

"And you've not seen him since?"

"No."

"Nor heard from him?"

"No—wait, you're right. I'd forgotten. I saw him in February of last year, only briefly. He was on his way south."

"Where?"

"To Göttingen, I believe."

"Yes, I was aware of that trip," said Korsch, hiding his vexation. That trail had been stone cold for a year and a half! "And you've heard nothing since?"

"Not a word."

"The two of you are friends, and you know nothing of his whereabouts?" snapped Korsch, too abruptly. The veneer of his casual interest nearly snapped, but he hastily retreated to conceal his error. "Excuse me," he said with oily aplomb, "that is, it only sounded odd to me when you said it, though I am certain there is a logical explanation."

"I have been an admirer of Pastor Bonhoeffer's," said Heinrich. "I have listened to and read his treatises on the Scriptures. But we have not corresponded personally."

"And his political inclinations?"

"Neither have I followed whatever political activities he may be involved in. I do not know where he is at present and have neither seen nor heard from him in all that time. To tell you the truth, Herr Korsch," he added with a laugh intended to poke fun at himself, "I do not follow politics all that closely."

Korsch took in the words with mingled suspicion and irritation, his training and nature telling him not to believe them for a second, and yet realizing they were probably true.

Somehow this man in front of him seemed incapable of lying to protect himself, and, illogical though it was, the fact made Korsch hate him all the more.

∽ 45 ∽

Renewed Friendship

After enduring two tediously long waltzes with Gustav, Sabina excused herself and sought refuge temporarily with her mother. The boy with whom she had grown up had become so pompous and preoccupied with himself that she scarcely knew

him. How could they ever have been such friends, she
wondered. And how much less believable did it now seem that
there had been talk of their marrying!

Oh, how I wish things weren't so awkward, Sabina said to herself.
She wished she could just leave and go home right now!

Almost identical thoughts had been flowing through
Marion's mind about Ingrid, and both mother and daughter
were saddened by what they felt.

Why was Gustav so intent on making a fuss? He refused to
accept the fact that however close friends they might have been
when they were younger, such times were past.

After a few minutes of reassuring talk with her mother, however,
Matthew McCallum approached. Immediately Sabina's face lit up.
It was so good to see him! She hadn't anticipated such a reaction of
pleasure deep down inside. He looked so much more grown-up, so
like a man! And the look on his face told her without any doubt
that they could start up their friendship immediately where they
had left off. Suddenly it was like no time had even passed.

"Hello, Frau von Dortmann. Hello, Sabina," said Matthew as
he walked up. "It's so good to see you both again."

"We've been looking forward to your visit with us."

"Thank you, Frau von Dortmann," he replied, turning to
Sabina. "I've been waiting for a chance to say hi to you," he
said. "You've been . . . pretty much tied up out there." He
nodded toward the dance floor.

Sabina reddened with embarrassment. "Oh, that," she said.

"Who is he, anyway?"

"Our neighbor, Count von Schmundt's son. I'd rather not
talk about him—we were children together, that's all."

"Would you . . . uh, like to dance?" asked Matthew, not without some awkwardness. Suddenly the suave maturity gave way
to the nervous teenager.

Sabina smiled. "I'd love to," she said, relieved to be with
Matthew before Gustav caught up with her again.

The young man and woman moved out onto the dance floor
to the melodic strains of Strauss's *Geschichten aus dem Wienerwald*.
Being so close to one another, and at a high-society function like
this—he in a tuxedo, she in a long gown—suddenly each seemed
to realize, though neither would have said so, that there was

more flowing between them than the mere frivolity and fun of friendship they had enjoyed together two years before. They were both so happy to see one another that they could hardly stand to be in such a stuffy and artificial environment. How much better to have been outside somewhere, though just being with each other was enough. It began to feel extremely warm.

"It's been a long time since your last letter," said Sabina.

"Yeah, I'm sorry I didn't write more often."

"Me too."

"I'm not a very good waltzer," said Matthew.

"Nonsense," rejoined Sabina. "I would say you're very good."

"As good as your neighbor friend?"

"Well, in all fairness, Gustav is an expert dancer. But I'd ten times rather be with you."

"You look very nice today," said Matthew. "I hardly recognized you." He stopped himself almost immediately and got a sheepish look on his face. "Well, actually," he said, "I recognized you the second I saw you, because I'd been looking at every face for yours. I mean, all I was trying to say was that you've grown and . . . oh, good grief, I don't know! You just look nice, that's all."

Sabina laughed. "Thank you, Matthew."

It is so nice to be with someone who isn't trying to impress or put on an act or show, she thought to herself.

"And you look quite the dashing diplomat yourself," she said merrily. "I shouldn't think it will be long before you are representing some United States president abroad yourself!"

"Don't I wish!" rejoined Matthew. "But to tell you the truth, I'd much rather be in a different garb and in a different place."

"Oh yes," exclaimed Sabina, "like in a garden?"

"Right! Or on horseback."

"Or romping through a pinewood!"

"Anywhere but in a tuxedo!" groaned Matthew.

"Diplomats can't hate tuxedos."

"This one does."

"How about . . . in a dungeon?" suggested Sabina playfully.

"Perfect! *Has* your father found the dungeon yet?"

Sabina laughed.

Never, thought Matthew, *have I heard such a beautiful laugh.*

"No, but he keeps looking," answered Sabina.

"I haven't forgotten that you promised I would hear the old legend of the place next time I came for a visit."

"I intend for you to hear the whole thing! How long can you and your father stay?"

"I don't know. I think two or three days."

Gradually they relaxed as they danced, hardly noticing when the music stopped. Another piece began and he took her in his arms again.

"Oh, *Morgenblätter*—it's one of my favorites," said Sabina as they started up once more.

Suddenly they found themselves brushing by Gustav, who was leading Sabina's cousin across the floor somewhat recklessly.

"If it isn't my provincial cousin," said Brigitte, laughing but with a sarcastic tone.

Sabina did her best to ignore the comment.

"Now, now, my dear," chided Gustav loudly, "don't speak ill of my future wife."

Matthew saw Sabina's face turn bright red. It was not the red of embarrassment but rather of anger. Her eyes flashed and nostrils flared.

How could he say such a thing . . . and in front of Matthew . . . in front of everybody? fumed Sabina.

Matthew tried to steer Sabina away from them, but Gustav kept himself and his partner close by. The smell of wine was evident about his presence.

"Oh, Gustav, she's only a country innocent. She's not nearly woman enough for you."

"You may be right, Brigitte," said Gustav, sighing and drawing his hand to his chest with affection. "But what can I do? The alliance was sealed when we were children, and the young thing is madly in love with me."

Sabina could do nothing to mask her fury. *How dare he!* she thought.

Matthew saw that his partner was about to explode. He stopped the dance, took her hand, and pulled her away. Obeying his lead, but in a fury of indignation, Sabina followed him, but not quickly enough to keep from hearing Gustav's voice behind them.

"Though perhaps I will have to reconsider *my* pledge to her," he said loudly, "*if* she continues to consort with American enemies of the German Reich. Ha! ha! ha!"

His wine-induced laughter was followed by the sound of Brigitte's, and the two danced merrily away in the other direction, Matthew and Sabina exiting through one of the open side doors into the fresh air outside. Matthew had heard the words too and was now warm inside on account of his own anger.

"What was that all about?" he asked. "Is it true what he said about you and him?"

"Of course it's not true!" rejoined Sabina heatedly.

"You're not engaged?"

"No! Our mothers just talked of silly things when we were young, and Gustav knows it irritates me."

"He does seem like rather a rude fellow."

"He's more than rude. If you only knew . . . "

"Knew what?" said Matthew, suddenly feeling very protective.

"Oh, I don't know . . . nothing I can say for certain. He's just gotten . . . a little spooky as we've grown. I don't like the way he looks at me. He comes around at odd times, sometimes even hangs around outside a long time without ringing the doorbell."

"That doesn't sound good."

"Sometimes I even get the chilly feeling he's watching me."

"It's a good thing, then, that your room is on the opposite side of the house from this villa. Even if he had a telescope he could never see you from here."

"I'll tell you one thing, I would never go down into the cellar of our house with *him!* He frightens me sometimes."

∽ 46 ∽

Outburst

One more waltz followed. Then the music stopped, and the sound of Countess von Schmundt's imperious voice raised itself above the din in an attempt to secure quiet. At last she succeeded.

"Meine Damen und Herren . . . bitte . . . " she said. "Today is a very special occasion. . . ."

Matthew and Sabina turned, standing now not far from the countess, who proceeded to make her brief speech in motherly, though somewhat pathetic, recognition of her son's twentieth birthday.

Gustav himself stood patiently at her side, too far gone with liquor by now to mind the embarrassment of a doting socialite mother whose better days had passed her by. He stood as erect as his tipsy frame was capable of, smiling in the adulation of her lauding words.

"And so, all you dear friends who have come to celebrate with us, won't you join me in singing a birthday toast to our dear and wonderful Gustav?"

Cheers and shouts went up, the loudest from some of Gustav's rowdy friends as they began to sing:

> *"Viel Glück und viel Segen*
> *Auf all Deinen Wegen,*
> *Gesundheit und Frohsinn*
> *Sei auch mit dabei."*

After everyone sang, Count von Schmundt emerged from the crowd, basking in the glow of the limelight in almost equal measure with his wife.

"I too have a few words," he said. "Mine, however, take the form of an announcement, which it gives me great pleasure to make. As you know, the glorious Reich of our beloved Führer is dedicated to the preservation of peace throughout Europe. To this end, it gives me great pleasure and pride to announce that my son and heir, Gustav, whom we have just been toasting, will, perhaps as soon as two weeks from now, be joining the illustrious *Luftwaffe!*"

Another round of cheers and applause broke from the assembly.

With a glow of self-satisfaction, Gustav grinned widely and bowed, then rose slowly, not without some difficulty, raised one hand in the air, and said deliberately, still grinning with a stupid expression of drunkenness, *"Heil Hitler!"*

After a brief silence had again settled over the hall, he continued, "Now, Papa, Mama—it's my turn. I too have an announcement, but first—a toast!"

He raised the glass still clutched in his left hand high in front of him. Everyone waited expectantly.

"To me!" he said at last, then followed his toast with a tittering laugh, put the glass to his lips, and drained off the contents in a single swallow.

"Hear! Hear!" said one.

"To Gustav!" cried out another voice.

"To the future hero of the skies!"

"Let's hear it for the *Luftwaffe!*"

The raucous tone gave clear evidence that Gustav wasn't the only one who had had just a little too much to drink.

The brief round of toasts and exclamations gradually silenced, and again Gustav raised his voice.

"And now for my announcement," he said, by now slurring his words badly. As he spoke, he turned and walked a few steps to a nearby table, upon which sat a huge arrangement of multiple bouquets and floral settings. He reached into the midst of one and pulled out a long-stemmed, perfectly shaped, deep red rose. He turned back, though instead of resuming his position beside his mother he continued shuffling forward, still with the wide grin plastered across his face.

Suddenly, to Sabina's horror, she realized he was coming straight toward the place where she and Matthew were standing!

Had Matthew divined his mean-spirited intent sooner, he would have found a way to get Sabina away and through the crowd. But by the time the truth dawned on him, there was Gustav standing before them, with every eye in the place riveted directly on him to see what would follow.

"I would like to make a birthday presentation of my own," said Gustav effusively.

Sabina stood gaping in mute terror and fury, knowing beyond any doubt that he was speaking to her. His eyes bored straight into hers.

"To a young heiress of Pomerania very special to me," he intoned in a voice that, though serious, Sabina knew for the mockery it was, "who has been the only love of my heart . . . all the years from my earliest youth, up to the present moment."

He hesitated but a moment longer, then handed her the rose.

"This, my dear Sabina," he said, "should seal the union of our estates."

He paused but a second for effect, then added, "And as you know . . . *the darker the red, the deeper the love.*"

Muted *ahs* and quiet exclamations of wonder spread through the women in attendance, who were well aware of the significance of the symbol and the drama that was actually playing itself out before them.

The countess didn't know what to think. Marion and Heinrich, in a distant part of the hall, did not become aware that their daughter was in the middle of a horrifying situation until it was too late to help without aggravating it further. Emil Korsch watched every move of Gustav's, gloating inwardly, with meaningful thoughts and possibilities flying through his brain.

Sabina stood like a statue of stone, her face alternating between the red of mortification and the white of wrath at his presumption, cruelty, and gall.

Still she stood, not moving a muscle, refusing to take the offered rose in front of her.

It took Gustav, in his condition, a second or two to realize that, though he'd intended to make a fool of Sabina, in her refusal it was very quickly he himself that was looking the idiot. The anger of alcohol, always as close to the surface as its merriment, began instantly to rise, and the natural bravado of his egocentric nature came forth.

"Take it, Sabina," he said, with some insistence in his tone.

The statue continued to stand before him.

"Take it!" he demanded.

The air was pregnant with suspense.

He moved yet a step closer and tried to force it into her hand. Then, as she still did not so much as twitch a finger to lay hold of the thornless stem, Gustav took hold of her hand and, holding the rose along with it, drew it toward himself and made an attempt to kiss it. She tried to pull her hand away from his lips, but his grasp grew tighter.

"Come, Sabina," he said, trying to make light of her refusal, "let us dance before my father's guests."

He turned and called out over his shoulder to the ensemble, "Another waltz!" then made as if to lead Sabina toward him to the open floor.

There was a deathly silence. Even the musicians had been spellbound by the tense drama unfolding before them.

Finally Sabina came to herself, and in a forceful and deliberate motion yanked her hand away from Gustav's clutch. The rose fell to the floor.

Immediately Matthew took her hand and pulled her a step or two through the crowd to lead her away.

Gustav was after them in a second, laying a rough restraining hand on the back of Matthew's shoulder.

"*Stop, Ame . . . !*" he demanded. "You swine—this is none of your affair! Leave my little Sabina to me!"

Sabina spun around. "*Your* Sabina!" she cried. "How dare you call me that, Gustav! And how dare you call my friend a swine!"

Without warning the forceful and undainty palm of Sabina's hand came slapping unceremoniously across Gustav's face with a loud *whack*, leaving an immediate red mark where it connected.

His eyes lit with the fire of passionate wrath at being so treated in front of so many.

He grabbed her arm, twisting it violently, and yanked her toward him. "We *will* dance, Sabina!" he insisted, "and later you will pay for your mistake!"

A cry escaped Sabina's lips from the pain of his rude grip.

The next instant, Matthew was at her side, attempting to wrest her away from the cocky and drunken young German who stood at least two inches above him.

"Look, Herr von Schmundt," he said, doing his best to be calm, "this has gone far enough. Sabina and I will leave, and you can continue your celebration—"

But in his present state, the calm words of an American diplomat's son were not the suitable unguent to Gustav's severely bruised ego.

The rest of the sentence never left Matthew's mouth.

Gustav's powerful fist came crashing into the side of his head. Stunned, Matthew staggered back a step or two. The natural fighting instinct of his own manhood suddenly awakened, he tried to shake his brain clear, then lunged forward toward his adversary. Hardly aware what he was doing, he felt his own fist crunch clumsily into Gustav's sharp jaw below his left cheek.

Gustav had anticipated no retaliation and had done nothing to defend himself against Matthew's blow. Unfortunately, it did not have the power to exorcise the demon of his anger.

Eyes afire, Gustav sprang back with a rapid parry of punches. Matthew, who had never been in a fistfight in his life, did not have a chance. He suddenly felt himself doubled over and gasping for breath from a wicked explosion against his midsection. Two more quick fists to the head, and a final vicious clout that landed somewhere between nose and cheekbone, and he toppled backward unsteadily, then crumpled to the floor.

"Take that, you American cur!" Gustav shouted, standing above him, fist still clenched and eager for more. "Yes, you can leave, when I'm finished with you! We need none of your kind here, you cowardly Americans. You're all as vile as Jews!"

By now Sabina was on her knees at Matthew's side.

"Ha! ha!" laughed Gustav. "Look at her! What did I ever see in the little shrew! She's nothing but a Jew-loving, American-loving tramp! You're no German! You're a traitor, you and your father too—the whole lot of you—traitors!"

By this time both Thaddeus and Baron von Dortmann had hurried to the scene and, within another moment or two, were helping Matthew to his feet. Thaddeus held a handkerchief to his bleeding nose, while Sabina dabbed away the blood oozing from a gash under one ear.

Gustav continued to laugh and shout anti-American and nationalistic oaths, though within another moment or two his father approached to attempt to calm him. The other guests watched the drama silently, several foreign diplomats wondering if what they had just witnessed was but a miniaturized version of events as they were now unfolding throughout the world.

Marion approached her friend and tried to speak some kind

words of thanks, best wishes, and farewell, since it was obvious she and her husband and Sabina would now be leaving.

The countess snubbed her rudely, accused her conceited and ill-mannered daughter of ruining her son's birthday and her own entry back into society, then turned her back and walked away, leaving Marion with tears rising in her eyes, wondering how someone could change so completely.

∽ 47 ∾

A Talk on Anger

Somehow the *Frühlingsgarten* did not feel the same with her spirits clouded over like they were.

Sabina had been walking the familiar pathways and trails for nearly an hour, going through all the motions of enjoying it as always, and had even clipped a bouquet of roses to take in to her mother.

But none of it could remove the fuming indignation from her breast. Her step was not light nor her pulse slow. Both kept a more rapid cadence than usual, and she could do nothing to calm them.

Her father had seen it immediately at breakfast when he had come in from the fields, but said nothing. Time was always a valuable forerunner to healing, and he would not rush whatever soothing preparatory influences the Spirit's breezes might bring.

He had more to tend to than just the harvest now in progress, or the matter of Sabina. He would have to speak with her, but first he must drive into town. Doctor Abrahams was on his mind.

Midway through the morning he returned and sought Marion to bring her up to date on what he had discovered. He then caught up one of his favorite walking sticks and headed briskly out across the courtyard, down the steps, and past the great oak. Thence he continued to wind his way down to the fields below, where he checked on the progress of the harvesting of one of the fields of wheat. Continuing on, he eventually

crossed the stream by the horse bridge, working his way gradually to the right, and ultimately found himself entering *Der
Frühlingsgarten* at its bottommost point through a narrow
opening in the tall, surrounding, green, bushy hedge not easily
noticeable to the casual passerby.

He did not know where his daughter was, or if she was still
even outside. He would stroll about and see what came. Never a
man to urge dialog unsought, the Spirit's breezes within him
and his own quiet prayerful upward communion kept Heinrich
von Dortmann attentive and ever ready for whatever and
whomever his Master had in mind.

He walked about slowly, enjoying the warm air and
fragrances of the countryside, knocking here and there a stone
from the path with the end of his stick, clipping off a spent bud
from a flower or snapping a dead twig from the branch of one
of the many miniature or flowering trees. The muscles of his
arms longed to share the work with his men. But there were
many fields yet to complete, and this growing, young, eternal
soul was the primary charge he had been given to nurture.

Eventually, as he drew near, Sabina heard him from the rose
garden and went to meet him.

They met at one of the particularly sunny and dry spots in
Der Frühlingsgarten, where, because of the protection and
warmth afforded them, the baron was able to grow a number of
plants indigenous to the Mediterranean region.

"What are you doing, Papa?" she asked.

"Savoring the day, my dear. How about yourself?"

"I am trying. But I'm afraid even the roses themselves haven't
succeeded in helping me enjoy it much."

"You are still upset over yesterday afternoon?" asked the
baron, continuing his stroll, stooping now and laying down his
walking stick in the path. On his knees, the baron proceeded to
carefully cultivate the earth around one of his prized crown of
thorns plants, gently massaging the dirt with his fingers. He had
started it from a cutting years ago and had grown especially
fond of its tiny orange flowers.

"It's getting ready to bloom again," he said, continuing to stir
up the soil, pulling out a few weeds as he did.

"Yes, Papa, but its thorns are so long and sharp and strong that I am not tempted by its blooms."

A quick contemplative look passed over the baron's brow, and he found himself wondering if his daughter's simple words mirrored all of life.

He scooted a little farther on and continued through the herb garden, abundant with parsley, and then around the trunks of the dwarf olive and fig trees, symbolically planted alongside one another. Then, rising, he walked a short distance to the small arbor of specialty grapevines and proceeded to pluck a few errant stringers.

Next to the rose garden, the area where he and his daughter now shared this solemn time was his favorite. Each plant bore a special significance. The bench they now passed he had placed here just for himself and Marion. When he came alone, he went to the rose garden. When he and Marion came together, they came here. There was nowhere on the entire estate that held as much significance for husband and wife, chiefly because of its reminder of the Master of them both and the land that had nourished him during his brief sojourn upon the earth.

At length he continued leisurely on up the hill. He was content to wait. He knew Sabina was thinking.

"Shouldn't I still be upset?" she said all at once after a minute or two. Her tone was abrupt and tense, almost as if the quiet fury boiling away beneath the surface was directed at her father.

He did not answer immediately, but continued to walk on ahead of her.

"You had every right to be angry," said the baron at length. "I was angry at Gustav myself for his treatment of you and Matthew also."

"Then why do I feel so unsettled?"

"Perhaps because you have not yet properly dealt with your anger."

"But how can I, after what Gustav did?"

"What someone else does cannot excuse our own responsibility, Sabina. Gustav's misbehavior doesn't remove from your shoulders the need to deal with this as Christ told us we must."

"How is that?"

"Surely you don't need me to remind you about forgiveness, do you, Sabina?"

"No, Papa."

"Gustav's wrong only increases the requirement on us to forgive. The higher truth is that we have been given an opportunity to allow the Spirit of Christ to flow through us. That is a far greater truth than whatever justification we may have to be angry."

Sabina was quiet a long while, obviously thinking.

"I know you are right," she said at length. "I don't like to say it," she added with an embarrassed tone, "but having to forgive someone feels like admitting you have done wrong—like I'm giving in to Gustav—and that is never pleasant."

"Well, you did do wrong," her father said, "in harboring your anger so long. Anger, held inside to fester, hurts you more than it hurts Gustav. And God knows that. So asking God's forgiveness, even as you must forgive Gustav, is no empty gesture, but a genuinely necessary prescription for your own spiritual health."

Sabina looked away.

The two were silent two or three minutes. The baron continued to stare about his garden, knowing that his daughter was conversing with her true Father, the Father of them both. Quietly he rejoiced that she was slowly learning to trust deeply and personally in her heavenly Father in her own right. He would likewise rejoice with every further lessening of the bonds of her dependence *on him*, as she exchanged them for trust *in God*. His was the prayer of the Baptist's, that whatever truth he was able to share with his daughter and others would turn those people not to him at all, but to the Savior.

He glanced at his daughter. A tear escaped from beneath her closed lids.

After a minute more, Sabina opened her eyes. They sat another five minutes in solitude.

"Thank you, Papa," she said humbly at length, with uneven breath.

"You are growing into quite a woman, Sabina," said the baron. "You are learning to look into yourself with the eyes of Psalms 51 and 139."

"Quote them to me again, Papa."

"'Create in me a clean heart, O God; and renew a right spirit within me. Search me, and know my heart: try me, and know my thoughts. See if there be any wicked way in me, and lead me in the way everlasting.'"

"I've heard them so many times, but I never tire of listening to your voice say them."

"It takes a mature man or woman to be able to pray those prayers, and mean them sincerely and openly and humbly— and to be able to respond properly and with prayerful humility, when God does reveal those black spots which we all have on our soul.

"I spoke a difficult word to you, my child. You uttered not a word of defense. The moment the truth was clear to the eyes of your heart, you took it to God in prayer and asked him to forgive you and make you whole. Such continual cleansing is the process of spiritual wisdom and maturity. I am proud of you, Sabina. You are truly God's daughter."

"Thank you, Papa. But I don't feel I deserve kind words right now. I see how wrong I was to hang on to my anger. I'm embarrassed for not behaving like you have taught me."

Again silence fell.

"I do have still one more question about it," Sabina said after a moment.

"Go on, my child."

"What about the Nazis, Papa? What about when evil is done in the world? Are we to be angry about it? They are doing evil against God's people. Does that justify what I have sometimes heard you call righteous anger?"

Dortmann sighed, and it was clear that his daughter's questions brought yet a flood of new questions to his own mind, questions he had discussed many times with the men at the fellowship.

"Ah, Daughter," he said with a sad and heavy voice. "You have asked the question that now is plaguing all true believers in this country we love so deeply. Honestly, I just don't know. I have been wrestling with it for years already. Such wrong is being done—what is to be the response of God's people? What would Jesus do if he were here among us?"

He paused and sighed deeply again.

"I saw our friend Aaron Abrahams an hour ago," he said. "He is angry, Sabina."

"Not at you, Papa?"

"Oh no—at the Nazis."

"What happened?"

"I went to his house. The windows had been broken and were boarded up. I knocked. When he appeared he did not even greet me.

" 'Go away, Heinrich,' he said. 'Go away! For your own good, for your family!'

"I tried to talk to him. I asked if I could come in. He wouldn't even let me through the door.

" 'Go, Heinrich! You are in danger—you must not be seen,' he said. 'You must forget you even know me.'

"I told him that was impossible, that he was our friend—and more than a friend.

" 'Go away, Heinrich,' he repeated a third time. 'I no longer exist for you!' And with that he closed the door in my face and would not answer it to my further knocking."

"Papa—that is terrible!"

"Yes, it is. I fear dreadful times are coming. Some may choose anger as their response. Perhaps under such circumstances it is right. But in truth, my daughter, I just do not know. What would the Master himself do?"

"What are *you* going to do, Papa?"

"I have no answers to these questions, Sabina," he said at length. "I just don't know."

∾ 48 ∾
The Red of the Rose

The morning following the party at the Schmundt villa, Thaddeus and Matthew McCallum took coffee alone in their rooms. Heidi brought them a tray of coffee and small white *Brötchen*, leaving it outside their door with a light knock. By the time they were up and about, the baron's harvesters were busy in the fields, Sabina and her father in the garden. It was late in the morning before they saw their host. The baron summoned their guests to join them in the family dining room shortly before noon after he and his daughter returned from the garden. Heidi was busily laying the table with sliced bread, cheeses, meats, butter, and jams. The smell of fresh coffee filled the room.

"I thought perhaps we might enjoy a light *Kaffee Trinken* together and then have dinner later, say around two-thirty," he said.

"That sounds fine, Baron," replied Thaddeus.

"After that I will be busy in the fields with my men, probably until dark," the baron went on. "I'm afraid that's not exactly the role of the host as I would like to play it, but when a field is ready to harvest, one mustn't wait, and rain is forecast before week's end. So we are trying to get as much of the grain under our storage roofs as possible before then."

"Think nothing of it, Baron," returned Thaddeus. "We would enjoy observing, if we're not in the way."

"Not at all. Please do! In the meantime, I have just checked on my men and they are doing fine, so I have about three hours before my presence will be required again—Matthew," he said, "you look battle-weary this morning."

The sheepish look on Matthew's face was almost as visible as the black eye and bandaged gash between left ear and cheek. His nose was red too, though the bleeding had not been serious and the baron was certain it was not broken. He wished he could have summoned Aaron to the estate to examine it but knew he would not have come unless it had been a matter of life and death.

"I don't know what it is with this place," he said. "I'm actually not so accident-prone as it must seem to you. But whenever I come for a visit—*wham!* Disaster strikes!"

They all laughed, Sabina not as lightheartedly as the rest.

"Just be happy you have such a willing and competent team of doctors, nurses, and friends standing by to help you, Matthew," said Marion.

"Well, at least I can still walk," said Matthew, sitting down and helping himself to a slice of bread as Marion offered him the tray, "though after your neighbor Schmundt plastered me, I wondered if I would ever walk *or* see again! My head was ringing with so many bells I thought I was in the middle of a church tower! He is really strong."

"Gustav is a powerful young man," said Heinrich, a cloud passing over his face.

"It saddens me to see what the count and Ingrid have allowed him to become," added Marion.

"A commentary on our nation," mused the baron. "We have allowed a bully to seize control, and now it seems there is nothing that can stop him. The effect seems to be contagious among many of our people."

"We in the diplomatic corps are still doing all we can to keep the peace," said Thaddeus, "though it is growing more and more difficult almost daily," he added with a sigh.

"Well, I certainly did nothing, diplomatically speaking, to keep the peace yesterday. I can't believe what got into me, going on the attack like that! Some diplomat I am!"

"You were just trying to protect me," said Sabina. "I don't care that Gustav did have the best of it, I can't think of anyone I'd feel safer with. I'm honored that you stood up for me."

"Well, thank you," said Matthew, "but he certainly did have the best of it. I'd have done better to try the diplomatic route."

"I doubt Gustav would have been any more inclined to listen than our Führer," commented the baron. "I fear they are cut out of very similar cloth."

"Still, I've spent a lifetime watching Dad here respond with gracious aplomb in some of the most hostile and crazy circumstances."

"I've had years of experience, my boy," said his father.

"Yeah, I suppose. But if I'm going to follow in your footsteps, I'm going to have to learn to handle things better than that. At least I shouldn't get into a scuffle unless I have an even chance of holding my own—which I sure didn't yesterday! That guy had me for lunch!"

A silence fell while everyone took a few bites of the food before them. Thaddeus found himself hoping that the incident involving his son was not prophetic with respect to the present world crisis involving the German bully Hitler . . . or, if it was, that the world community would be more able to resist his threat than Matthew had Gustav's.

"What was all that business with the rose?" Matthew asked.

Sabina reddened.

Matthew saw it, realized perhaps he'd stumbled into something touchy, then awkwardly tried to withdraw the question.

"No . . . it's all right," said Sabina. "But—don't you have the same custom in America?"

"What custom?"

"About the giving of roses . . . about *red* roses?"

"I don't know. People give roses to each other all the time, and I guess red is the most common color to give."

Sabina glanced at her mother.

"In our country, Matthew," Marion said, "the giving of a red rose signifies one and only one thing and carries with it that single, important meaning."

"What is that?" he asked.

"Red roses are given *only* between lovers," Sabina's mother replied. "The exchange of a red rose is perhaps of equal significance with an exchange of rings. It is *only* husbands and wives, or those who will soon be united in matrimony, who do so. Roses of mere friendship may be of any other color—but never red."

"So Gustav's action was more than mere rudeness?" said Matthew's father.

"Far more," replied the baron. "No one in that hall would have mistaken his meaning. It was not just in bad taste, it was insulting and demeaning. He put Sabina in a very awkward and compromising position. No man of integrity would offer a woman a red rose unless she already is, or unless he intends to make her, his wife. It had already been made clear enough to both Gustav and his parents that Sabina was not interested in marrying him, so what he did yesterday was highly offensive. You showed yourself well for standing up for my daughter. I am proud of you, and I thank you."

"It's as though the rose has a secret," said Matthew.

The baron glanced at his wife, and a special smile of significance passed between them. "We've always felt that way," he said. "That is one of the reasons we grow roses and are so fond of them. They contain many secrets, only one of which is the depths they silently speak between the hearts of lifelong lovers. Yet between two who have come to love their multitude of secrets together, the secret the red rose tells is the best one of them all."

A silence followed.

"Well, I think we've ruminated enough about yesterday," said the baron. "It's time to put it behind us! And since we're on the subject of roses, what about a walk to the rose garden and we'll see what varieties and colors and fragrances happen to be blooming."

They all got up and left the house together.

∽ 49 ∾

The Three Parents

"As much as I love your garden, Baron," said Matthew, "there is something else I have been waiting even more impatiently for."

An hour had passed. The five of them strolled all the way down to the bottom of *Der Frühlingsgarten* and back up the other side, pausing for the baron to give them a short tour of his and Marion's special place, and on to the rose garden, where they now had been sitting for some time chatting freely.

"And what would that be?"

"I want to hear the ancient legend of the house," he replied. "And now that I can walk and don't have to drag that cast around behind me, I want to see the cellar again. I want to see if I can find your secret dungeon."

The baron laughed.

"Good luck! My hat will be off to you if you succeed. I shall be eternally grateful besides. I have been searching for it for years and have finally concluded there is no such place except in the mind of dear old Eppie. Like all of Eppie's tales, there is more imagination and shadowy fable associated with it than fact."

"Can we take them to meet Eppie, Papa?" asked Sabina excitedly.

"How is she feeling, Marion?" asked the baron.

"She's doing very well. I have no doubt she would love the opportunity to try to frighten some new unsuspecting visitors—especially if we tell her they are Americans!"

"But it has to be at night . . . after it's dark, Papa!" added Sabina, hardly able to contain her anticipation.

"We'll gather with Eppie then, this evening."

"Then come on, Matthew!" said Sabina, jumping up. "Let's go explore again!"

She was already out of the garden and running up the hill.

They were children again, and like a shot, Matthew was after her. The three parents sat, listening to them yelling and laughing all the way to the house, then sat alone together in silence a while.

~~~

In the distance, two flaming eyes squinted through their binoculars and watched the proceedings from a distance, livid to witness all too clearly that happiness and gaiety still ruled at *Lebenshaus*.

It was as though nothing had happened!

He could just barely hear the high-pitched squeals of delight as Sabina ran up the hill trying to outsprint Matthew up and across the courtyard to the house.

The very sound of her merriment struck into his icy heart like a knife. He vowed yet again that the day would come when he would make her pay for her folly and for making him look the fool.

He would possess her yet!

It mattered not how long it took, years if need be. He could wait. He would make them all pay dearly for being so high-and-mighty! He would bring them down, and a mighty and painful fall it would be.

Her laughter would turn to weeping! She would beg him for mercy. She would beg to be his!

Who would be laughing then?

സ്ലൈ

"You have no idea what a tonic your daughter is for my Matthew," said Thaddeus at length, still sitting in the rose garden, out of sight of distant, snooping eyes. "He has not had many quality relationships with young people his own age. It is one of the disadvantages of my work."

"He is very mature, though, Thaddeus," interjected the baron, "which is certainly an advantage."

"Yes, he is. I am proud of him."

"I have not always been convinced that having children of similar age around is a great advantage in character development. In fact, my experience tells me just the opposite is the case."

"I see your point. And yes, Matthew is a good, solid young man. But he expects a good deal of himself—too much, I fear sometimes. Being mostly around people much older than he, and especially the diplomatic crowd where all is pretty staid and orderly and by the book, if you know what I mean, he hasn't had many opportunities to just romp and play and run free since he was quite a bit younger. I suppose I can't help feeling a little guilty myself, like I've caused him to miss some of his childhood."

"Circumstances came to your life that you could not prevent, Thaddeus," suggested Marion sympathetically.

"You mean . . . my wife?"

"Yes, her death, but also your work, your appointment here in Germany. As I look at it, it seems the two of you have not merely made the best of it you can but have made a very good thing of it indeed. You are close to each other, after all, and that is not a thing all fathers can say concerning their sons."

"Yes, and I am thankful for that. You are right."

"Still, you feel sorry for Matthew, is that it?"

"Perhaps," agreed Thaddeus. He thought a moment. "I suppose I cannot help seeing a great deal of myself in him," he added after a moment. "As I said, he sets high standards for himself—too high. He gets that from me, I think. But again, being in the circles we are, where there's such an air of sophistication and everything being just so, it almost can't be helped that he would see all this and want to fit in. Rather than just being a boy, he has striven to grow up before his time, trying to be the perfect diplomat's son, if you know what I mean."

"He doesn't seem any the worse for it," commented Marion. "He is very grown-up and personable, able to handle himself and converse very easily with others."

"Being close as we are, and being my friend as well as my son, I have taken him everywhere with me. He's been around adults most of his life and has been comfortable with it. He's been treated as older than he was and learned early to be gracious, to act as an adult would. You may have noticed that he tends to feel awkward and sheepish and embarrassed easily when the smooth diplomatic covering gets stripped away or when he feels likes he's lost control of himself or done something foolish."

Thaddeus laughed. "He didn't stop talking for months about what an idiot he felt like after falling in the pond at that garden party two years ago! He doesn't realize that everybody sticks their foot in their mouth and commits a faux pas now and then. He doesn't know how to allow for that in himself."

"He'll learn."

"That's probably my major concern, that he doesn't know when and where it's acceptable to be . . . well, to be childish and frivolous."

"He seems able to enjoy himself here," said Marion.

"That's your daughter's influence," rejoined Thaddeus. "I can see that Sabina brings out the child, the playfulness, even an impulsiveness in him. He thinks a great deal of her, but mostly he finds her fun to be with. He has told me so. She brings a part of his nature to the surface that he has never had the chance to discover before now."

He laughed again. "Though to tell you the truth," he added, "I can't help finding it humorous."

"What's that?" asked the baron.

"It's obvious that the two *aren't* children any longer. Your daughter is every inch a woman."

"And your son is a striking young man."

"Exactly," rejoined Thaddeus, still chuckling. "I can see in Matt that he doesn't know when to be a boy and when to be a man when he's around Sabina. They both are very grown-up and mature for their ages, and yet so young and innocent in so many ways. It's interesting to watch them work out the growing process while they're right in the middle of trying to figure out what they think of one another."

"I see the humor in it," agreed the baron, smiling. "It's a delightful thing to watch unfold, because of who the two young people are."

"They are rather an unusual pair," added Marion.

"Now that you've told us all this, I do understand Matthew better than before," said the baron. "I thank you for sharing as candidly as you have."

"You just can't know how thankful I am for these few times he's been able to enjoy being here. *Lebenshaus* has indeed been life-giving for my son—in no small measure because of your daughter. She is . . . well, she is quite a young lady."

"We would say the same of her friendship with Matthew," said Marion. "We too are thankful, especially after this unpleasantness with our neighbors began. . . ."

Her voice trailed off, and the sadness from what went unsaid was more than evident.

"Your son is just the caliber of young man we have hoped for Sabina to meet," said the baron, stepping to his wife's rescue. "But such come along but rarely. We too would express deep thankfulness for Matthew on behalf of our daughter. She will have a standard with which to measure other young men. Whatever your reservations, I would certainly commend you for the job you have done with him. He is clearly a young man of principle and integrity and fiber, and such qualities are not ingrained by accident. You have given him more of the mettle of manhood than perhaps you are aware."

"Thank you, Baron," said Thaddeus humbly. "You are very kind."

There was a pause. It was the American who broke it after a few moments.

"Do you mind if I ask you a question?" he said. "About your daughter—yet, I suppose, not only about her, but concerning your whole way of life here?"

"Not at all," replied the baron. "I would be honored to attempt to answer any question you might have."

"All right," said Thaddeus. "Here it is: How are you preparing your daughter for a world that, it is all too clear, may not be pleasant? All this here—it seems too perfect, too serene, too idyllic. Don't get me wrong—I love it here at *Lebenshaus,* as I have said, and it has been so wonderful for Matthew. But don't you fear that, if the worst does come, perhaps your daughter will be ill equipped to cope with it because she has been so completely protected from the harshness and cruelties of life?"

The baron nodded as Thaddeus spoke, deep lines of concern etching themselves across his forehead and becoming apparent around his eyes. He was clearly deep in thought. He continued to reflect a few moments after his friend was through, then spoke.

"You cannot know how long and hard and earnest have been our times of discussion and prayer over this very concern, Thaddeus," he said. "Marion and I have spent countless hours asking ourselves that very question in a hundred different ways, quite literally since the day Sabina was born. Haven't we, dear?"

Marion nodded.

"There are times and seasons, Thaddeus," the baron said, "periods of life, now for one thing, now for another. God gives seasons of serenity at certain times, often with the purpose of preparation for difficulties that lie ahead. It is a mistake, in my view, to think that only hardship prepares one for hardship. There is, of course, a sense in which that is true. But there is another sense in which serenity is of equal strengthening value.

"Take growing plants, for example, such as any of a hundred we could examine around the garden here. Nurturing a tender young plant in a greenhouse early in its life, and then exposing it to the harsh winds and frosts of winter *could* kill it. On the other hand, if the years of its early life are such that its roots go deep and its stalk and trunk and branches grow strong and vital, then it becomes a plant of such virility that it will flourish under any adverse circumstances. So the greenhouse yields two very different possibilities of result.

"Likewise, imagine a tree having grown from a seedling high on the slopes of a rugged, rocky mountain where all nature did her best to destroy it. If that tree survives, it will indeed be tough and sinewy and hardy, able to withstand most anything. Yet most such seedlings die on those fierce slopes before reaching maturity. Those that do survive are usually dwarfed and deformed and never shaped and fruitful as they might have been had they spent their early years in a more protected environment.

"So which is the best way to grow a healthy and vibrant plant, Thaddeus," laughed the baron, "in the greenhouse or on the mountain slope? Both contain inherent risks."

"You do enjoy making the earth's growing things into your object lessons, don't you?" said McCallum, joining in his laughter.

"If you only knew!" added Marion. "Positively *everything* in the mind of this husband of mine comes back to roots, soil, plants, and God's creation! He *loves* to find the lessons of nature for everything else in life!"

The baron roared with good-natured laughter to hear his wife talk about him so.

"I confess to every word!" he said. "She's absolutely right, I do love it."

"I have the distinct feeling you're not talking about plants, though, Baron," said Thaddeus.

"What are children but tender, growing *live* things?" asked Dortmann in reply. "I happen to be a strong believer in giving all things that grow a strong and healthy beginning in the protected environment of the greenhouse. Figuratively speaking, of course."

"Please, explain what you mean more specifically," said Thaddeus.

"Let me give you an example," replied the baron. "When I travel to Berlin to find a certain new specimen for my garden here, or to purchase seedlings, or when I visit one of my many horticulturally enthusiastic friends around Neidersdorf to obtain a cutting or start of some plant I want to try, I go to extreme lengths to give that plant all the help I can to make sure it begins its life in a healthy manner. Whatever strength it will carry with it throughout the remainder of its existence depends on the help I give it in its first year or two. What I must do mostly at first is protect and shelter it from all sorts of effects that would kill it if left to itself—snow, frost, wind, pests, various fungi, rabbits, deer, snails, and so on. I am extremely protective of my young plants, and often I cover them with small shields until they are well under way. I also fertilize and prune as needed. I spare no effort during the critical first two seasons."

The baron paused, glancing toward the sky in the east.

"Do you see those dark clouds off in the distance, Thaddeus?" he said.

McCallum looked, then nodded.

"From the smell of it, and the feel of the breeze that kicked up about twenty minutes ago, I can tell they are moving this way. There will be rain on the ground under our feet by this time tomorrow. I guarantee it. Possibly a severe rain. And if I had any plants or cuttings I had recently put in the ground, I would this very afternoon take necessary precautions to protect them from getting blown about too much, or the topsoil washed from them.

"You see, it's all a matter of getting their roots deep into good, rich soil so that the growth of stalk and trunk and stems and branches and leaves above ground is vital and healthy. Without deep roots, and if outside influences continually come to eat and destroy the first tender green sprouts, a long and healthy and productive future is doomed.

"I happen to believe that the same thing is necessary in the matter of one's children.

"*Roots*, Thaddeus!

"Roots must be nurtured carefully so that they extend deep into good soil. At the same time, pests and winds and frosts and snails must be kept away so that the first tender shoots of life have sufficient protection to grow strong as well."

"There are many who would disagree with such a parallel," suggested McCallum.

"Yourself?"

"Not necessarily. Frankly, I've never thought about the things you're saying before. But I do know everyone would not agree with you."

"I run counter to the prevailing notions in most things, Thaddeus," laughed the baron. "Of course, you are correct—not only would *some* not agree, I would go so far as to say *most* would disagree with the whole notion of greenhouses as being appropriate for children. But then all you have to do is look at a young man such as our neighbor Count von Schmundt's son, and you see all too clearly the results of a plant's being allowed to grow in any and all directions its sinful nature sees fit, without sheltering, without fertilizing, and without pruning. I feel sorry for the young fellow. In a way it is not really his fault," sighed the baron. "The tenders of his garden, I fear, let him go to seed early, and they are all now paying the price."

"What about you, Frau von Dortmann?" asked Thaddeus. "Are you of one mind with your husband?"

"Of course," answered Marion. "But then my family background is such that these concepts are not unusual nor—"

She stopped suddenly, as if having said something she should not have.

"I . . . I don't understand," said Thaddeus. "What kind of family background?"

Marion glanced at her husband.

"If you don't mind, Thaddeus," the baron said, "the subject is a ticklish one."

"I am very sorry. Forgive me."

"Think nothing of it, Thaddeus," said Marion.

"In any case," the baron went on, "such was the Father's way with his own Son. To insure Jesus' protection and nurturing, his Father chose the most godly woman of the time, young Mary, to act as his greenhouse, so to speak, to shield him from all that could thwart the Father's plan. If such was the Father's way, it is the example I for one desire to follow."

"But how long is such to last with children, Heinrich?" asked Thaddeus.

"Jesus remained at home with his mother for thirty years, so I suspect it is longer than most people realize."

The baron paused, then grew reflective. "As parents concerned for our daughter," he said, "we struggle frequently with this question. One can never anticipate everything that lies on the horizons of life. It has been our hope and prayer that by providing a serene life for our daughter, as you said to begin with, and by giving her an environment where there is a minimum of conflict, internally, so to speak, that she will be strengthened within herself to face the external conflicts that will come upon her later in life.

"It is exactly how I tend my garden. In a larger way, it is this very foundation upon which the ministry of *Lebenshaus* is built—by the peacefulness and serenity and harmony of our internal relationships and lifestyle and even this country setting we are blessed with, we are able to offer a retreat and peacefulness to others whom God sends us.

"There have been times we have wondered if we have created an unreal world for Sabina here. Will she be able to deal with life's stresses and conflicts and heartaches when they overtake her, as they inevitably do everyone? We don't have the answers to all these questions."

"Yet this is exactly what we set out to do in the beginning," said Marion. "We desired to show Sabina what life and relationships were *supposed* to be like, how they could and should function in an ideal setting, in order to, as my husband has said, give her the roots and strength necessary when later trials come. You come to know the *true* and the *real* by being surrounded by it, not by going out into a world where *false* values and *wrong* attitudes and *shallow* relationships are the norm."

"I have always felt that the way to be strong for battle was not necessarily to be a fighter yourself but to be a person of courage down inside," added the baron.

"So how long *do* you intend for the process to last with your Sabina?" asked Thaddeus, after a pause.

"Ah, you've put your finger on the most difficult question of all, my friend! Plants and children both must gradually be allowed to grow on their own, by degrees. With children it takes many, many years, steadily allowing more and more of their life to come from their own roots rather than from parental influence. Fertilization of those roots must, of course, continue, and even after twenty years there remains much nurturing to be done. Witness our own two—they have well-established root systems and are growing independently. Yet both are still children in so many ways. They are flourishing—tall and strong and hearty—yet the full maturity of their adulthood has not yet come."

"It approaches rapidly, however," said Thaddeus.

The baron sighed. "Adulthood always approaches more rapidly than we think," he added.

∞ 50 ∞
Corridors High and Low

Meanwhile, as their parents conversed in the garden, Sabina and Matthew had been running from one end of the cellar to the other, laughing and still in full flight of the chase.

Sabina had flown up out of the garden, across the courtyard, through the kitchen door, through the long corridors, into the south parlor, down the stairs into the cellar, and all the way along the narrow corridor—Matthew on her heels every step of the way—and into the empty cellar room at the far north side of the house. There she collapsed on the stairs that led up to the guest *Stube*, laughing harder than she ever had in her life. He had just caught up with her, and now he leaned back against the stone wall next to her, laughing equally hard himself.

"How can you run so fast?" Matthew asked breathlessly.

"I know the house like the back of my hand," Sabina replied.

"I'll have to get you back outside in the open!"

"I used to pretend I was escaping from bad people trying to get me," Sabina went on, recovering her breath. "Actually," she laughed again, "I used to pretend I was escaping from Gustav—I'd forgotten all about that, till just now!"

"Does he know about all this down under here?"

"Oh no, I never brought him here to play."

"Why not, if you used to play down here?"

"I don't know, something just told me I shouldn't. I guess I never thought about that either. I just . . . didn't bring him down here. He knows nothing about it."

"How about all the secret places upstairs?"

"What secret places?"

"Up on the top floor?"

"They're not all that secret, just mysterious."

"Did you and Gustav used to go up there together?"

"No, not much . . . I don't know, I can't remember—that's been so long ago. I'm sure he's been on the balcony, but I don't recall ever going through the rest of the second floor with him. We mostly played outside when we were small. My parents liked to be around when we played together."

They were silent, both still breathing deeply. Then Matthew began to wander around the small room.

"Just like I remember it," he said. "Even the earthy smell . . ."

He glanced around the small room, eyes falling on the stone or brick indentations on the interior wall where a few broken pots stood.

"Hey," he said, "look up there! A great place to hide a key to a secret room or hidden dungeon!"

"Matthew, your imagination is running away with you!"

"No, come on—I want to look."

He strained on his tiptoes but still could not see over the top of the ledge.

"Come here," he said. "Stand in my hands."

Matthew knelt down, pulled Sabina's foot toward him, and cupped his fingers into a makeshift ladder rung. "Come on, stand on my hand and I'll hoist you up to see if you can see anything."

Sabina did so, peering and feeling about and shining her light toward the corners, discovering nothing but dust and dirt.

"Aw, shucks!" said Matthew. "I know it's around here somewhere."

"Matthew!" laughed Sabina. "I tell you there's no key!"

"Well let's go find the dungeon without it then!" he said, leading the way back into the corridor under the house.

"I tell you, it's no use," said Sabina, getting up and following him. "Papa's been over every inch of these walls, up and down both sides of the hall all the way from one end of the house to the other."

"Then how about the floor . . . or the ceiling?" suggested Matthew, inching his way along the dark, damp, dirt corridor, scanning here and there with his eyes.

"The floor?" repeated Sabina.

"Sure, maybe there's another level down below this and

there's a trapdoor over the stairway all covered over with layers of dirt."

Sabina laughed.

"Dungeons are always deep down in low hidden cellars," said Matthew. "I bet that's it! The dungeon's below us!" Immediately Matthew fell to his hands and knees and began digging with his fingers in the dirt.

Sabina continued laughing.

"You are silly, Matthew! There's nothing there but dirt. Even if there was something to find, you would have to go over every centimeter of the whole corridor to find it."

"Do you have a rake, or a shovel or hoe? If we started from one end and worked our way to the other, digging down a few inches, I'm sure we'd find a trapdoor somewhere."

As he spoke he continued to dig about.

"Hey, what's this!" he exclaimed, digging now more furiously. "I've found something!"

Sabina knelt down beside him and looked.

"Feel right there," he said, taking her hand and guiding it into the dirt where he had been digging.

"It's nothing but a big stone," she said after a moment. "See . . . here are its edges." She pushed at the dirt, and after a moment her efforts yielded the outline of an irregularly shaped rock buried in the earth below.

"All right, all right, maybe the trapdoor's not right *here*," said Matthew, standing up. "But I bet there's one someplace!"

"I'll tell Papa your theory," laughed Sabina. "In the meantime, he won't want the whole floor dug up. Come on, let's go to the top floor. I want to show you the rooms up there again."

"And the armory?" said Matthew, following her.

"If you like!"

She ran on ahead, then stopped.

"Here's the stairway up to the guest bedroom, where I fooled you last time," she said. "Let's go up here."

He followed. They entered the room of his earlier convalescence, then made their way along the main hallway to the west stairway, which they then took all the way to the second floor. Matthew followed Sabina first to the armory, then to the east wing of the house, where they ran and hid, laughed and explored, and chased one another about until two-thirty and time for dinner.

Both declared upon entering the dining room, disheveled, hot, perspiring, laughing, and still talking freely, that they had not had so much fun in years.

Matthew had completely forgotten the wounds on his face.

∽ 51 ∽
In the Harvest Field

Immediately when they were through eating, the baron excused himself.

"I must go see if those oats are ready for me," he said. "This is one of the most difficult of all our fields to harvest—next to the wood, quite bumpy, and with many stones. The *Mähdrescher* is such a temperamental beast, if something goes wrong or we pick up a large rock by accident, I would rather it be me that does the damage than one of my men."

The moment the door was closed behind him, Marion added, "My modest husband is, in truth, the most skillful harvester east of Berlin. He knows the field is a difficult one and knows that he is more likely than any of the men to get through it without a breakdown."

"He does a great deal of the work around here himself, doesn't he?" said Thaddeus.

"A very great deal," replied Marion. "Far more than most people realize. He makes no show of it, but he is the reason our farm is so profitable year after year. He is up at dawn every day. He is a very skilled agriculturalist, as well as other things."

Before Thaddeus had the chance to ask Marion what she meant, Sabina rose to follow her father.

"Come on, Matthew," said Sabina. "Let's change clothes and go to the fields. I want to show you what they're doing. I think Heiko and some of the other men are pressing straw in the wheat field Papa finished harvesting yesterday morning before the party."

"Pressing straw?"

"Yes. Making it into bales for the cows. Papa has a brand-new baling machine. It's so clever what it does with the straw on the fields."

They left the house, while Thaddeus and Marion engaged in a fascinating discussion—mostly about the baron and his very interesting past.

The field of ripe oats lay some distance from the house. The baron had ridden by horseback, while Matthew and Sabina went on foot. By the time they arrived, therefore, he already stood high on his perch, dust and chaff flying in his face, aboard the clattering, gigantic, metallic spider called the *Mähdrescher* as it went raking and clawing and cutting and clanking through the tall stalks of grain behind the tractor pulling it.

Sabina's father waved to the two young people, but then quickly returned his hands firmly to the controls. He had to mind what he was about. Matthew could see immediately that the field was indeed an uneven one, and the contraption seemed so rickety and had so many moving parts that he scarcely imagined it being able to hold together for an hour.

In mesmerized fascination, they stood and watched the baron make two complete passes of the long rows of the field, then Sabina led Matthew farther on, to the wheat field beyond, which now lay reduced to stubble sticking out of the earth, strewn with the remnants of straw left behind after the combine had done its work.

"There they are!" shouted Sabina, pointing across the field. "Heiko and Hans are pressing the straw into bales—let's go!"

She took off across the stubbly field, and Matthew gave chase. He caught her, and they ran side by side across the vast former wheat field, until they arrived at the scene of today's labors. A tractor pulled another of the baron's new mechanical devices, a smaller clattering, clanking, spidery apparatus, which was in turn attached to a flatbed wagon that was pulled along behind.

Sabina fell in immediately with the three men present, one of whom drove the tractor in front, another who walked alongside hoisting the bales of straw as they fell from the baling machine, up to the third man perched precariously on the bed of the slowly moving wagon. It was clearly rigorous work for just two men to keep up with the progress of the tractor, for the bales came more quickly than they could easily get them off the ground and stacked neatly on the wagon.

It was not hard to tell what was to be done. As the tractor continued to pull the baler and wagon along, Sabina clambered up onto the half-full wagon, jumped to her feet, and began helping the man already there to stack the bales ever higher as they continued to be tossed up from the ground. Observing for a moment, Matthew easily caught on and began helping the fellow on the ground with the bales as they came tumbling out onto the ground from behind the machine.

The next time he looked up, Sabina was alone on the back of the wagon. She shouted at him to climb up.

"Where'd the other guy go?" he said, hoisting himself over the edge of the wagon as it bounced slowly across the dirt field.

She pointed to his retreating form already halfway across the field.

"He's going to get another empty wagon and to see if Papa needs any help with the oats. There are several fields in progress right now, so the minute any extra help shows up, they put you to work and go on to something else."

Suddenly a bale from the ground flew up, knocking against the side of Matthew's legs, sending him sprawling across the bales onto his back.

"You won't be much help to me up here if you can't keep your feet any better than that!" laughed Sabina.

"I didn't see it coming."

"Watch out—there's another one!"

One more bale tumbled onto the wagon beside them.

"What do you want me to do?" said Matthew, climbing to his feet.

"You stand here, and when Hans tosses them up, you bring them back to me. If you can set them at my feet, I'll be able to stack up the back of the wagon without having to go back and forth."

"Sounds simple enough."

"As my pile moves, though," said Sabina, "you'll have to adjust your position too—look out!"

Another bale tumbled up.

"Hey, these things come fast!" cried Matthew.

"And they get heavier and heavier as the day wears on, as your fingers get rubbed raw from grabbing them by the twine. We should have brought gloves! Oh well . . . grab it and toss it back to me."

Matthew did so, beaming with satisfaction, while Sabina placed the bale in place. By the time Matthew turned around, another bale was already at his feet. He reached down, laid hold of the twine, took two or three steps to place it at Sabina's feet, and turned again just as another bumped into his knees.

"Did I forget to tell you that they keep coming and coming, seemingly faster and faster?" laughed Sabina. "You've got to be ready for them."

"I'll try!" shouted Matthew.

Within five or six minutes they had completed the third layer across the entire bed of the wagon, and at the back end Sabina began with the stacking of the fourth. Gradually Matthew discovered the secret of using the momentum of the wagon and his own body weight to toss the bales with less strain on his arms.

"You look like you've been doing this for years!" Sabina called out to him. "I had the feeling you were a farmer at heart!"

In less than an hour the wagon was full, seven layers high. By that time Heiko had returned with another empty one. They all stopped, unhooked the full wagon, attached it to Heiko's tractor, hooked up the empty flatbed, and were ready to begin piling up another load while Heiko pulled the full wagon, slowly and carefully, back to the barn.

The driver of the tractor ground it into gear once more, and again the baling contraption, followed now by an empty wagon, lurched across the field. Soon the bales were flying again, and Matthew and Sabina busily stacked them in place.

Just as the first level neared completion, the machine hit a snag and stopped. The two men proceded to investigate the problem. Matthew stood watching, then all of a sudden found himself sprawling again onto the row of bales. The laughter behind him told clearly enough that the bale that had sent him flying had been intentionally thrown.

"Hey!" he called, turning around. Scrambling to his knees, in one swift movement he leapt forward, threw his arm around Sabina's ankles, and yanked her feet out from under her. With a cry of laughter she fell onto her back.

Now the fight for supremacy began in earnest, as first one, then the other found themselves knocked, tripped, or shoved off their feet. Laughing so hard they had to struggle for breath, neither could maintain their legs under them long enough to gain control. At last, both Sabina and Matthew stood, facing each other as two wrestlers, circling about, hands poised in readiness.

All at once the wagon lurched forward again into motion. Both toppled over backwards in a heap, giggling like children. A moment later, Hans tossed a bale onto them.

"Hans, you did that on purpose," laughed Sabina, struggling to climb to her feet.

The old field hand, who had been with the estate for more years than Sabina was old, smiled up at the two with the look of a prankster gradually spreading over his own face. Their playfulness made the work more enjoyable for him, and the rest of the day's work proceeded at a slower, though hilarious pace.

At day's end, with the baler off and the tractor proceeding slowly across the field back toward the house, Hans sitting on the edge of the wagon behind it with his legs dangling over the edge, and Matthew and Sabina perched high and triumphant on the topmost bundles of straw, the baron saw the returning workers from the middle of the field of oats. He shut down the combine, climbed down, and walked forward to meet them.

The driver of the tractor stopped. The baron glanced up at his daughter and her young friend, examining Matthew's brown, dust-smeared face, his puffy eyes made red from the wind-tossed chaff, his sweat-streaked neck, and the shirt and jeans coated from top to bottom with grime and dirt and bits of straw. He smiled and jumped up himself, giving the signal to Friedrick in the tractor to continue on. He climbed up and sat just below his daughter.

"Your father would be proud of you, Matthew," he said.

"Sabina warned me it would be hard work."

"You should have seen him, Papa. He's so strong he threw the bales around like they weighed no more than a feather."

Matthew laughed.

"Don't lie to your father, Sabina!" he said. "You handled them more easily than I did!"

Now it was her turn to laugh.

"What do you think of our farming life, Matthew?" asked the baron.

"It is hard work, but I don't think I've ever had such a satisfied feeling, even with my arms and legs so tired, in all my life."

"You are right," returned the baron. "It is a satisfying life, like no other. But now we have to make sure we get all the day's grain and straw under the roofs before the rain."

"What about the *Mähdrescher*, Papa?"

"I'll come back for it. I never miss a chance to ride back on top of a wagon piled high with straw. It's the best part of the whole harvest!"

Laughing and talking together, they continued on back to the house.

∽ 52 ∾
Old Eppie's Tale

Later that evening, though weariness from the day's work was keenly felt in the muscles of more than one of the bathed and scrubbed bodies present, the baron and his wife and daughter gathered with their visitors in the guest parlor. With them was the most special guest of all, the servant who had lived at *Lebenshaus* nearly longer than the baron's and his wife's ages put together. She was known affectionately to family and staff simply as Old Eppie. Hearing that foreigners were in the house, and having received a personal invitation from the baron to join them for tea and cakes in the evening, her eyes were already aglow, and both Heinrich and Marion knew it would take very little prodding for tales out of the past to begin flowing from her ancient tongue.

The atmosphere for the occasion was rendered all the more

suitable in that the black clouds from the afternoon had continued to approach, engulfing the entire north of Germany by the
onset of evening, threatening severe thundershowers certainly
before morning, possibly by midnight.

Once they were all seated and suitably introduced, Marion
and Sabina served small plates of cakes and tea.

"We've told our guests, Eppie," said the baron, "that you've
lived here longer than any man or woman alive."

"Longer than any man or woman *should* be alive!" rejoined
Eppie in a shrill tone that was followed by a cackling laugh.
"But you've been good to me, Baron," she added. "Though you
could have put me away years ago, you keep me like I was
family, just like you did my mother before me."

"You *are* family, Eppie," laughed the baron. "But I'm afraid it
was my grandfather who saw to your mother, not me."

A brief look of question passed over the grizzled countenance.

"You didn't know my mother, then, Baron?"

"No, Eppie. She may have known me, but I'm sorry to say I
did not have the pleasure. She died when I was five, I think it
was."

Eppie was silent, brow still crinkled in bewilderment. In
truth, it would have been impossible to distinguish the furrows
of confusion from the wrinkles of age. Her cheeks, forehead,
neck, and chin were crisscrossed with such a multitude of inter-
secting lines and folds and crinkles of white skin that one could
not help thinking she bore some resemblance to the reptilian
species. She still possessed an abundance of hair—though it
had thinned considerably and her scalp was visible—every
strand of it white as her skin and most of which stuck nearly
straight out from her head as if she had just seen a ghost, which,
in truth, was more often than not precisely the case.

"Were you here for the premier's visit, then?" she asked,
suddenly in a very faraway tone.

"I'm sorry, Eppie," said the baron. "Whose visit?"

"The premier's—Bismarck . . . of Prussia."

"When was it?"

"I must have been ten or twelve at the time," she said, doing
her best to make her brain work clearly. "My mother will

remember . . . we must ask her. Yes, Bismarck was here—when he was fighting against the Austrians it was."

"He was always fighting against the Austrians, was he not, Eppie?" said the baron.

She chuckled. "A fighting man, he was—that's what the old count found out soon enough!"

"The count? What count, Eppie?"

"The count from next door, who else!" As she spoke her eyes grew wide, and the baron knew she had been transported back in time to some era long before. But as many times as he had heard Eppie's tales from the past, he had never before heard of a connection between Bismarck and ancestors of the Schmundt clan, if that was who Eppie was even talking about. He had heard her allude to Bismarck upon occasion, but never so directly.

"He was a spy for the Austrians, though his blood was Prussian. But Bismarck found him out and dispatched him through the heart with his sword, the very sword hanging up there."

She motioned feebly with her hand, indicating the floor above them. They were, in fact, directly below the armory.

"Where did it happen, Eppie?" asked the baron.

"In the dungeon, where else? He found the count hiding out, right behind our very walls! He snuck in from the fields, into the cellar, down the two corridors—it was the dead of night when he came—and there he plotted mischief against the baron and against all of Prussia. But Bismarck discovered his hiding place, secret though it was to all but the baron, and he threw open the door, and there was the count. 'Prepare to breathe your last, traitor!' shouted the premier, and the next instant the evil count lay dead, his blood soaking into the dirt floor of the dungeon, and Bismarck standing above his evil corpse, drawing out his sword and wiping the blood on a towel that lay on the table in the center of the room."

Eppie stopped, breathing heavily, eyes still wide as the saucers under the teacups of her listeners. The room was quiet as death.

Suddenly a tremendous crash shook the house.

As if in one accord, everyone jumped straight up out of their chairs and the hair on nearly every arm stood out as if suddenly charged with an invisible current of electricity.

The baron smiled. "It would seem the thunderstorm has arrived earlier than I expected," he said.

Flashes of lightning could faintly be seen through the door that stood open to the corridor, from windows at its end and the guest rooms opposite. More echoes of thunder sounded.

"Go on, Eppie," said the baron.

"The dungeon was never used again," she said, "though the chancellor checks it every time he comes."

"The chancellor—I thought you called him the premier."

"He was made the chancellor later, after the defeat of Austria and the unification . . . you should know that, Baron."

"Ah yes, Eppie—I had forgotten."

"You must call him the chancellor now—times are not what they once were."

"I understand."

"He has his dignity to maintain, Baron."

"He has been here again?"

"Oh yes, I saw him recently. He always checks to make sure the wicked count is still dead. Sometimes he takes me, so that someone in the house will know the count's whereabouts in case he tries to cause more trouble. He is a traitor, you know, a spy. He wants the estate for himself. And there's the gold, you know, as well."

"The gold?"

"The cache from the Prussian vaults, spirited away for safe-keeping during the Prussian war. It is still here, Baron."

"Where?"

As she spoke, Eppie's voice lowered to a whisper, and she raised her hand to her mouth so that no one but the baron would hear.

"Somewhere in the dungeon."

"Have you seen it?"

"No, he never showed it to me."

"How do you know it is there?"

"He told me he had hidden it safely until he would need it again. Then he would let me know."

"Then what?"

"We would dig it up together."

"I see."

"He said—"

"Who, Eppie?" interrupted the baron.

"Otto, who else . . . von Bismarck—he allows me to call him Otto sometimes."

"Go on—the gold?"

"He said some of it goes as far back as to be part of the missing Hohenzollern treasure from the days when Albert of Brandenberg created the duchy of Prussia. That was years ago, you know, Baron, during my grandmother's time, I believe."

In truth, the duchy of Prussia was created in 1525, easily three or four generations before the construction of the present house and three hundred years before Eppie's grandmother's day.

"And the count is after the gold, you say?" asked the baron, speaking in hushed tone as well.

"Oh yes. He lusts to possess it all—the gold, the estate, all the land of Pomerania. He always has. The baron would have had to kill him eventually, but Otto discovered his treachery first, an even greater treachery to all of Prussia, and had to kill him."

"Do you know where the dungeon is located, Eppie?" asked the baron.

"Of course, don't you?"

"I seem to have forgotten, it has been so long. Could you take me there?"

"Of course," replied Eppie, trying to rise immediately out of her chair. "You will have to bring a light, Baron," she said. "It is exceedingly dark, you know."

"Yes, that much I do recall about the place."

The baron glanced around at the others, now all wearing expressions of anticipation and looking out of eyes as wide as Eppie's own. Then he rose, gave Eppie his hand, assisted her in getting to her feet, and said, "Here, Eppie, take my arm. I will lead the way as far as I am able, then I will let you take the lead. Marion," he added, turning to his wife, "if you will fetch us a candle."

The others all rose quietly, no one breathing a word lest they break Eppie's spell, and followed the baron and Old Eppie from the room. They slowly made their way to the grand staircase, down to the ground floor, and to the south parlor. There the baron gingerly and with sturdy strong hands assisted Eppie down the old stone stairway. This was more than anyone had expected, and even the baron could hardly contain himself over a hope that perhaps the legends were true after all! She seemed to possess her wits and from occasional comments knew very well where they were going.

In another ten minutes the small group stood in the dark underground corridor directly below the south parlor.

It was with an eerie feeling of ghostly reminiscence that Matthew walked along the darkened passageway behind Sabina, who, behind her father, trailed the ethereal figure of Old Eppie, carrying a candle which lit up her wild white hair and appearing in almost every detail the exact personification of the ghost in his dream of two years earlier. He could hardly believe this whole reenactment wasn't a new dream, yet the soft voices of his father and Frau von Dortmann whispering behind him confirmed otherwise.

Almost at the precise place he expected, suddenly Eppie stopped.

She turned first to the right, then to the left, seeming to expect to find an opening.

"The door . . . it should be . . . " she mumbled, though he could barely make out her words.

She handed the candle to the baron, then proceeded to feel about the walls, obviously growing confused.

The baron spoke to her, but without effect. She took the candle and continued on, more hesitantly now, still glancing back and forth as if expecting to come upon an opening. At length they all reached the end and gathered into the empty, earthy cellar room at the north end that Sabina referred to as the icehouse.

Confused, Eppie continued to glance about.

"This is not the dungeon," she said. "The table should be there—"

As she spoke she pointed with her finger.

"And the body of the count has been moved . . . we must tell the chancellor. The traitor may be on the loose again! We must tell him, Baron!"

"I'll see to it, Eppie," said the baron. "I'll make sure word gets to him tomorrow."

"And the gold—it must be guarded, for the sake of the Prussian empire! The Austrians mustn't be allowed to find it! Nor the count. He is an evil man . . . they are all evil, the count and the Austrians!"

"We will take precautions, Eppie," assured the baron. "But it is late now. I think it is time we were all returning to our rooms for the night."

He took her gently by the arm and led her back the way they had come.

Once Marion had seen Eppie safely to her room and was assured she was resting comfortably after the excitable state her mind was in, she returned downstairs to the *Gute Stube*, where the baron had taken the others. As she entered they were still discussing Eppie's remarkable tale about Bismarck's visit to *Lebenshaus*. They had heard snatches of the story previously, but never in quite so complete a narrative.

Fifteen or twenty minutes later, a few yawns and glances at watches were sufficient to bring the unforgettable evening to a close. It was quite late.

The five friends rose and slowly climbed the grand circular staircase together. The baron and his wife turned left, Thaddeus McCallum to his right, toward their respective rooms.

"Thank you for everything, Heinrich . . . Marion," said Thaddeus.

"Good night, Thaddeus," returned Marion.

But Sabina was not quite ready for the evening to end.

"Matthew," she whispered, "come with me!"

With a look to his father as if to say, *I'll be back in a minute or two . . . I think!* he followed Sabina down the corridor to the right, past the guest rooms. He followed as Sabina climbed the library stairs.

Emerging next to the armory, she led the way along the silent darkened hallways into the mysterious east wing. As the corridors narrowed, he fell into step close behind her. Neither said a word. In a few moments, Matthew knew exactly where they were.

Sabina stopped.

She turned and faced Matthew. The small light she held in

her hand was just barely enough that they could see one another's faces.

"This is one of my favorite times and favorite places," she said. "I've come here alone so many times, but have never had anyone to share it with. But now . . . I can't think of anyone I would rather share it with . . . than you."

"I am honored," said Matthew seriously, looking deeply into the eyes he could only barely make out in the darkness. It was perhaps good that there was not more light, for both of their hearts were pounding inside them, and the expressions on their faces would probably have revealed more than either knew they wanted to tell.

Already Matthew suspected why they were here, for he could hear an occasional peal of thunder behind the door in front of which Sabina stood.

Just a moment more she stood gazing into his face, then she turned and opened the door.

The sudden rush of the stormy midnight greeted them with all its windy fury.

They stepped out onto the balcony.

The storm had continued its westward move, but occasional lingering flashes of lightning, followed now by distant rumbling, continued. The wind was fierce, and huge pellets of rain slammed down onto the stone floor of the balcony with such force as to be audible.

"Stand here!" shouted Sabina above the din. "With your back up to the wall on the side of the door. See, you won't get wet!"

Matthew obeyed. They stood side by side for perhaps five minutes, saying nothing, enjoying the fierce display of the elements.

"But the storm is moving toward us," said Matthew all at once. "Why is the wall protecting us against the rain? The wind should be blowing the other direction."

"I asked Papa that once," returned Sabina. "It is something about the circular motion of the wind within the storm blowing one direction on the ground, while higher up in the atmosphere the whole storm is moving in the opposite direction. I don't understand it, but here it is . . . whatever the reason—we're dry like this!"

Again they stood, side by side, both their hands beside them.

Unconsciously, with neither having intended it or attempted to initiate it, Sabina suddenly found her hand creeping slowly inside Matthew's, and Matthew found his large palm closing about the tiny soft dainty thing inside it.

For several more long minutes they stood, feeling more quiet bliss and happy contentment than ever before in their young lives. Both could have stood there all the night long. In the innocence of their love as friends first, and brother and sister second, the whole world was for them right here, right now. They were oblivious to the crises and wars and threats all around them. Gradually they even grew oblivious to the storm.

Suddenly, able to contain her exuberant joy no longer, Sabina leapt away, regretting her impulsiveness the moment she did, for another such moment at Matthew's side might never come again. She ran several steps out into the middle of the balcony and cried out:

"Oh Matthew! It's just so wonderful! I'm so happy! *Whee!*"

She tossed her head back into the driving rain, threw her hands into the air, and yelled with childlike abandon and glee.

Matthew was at her side in a moment, and the two of them spontaneously danced an impromptu little jig in the rain, spinning and twirling, then stopping to stand in the downpour, both laughing in sheer pleasure and delight.

Gradually the mood subsided.

Still the rain plummeted down onto their heads. Slowly they walked toward the door, both drenched to the skin, and made their way back through the quiet corridors to their rooms.

"Good night, Matthew," was all she said, when they paused outside his room.

He looked deep into her eyes again. She returned the gaze. It lasted but a second.

"Good night, Sabina," he said.

He turned and went inside, and Sabina continued on down the hall to her own chamber.

The storm was mostly gone by morning, and midway through the afternoon, Thaddeus and Matthew returned to Berlin.

∼ 53 ∼

The Coming of War

Three days later, Sabina found herself awakened before dawn with a vague sense of anxiety. Her sleep had been filled with dreams, though formless and strange, and she remembered nothing. When she awoke, suddenly, even though she had been only partially asleep, it was with the fading of a far-off sound in her ears.

She glanced outside. It was still dark. *It must be another thunderstorm,* she said to herself. Immediately her thoughts turned to Matthew.

Wide awake, she leapt out of bed, dressed hurriedly, and ran out into the corridor.

There was only one place she wanted to be at a time like this. If she could not actually share the special moment with Matthew, she could at least think of him while she enjoyed it. Two or three minutes later she ran out onto the balcony, which looked east. Sabina was oblivious to the date.

It was the first day of September. The year was 1939.

There was no rain this time, and the air was warm. Sabina sucked in large gulps of it, cleaning away the last of the haze of her fitful night. Curious, she thought to herself, there was no wind either. The morning was calm and still. Yet far in the distance to the east, more occasional thunder could be heard. She thought she saw tiny flashes of light too, but they didn't look like lightning.

Slowly Sabina walked around the edge of the balcony, the grey light of dawn now beginning to show itself in the distance where the storm was.

She returned to the door, then leaned back against the wall, remembering the stormy night here with Matthew and how peaceful and good and warm she had felt all over.

She stood there a long time, dreamily turning many things over in her thoughts. When she came to herself she realized it was no longer dark. It was still early, but light enough to see out across the rural landscape. The orange glow of the sunrise had begun to gather itself along the horizon.

Something was wrong.

The sky was cloudless and clear. Above the approaching sunrise, the pale blue of what promised to be a warm summer's day was beginning to show itself.

Still the thunder sounded, more frequent now, Sabina realized. But where were the clouds . . . where was the storm causing it?

And there was more wrong than just the cloudless dawn. The sounds were wrong too!

Gradually Sabina became aware that more and different sounds could be heard—deep rumbling sounds, as of the movement of huge equipment coming from somewhere south of them. And overhead she now realized planes were flying.

Though all the scattered and distinctive noises were muffled and in the distance, the quiet dawn had become filled with forebodings of terror.

Sabina's heart began to pound violently within her breast.

It was all wrong . . . very wrong!

A chill swept through her body, and suddenly she felt very young again, alone and vulnerable . . . and afraid.

She turned and ran back through the door, flying through the corridors and down to the first floor. She did not even stop at her own room but burst straight into her parents' chamber at the corner of the wing.

They were not there!

Sabina glanced around in panic. The door to the sitting room she shared with them stood open. She flew to it.

The sitting room, too, was empty. She saw her mother and father through the window, standing on the balcony. Calming, she walked toward them from behind.

Her father had his arm around Marion's shoulder, holding her close to him. They both stood, still in their nightclothes, motionless, gazing, as their daughter had been, at the portentous events unfolding before their eyes and ears in the distant east.

Sabina approached and stood at her father's side.

Slowly he stretched his other arm around her and likewise drew her toward him. They were silent, and neither moved their head.

Sabina followed their gaze for a few moments, then glanced

up toward them. Silent tears streamed down the faces of both
her father and mother.

She watched their mute expressions for several long minutes.

"But . . . what *is* it, Papa?" she asked at length. "What does it
all mean?"

The baron did not answer immediately, but continued to
stare across his fields and toward the distant sounds. The high-
pitched drone of an airplane somewhere in the sky not far away
came to their ears, then gradually receded toward the east. An
explosion sounded, coming from the same direction, but they
could see nothing.

A moment of silence followed, and it seemed the peaceful
dawn of a late summer's morning had returned.

At length the baron spoke.

"The dark midnight of our history approaches, Sabina," he
said solemnly.

His words filled her with a chilly feeling of dread. "I . . . I
don't understand you, Papa."

"What you hear, my daughter," said the baron, "is the sound
of guns, tanks, planes, and bombs—war. My guess is that our
Führer has sent his army to invade our own people, our own
Prussia."

"*Invade*, Papa?" said Sabina in astonishment.

"I believe Poland is being attacked," said the baron. "Within
days, I have no doubt, like Austria before her, Poland will no
longer exist, but will be consumed and swallowed up by the
German Fatherland."

∾ 54 ∾

Heart-Wrenching Offer

Heidi knocked at the Baron's study to inform him that there
were visitors downstairs.

"But I'm expecting no one," he said, rising and following her.

He went to the waiting room, shocked to see Thaddeus and
Matthew McCallum standing there.

The look of joy on the baron's face as he greeted his friends was quickly dampened by a corresponding expression upon Thaddeus's countenance that told him he was bearing evil tidings.

"It is not good, my friend," he said. "I would have called or written, but as things now stand, I feared doing either could put you in danger."

"Nonsense, Thaddeus, you are my friend!" said the baron.

"The world has changed, Heinrich. All is changed overnight. If you do not fear for yourself, I *do* fear for you."

"You did not come to tell me that," said the baron.

"No, I bring news that was inevitable under the circumstances . . . I have been summoned back to the United States."

"No!" exclaimed the baron. "When?"

"I'm afraid immediately. We came," Thaddeus said, glancing at his son, "to try to implore you to come with us, you and your family. It is still not too late. There are ways . . . I have connections that would make it possible."

"But . . . but, Thaddeus . . . what are you saying? How could we leave?"

"Otherwise, Baron, I am afraid our visit is for a most unpleasant purpose . . . to say good-bye."

The baron motioned his unexpected guests to two chairs, then slumped into one himself opposite them, a devastated look on his face from the blow of McCallum's words.

It was exactly two weeks since Dortmann and McCallum had seen one another. Great Britain and France had formally declared war on Germany on September 3, followed by Australia, New Zealand, India, South Africa, and finally Canada.

The dawn invasion two days later of the German *Luftwaffe* sliced into Poland in a dozen places—through East Prussia, Pomerania, Brandenburg, and Silesia—and was aimed directly at the heart of Poland. A million men—forty-seven divisions, nine armored divisions, and fifteen hundred planes—were mounted for the surprise and treacherous assault. The Polish forces were hopelessly outmatched, and resistance collapsed within a week.

The Second World War had begun.

Though the United States would officially remain neutral for more than two years, realistic neutrality was impossible. McCallum and much of the rest of the diplomatic staff had been summoned back to Washington for high-level meetings, briefings, and discussions.

"When do you leave, Thaddeus?" asked the baron at length.

"In two days. But seeing you, and trying to persuade you to come with us, has been one of the highest-priority items on our agenda—speaking for both my son and myself. That is why we drove out here at the absolute soonest possible opportunity."

Again Baron von Dortmann was silent and thoughtful. He glanced down at his watch. He was obviously moved by their concern and care.

"The day is already well advanced," he said. "You will stay the night?"

McCallum nodded. "But we must be off again for Berlin in the morning. We fly out the day after that."

"Then we must make use of every possible minute," said the baron, rising. "I will find Marion and Sabina. Why don't the two of you go down to the *Gute Stube?* We'll meet you there shortly and discuss this all together."

He disappeared from the room.

An hour later the five friends were deep in thought. The baron had told his wife and daughter of McCallum's offer to take them out of the country before the ugly prospects of the war overtook them.

Thaddeus had been bending his best diplomatic eloquence to the task of persuading his friends that it was in their best interest to leave Germany, if not for the United States, then for England or Switzerland.

"But . . . this is our home, Thaddeus," each of the three Germans had said, in a dozen different ways. "Our home, our country, our people."

"Don't you realize what is at stake?" the American had implored.

The baron and his wife looked at each other. Their expressions seemed to say that they did know, perhaps even more intimately than they could let on, exactly what the cost of remaining in Germany might be.

"People are going to die—perhaps millions," Thaddeus continued. "I simply do not want you dear friends to be caught up in the terrible conflict that is sure to come."

A heavy silence descended over the room. All present knew that destinies and futures hung in the balance. The dilemmas and decisions facing them were heart wrenching, as would be their parting, if such was indeed inevitable.

"I have just learned," said the baron in a low tone, "something of the whereabouts of our friend and Christian brother Dietrich Bonhoeffer. The information only came to me days ago. I thank God I did not possess it when interrogated at the count's by that fellow who was intent on finding him. What I have learned is that Dietrich is back in Germany, after a long absence."

"Where was he?" asked Thaddeus.

"Initially in England, then in the United States," answered Dortmann. "But he has recently returned. He has said that he decided that he must live through this difficult period in our national history with the Christian people of Germany. Even above his own personal safety, he feels compelled to remain here with his people."

The baron paused, then added, "He is a courageous man, and I feel such is my calling as well. We may be able, in some way, I know not how at present, to help God's people endure this time of darkness. God may have a work for me to do here, among my people."

"Won't you reconsider, then, on behalf of your wife and daughter?"

The baron glanced at his wife beside him.

"It may become . . . dangerous," he said softly, " . . . especially for you, my dear. I would rest easier if I knew you were safe and—"

"Heinrich, please," Marion interrupted. "We have been over this already many times. You have already tried to persuade me to go, and my answer is still the same. I belong at your side, and that is where I shall remain. I too am a German, whatever else I may also be, and I have no wish to leave my homeland."

The baron nodded. He knew it was no use trying to change her mind.

"The work God gives us may be to my wife's people as well, Thaddeus," he said. "She would not allow me to carry out that work alone."

He paused briefly.

"Sabina," he said, glancing across the room toward his daughter. "Matthew and his father have offered to take you with them—it would only be for a time, until the danger is past. You have my blessing to accompany them. I would like you to, in fact, though your mother and I would miss you desperately. We would make any sacrifice to see that no harm comes to you."

"Thank you, Papa," said Sabina.

"But you are eighteen now, and this is a life-changing decision . . . one I must leave in your own hands."

"Will you come with us, Sabina?" asked Thaddeus.

"I . . . I don't know," she answered. "I will need time to think and pray."

"The time is short," said Thaddeus. "Events are closing in upon us."

∾ 55 ∾
Testimony of Urgency

That evening, after they had eaten supper, Baron von Dortmann requested that the five gather together again.

"I've asked you here," began the baron after they were seated, "for some extremely important business—to share something with the two of you, Thaddeus and Matthew, that is of vital significance, because its impact upon you is even greater than this war which has broken out and now seems likely to engulf us all."

Thaddeus and Matthew glanced at one another with questioning looks, wondering what information the baron could possibly possess about them that was on the level of international security.

"I'm afraid I'm really a rather mid-level diplomat, Baron," laughed McCallum. "When all is said and done, my job is mostly bureaucratic. Perhaps I should contact my superiors and have you talk—"

The baron waved off the suggestion in midsentence with a chuckle and wave of the hand. "No, Thaddeus," he said, "you

misunderstand me. It is you and your son I desire to talk to.
What I have to say is of an altogether different nature than
world diplomacy. You came here to see if you could help us.
You cannot know how much your concern means to me and
my family. But now, as I have been praying for the past two
hours, it has come to me that I too have something of equal
importance that I must share, even offer to you. Since in all likelihood this will be our last evening together for a long time, it is
now or never, as they say."

Thaddeus nodded, though still not comprehending Baron
von Dortmann's meaning.

"Would either of you like some more coffee?"

Thaddeus nodded.

Marion rose from her seat next to her husband and refilled
his cup, then the baron's.

"Sabina, more tea?" she said, glancing toward her daughter.

"I have enough, Mama, thank you."

Marion resumed her seat.

A brief pause followed. Then the baron began.

"I hope you'll excuse my speaking very candidly, and, it may
be, at some length."

"Not at all," said Thaddeus. "If something is as important as
you say, I want to hear the unabridged version. We'll stay as
long as it takes."

"Good. All right then, I'll begin by affirming that I do not
believe in chance encounters. Everything has a purpose. There
are no accidents. All that is by way of saying that I do not
believe our friendship together—my wife and daughter and
myself, and the two of you—is merely coincidental."

"Nor do I, Baron," interjected McCallum. "My son and I have
been greatly enriched from knowing you—knowing you all,"
he added, looking toward Marion and Sabina.

"Thank you," rejoined the baron. "The sentiment is entirely
mutual. Which is precisely why I felt an urgency upon me to
share these deep matters with you. None of us can tell what the
future may hold. These are dangerous times. I fear the world is
approaching disaster because of our reckless Nazi leaders. The
thought causes me nothing but sadness, but it may be that we
will not see one another again, my two friends. . . . "

As he said this, the baron looked first at Thaddeus, then over at Matthew, and in his eyes there could be no mistaking the deep love he felt for both men.

"You are leaving in two days. Marion and I will remain here. Sabina must make her decision, and I know she is praying with both diligence and anguish. These are terrible times for those in whose hearts love dwells."

He paused again, struggling over the words.

"I pray this conflict will soon be over," he went on. "But if not, I would never forgive myself had I not spoken very directly to you about the very foundation of my life, of my family's life, and of all we stand for here at *Lebenshaus.*"

He paused briefly.

"I'm sure by now you realize I am speaking of our faith, of our perspective as Christians, of how we try to order our home and our life and our attitudes and behavior according to God's ways. I have been outspoken about my Christian beliefs from the outset of our relationship. We have spoken about many matters of belief together in the two years we have known one another. Though we have not spent as much time together as I might have wished, what we have enjoyed has been rich, and I feel we have come to know one another deeply and with a mutual kinship and respect."

He stopped, took a sip from his coffee cup, then sat thinking. The other four in the room waited patiently.

"I do not happen to be one who believes," he continued after a few moments, "that the calling upon a Christian is to convince others that the tenets of the Christian faith are true. There are those who make that the chief aim of their existence. They are what I call Christians of *persuasion.*

"I have always taken a different view. For many years I have felt that my duty was to *live* my faith, not persuade others as to its veracity. At every opportunity afforded me I will happily, even eagerly, give testimony as to the values and beliefs by which I attempt to live. But I do not feel it my duty to convince. Such a responsibility has not been placed upon my shoulders as a Christian. The only injunction placed upon my shoulders . . . is to *live* the principles I profess. I would hope to be able to say I have not made such an attempt when speaking with the two of you . . . have I?"

"No, I have never felt the least sense of that common persuasive element you speak of," answered Thaddeus. "In fact, you are no doubt the most gracious and sensitive man of outspoken beliefs I have ever encountered. Not only do you not push your views onto others, you seem genuinely to enjoy listening to alternative perspectives."

"I do indeed," rejoined the baron, "except when those others are fellow brothers and sisters who speak narrowly of my Father and his ways."

"You are not in the least threatened by opposing viewpoints," Thaddeus added. "I would even say you seem eager to hear them. You have always treated me with the greatest of respect, even though I have known we were in disagreement about some fundamental issues of belief."

"You are right. I see nothing whatever to be anxious about in such disagreement. Perhaps it is because I so strongly believe that all truth will in the end be known that I feel so little anxiety to right every error here and now. As if I saw clearly enough with my earthbound eyes and senses to do so anyway! It has always been a mystery to me how so many believers talk as if theirs are the only eyes in the universe, except God's perhaps, to perceive truth without distortion. But there I go off on a detour again! I apologize."

Thaddeus laughed. "I am glad to know you harbor frustrations of your own."

"Many of them," rejoined the baron. "There are such a multitude of things I do not understand. I remain very much still an eager young learner in the things of faith, believe me!"

A momentary break of silence followed.

"The point I was attempting to make," the baron went on, "was that living my faith occupies my full energies. Persuasion is not given to me. Living is. That is why we call this *Lebenshaus*. I perceive my duty as a Christian is to live as Jesus instructed and to give voice to my faith whenever I am asked. But even then only to *lay before* another, such as yourself, Thaddeus, what I believe, so that you may examine it and respond to it in your own way and in your own time. I can only say, 'These are the principles by which I try to live. They seem good to me. They have helped me come to know my heavenly Father better. I therefore commend them to you for consideration.'

"As I read the Gospels, this is the example I witness—Jesus laying the truths of the kingdom of God before his disciples and his listeners, but making no persuasive speeches. He spoke the truth, laid out the values and attitudes and priorities by which life in the kingdom was to function . . . but then he turned and left the crowd to think about what he'd said and to make up their own mind. He didn't even try to persuade his disciples, but merely kept placing the principles of the kingdom of God before them."

The baron stopped. A long silence followed.

When he began again, a subdued emotion of concern and love and urgency filled his voice. Though he continued to speak in low volume, the whole room was filled with an intensity and passion none of those present could mistake. A heavy sense of import fell upon all, and they knew, each in his own way, that the Spirit of God was in their presence.

"We now come, my two dear friends," the baron resumed, "to that point for which I wanted to speak with you before we part on the morrow. I said a few minutes ago that there was one aspect of my faith that I had not shared with you, do you recall?"

Both men nodded their heads.

"This is something I rarely say to anyone, because, as I expressed, I do not feel such is my duty. But the times compel me to do so now, and the circumstances of our friendship."

"Go on," said Thaddeus. "You need fear no adverse reaction from me."

"Nor me," added Matthew. "I am eager to hear what you have to say to us."

"You are both very open men," said the baron. "Were there the slightest hesitation on either of your parts, I would stop immediately. What I have to say now cannot be said except where the door to the heart and mind is open. Where it is not, only harm is done by speaking prematurely—sometimes permanent harm."

"Our doors are open. Please proceed," said Thaddeus. "You

have earned our respect with your life. Now speak to us . . .
please, we *want* whatever you have to tell us . . . Matt?" he
added, looking at his son.

"Yes, so do I, Baron von Dortmann," said Matthew, confirming his father's request.

"Very well," replied the baron. "I commend you both for
your openness. It is most refreshing! So . . . here it is, then.
There comes a time in every man or woman's life when to sit
back casually observing the principles and truths of the kingdom of God is no longer enough.

"There are occasional passages in the Gospel accounts when
Jesus did more than simply lay truth before his hearers. In such
passages we find Jesus looking straight into a man's face and
forcing him to confront the meaning of his life and his whole
future. They offer the example of what I mean, that such a
moment ultimately comes for everyone."

He paused. The others waited.

"You have, I'm sure, heard of the young man known as the
rich young ruler. He came to Jesus and asked what he had to do
to inherit eternal life. Jesus told him to keep the command-
ments. The young man replied that he had kept them all his
life. Then Jesus said that there was only one thing he lacked."

The baron paused, then asked, "Do either of you know what
it was?"

They shook their heads.

"You see, here is an instance where the moment of decision
had come. In this moment, Jesus looked at the young man,
loved him deeply, and then this is what he said to him. 'One
thing you lack. Go and sell everything you have and give to the
poor, and you will have treasure in heaven. Then come, and
follow me.'"

Again the baron paused.

"And . . . what happened?" asked Thaddeus.

"When such moments of decision come, there are always
two choices we can make. This young man made the decision
not to obey what Jesus said, and not to follow. The passage says,
'He went away sad, because he was very rich.'"

A long silence followed.

"Do you understand what I am saying, and why I have told

you this story?" he asked at length. "You see, Thaddeus . . . Matthew, the point I'm trying to make is not that you should go and sell your possessions. Look around—I haven't done that. God has not told me to. If he did, I would . . . but he has not. What he will tell you or me or anyone else specifically—it will be different for all of us. Different things stand in each of our ways to enter into kingdom living. For the young man in the story it was wealth, for me it may be something else, for you it will be something else again. But the point of the story is that such a time *will* come for everyone . . . including each of you too."

"Are you saying that . . . *now* is such a time . . . for us?" asked Matthew.

"Oh no, by no means, Matthew!" replied the baron. "I mean, perhaps it is, perhaps not. I could not say one way or the other. I am not the one who sets the timetables for such things!"

"Who is, then?"

"The Spirit of God, working inside each one of us. He sets the season and the circumstances and the place and the hour. He alone. And when the moment comes, he makes it known, and he speaks to the inner ear of our heart as clearly as Jesus did to his disciples as they were walking along and as clearly as he spoke the word of challenge and commitment to the rich young ruler. *At that moment, whenever and by whatever circumstances it comes, all of life hangs in the balance. The moment of decision has come. It comes to all sooner or later, and when it does, there can be no avoiding the confrontation.*

"I use that word intentionally. Though it is gentle and quiet, though he will never use force or coercion or even persuasion, that it is a confrontation there can be no doubt.

"It is the moment when he stands before us, and we before him. The Master has come, he has looked us in the eye, and at that moment, though he uses ten million different sets of circumstances to utter it, the words are always the same—*Follow me!* When those words sound in our heart, there are only two paths to take: forward into life *with* him . . . or else to turn your back and walk away.

"But you can depend on one thing—that time *will* come in each of your lives. My reason for saying all this now is so that you will be ready when it does. I want only the best for you, for

I have come to care about you and love you both deeply. Because of that I suppose I feel a certain urgency about all this, because of what the times may portend."

There was a great deal to ponder. All five sat silently for some time, reflecting on the implications of the baron's words for each of them personally.

"How do you know when such a moment has come?" asked Matthew.

"You will know."

"How?"

"He will not let you mistake it."

"What if you don't hear him?"

"He will speak again."

"If you still don't hear?"

"Then he will speak once more, louder."

"If still you don't hear?"

"He will continue to call your name. He will speak until you have heard, and until you *know* you have heard. And always the words are the same—*Follow me!*"

"Then what?" asked Thaddeus. "When you have heard and you know he is speaking to you, what do you do then?"

"That's the moment of decision," answered the baron. "*You must decide whether you are going to obey and follow him* as his disciples did when he said it to them . . . or take the sad path of the rich young ruler."

"And if you *want* to follow him, and that *is* your decision, then what do you actually *do?* How do you begin to follow him?"

The baron smiled. The words could not have rejoiced his spirit more. He knew the truths of God were taking root!

A man with less faith in his Father would have, then and there, pressed Thaddeus and Matthew toward a handful of artificially framed decisionary words of his own devising. But Heinrich von Dortmann was too much a son of his Father, and too faithful a younger follower of his elder Brother, to interfere with their work by erecting signposts of spirituality of his own construction. He would not tamper with the inner dialog between either man's spirit and the voice of his Maker by intruding himself into the center of that eternal discourse.

He would but point. They would have to walk the path individually, with only the Spirit of Truth, and the obedience of their hands and feet, to guide them.

"What do you do?" he repeated softly.

"Yes," said Thaddeus.

"Two things," answered the baron. "I can tell you in a few seconds. If you are in earnest when that moment comes, it will take the rest of your life for you to carry them out. And when you reach the end of your life, you will look back and realize that you still have only progressed past merely the first steps of beginning. But then, of course, this whole life of ours on earth is only a beginning!"

"What are the two things?"

"First, read John 3 and John 15. In those passages Jesus explains what it means to be his disciple and how to become one."

"And the second?"

Again the baron smiled.

"This is what takes a lifetime," he said. "It is simply this: *be* a disciple of the Master. How that is accomplished is quite simple really. Extremely difficult . . . yet simple. Read the four Gospels of the New Testament. Read them over and over and over. Immerse yourself in them. And as you do . . . do whatever Jesus tells you to do.

"*Every word that proceeds out of his mouth, as recorded in the Gospels, is meant for us to heed and obey.* That's all there is to it— after that moment comes when he bids you to follow, and after you make the decision to be his disciple, all you must do is obey his every word and teaching.

"*That's what a disciple does—he obeys his master.*"

∽ 56 ∽

Parting

The mood at breakfast the following morning was quiet and subdued.

The realization had deepened upon them all through the night that a painful parting was at hand. Few words were spoken. These were times that tested the mettle of character and the fiber of relationship. Everything that needed to be said had been said.

"It is with a heavy heart that I say it, Baron," said Thaddeus when the meal had been completed and they had been sitting for some time in silence, "but we must presently be on our way."

Baron von Dortmann nodded gravely.

Suddenly Sabina rose from her chair, burst into tears, and ran from the room.

The other four sat in awkward silence a moment more, then Marion began to rise to follow her. The baron gently placed a hand on her arm and glanced at her with a barely perceptible shake of the head. Marion resumed her seat.

It was Matthew who got out of his chair and left the room. The baron let him go, saying nothing. All three parents sensed that a special bond had been developing for some time between their son and daughter. Though it seemed destined to be torn asunder by the tragedy of war, the baron knew that this moment with his daughter belonged to Matthew, not to himself or his wife.

Matthew went first to his room, then to find Sabina. He made his way along the now-familiar corridors, heavy of heart. He knew where she would be.

He stepped out onto the balcony and saw Sabina at the far end, standing at the edge of the battlement, looking over the fields.

Slowly he approached, his hands held behind him.

She sensed his presence, but kept her back turned. Matthew knew she was still crying, though softly now.

"I've decided to stay," she said after a moment, her voice full of tears. "I couldn't possibly—"

"I know," said Matthew.

"But how? How could you know? I only just came to the decision a minute ago."

"I guess I just had a feeling. Maybe it's because you're so much like your father."

"I could never leave them," said Sabina, "no matter what happens."

It was quiet a moment.

Slowly Sabina turned. Her face was red. She smiled, though her cheeks were wet, and took in a deep breath to try to steady herself.

"I must look a dreadful sight," she said, coming as close to embarrassment as Matthew had ever seen her.

"You look wonderful," he replied simply.

She laughed again, regaining her equilibrium and trying to wipe some of the wetness from her face.

Now it was Matthew's turn to draw in a deep breath.

"I'll never forget you," he said.

"Nor I you."

"I've never known anyone I've enjoyed so much."

"Oh, Matthew—don't," she said, half smiling, half imploring. "You're going to make me cry again!"

"It's true, Sabina. You are one of the best friends I've ever had."

She returned his earnest look with a deep smile of gratitude.

"I brought you something," he said. "I know it's probably not so special—after all, you have them all over the place here. But . . . well, it was . . . that is, I wanted to find one that was just perfect. I went to three shops in Berlin until I got exactly the one I wanted, though I'm afraid it's starting to die."

"Matthew—what is it?" asked Sabina, laughing. "Are you going to keep me in suspense all day?"

He pulled his hands out from behind his back, and held toward her the perfect bud of a single yellow rose.

Tears filled Sabina's eyes.

She reached forward and took it from his hand. She struggled to speak, then turned aside, choked with emotion, unable to find a single word.

"There's a little card I wrote to go with it," said Matthew. He handed it around to her. Still looking the other way, she took it from his hand and looked down at it. It was a tiny slip of paper with but two words handwritten on it: *Friends forever.*

It was a minute or two before she turned back to face him.

"How dare you say it's probably not special," she said in a husky voice barely above a whisper. "It's the most special rose I've ever been given. I will treasure it—always! Thank you, Matthew."

A moment more they stood.

Suddenly Sabina brightened, took in another deep breath, and said, "And I have something for you! But it's not here. I didn't expect to see you here when I ran out downstairs. It's in my room."

She walked back toward the door into the house. Matthew fell in beside her. She led him to the sitting room off the small private balcony.

"Wait here a minute," she said. "I'll be right back."

With the words she disappeared into her own chamber, reappearing a moment later. She reached out to Matthew.

She placed within his hand a small rectangular box of bone china, some five centimeters by ten centimeters, and five or six centimeters high, with a removable top upon which had been hand painted a perfect pink rose. Matthew took it gently, lifted the lid, and looked inside. It was empty.

"My father gave it to me when I was confirmed," said Sabina. "I was fourteen. He told me to keep it empty until the day I knew the secret of the rose."

"But . . . but I could never accept this," said Matthew. "It was a gift from your father!"

"I spoke to him about it last night," she said. "I asked him, if I decided to stay here, if he would have objection to my giving it to you as a gift . . . to remember me by. He thought it was a wonderful idea."

"I told you up there on the roof, I won't forget you."

"I would still like you to have it."

Matthew stared down at the white china box in his hand. "I . . . I don't know what to say," he said.

"Say you'll take it."

"All right . . . I'll accept your gift," he said, his face suddenly coming alive with an idea. He looked into Sabina's face. "But I won't *take* it!"

"I don't know what you mean."

"I'll leave it *here* . . . with you—for safekeeping!" exclaimed Matthew. "That way—don't you see?—I'll have to come back for it! It will be my pledge, my promise to come back and visit you again . . . *and soon!*"

"Yes—yes, I see!" said Sabina, brightening, too, now that she caught his meaning.

While their parents weighed the severity of what had come, in their youthful innocence, the two young people suddenly made their parting a game, with a promise that it would not be a long one.

"I know," said Matthew. "Let's each put something inside the box—now—today!"

"Then we'll hide it."

"And open it again when I come back!"

"Oh yes, how fun!" exclaimed Sabina with delight. "Where shall we hide it?"

"It's got to be where no one but us can find it."

"No one but the two of us can know."

"In your father's garden?"

"No, somebody might dig it up."

"Somewhere in the house then."

Their eyes locked for a moment. "The dungeon!" they both said in unison.

They both laughed. "Oh, if only we knew where it was!" added Sabina.

"What about that room at the far end of the corridor?" suggested Matthew. "Where you said no one ever goes?"

"That will be perfect!" cried Sabina. "Let's go!"

She jumped up and ran from the room.

Still holding the box, Matthew followed.

At the top of the stairs suddenly Sabina stopped.

"But what will we put in it?" she asked, facing Matthew.

They both found themselves staring down at the china box in Matthew's hand with the tiny painted flower on its lid. As with one accord they both seemed to think of it at the same moment.

"A rose!" said Matthew.

"We'll *each* pick a rose . . . just the bud, without a stem!" said Sabina, then turned and the next instant was flying down the stairs, through the house, outside, across the courtyard, and down into the garden. A few minutes later, both Sabina and Matthew were catching their breath and walking slowly through the baron's many varieties of roses, looking for just the one each wanted to select to put in the china box as a seal of their friendship, and their mutual pledge to meet again.

After ten minutes they approached one another, each with a hand held behind the back.

"What color is your bud?" asked Matthew.

"I don't know, what color is yours?" Sabina asked with a coy smile.

Matthew returned the smile. "Not red," he said. "I would not want to make the mistake your neighbor did."

"Yellow then?"

"I have other favorite colors too, you know." Matthew smiled. "What about you?"

"So do I," rejoined Sabina, laughing now. "I love *all* my father's roses!"

"All right," he said, "I can see you are determined to be difficult. So . . . that will be another condition of the hiding of this friendship box. We put the buds inside in secret, and we won't see the other's rose until we open it again . . . together. Then we'll tell why we chose whatever colors we did. Agreed?"

"Agreed," said Sabina.

Matthew knelt on the ground, set down the tiny box, and took off the lid. Sabina knelt beside him.

"Now we'll both close our eyes," he said, "and put our buds inside."

They both closed their eyes.

"Are your eyes shut?" he asked.

"Yes."

"Then I'm putting my rose in the box . . . there—I'm finished. Now it's your turn."

Sabina fumbled with her fingers, found the box, and put her rosebud in it.

"Done," she said.

Still with his eyes closed, Matthew felt to see that both little flowers were inside. Then he replaced the lid.

"Open your eyes," he said.

They looked at each other, laughed, and stood.

"We did it," said Matthew. "Now let's go hide it!"

They hurried from the garden, and in a minute or two found themselves, once more, standing in the dark, quiet, earthy room under the small library with only the dim light of Sabina's small flashlight.

"Where shall we hide it?" said Matthew, glancing all about.

"Those stone shelves up there," said Sabina. "There's nothing on them but a few pieces of old broken pots."

"Somebody might see it just sitting up there."

"No, we'll stick it at the back, and it's up so high, from down here no one could see."

"I don't like it. Someone might take to cleaning this room up."

"Not without me knowing about it," said Sabina.

"Isn't there someplace that would be out of sight?" said Matthew, still looking around the room. "Why don't we try to loosen one of the stones in the wall, or even one of those shelf stones?"

"Do you think we could?"

"If you—could you go up and bring a chair down here?" asked Matthew. "If I had something to stand on, maybe I could look behind that tallest shelf there and see."

The next instant Sabina was gone up the nearby stairs, and a minute or two later was crashing back down, clumsily bearing one of the high-backed wooden chairs from the guest *Stube*.

Matthew set it in place and jumped onto it, standing on his tiptoes and peering over the ledge of stone that was built into the wall.

"I think I could loosen one of these rocks in the wall," he said, "if I had a knife or implement of some kind."

"I'll get a trowel from the gardening room," said Sabina, and she disappeared again.

This time she was gone four or five minutes, but presently returned with the instrument. She handed it up to Matthew, and he began chipping and knocking at the hardened dirt around one of the wall stones. In three or four minutes he pulled out a chunk of rock about three times the size of his fist.

"Nothing to it!" he exclaimed, showing Sabina his prize.

"Will the box fit into the hole?" she asked.

"Easily! Hand it up."

She picked it off the ground where he had set it and gave it to

him. He shoved it into the cavity in the wall, then jumped
down off the chair.

They both looked up.

"You see," said Matthew, "the ledge hides it completely. You
can't see a thing!"

Sabina jumped onto the chair so she could see the box in its
new home.

He stooped down, put the rock on the ground, and began
whacking it with the trowel.

"What are you doing?" asked Sabina.

"Breaking the stone in half," he answered.

"Why?"

"You'll see."

He went on, and in a minute or two he had chipped enough
off the rock for his purposes. He stood on the chair again,
replaced the half-stone in the front of the tiny cave he had
made, then with his fingers squeezed dirt in around its edges,
brushing and blowing at it to make it look undisturbed.

Again he stepped down.

"There," he said with satisfaction. "Even if someone was to
look straight at it, they would never see where we have hidden
the box."

"Let me look," said Sabina.

She stood up on the chair.

"It's wonderful, Matthew . . . perfect!"

She stepped back to the ground while he wiped at the dirt on
his hands.

They stood a moment looking at one another, suddenly realizing they could not prolong the difficult moment indefinitely.

"Oh, Matthew—I can't stand it!" said Sabina.

"Come on," he said cheerfully. "That's why we hid the box—
it's my promise to be back soon."

She sniffed and brushed at her eyes.

"I know."

"And you must promise that *you* won't open it until I am here
with you again," he added, in the tone of a command.

Sabina smiled, and nodded. "I won't look at the roses until
we can enjoy them together."

Again they stood, looking at one another, each with worlds

they wanted to say, but with no way to summon forth the words.

"May I keep writing to you?" said Matthew.

"I'll be furious with you if you don't!" rejoined Sabina.

"And you must answer me back."

They turned to leave.

"The chair," said Matthew.

"I'll get it later," said Sabina.

They entered the long corridor, walked it in single file silence, and presently emerged once more up the stairs into the south parlor. They found their parents out in the courtyard.

"Where have you two been?" exclaimed Marion with a laugh.

"All over, Mama—the balcony, the rose garden, and the cellar. I had to give Matthew one last look around the place."

"We've got to be off, Matt," said Thaddeus, with an urgency of resignation. "I've already brought your things down to the car."

Matthew nodded.

Handshakes followed, all around, in the stoic German tradition. The prolonged grips, however, and the accompanying deep penetrating gazes that each liquid set of eyes gave the other, spoke of attachments and emotions far beyond the ordinary.

When Matthew offered his hand to Marion, she ignored it, taking him instead into her arms and giving him the full embrace of a mother. When they stepped back, she was weeping.

They walked slowly around to the front of the house, where the car sat awaiting departure.

A few final attempted words struggled out. None seemed to accomplish their purpose. There were no dry eyes.

"Write . . . ," said Matthew to Sabina.

"I will—and you!"

"I promise."

More handshakes, looks, and sighs . . . then Thaddeus and Matthew opened their respective car doors and got inside.

"God be with you, Thaddeus . . . and you, Matthew," said the baron. "You will always be in our prayers."

The engine turned over and came to life. Slowly the automobile pulled forward, around the circle, down the winding drive, and out of sight.

Sabina turned and ran inside the house and up to her father's study. She would give her tears full vent by staring after the car until it was completely out of sight.

Heinrich and Marion, hand in hand, were already making their way to their private place of prayer and retreat in the midst of *Der Frühlingsgarten.*

Only the rearing equine sentinel of stone was left in front of the house gazing after the disappearing automobile, the fierce expression of defiance in his eyes eerily reminiscent of the dictator in Berlin, who had now challenged every nation on earth to see if any possessed the courage to stop him.

∽ 57 ∾
Prayer for Direction

The hour was early.

Dawn was abroad throughout the land, though the sun had not yet risen over the horizon.

Baron Heinrich von Dortmann, landowning farmer, German aristocrat, husband, father, and man of God, lay in his bed, eyes staring wide at the ceiling.

It was probably five o'clock, perhaps fifteen or twenty minutes after the hour. He had not looked at his watch.

His men would shortly be with the cows, and the field workers would be up for breakfast within the hour. But there were matters of weightier concern on the mind and heart of Baron von Dortmann.

He had been awakened out of a sound sleep, almost with the sense of hearing an audible voice in the room. He knew his Father had spoken to the inner ear of his spirit, bidding him rise and seek him.

Careful not to disturb his sleeping wife, he rose, dressed in silence, and, taking his Bible, which still lay open on his nightstand where he had been reading it before falling asleep, sought the chilly, damp, early-morning air.

He did not immediately go to the garden, but sought a longer route, across the stream, through the fields, and deep into the wood, before, after a long walk of quiet reflection and prayer, his steps eventually took him back toward the house.

He loved this time of the morning and always felt more keenly in tune with himself, his surroundings, and his heavenly Father when he could get out and alone well before the day's concerns and activities began to press upon him.

Though the summer's zenith had only passed five or six weeks earlier, there were unmistakable signs to the baron's senses that autumn was approaching. The pinewood contained a slightly more earthy fragrance, brought on by increasing dampness in the ground at night. The warm, summery aroma of dried pine needles and sap, warmed by the sun, had given way to the smells of dew, of moisture, of dirt, and of humus, decay, and dead leaves. He loved the smells of summer, he loved these new smells, each one intrinsic to the ongoing cycle of ever-renewing, ever-changing, ever-growing life.

He looked down as he walked. His footfalls did not make crunching noises across the dry forest floor as they did in July. The ground, now moist and soft, gave way silently to the indentation of his boots; dew still gathered on the patches of grass throughout the forest. He stopped to examine the tip of a pine branch, its rough green needles holding back droplets of water, clinging to them till the very last moment, then suddenly releasing them—one tiny, shimmering, liquid crystal at a time—to fall noiselessly to the ground.

"Oh, Lord," he sighed over and over as he walked, "what is it you have to tell me?"

He had been here before many times. He could always sense when something was being spoken to the inner ear of his spirit, though he could not always immediately discern what the message was. The voice that called to men like Heinrich von Dortmann was not a voice most mortals could hear. He had been tuning his heart to descry its peculiarly quiet, divine timbre for thirty or more years, and still the indications were sometimes so faint as to require much prayer and numerous lonely walks and many mornings of solitude before clarity was obtained. But until that translucence of supernatural vision came to him, he would make no move within the motions of his own flesh. He would go about his work as any working man must go. What had been given him to do, he would do with energy and faithfulness. Where he had not yet been given direction, he would wait.

No one would look upon his face and hear the rippling of the subterranean streams that flowed within him, bringing the essential elements of life with daily renewing *into* his soul, and carrying those same ingredients *from* his innermost being out and into the lives of those around him. Only his wife and daughter fully knew what manner of man this was who lived with them, provided for them, protected them, and helped bring out of them the full maturing of their own beings. Visible or not, his was a life lived on an altogether distinctive plane from his contemporaries of society. Truly he was a citizen of another kingdom.

"What did you want to show me, Father?" he breathed softly as he walked. "What do you have for me to do . . . what is it you want me to see . . . why did you awaken me . . . what are you trying to speak . . . help me to hear your voice. . . ."

His prayers became once again inaudible, mingling with his own thoughts.

His dear friend of many years—Aaron Abrahams—had been on his mind ever since he had last seen him in Niedersdorf. Indeed, Aaron was far more than a mere friend to himself and Marion, though they had both, against their own wishes, consented to Aaron's demand that they promise never to reveal his secret to another human soul—even to their own daughter. And so, all these years, no one ever knew. And now that the doctor had troubles with the authorities, being powerless to help nearly killed Heinrich.

He was not the first, and he would surely not be the last. The persecution had been mounting for years.

Hitler's diatribe *Mein Kampf* had outlined his demented race-superiority theory, and now his powerful secret network of army and police and spies were carrying out his evil schemes against the Jews with greater and greater abandon. That evil night of rioting, looting, destruction, and killing, known as *Krystallnacht*, was already a year in the past. It could only grow worse. And now it had spread from Berlin to a small village like Niedersdorf!

Both his own daughter and his friend Bonhoeffer had challenged him to consider what he would do, what he should do, as the policies of the Nazis came ever closer. What was right? What was the call upon the people of God?

"God . . . oh, God," he cried out in an agony of frustrated confusion, "what would you have me do? How can I help your people?"

He walked on another few steps, then stopped and fell to his knees, covering his face with his hands.

"Oh, Father, I fear for such grief and pain and suffering coming for your people, for Jews and Christians alike. I cannot stand idly by, Lord . . . that cannot be what you desire of me. There is such evil and wickedness spreading over our land. What is your purpose for me? My heart aches for Aaron, Father . . . what can I do . . . and Marion . . . oh, God. . . ."

The words of prayer turned to inarticulate groanings, as unconsciously he rocked slowly back and forth on his knees.

"Lord, break me . . . break my soul so that none of my self remains . . . fill me only with yourself, my Father . . . fill me with your Spirit . . . let my life be nothing but a reflection of your being and your character and your goodness . . . purify me, O God . . . circumcise my heart . . . cleanse me from all motive . . . search me with the finger of your cleansing fire . . . I want nothing, Father, except to be more and more transformed into the image of your Son . . . make me, O Lord, like Jesus . . . let me become the son you desire me to be . . . and show me, Father— please show me . . . what you want me to do . . . open my eyes to your purpose, your will . . . let me do nothing, say nothing, think nothing that is contrary to your purpose . . . help me, Lord . . . instruct me . . . guide my steps in your way . . . fill me with your wisdom and your life and your very being. . . ."

Again his words gave way to the silent pleadings of the Spirit inside him. When he rose from his knees ten minutes later, his eyes shone with the cleansing rains of self-abandonment, and his cheeks were stained with its tears.

He continued his walk, still praying and thinking quietly—

though the storm in his heart had been stilled—and asking his Father for direction.

A passage of Scripture had been on his mind since the moment of his awakening. He had read it several times. Still his finger marked the page as he held the Bible at his side. Once again he opened it and read the words.

These are the words of the holy one, the true one, who holds the key of David; when he opens none may shut, when he shuts none may open . . . and look, I have set before you an open door, which no one can shut.

"The key . . . what key, Lord? What open door?"

Your strength, I know, is small, yet you have observed my commands and have not disowned my name.

He thought of his friend Dietrich, and then of the many German church leaders who had given in to the Nazi demands, signed oaths of allegiance to Hitler, and thus disowned the name of their true Savior. "But Lord," he prayed, "are you speaking to me, too?"

He continued to read.

So this is what I will do: I will make those of Satan's synagogue, who claim to be Jews but are lying frauds, come and fall down at your feet.

"Who do you mean, Lord . . . who are these false Jews . . . what is Satan's synagogue?"

And they shall know that you are my beloved people.

"Beloved people . . . they shall know that *you* are my beloved people," repeated Heinrich to himself. "What people, Lord . . . who are these beloved people?"

Because you have kept my command and stood fast, I will also keep you from the ordeal that is to fall upon the whole world and test its inhabitants. I am coming soon; hold fast to what you have, and let no one rob you of your crown. He who is victorious—I will make him a pillar in the temple of my God.

"Oh, Father, what *are* you saying to me?" implored Heinrich. "I must know, Lord. Make your voice clear, so that I can obey, and do exactly as you desire!"

Words from the Scripture began to come back to him, and as they did, thoughts tumbled forth out of his brain so rapidly that he could not piece them together in an orderly flow. But he knew that in some way God was beginning to answer his prayer for clarity.

Satan's synagogue . . . that was not the true church, the true nation of Israel, but an utterly false one, not claiming to be Jews as the verse in Revelation said, but claiming to be the true descendants of an "Aryan Christ."

False Jews . . . Satan's synagogue . . . but they shall know that *you* are my beloved people . . . *true* Jews . . . the *true* church . . . the *true* people of God!

I will keep you from the ordeal that is coming . . .

"Who, Lord . . . who will you keep from the ordeal?"

I will keep you from the ordeal . . . they shall know that you are my beloved people . . . my beloved people . . . my beloved people . . .

"Lord, what would you have me hear? Open my ears, Lord, open my eyes."

Hold fast to what you have . . . what you have . . .

"What do I have, Lord . . . how will you keep them from the ordeal . . . ?"

I have set before you an open door . . . an open door . . . open doors . . . open doors . . . many open doors . . .

As he walked and prayed, Heinrich had retraced his steps and had now come to the edge of the wood. Out before him in all directions spread his land, the land of his fathers, land that he loved. Straight before him, on the hill rising out of the plain, sat his beloved *Lebenshaus*, with *Der Frühlingsgarten* spreading down the slope in front of it toward him.

He stopped.

Gazing upon it all, his mouth was just voicing the quiet words yet again, "Open my eyes, Lord . . . " when all at once an expression of incredulity broke upon his whole countenance.

Eyes wide, he gazed around, first at the garden, then at the house, with sudden amazement.

"Of course . . . that's it! *Hold fast to what you have* . . . I have open doors, my house has many available doors, *many open doors for God's beloved people to help keep them from the ordeal that is to fall on the whole world.* How could I have not seen what you were trying to show me before! Oh . . . Father . . . thank you!"

He broke into a run, across the field, and back toward the house.

There was not a moment to lose! There were more Scriptures he had to look up, but he needed his study for the task. If he *had* correctly divined the Lord's voice and direction just now, he would find ready confirmation.

An hour later, the baron set his pen down on the desk and sat back in his chair. Several open Bibles and other books lay about his desk. The paper directly in front of him was full of a half-dozen or so portions of Scripture, which, beyond any further doubt, confirmed what had come to his heart an hour before.

There were many precautions they would have to take, for what had already happened once would be likely to happen again. They might still be watching him. There would be enormous risks. There would be walls, doors, passageways to alter. So much to do! But, if the Father was truly breathing life into the plan, all would fit together.

It was time to tell Marion of his walk, of what the Lord had spoken to him, and to show her this list of scriptural precedents for what he had in mind.

He rose, picked up the sheet on his desk, and went to find his wife. They must now make it a matter of serious prayer together.

∽ 58 ∾

Clandestine Assignment

The room where the two men were seated was as stark in its furnishings and decor as their voices were devoid of emotion. A more suitable setting for the transaction of their business could not have been found. The walls were barren, the floor of cold cement, the single high window dirty and admitting but scant hints of the light that shone outside.

Two straight-backed chairs sat opposite one another. In one, a man of approximately thirty-three was speaking across to the occupant of the other, a young uniformed man some twelve or thirteen years his junior.

"You have shown yourself well," the older of the two was saying. "I have spoken to your superiors. They say you have a bright future in the *Luftwaffe*. The command of your own squadron, they say, will surely be yours."

"I am gratified my service to the Reich is found satisfactory."

"I am certain such a future would be enough to satisfy most loyal young German men."

The other did not reply.

"There are, however, avenues of 'service' to the Reich and our beloved Führer that require a higher, and what I might call a certain fearlessness of devotion beyond that which most men are able to demonstrate. Do you understand my meaning?"

"Perhaps."

"I had hoped you would come with us when my man spoke with you two years ago. I was disappointed to learn of your decision about the *Luftwaffe*."

"My father thought it was best."

"Do you only do what your father tells you?"

The young man eyed the other with irritation.

"I make my own decisions," he said.

"It might be worth your while to reconsider. I might insist that you reconsider."

"Reconsider . . . I don't understand."

"I am in need of one who *does* understand and whose loyalty I will never need question."

"Loyalty . . . to whom?"

"To *me*, you fool! Who else!"

"Forgive me," said the younger man, the word implying no repentance, only that he knew such a tacit apology was expected. "I was only thinking of the Führer."

"When I speak, the Führer speaks!" rejoined the other. "Loyalty to me *is* loyalty to my superior, who is the Führer's closest associate. Loyalty to me *is* to the Fatherland and the Reich!"

"Of course."

"Are you one capable of such loyalty?"

"If you deem me worthy to fulfill the assignment you speak of, then my loyalty will be absolute," he answered, thinking it best to sound conciliatory.

"Whatever it may require of you?"

The young man nodded. "I am not unaware of the nature of your activities."

The older man smiled a sinister smile. "The assignment I have will require your relinquishing the uniform you wear."

"It is a price I could be persuaded to pay. . . ."

His voice trailed off in a significant tone.

"*Persuaded?*" repeated the other with equally knowing intonation. "For the right price, as it were?"

"I think we understand one another, Herr Korsch."

"There is no *price*," snapped the older man. "If I want you in my service, you have no other options. Do you still not grasp who you are talking to?"

The other merely nodded his consent.

"Yet," the older of the two went on, moderating his annoyance, "there are, to be sure, certain *compensations,* as I am sure you must be aware. Power, and the prestige that comes with it, do not always carry financial rewards, and yet . . . confiscations *are* occasionally diverted to assist in the funding of our activities. I am in the process of such a diversion on my own behalf even as we speak. Once this conflict is over, however it should turn out—and whatever the outcome, I intend to land on the victorious side—there will be those who will profit handsomely from it. If you are loyal to me, I will see that you are one of them."

Both men smiled knowingly.

"Additional confiscations in the sector in which I feel you might be most useful can sometimes be extremely lucrative. *They* do have extensive assets, you know, which are not lawfully theirs."

"So I have heard."

"Your friends may be among them."

"They are not *my* friends."

"You are willing, then, to join my efforts to purify the Reich of these seditious lawbreakers?"

"I will follow your command."

"Good. I knew I could count on you. I know the Führer will likewise be pleased!"

There was a pause.

"Now, I have already confided some of my suspicions to

you," Korsch went on. "Do you have any immediate information that might be helpful to me as I prosecute my inquiry further?"

"Only that in addition to the fellow you are seeking, they also make it a habit of entertaining Americans."

"Americans, you say. No, I wasn't aware of that! This could be very useful, very useful indeed! You are a shrewd young man."

"Thank you, *mein Herr.*"

"How do you manage to fall privy to as much information as you seem to possess?"

"I have my ways, *mein Herr.*"

"Yes, and if you work for me, I want to know what they are!" snapped the agent crisply.

"I have a vantage point from which I can see much of what goes on. I have been using it for years."

"For what purpose?"

The younger man did not answer immediately.

"Ah yes," said the other, "the girl! Of course. I had forgotten. You made a practice of keeping a private watch on her, is that it?"

He broke into a villainous laugh.

"Yes, you will do fine! There's nothing we want more than agents with secret battles of their own! Ha, ha, ha! Well, my lovesick young friend, if you pull this off and we bring them all down, I'll make sure you get the girl in the end."

PART V

The Mystery of Lebenshaus— 1942

Darkness over the Land

Darkness had fallen over the small Polish city of Wloclawek. The hour was not late, perhaps only eight or nine. But in these regions at this time of the year, dusk arrived early.

The blackness across the land came not merely from the season. Indeed, darkness had closed in over all this region three years earlier. The Poland of their forefathers, the Prussian and Polish kingdoms of the Hohenzollerns and the Great Otto von Bismarck, the very kingdoms out of which a united Germany had sprung, existed no longer.

The midnight of their long history had come, and none had stepped forward to their defense. No modern-day Bismarck had emerged to save the once-proud empire.

Now only black hopelessness engulfed the land.

The Polish army had been paralyzed by the massive *blitzkrieg* of September 1939. Against modern German bombs and numerous armored divisions and fifteen hundred swift fighting aircraft, the Poles sent out but scant numbers of foot soldiers, a single armored division, and, unbelievably, twelve fully booted and spurred cavalry brigades mounted on their trusty steeds.

The campaign was decided in days. Poland collapsed in a week.

According to the August Moscow Pact with Russia in the middle of September, Soviet troops now invaded the eastern frontiers. Hitler's representatives met once again with Stalin's, and the two autocrats proceeded to divide the spoils. Poland was partitioned in two. Half now became part of Germany, the other half part of Russia.

The declaration of war by Great Britain and France and their few allies, far from stopping Hitler's thirst for conquest, only exacerbated it.

With much the same speed, force, and lightning success, Hitler proceeded to invade France, Norway, and Denmark in 1940; and Yugoslavia, Greece, and North Africa in 1941. Only

Great Britain (despite punishing bombing by the German *Luftwaffe*), and to a lesser degree the Soviet Union (who now found Hitler, their temporary ally, launching an invasion against them as well), held out against the vastly superior German forces.

Japan's attack on the United States at Pearl Harbor in December of 1941 at last brought America aggressively into the conflict on the side of the British. As the year 1942 opened, the entire world was engaged in a global war such as the community of nations and peoples of the earth had never seen. Utterly irreconcilable ideologies between the Allies and the three Axis powers of Germany, Japan, and Italy rendered a compromised settlement of peace unthinkable. Only total defeat and unconditional surrender could decide the outcome of such a monstrous clash.

Territorial conquest, however, represented but a portion of Adolf Hitler's megalomaniacal objective. Even greater proved his growing obsession to rid not only Germany but all of Europe of what he considered the scourge of the Jewish race.

The resolution could be nothing less than complete extermination. The only permanent remedy, as he saw it, was the eradication of the Hebrew race from the face of the earth, beginning with Poland, now in his hands and by far the largest territorial home for European Jews, and including not only those of Polish descent but recent immigrants from Russia and Germany.

The details of this objective were first carried out by special *Einsatzgruppen*, who rounded up Jews in a given area, loaded them like animals into trucks, and drove them to a predesignated and prepared location in the country, where they were thrown into large ditches and shot from above with machine guns.

Gradually, as the war progressed, methods and techniques of this genocide became more refined, always with the end in view of killing more people more quickly. Death vans were devised, gassing their victims while the vehicles sped on their way to whatever final resting place had been prepared for the bodies.

By the end of 1941, a decision was made in this evil high

command to undertake what its architects termed the "final solution of the Jewish problem." To this end, orders were passed from Hitler and his chief architect of the plan, Heinrich Himmler, to the SS commanders, thence to the Gestapo chiefs Heinrich Müller and Adolph Eichmann, who then forwarded specific instructions to the local officials, who carried out the gruesome deeds of mass murder.

Though the shooting continued, and many were killed by phenol injections, hanging, malnutrition, and disease, the apex of this horrifying tale of human depravity was reached with the construction of special camps whose only purpose was murder. Gas chambers and crematoria were designed for mass slaughter, carried out efficiently and cleanly.

From all the conquered countries of Europe, Jews were gathered and transported, either to locations throughout the Reich for needed slave labor, or to such death camps in Poland as Auschwitz. In addition to mere slaughter, many Jews were selected for fiendish and usually fatal medical experiments at the hands of Nazi scientists. Before or after the chambers and flames and ropes and bullets had accomplished their work, the clothing and shoes and bones and gold fillings and jewelry of the victims were gathered and collected—bones for fertilizer, clothes for the German poor, gold and jewelry to deposit in the banks of the Reich.

Emigration became impossible. There was no place to go. Getting out of Poland or Germany served no end, for all Europe had been taken over by the madness. Jews whose identities were known could only hide from the SS and Gestapo squads or seek escape in a safe house. Some moved into attics or basements with sympathetic friends or relatives.

Danger lurked everywhere. There were few corners of refuge. Underground networks began forming, some in association with the anti-Nazi resistance movements in each country, others independently. All who chose to participate in this invisible humanitarian effort to preserve Jewish life immediately put themselves at huge risk.

Spies were legion. One could not even trust family and neighbors and friends.

Some chose to remain in their homes, at their jobs, hoping

against futile hope that the roots of their Hebrew lineage would not be discovered. Others attempted to change their names and obtain forged documents. But all waited in constant terror for the heavy-booted tramp of Gestapo feet, knowing that if the truck came to the front of their house, its destination would be death.

~ 60 ~

Nighttime Vigil

In an upstairs bedroom, a father and mother huddled in the darkness with their seven-year-old son and five-year-old daughter, waiting for the lonely hours of the night to pass.

They could no longer merely go on with their lives and hope to elude discovery. The man called Jakob knew it was too late for that. The Gestapo would be here tomorrow. Tonight was his last chance, his only chance, to remove his children from Wloclawek and, he prayed, to safety.

They would take only what they could wear. Such were the instructions he had given his wife. Only one small handbag of a few needed personal belongings he would carry with them. Appearance of travel or flight, if they were seen, would result in being reported.

When Jakob had returned from work only three hours ago he quietly announced to his wife that what they long feared had come upon them at last.

"We must leave immediately," he said.

"When, Jakob?"

"In the middle of the night."

"But . . . but—how . . . what will we—"

"It's already been arranged."

"But Jakob, we can't leave—just like that, without—"

"We *must*, Ulrike," interrupted her husband with yet more urgency. For the first time she apprehended the panic in his voice. She looked deeply into his eyes. She realized what fear he carried on behalf of his family. "We must," he repeated, softer now, but with no less insistency.

They stood silent a moment.

He took her gently into his arms and held her close. For the Jews of Poland, this hour was never far away. Now for Jakob and Ulrike Kropf, suddenly it had come. They were more fortunate than most. They at least had a few hours' warning. Though but an unskilled textile worker, Jakob Kropf was a shrewd man. He had been watching developments and making plans on behalf of his wife and son and daughter. No modern-day Moses, he yet took his little charge as seriously as did the great deliverer his ancient flock of millions. For these three children of Israel, the Pole and faithful follower of Yahweh Jakob Kropf would give his life, if necessary, to rescue them from the bondage of their twentieth-century Egypt.

"The Gestapo came to the factory today," said Jakob at length, still holding his young wife. "I watched from far away across the floor. I saw two agents—I knew immediately they were Gestapo—go into the glass office of the superintendent. He showed them papers. They took them. I know they were employee lists. It is their way. They came back later. I was watching. I was afraid I would drop a box and bring attention to myself. This time I found an excuse to move closer and watch. They showed the superintendent the list again, pointing to certain of the names. He went to the cabinet and brought out more files. You know what they were, Ulrike! My personnel file, and the others'!"

"What did you do, Jakob?"

"What could I do? I tried to keep my mind on my work! I knew it was my last day at the factory, that I would never see another paycheck, and that tomorrow none of us would be back."

"Can you be sure?"

"It is happening everywhere, Ulrike. You cannot have forgotten the steel plant. The Gestapo came, and the next day every Jew employed in it was arrested—and their families. That was only last week. They have set their sights on Wloclawek. They will be here tomorrow. We have only tonight, Ulrike—*only tonight.*"

That had been some hours before.

They had eaten hurriedly. Ulrike had packed what food

could be carried, and they had hastily assembled what few things they could manage. It was winter and cold. They would wear several layers of clothes and in that way pack most of the wardrobe they would need. They could take little else and hope to survive the arduous trek. Jakob Kropf well knew the risks. But it was a risk that enabled him to *do* something. Should they remain, passively waiting, he would be impotent. The man in him must do all he could to actively help his family.

He also knew that to remain meant one of the camps.

After they had eaten, Ulrike had tearfully gone about the house saying good-bye to so many things she would never see again—the baby rocker Jakob had made, the dresser with mirror that had been her mother's, all their well-worn clothes, trinkets here and there, a china tea set, a table that had been her uncle's. She ran her fingers over the brass candle holder, then continued to walk about the room. So many mementos from the past! Possessions that, while not of great value, meant more to her than she could have said. She quickly grabbed up the dreidel off a shelf—the children might enjoy playing with it, and it would be a reminder of happy family celebrations.

Jakob, meanwhile, in his own way, carried out the same nostalgic and painful litany to a life they would know no longer. He forced himself to remain calm. He could not let his emotion spill over the dam behind which he contained it. His family must gather courage and strength from him, and he must not reveal his inner fears.

They had eaten supper as usual, then turned the lights out at their normal bedtime. Everything must appear as always. Not even their neighbors and friends must suspect what they were about to do, or they would be in danger as well.

Now, in the quiet hours of the advancing evening, they huddled together in the darkness, waiting for the minutes to pass. Jakob had arranged to meet the man called Luddoff at midnight.

No hour was safe anymore, but the fewer eyes awake, the better the chance to get out of the city and into the country unseen. Then they would be, temporarily at least, hidden from the eyes that now knew Jakob Kropf by name, possessed his file, had his address, and planned to round up his family probably at dawn. Such the Gestapo had been doing for some weeks, ever since the SS came to this area to carry out their program of cleansing.

It was not yet so late, but the darkness made it seem later than the clock. Not wanting to alarm the children, and trying to remain calm, Jakob and Ulrike spoke but little, hoping to coax them to sleep.

The evening deepened. Gradually Jakob himself felt the weariness of the stressful day stealing over him. His arms, then his whole body, and finally his eyelids began to sag. He had to remain alert, he told himself. They must not miss the appointed meeting, lest they lose their only chance of escape.

He clutched his sleeping son more tightly in his arms and, fighting sleep himself now, continued his nighttime vigil. . . .

➣ 61 ➢
Gestapo Schemes

The Gestapo section chief strode back and forth in the small room with a determined step. His eyebrows were knit in thought, causing the black eyes beneath them to appear even more sunken into the depths of his head than they actually were.

He had been absently glancing over a stack of routine files a few hours ago. He'd not even seen them on his own desk, but had absently noticed them among the papers of a subordinate.

Something had flashed back into memory and with it, the question whether there was more here than met the eye.

The trail of Rabbi Wissen had been his private search for months. In hopes of finding the man's whereabouts he had ordered the net dropped on this region several weeks ago, stretching from Torun down to Inowroclaw, and east to Wloclawek.

Many Jews had been rooted out, but not the rabbi.

He knew the rabbi was in this area; he could smell the dirty, olive-skinned Semite! The professor's hometown was Plock. After leaving Warsaw, he had traced him there, and at last report the Jewish leader was said to be heading west. He had the feeling the rabbi was right here in Wloclawek!

He hated to be made to look foolish, and the rabbi had eluded capture far too long!

The assignment had been an unwanted one. He hadn't clawed and backstabbed his way up through the ranks of the Gestapo for this. Actually, it hadn't exactly been *offered*. *Reichsführer* Heinrich Himmler had ways of pretending assignments were voluntary when in fact they were nothing of the kind. He had accepted the offer, not because he had the least interest in being sent to Poland, but because it was *Himmler* personally who had done the offering. *He* was a man you did not refuse.

As it turned out, the move represented an advance, more power, the chance to lay important groundwork for further promotions within the SS, and the opportunity to survey options eastward if such ever became necessary. The Russians had invaded this far back in '39, and, though they were on the retreat at present, one never knew how the fortunes of war might shift.

In addition was the fact that Himmler had already shown a kindly disposition toward him. The future for the Jewish sphere of the SS's mission lay in Poland. As despicable as the Christians were, or anyone, for that matter, with religious superstitions, it must be admitted that it was on the coattails of the Semitic solution that advancements in the SS were based. The hated secret police were already constructing more advanced facilities throughout this country. If he could make himself look good, perhaps he could make a name for himself here, however it turned out.

So far everything had gone well . . . until the order had come—from Himmler personally—to find and capture this rabbi. The order had, in fact, been so specific as to leave little doubt about the Jew's importance—he was to drop everything else and concentrate all his personal efforts on the capture of Rabbi Wissen.

The rabbi's eluding him didn't bode well for his record. It had been such an easy assignment—arrest a bearded history professor, who knew every important Jew and synagogue leader in Poland, and who also maintained a file of certain key undiscovered Jews in the Nazi government who wanted to privately stay in touch with their faith, and bring him to Berlin.

The section chief was angry with himself to think how he had allowed the thing to be botched. If Himmler learned that information had been withheld about the artifacts the man possessed, it would be his head. Himmler wanted the swarthy traitor only to torture information out of him, but the section chief had himself learned that the rabbi possessed treasure of a far more valuable kind. Hitler would give anything for it—that much he knew without the least doubt—once the power of the stones was known. With the contents of the rabbi's box, as much as he believed in all that cultish hocus-pocus, Hitler might be able to win this war after all!

If he chose to take them to Hitler, the chief thought to himself, he would be able to name his price. Himmler just might find himself the subordinate in the end! Or perhaps he would just keep them. Those stones would be worth more after the war than any bank account! And who was to know about them?

But the Jews could be clever people, and the rabbi-professor had gotten out of the city and taken the holy box with him.

Yet . . . if he *could* bring in the rabbi, and his ridiculous sacred stones—whether or not he decided to turn them over to Hitler—he might be able to deal himself even further up the line, even past the echelons of Heydrich and Kaltenbrunner, right into the inner circle.

The Führer's obsession with objects of art and historic relics was not a fetish the chief understood. All the Nazi leaders, from Hitler and Göring down, unrefined as they were, had engaged in an enormous program of artistic and cultural looting from every city and country their armies had overrun. From Vienna to Prague to Paris, they grabbed paintings, gold and silver relics, tapestries, jewels, rare books, and all manner of articles with inestimable historic and real value. Entire museums and libraries and galleries were sacked, and the contents now filled both public and private Nazi collections. Every top Nazi leader engaged his own agents to secretly remain on the lookout for cultural and artistic treasures, and they raced and competed against one another to lay hold of especially desired objects. An entire military unit known as *Einsatzstab-Rosenberg* accompanied every invading army, whose purpose was to seize all such valuable property of Jews and other "ideological enemies of national socialism."

And now *he* might well have discovered the most valuable item of all! Or so the information the chief had stumbled onto six months ago led him to believe. Only he knew about it—not Hitler, not Himmler nor Göring, not Alfred Rosenberg.

The power to divine the future, to discern the will of God! Whether or not you believed in such a being hardly mattered. The possibilities were infinite regardless! And Hitler was enough given to the occult and mystical to believe in the power of the stones.

The cringing imbecile he had beaten the information out of certainly believed it!

The fool had been so afraid of the wrath of God and had babbled like an idiot in terror of betraying the rabbi's secret. But in the end he had been *more* afraid of the butt of a rifle crashing against his skull one more time and had finally divulged the information.

That had been one beating he had taken particular pleasure in. *The fool,* he thought. *He could have kept his knowledge of the rabbi's box and taken it to the grave.* He grinned a sinister smile at the memory. He was going to kill the fool anyway. Especially when the Jewish moron began to chant a prayer and incant ridiculous words of Scripture. Imagine the lunacy of it—praying for the man who was about to kill you!

He had slammed the butt of his rifle once more into the man's midsection, hearing several more ribs crack, before finally putting a bullet between his eyes.

They were so heavenly minded! Well, thought the chief, he'd be happy to send them there immediately!

He had discovered *what* the rabbi possessed. But finding the professor *himself* had not been so easy. The cur had escaped from the *Universität*, fled Warsaw, and was now reportedly linked to some network of Jewish sympathizers who got resisters and traitors out of the country, even in some cases off the continent.

The chief began sorting through the files again.

His men had a raid planned for tomorrow morning. It was routine. Nothing more than rounding up those identified in normal investigations of factory personnel files.

But something he had noticed here stuck with him. He was certain it bore a connection to the rabbi.

A word he had seen mentioned on one of the documents . . . what was it? Yes—there it was!

He grabbed up the single sheet of paper with the group of names listed on it—*Luddoff* . . . where had he heard that name before? Here it said he was thought to be one of the network's organizers. Further, the report indicated that if any of these newly discovered workers were contemplating flight, the fellow Luddoff would likely be involved. It was sure to be a code name, the report said, but it was all that had been discovered thus far.

Where had he heard the name?

He continued to pace back and forth, more rapidly now.

A moment more . . . then suddenly he stopped. His eyes shot wide open in remembrance, then his right fist slammed into his left hand with triumph.

Of course! It was the little weasel he had killed in Warsaw! *He's* the one who had said the name Luddoff while he was beating him. He'd thought nothing of it then. He was only after information concerning the rabbi's treasure, and he had hardly paid attention to anything else.

What had he said? He could remember nothing.

Whatever it was, there had to be a connection between the professor and the fellow Luddoff. A fact which linked Professor Wissen to this area, right here to Wloclawek!

If Luddoff belonged to the escape network, he had to be involved with the rabbi! There could be no doubt. Either the rabbi had already passed through his hands, or soon would!

Luddoff might hold the key!

He grabbed up the papers again, scanning them now with breathless anticipation. If some of these factory workers had indeed contacted the network, he couldn't risk letting them slip through his fingers. It might be his only chance to lay his hands on the fellow Luddoff . . . and the rabbi!

Tomorrow might be too late.

He would order the arrests of all these people tonight! He would question them, beat them, do whatever it took to learn the whereabouts of Luddoff!

Still clutching the papers, the section chief ran from the room, shouting orders to two men in an outer office, then raced outside and to his car.

He would supervise this series of raids himself.

❧ 62 ❧

Flight in the Night

They were close behind them!

"Run, run!" cried Jakob.

Across the long, desolate field they flew, Ulrike a few strides in front of him, all four of his limbs about to collapse from the weight of the two children he held, one in each arm.

If only they could reach the cave, they would be safe there!

Behind them suddenly flashed the twin headlights of the evil vehicle of death. Its engine roared as it bounced across the rutted, open, grassy pasture. Already, Jakob knew, the back of the truck contained a dozen or more of his kind, rounded up this very night, hunted down like animals. Now the agents driving it sought to add him and his family to the number of those who would be shot before the night was out.

He urged his exhausted legs on, heart pounding, afraid that one of them would stumble in their flight and be found by their pursuers.

Behind them he heard the truck, at reckless full throttle, speeding toward them. But the menacing eyes of its headlamps, like thick arrows of light, probing the night with fiendish, bouncing glares through the blackness, still had not illuminated their fleeing forms.

Gasping for breath, Jakob felt himself slowing. He knew that every step might send him and the children sprawling over the grass and dirt, announcing their presence with cries and screams, to be followed the next instant with a spray of machine-gun fire!

With agonizing slowness he lifted his feet, step after step, feeling that each of his boots weighed more than the two youngsters in his arms.

In front of him, Ulrike had reached the cave!

If only he could get his family into it and out of sight in time!

The sounds of the truck grew louder. The luminescent beams panned the field.

Jakob reached the cave. Ulrike was already squatting down inside. Lungs heaving and scarcely able to stand, he set each of the children down, then hurriedly guided them down into the subterranean hole where their mother waited—first the girl, then his son.

"Jakob . . . Jakob, please don't leave us here alone!" cried Ulrike from the depths of their hiding place.

"It is the only way you will be safe," replied Jakob.

"Please, Jakob—please stay with us!"

"I must know you are alive! They will search until they find us. I must be a decoy and try for the woods. I will come back. If I do not, you must find the man they call Luddoff. He will take you to safety."

"No, Jakob—"

"Be sure to place the pole against the boards for support."

Jakob backed away from the hole, then grabbed the two large slabs of wood to set over it.

"Jakob, no . . . please—"

But his wife's final pleas were lost to his ears with the thudding against the earth of the planks as he dropped them into position.

Hastily he tore at grass and weeds with frantic fingers, throwing clumps and chunks of dirt and sod over the opening to the makeshift cave to camouflage it.

Then once more he took off at a desperate run across what remained of the field. If only he could make the woods on the other side!

Suddenly the truck sounded close behind him!

Shouts mixed with the revving of the engine, angry shouts, crying out in German for him to stop. They had spotted him!

All at once the headlights found him. The next instant his body and path of escape were exposed in glaring illumination.

He continued running, but knew it was no use.

Shots sounded behind him, the sharp report of rifle fire!

The trees were too far in the distance. He could never make it. Still he ran, over the rough terrain.

Suddenly all went black as the searing pain of a bullet ripped through the flesh of his back. . . .

◈

Jakob cried out, jolting awake where he sat.

He breathed in and out heavily. A cold sweat covered his damp body.

How many times had he relived the same nightmare? More than he wanted to remember.

"What is it, Jakob?" whispered Ulrike.

"Nothing . . . only a bad dream. Is she still asleep?"

"Yes."

"The contented innocence of childhood."

"How much longer?"

"An hour perhaps. I will check my watch at the window."

Adjusting the body of his sleeping son, Jakob began to rise.

Suddenly a sound came through the stillness of the night. A cold shiver ran through his body though he had been perspiring only moments before.

Jakob strained to listen with an anxious sense of foreboding growing in his breast.

There it was again—the screech of tires sounding in the distance!

It could be nothing, but . . . he listened again, more intently.

A car—no, several cars by the sound of it—sped through the night streets of Wloclawek.

There could be no mistaking it now—they were coming this way! It couldn't possibly have anything to do with the factory and what he had seen.

It couldn't—but he would take no chances!

He glanced toward Ulrike at his side. Her terrified eyes were glued on him, huge as the moon that had risen just half an hour before. Her face was just as pale.

"We must go," he said.

This time she did not hesitate or pause to question him. Waking the youngster in her arms as she did, Ulrike rose to her feet.

"Come, Son," Jakob said to the boy, setting him on his sleepy feet, taking his hand, and leading him to the stairs. Seeing that his wife still held their daughter, he stopped and took her in his arms. Then, carrying the young innocent who knew not that they were risking everything that she might live, he led the way down the darkened stairway, followed by Ulrike and their son.

Already the sounds in the street had grown louder. By the time the little family reached the back door, Jakob knew the automobiles were those of the Gestapo, and that they sought *them!*

Why were they coming now?

What would they do? He was not supposed to meet his contact until midnight!

Jakob gave the girl back to Ulrike and scooped the boy up in his arms. They were running now, through the back door and onto the porch.

The air was filled with more than screeching tires. The sounds of car engines roared only a block or two away.

Headlights shone around and over the buildings through the night! The sounds grew louder. Just as he had sleepily imagined, the lights seemed to be searching the darkness for them!

With an eerie feeling of somnolent déjà vu, Jakob Kropf hurried his little band out, not into the field of his nightmare but into their own little yard!

The young Jewish parents, arms already wearying with their loads, now prepared for the dash across the open space behind their home, sweating, terrified, and knowing they were running for their lives.

This was no dream!

As terrifying as his nightmare had been, Jakob now knew its fear for the counterfeit it was.

Ulrike stumbled as she stepped off the porch and cried out.

Managing to keep a grip on the bundle in her arms, she fell to one knee, stifling a cry of pain.

Jakob stopped, helped her up with his free hand, then continued, half running across the thick, uneven grass and dirt.

The cars screeched to a stop in front of the house.

There were voices now—loud, angry voices. Another car roared around back. Headlights shone through the night!

Sounds and voices and stomping feet echoed behind him. Jakob glanced back, still running. Lights shone throughout the house. Men were moving about, storm troopers with guns.

Another car emptied in back, not far from them. Three men ran inside the door Jakob had just closed behind them less than a minute ago. The headlights of the car still pierced the darkness like two evil, menacing eyes, reflecting brightly off their neighbor's house only twenty meters from them.

Now he heard angry sounds of shouts and orders. Men ran outside again, shouting that the house was empty. Jakob's head was swimming, lights and sounds fading into blurry confusion.

Still they ran . . . it wasn't supposed to be so far . . . why was it taking so long to reach it . . . if only they could make the hiding place . . . lights and voices . . . headlights and lanterns . . . more shouts . . . all looking for them!

The nightmare had suddenly become all too real! Was he dreaming all over again. . . ?

∞ 63 ∞

Savage Search

The Gestapo section chief had sent the men on ahead in two cars. He had followed in his own. This was one night of arrests he determined to be part of himself. He wanted to look into their faces and see the terror of knowing they were at last in the power of the Gestapo! Then he would question each one until he found out the information he wanted.

Thirty minutes later, at the first of the seven locations they had to search, he stood by while the men under his charge dragged the family of six from their beds. He hated it when they begged for mercy. Screaming he could tolerate. Begging filled him with nauseating disgust. It made him want to plunge a knife into their hearts right on the spot.

He remembered the night last year at Poznan when the big hulking fellow had gone down on his knees, begging for mercy to be shown his wife and three youngsters. The cowardly display had made him sick. He had nearly vomited all over the dog! What kind of men were these Jews that they would allow themselves to fall to such depths of depravity? *They* were the ones who supposedly believed in some future life—why couldn't they face death like men!

Begging hadn't saved a single one of them. They had their religion and their God. Let them silently say their prayers and let the inevitable come without so much fuss.

What good had the big fellow's begging done anyway? Only that his wife had to see the blood oozing out of the side of his head a moment later as he slumped senseless to the ground. She had only made matters worse by then falling upon his body, screaming hysterically and calling out to their desert God.

The chief smiled at the thought of her invoking the wrath of Yahweh, whoever she meant, to destroy the evil Nazis with the fire of his vengeance. *The Nazis might be destroyed one day*, he thought to himself, *but certainly not by some celestial bolt of lightning!*

They were fools, every one! He had made a special point of taking up a rifle later that night and aiming it at the whole lot of the cowardly family.

He liked to take a personal hand in the executions whenever it was convenient. It kept him from getting too soft.

The crying of a little urchin at his feet brought the section chief back to the present. He whacked him across the face with the back of his hand, yelling out a foul oath as he did, commanding the parents to keep their brat quiet.

He was in no mood for all this. He wanted that rabbi!

But it was clear there was no information to be gained about either him or Luddoff here. These poor idiots were such fools it was obvious they were making no plans to escape. They had no

idea what was about to come upon them! It would do no good
to torture them. They would know nothing about Luddoff!

He walked back to his car and lit up a cigarette, while the
storm troopers threw the six into the back of the wagon. He
climbed in behind the wheel, waited for the cars and truck to
rumble off, then followed them to the next house on the list.

As the two automobiles, the truck, already accumulating its
cargo of victims, and the third car rolled up to the darkened
house, immediately something appeared wrong.

The place was too dark, too still.

His men ran inside. The chief saw the lights go on, and now
saw the silhouetted figures of his own troopers running about
the rooms. It was obvious they had found no occupants.

As he approached, he signalled to the men of the second car
to drive around back and search the alley and nearby streets.

He ran up the steps and inside.

"Es ist ganz leer, mein Herr," said one of the men, meeting him
at the door, rifle at his side.

Brushing past him without reply, he slowly entered and then
walked through the rooms of the small dwelling. Just as the
man had said, the house was empty.

They must have been tipped off. The very thought filled him
with anger. He did not like to be anticipated or second-
guessed!

By now several of his men were running through the back
door, having encircled the house. In answer to his inquiring
look, they shook their heads.

He turned back inside and walked through each of the rooms
again, more slowly now.

He paused in one of the two tiny bedrooms. The quiet rage
boiled inside. *They are not far away,* he thought. His preternatu-
rally keen sensibilities told him they had left just minutes
before he and his men had arrived.

In the room yet hung the faint odor of humanity, even a hint
of bodily warmth. He could *sense* the lingering feel of their presence.

The yellowed teeth clenched invisibly against themselves, as
the hands at his sides unconsciously assumed the white-
knuckled formation of a fist.

How did they know?

He stood thinking a moment or two longer. *They can't have gone far! They have to be somewhere in the vicinity!*

With sudden determination, he spun around and strode to the front of the house.

"Search everywhere!" he said to his men. "Don't give up till you find them. These are the ones we've been looking for. Search the yards nearby. Roust the neighbors, arrest them if necessary. Someone had to see them or know of their plans!"

Instantly the men dispersed in a flurry of directions, while their superior quietly turned and walked again through the house. If they were unsuccessful, after the rest of the night's business, he would bring dogs back in the morning.

The chief opened the back door, stood for a moment, then lifted the lantern in his hand toward the blackness of the yard behind the house, peering into it as with the intent of a sorcerer, attempting to divine what no human eye could see.

He could make out no forms in the darkness, other than a handful of his own men as they ran into his field of vision. They continued the search yet farther from the house that stood now empty and silent behind him.

The moon had risen over the distant horizon, though black clouds higher in the sky waited to obscure it.

He could still feel his prey, yet neither moon nor lantern could give sight to his eyes for what they sought.

∽ 64 ∾
Tomb of Safety

From where they huddled in terrified silence, Jakob and Ulrike Kropf heard the dull thudding of booted feet above them.

These quarters were more cramped than where they had gathered together for the evening—only a few moments had passed, yet now it already seemed a lifetime ago—in the warmth of the house that had been their home for the last three years. Where they now found themselves was cramped, pitch-black, wet, cold, and pungent with the musty fragrance of earth.

Never, thought Jakob Kropf, had ordinary dirt smelled as such a rich perfume!

A cry of belated fear suddenly escaped the lips of his daughter, so rudely coming awake in a strange and fearful place and feeling bodies and arms and legs too closely about.

With an unintentional sharpness, Jakob clamped his hand quickly over her mouth. The Nazi troopers were only an arm's reach away!

He could feel her trying to cry. As he kept his hand still pressed firmly against the frightened little lips, Ulrike began speaking soothing words into her daughter's ear, then, in the quietest of possible tones, began singing a familiar whispered Hebrew lullaby in the young one's ear.

Jakob had dug this hole over the past year, rising after midnight, folding back the thick layer of turf he kept growing over the board that concealed the opening to the little cave, and then digging a few more precious centimeters. For a year he had been working here, for just such a moment as this—a bucketful of earth scooped out every few nights, carefully concealed in his own garden, sifted into the gutters of nearby streets, or carried and sprinkled through the fields at the edge of town.

He told no one, not even wife or son, though Ulrike knew he was about something secretive.

Jakob well knew the lesson of Belshazzar in Daniel 5. He too, like the ancient Babylonian king, had seen the handwriting on the wall. He knew the Jews of Poland were at great risk. He had seen the signs. After the raids in Poznan and Torun, he knew it was only a matter of time. He had then first begun making preparations to contact the fledgling escape network and had begun digging the cave thirty meters from the back door of his home, in case there was no other way to save his family's life.

He had envisioned this night many times.

Always in his nightmares he helped Ulrike and the two young ones down into the earthen tomb, giving her last-minute instructions of whom to contact, of how to place the pole tightly under the board so it would not sag or bounce if stepped upon. Then he would lay the heavy board down over them, carefully replacing the thickly cut square of sod on top of it, and would run away from the cave himself, as a decoy, waiting for the moment when an explosion of gunfire awakened him. Every dream ended the same.

But here he was, crouched in the blackness *with* them, not running for some nightmarish woods that ever receded farther into the distance, but still alive, listening, afraid each second that he would feel the earth tremble with a booted foot crashing down on the board above them, followed by yelling. Then the loose sod would be discovered and torn back, the board removed, and suddenly lights and rifles would be sticking in their faces, angry shouts, and they would be dragged out of the hole and to some pit of murder.

He could hardly believe his plan had worked! Yet they were alive and undiscovered.

The dimensions of Jakob's little cave would not appear sufficient to hide an entire family. He had intended to enlarge it further, even to supply it with emergency water and a few other helpful articles. But the moment of need arrived sooner than expected. Now they were crammed tightly into a space no more than a meter deep and probably not eighty centimeters square.

He rejoiced that he had had time to get it this big!

Jakob strained his ears to hear. All he could make out were the breathing sounds of his terrified wife and son. His daughter, calmer now, did not realize enough to be scared. Now that she was aware of her mother's arms wrapped tightly around her, she felt safe again.

Jakob knew storm troopers still ran about, for he felt the earth tremble slightly from nearby footfalls. Occasional muffled shouts penetrated the cramped hiding place.

Gradually it warmed from the heat of their bodies. How long, he wondered, could they stay alive down here without suffocating? Had he unknowingly dug his family's tomb? Might they huddle here in one another's arms until they were dead?

It would still be better than dying by gas or bullets at the hands of the Nazis.

Suddenly a terrible jolt interrupted his thoughts. Someone above had crashed down exactly upon the middle of the board he had carefully let down after himself, the sod on top of it. The jar of the heavy footfall had hit squarely in the center, where he held a thick pole for support. Would it be enough to conceal that emptiness was beneath the ground?

Anxiously he awaited further sound.

None came. The post must have absorbed the shock as he had hoped. Jakob could hardly believe that his long-imagined, long-anticipated plan had actually worked and that they had eluded the feared and ruthless Gestapo—for now.

Time passed. He could not judge how much.

Slowly Jakob could feel the air getting stale and thick and more difficult to breathe. All was black.

Hear O Israel, he began to whisper, and as he did Ulrike and the youngsters joined with the Shema, *the Lord our God is one, and thou shalt love the Lord thy God with all thine heart, and with all thy soul, and with all thy might* . . .

They continued to quote favorite passages, first from the Psalms, then from Deuteronomy.

It must be nearly midnight, thought Jakob.

He wondered if his contact would still be at the designated location. Would he wait, or would they be left on their own, to wander through the night until the Gestapo picked them up at the break of dawn?

Carefully he wriggled his cramped legs free from the weight of his son's now-sleeping body, put his hands above him, pushed up the lid, stretched himself upward, and dared a peek into the open yard.

The immediate rush of the cold, fresh, night air felt like a bracing tonic against his face. His eyes peered about, heart pounding.

Behind him, the lights of the house were still shining. He wondered if someone was inside, awaiting their return. They probably had someone guarding it.

He lifted the makeshift roof a little farther, then enough to poke out his head. He glanced about quickly.

All was still. It looked safe enough. The Gestapo appeared to be gone.

Gently and quietly, he laid back the sod and board, then stood and climbed out. Adjuring Ulrike to silence with a gestured finger against his lips, he knelt down and took the sleeping little girl from her arms.

ᴄ⚬ 65 ᴄ⚬
Night of Death

In a distant part of Wloclawek, the final search on the list had just been completed.

Neither rabbi nor kingpin of the Jewish escape network had been found. Only more Jews. None of them knew anything. These mostly came from the day's investigation of the textile factory. Where did these Jews come from, the section chief wondered. Why were there so many in Poland and Russia?

He climbed into his car and waited, then started the engine and fell in behind the truck.

It was one or two in the morning. The city was silent save the two SS cars, a truckload of God's children about to be purged forever from the German Reich, and the lone car following behind.

Slowly the four vehicles snaked their way to the outskirts of the city, then four or five kilometers southward into the country, to a lonely forested area along a dirt road some distance into the trees, where at last they stopped beside a great mound of earth.

Beside it a deep pit yawned black, broken with macabre shadows from the moon's pale light. He got out and stood beside the wide mouth of the mass grave. Not even the thick layer of dirt over them could keep away the foul stench from the rotting corpses that had already been dumped here. He turned away, walked a few paces into the woods, and lit a cigarette.

He watched silently as his men dragged their evening's quarry out of the back of the canvas-covered truck. He took a long drag on his cigarette, the glowing tip shining orange in the night, casting but faint illumination against the menacing, deep-set black eyes and angular features that watched over the cruel proceedings.

A moment or two later the screaming began again.

Let them scream, he thought. *No one can hear them here. It will all be over in a minute or two.*

"Please . . . please, in the name of God—"

The words were cut short by the sound of a club against the side of a skull, followed by a thudding of the unconscious body into the pit. Sighs and screams and prayers began now in earnest. But they were immediately replaced by cries of pain and anguish as the guards rudely shoved and kicked the small assembly tumbling down into the hole. A bright light was directed downward. The next instant the night exploded with machine-gun fire.

Five or ten seconds was all it took.

The echoes slowly died away. There was no more screaming or wailing. No voices could be heard in Rama, no weeping nor lamentation nor mourning. Neither could Rachel be heard weeping for her children, for she and they were no more.

He dismissed his men.

He would watch himself to make sure the job was to the Führer's satisfaction. In the darkness, sometimes it was difficult to tell.

He took out his own rifle and poised his lantern on the hood of his car, while his men drove away.

He detected a movement below him, a twitching of one of the bodies. Several rapid rounds burst from his gun. Blood splattered about. The body slumped and fell still.

Again he waited, thinking once more of the rabbi he had hoped to find tonight, growing angry all over again at his failure.

What was that sound he heard?

He listened intently.

It was the whimpering of a child! Those fools of his! Couldn't they even get them all thoroughly disposed of!

He squinted into the pit. He had noticed that most men facing death had the preposterous predilection to throw themselves on top of women and children, as if such an absurd gesture could save them from the spray of bullets. That had probably happened this time.

He could see nothing, but something was still alive in there.

He squeezed the trigger and sent five seconds of gunfire throughout the entire pit. He would make sure there were no more sounds.

When the sounds died away, his objective had been achieved. All was now quiet—permanently.

He turned off his lantern, but stood a while longer beside his car, taking an occasional draw on the cigarette held carefully between thumb and forefinger.

As the smoke drifted out of mouth and nose, again he fell to reflection. Momentarily he held in the smoldering acerbity of his bitter disappointment over the rabbi and mentally surveyed the dimensions of his defeat. The sharp sunken cheeks and chiseled jaw shone eerily in the pale moonlight, portraying an accurately fearsome image of the soul of stone that resided somewhere beneath the leather trench coat he wore. To say it dwelt near his heart would convey altogether an inaccurate psychic proximity, for that he possessed what is commonly referred to as a *heart* was doubtful at all. If he had ever had a conscience, that watch hound of the now-frigid soul had not given him nearly enough trouble during the time of his life when it should have barked the loudest. Alas, as such spiritual dogs are prone to do when not heeded, it had now become silent as a statue.

He had not laid his hands on either the rabbi or the network contact whose name he had heard in Warsaw.

Yet, he could not help his thoughts going back to that one empty house from earlier in the evening. Perhaps his instincts at the time had served him faithfully, and the clue he sought *was* in those silent rooms after all.

There must be some connection!

If so, he would find it. If the man called Kropf had contacted the escape network, he would leave a trail, no matter how hard he tried to disguise his moves. He would *have* to have talked to someone. No one—Jew, Pole, Russian, or German—just disappeared without a trace.

Whatever that trace was, Emil Korsch vowed to himself, he would find it!

He would dig into every file—past and present—to locate where this fellow Luddoff might have left a footprint. He had been so intent on the rabbi he had given but casual notice to local regions through which he must pass.

How could he have been so blind! The path to the rabbi's door would necessarily lead through streets and neighborhoods just like this one.

The place to begin was back at that empty house!

He would put a man on it for the rest of the night, then he himself would return in the morning, with the dogs. He would find someone who knew something.

He would infiltrate the network! He would find the miscreant Kropf. He would break the network.

He would chase them all over Poland, all over Europe if necessary. He *would* get his hands on the rabbi's holy box if it took him the rest of the war!

∞ 66 ∞

The Network

On a lonely stretch of dirt road three kilometers west of Wloclawek, three figures—a woman, a boy, and a man carrying an awkward blanketed bundle—trudged forward through the night.

A drenching rain had made their progress miserable, though it would ensure that the dogs sent to find them a few hours from now would find muddy and unsuccessful work of it.

Some distance on, at a small bridge across a creek, the man, leading the other two, turned right and pursued a course along the edge of the stream that bordered a fallow field. Half a kilometer from the bridge, he paused, glancing about the unfamiliar terrain with the aid of the moon, which was still battling the saturate clouds for supremacy of the night sky, then continued, bearing now on an angle away from the field, but still following the stream.

At length they came to the edge of a grove of birch and pine. He stopped, set down his burden, glanced nervously in every direction, and waited.

From the dark interior of the wood fifty meters away, a brief flicker of light flashed, then disappeared.

"That is the signal," whispered Jakob.

"What if it is a trap, Jakob?" said Ulrike. "What if it's a Gestapo agent?"

"It is the signal I was told to watch for. Come."

Each of the two picked up one of the youngsters, then entered the wood, making their way through the trees, stumbling now and then, for there was no path.

When they had gone the distance Jakob calculated to be far enough, they stopped.

Several meters in front of him he detected the form of a man. It was only a shadow in the blackness. It moved. A voice spoke. It was Polish.

"Mr. Kropf," he said.

"Yes, I am Jakob Kropf. Luddoff?"

"Come with me," said the man without answering. "You are late."

"The Gestapo raided our house. We had to hide for two hours."

"We are an hour behind schedule. I must get you to my house before daybreak or all will be lost."

The man began walking briskly through the woods. Jakob and Ulrike each did their best to keep up, still carrying the heavy children.

As the man set off, a second figure emerged from the trees and fell into step with them.

"Who is this?" asked Jakob. "I was told there would be only one man."

"This, Mr. Kropf, will be your traveling companion."

"I thought it was but my family and me."

"There has been a change of plans. It is imperative he get out of this region and to a safe house away from here. His family will join you tomorrow."

The second man stopped and turned around.

"I am sorry to be inconvenient, Mr. Kropf," he said in perfect Polish. "I pray I do not endanger you in any way. Perhaps I will be able to help you and your wife with the children. My name is Heziah Wissen."

He stepped toward Ulrike and took from her the burden of her daughter, then all three hastened after Luddoff, already nearly out of sight among the trees ahead.

∽ 67 ∾

Reunion

Three women huddled together on a loose pile of straw against an interior stable wall. It was the warmest place they could find in the barn, whose ancient brick walls had enough holes and cracks to admit any weather—wind or rain or snow, and especially cold—wanting to get through. But the roof was sound, and the stable against which they leaned hadn't seen occupants in some time.

Therefore they were dry. And the warmth of their own bodies, with straw piled above the two blankets they possessed between them, had made the previous night a tolerably comfortable one.

Today, however, had been long and chilly. With night again descending, and the wind whistling mournfully through those cracks and holes, their spirits had finally begun to sag.

The mother of the two teenage girls did her best to keep worry and melancholy from overtaking her, but the silent prayers she sent heavenward were evidence that she was all too conscious of the danger to women found alone and defenseless by enemy soldiers.

They had heard footsteps, or thought they had, all day.

It was hard to tell. The blustering wind outside gave a fearsome tone to everything. There had been what sounded like a wagon passing once, a herd of cows—that could not be mistaken!—and then, midway through the afternoon, what could not have been other than six or eight soldiers. They tried the padlocked door—and shook it two or three times—while the three women crouched inside in terrified prayer. Apparently thinking better of busting it to pieces, finally they continued on.

Now night was falling again. And the hours dragged tediously by.

Suddenly voices sounded outside!

The mother pulled the blanket up around their shoulders, then stretched her arms around the two girls and pulled them toward her tightly.

The door shook. They could hear people talking! Hands fumbled with the lock!

Suddenly the rickety wood door swung wide. A blast of frigid wind sent straw and dust flying, as the glare of a lantern illuminated the darkened enclosure.

A large man stood in the windy light. They recognized nothing of him! Who could it be?

He stood but an instant, glancing around as if seeking them. They slunk deeper into their hiding place of straw.

Now the man walked forward into the barn. What looked to be a young family followed him. Who were these people?

Suddenly another silhouette came into view! The aching eyes of the three fell upon a familiar face bringing up the rear—a familiar bearded face!

Now the six newcomers were startled in their turn. The next instant gasps of joy erupted from amid straw flying in the air and three bodies rushing toward them from out of the barn's darkness.

Jakob and his family stepped back in fearful astonishment as the three women rushed past them and into the arms of their fellow pilgrim.

"Oh, Heziah, we have been so worried!" exclaimed the mother of the two girls, after getting as close to the man's cheeks with her kisses as his long beard would allow.

"Papa, what took you so long?" said the younger of the two, as the rabbi hugged and greeted and soothed and kissed the three women who had been waiting for him. "A man left us here, and we have been in this barn all night and all day wondering if you would ever come!" added the other girl.

Meanwhile, Luddoff had closed the door behind them and now interrupted the reunion.

"I've given you men the instructions," he said. "You are to meet Polatski under the rail bridge four kilometers due east of here at ten o'clock tomorrow night. Do not be late. He will take you in the back of his wagon to the man who will get you safely to Ciehocinek. That will be your first safe house. There is a stream down the hill from here where you may get water and bathe. You should have enough provisions to last until tomorrow night. Lock the padlock when you go. Keep the children quiet. There are ears everywhere."

He shook each of the men's hands, handed Jakob the lantern, then reopened the door a crack and disappeared into the night.

Suddenly eight strangers stood facing each other.

The rabbi was the first to speak.

"Jakob, Ulrike," he said, "may I happily present my wife, Helga, and my two daughters—Ursula and Gisela. Helga . . . girls," he added, turning to his family, "these are my friends and our traveling companions, Jakob and Ulrike Kropf, and their son, Dieder, and daughter, Angela."

Handshakes and greetings and questions followed.

An hour later, after a sumptuous cold meal from their joint provisions, the two older girls entertained the younger two children on one side of the barn, while the four parents spoke together in low tones.

Already the circumstances of their plight had begun to forge a camaraderie between them.

᧏ 68 ᧏

Wilderness Wandering

Thus had begun the long trek across the former Poland of their grandparents and great-grandparents, a Poland now swallowed up in the insatiable territorial lust of the Third Reich.

As they walked, many thoughts went through the minds of each of these individuals whose lives fate had so suddenly thrown together. Those first two nights, in the wood and then in the deserted barn, they hadn't known a thing about one another. Their common Jewishness was the only bond they had to depend on. But if they were going to survive, if they were going to learn to trust one another, and especially if by some chance they might learn even to love one another, bonds would eventually have to fuse them on deeper levels.

Such things only time could determine. In these days of danger, however, time was not a commodity one could always depend upon.

Ulrike Kropf glanced up at her husband walking side by side for the moment with Rabbi Wissen.

Two more different men she could not imagine: the learned rabbi, a respected university professor, well known, educated, wise; and the factory worker from peasant stock, uneducated in the ways of the intellect, a father and a husband and a practical man. The one used his brain, the other his hands. Now the fate of this small band of Jewish pilgrims walking through the night toward an unknown destiny lay in the care of them both.

"God help them," Ulrike quietly prayed. "Give them wisdom. Let them guide us as one."

Ulrike Kropf, like her husband, was a practical woman, though she was a thinker in her own way as well. It had now been two weeks since they had left their home and begun this journey through unfamiliar land. She could not avoid almost a tingling quiver of kinship with the ancient children of Israel, though her heart could not keep away a constant fear on behalf of her children. She knew nothing of where they were bound. But neither had the children in the desert. They had had only the promise of God to guide them.

Ulrike too knew the promises of Yahweh. He would keep them in the palm of his hand.

There was this difference, too, between those who followed Moses through the desert and this little band of Jewish wanderers. She and Helga and their children and husbands were fortunate to encounter untold numbers of friends willing and eager to help them. This was no aimless desert experience. Though she might not have understood everything, it was clear a distinct plan and schedule guided their movements. She had found tears rising daily within her from the sheer kindness and sacrifice of so many on their part.

Most did not even share their faith or race. Most were Christians. Some professed no religion at all. Yet these vast numbers of underground servants for good in the midst of the Nazi plague risked their lives on behalf of the safety and care of people they did not know and would never see again.

What was it that motivated such people, Ulrike wondered anew each time. In what deep recesses of being did that altruism originate prompting some men and women in times of trouble to make sacrifices for their neighbor, while others thought only of safety for themselves?

Was it disaster that brought out the deepest goodness or the deepest selfishness of people? She especially wondered about those calling themselves Christians, both Catholic and Protestant. Most welcomed them like fellows of belief, speaking of their worship of the same God.

They treated them like kinsmen. They called her *sister*, and her husband *brother*. She did not understand it. But she could feel it changing her. She would never be the same.

Ulrike glanced down at her son just in front of her, and then to her daughter at her side, whose tiny hand lay in hers. She gave it an unconscious squeeze.

She hoped the youngsters would in later years remember more from the experience of these weeks than fear. However it all turned out, something deep was at work. She found herself praying for the youngsters, that they would grow to be the kind of people who would serve others as they were themselves being served by the loving hands of God's family—a family much wider and more encompassing than only the boundaries of their Jewish faith.

Her husband and the rabbi still spoke together, more animated now. The air was punctuated with their gestures. Occasionally she heard one of them laugh.

She could not explain why, but the sounds of their voices mingling as one sent strange rays of warmth through her heart.

∝ 69 ∝

Even the Petals Have Fragrance

The eight weary travelers awoke one at a time from a fitful and uneven afternoon's sleep.

When Heziah came to himself, he saw Jakob standing at one

of the windows of the barn, staring out into the gathering darkness. He walked quietly across the wood floor to join him.

This was supposed to be the final leg of their trek.

"Could not sleep—eh, my friend?" said the rabbi softly.

Kropf turned toward him and nodded.

"I suppose I am anxious to be gone from here."

"It has been a long six weeks. I too will rejoice to sleep more than two nights in the same place."

The two men fell silent.

The factory worker and rabbi, by common Hebrew heritage, had suddenly been thrown together in this nighttime life-and-death journey across the Poland of their ancestors in which they had suddenly become outcasts. They were the hunted who knew that any day, any night, the slightest mistake, the slightest slipup could mean death to their family. They had learned to depend on one another, to trust one another . . . and to consider one another brother and friend.

"What will you do?" asked Jakob at length. "What will you do with the box and its contents?"

"If we reach the safe house all will be well. Hopefully it will be protected there for a time. Then I must try to contact the southern network," replied Wissen. "We must do what we can to get as many as possible across the southern borders."

"Your wife will object."

The rabbi sighed.

"Yes, you are right. I will not like leaving her and the girls again. But sometimes there are works given men that require sacrifice of their family. This is such a time for all Jews, in one way or another. Many lives may depend on my success."

Another pause.

"What about you, my friend Kropf?"

"What about me?"

"What will you do?"

"After the safe house?" Jakob sighed. "I do not know. We have no place to go, no hope for safety. I suppose we must keep hiding until this terrible time is past. Perhaps we can obtain new identity cards, change our names—*how*, I have no idea—and somehow find a way to start a new life . . . as Gentiles."

The network the rabbi spoke of was one of many small organizations within the overall resistance and underground movement, joined but intermittently with one another. There were many such peopled lattices of help, some attempting to move families eastward into Russia; some toward Switzerland, where Dietrich Bonhoeffer's sister and many like her now resided in safety. Others simply connected safe houses, large and small, in a loose, invisible confederation of compassion for those who had no place to go.

It was an uncertain life for the Jews who found themselves at the mercy of those they did not know, made all the worse by realizing they were endangering the very lives of those who showed them mercy.

But it was better than the camps.

Their conversation was cut short by the approach of young Angela behind them.

In a few minutes Ulrike and Helga were also up, followed by the entire troop.

The previous night had been like so many of the others during their three-hundred-kilometer westward pilgrimage across northern Poland, all of which faded into a continuous string of fields, barns, woods, back streets, basements, attics, darkened rooms, unfamiliar voices, hushed conversations, and constant fear of discovery. They had been huddled into the back of a rickety old wood farm wagon, covered first with blankets, then with hay and straw, and transported over bumpy terrain, eventually arriving, just as the sun was coming up, at this deserted building, which had served as their accommodations for the day's repose.

It was never easy to get all eight of them to sleep at the same time. Sometimes weariness overtook the children at the most inconvenient moments. Angela often had to be carried by one of the four adults. But on this day, by noon, all had slept, for some hours at least. Now, with dusk falling, it was time once again to be on their tired and travel-worn feet.

The remaining four kilometers they must travel alone, without benefit of a guide, they had been told.

Sometimes this was the way. The network had to be regularly broken so that the people involved did not know one another.

It protected them all. Only those moving along the network encountered more than two or three of the links of the chain.

The greatest precaution against discovery was that no single individual knew *too* much, and those who helped were familiar with a minimum of others like themselves. They must not know what went on before or beyond the time when travelers in danger came into their hands.

The farmer who had deposited them at this particular site, which was not his, did not know whose building it was or where they were bound next. He only knew sufficient instructions to take them halfway. Then they would be met by another, in the middle of the night at a prearranged point, one who knew nothing of the farmer, his hay wagon, *or* the building, but who *did* possess the directions necessary for the remainder of their night's journey and the password that would be required of them at its end. He knew nothing beyond that.

There was a small moon. They set out alone with the scant instructions they possessed.

Through the deserted countryside they walked, Jakob, as was his custom, leading the way. The partnership could not have been more perfect under the circumstances. Heziah Wissen listened to and memorized every detail of every instruction, which Jakob Kropf then let his hands and feet interpret in leading the little band. Each needed the other. The rabbi was happy to submit to the leadership of Jakob's feet, Jakob to the wisdom of Heziah's judgment.

The mutuality of friendship and trust between them was of a very practical sort.

It worked. And it had kept all eight of them alive and moving steadily toward their unknown destination.

They met what was supposed to be their final contact sometime between one and three in the morning, in a deserted field next to an abandoned shack.

Words between them had been scant. It was always best that way. The network was in the business of helping and saving lives, not making friends. The man had given the rabbi their directions for the rest of the night and the password, which he must not forget if they were to gain admittance.

They thanked him. He disappeared.

They continued on.

They would meet no one else. The rest of the way they would have to make on their own.

By daybreak they had still not reached the edge of the wood. Under cover of the trees, the moon's light had not been sufficient to keep easily to the paths and dirt roads. They had made some errors, had to backtrack, and Jakob had done well to keep them moving in the right direction at all.

Now it was dawn, and he knew they could not make their destination. The man by the shack had been specific and insistent.

"If you have not arrived by first light, *do not* continue. Hide amongst the trees until nightfall. You may be so close as even to see across the clearing to your destination. You will be weary, hungry, thirsty, and your children may complain. But to attempt to cross even that short distance after the grey of light has come could endanger the entire operation in this region. There are reports of heavy SS activity, and no matter how safe it seems, you could be seen. It *must* be black before you make your final approach."

"If such does befall us," asked the rabbi, "where should we spend the day?"

"In the wood. It contains many dense places. Find one of them, stay there, and keep your children quiet. I have not been there myself, but that wood is reported to be extremely dangerous."

The professor had nodded.

Now, indeed, it had come upon them exactly as the man had warned. Day was rapidly approaching. Jakob and Heziah began looking about for a place to rest and spend the daylight hours.

They found a small clearing in the midst of the wet woods, surrounded on all sides by trees and brush, and with the blankets they had, they were able to make the children tolerably comfortable.

Not long after they were settled, suddenly Jakob began making wild gestures with his hand, signaling for absolute silence.

The tramping of footsteps could be heard through the trees!

Jakob fell silently to his belly and strained to see out of their little hollow through the trunks of the pines surrounding them.

Yes, his ears had heard correctly! Two booted feet strode through the desolate early-morning forest.

What if it was their next contact, come out looking for them, he thought to himself.

Should he call out?

What was the password again? Something about plants or trees or woods or flowers.

Heziah would remember. Maybe he should call out the password.

He glanced back at the others. They all stared at him with anxious faces. He didn't want to wait all day before moving on, not when they were this close. He'd get the exact password from the rabbi. What was there to lose?

He began inching back toward his companions. An inner urge compelled him to look out through the trees again. His gaze fell on the boots, now retreating through the forest. If he did not call out the password soon, it would be too late.

An involuntary chill swept through him. Suddenly the boots disappearing through the trees seemed unfriendly. Jakob watched them, keeping silent.

What had he been thinking?

How could he have come so close to betraying their position! What a fool! The man had been very clear—hide until day is done. Even the woods were dangerous!

When the sounds of the heavy feet were gone, he crept back to the others. No one spoke. The look on Jakob's face said clearly enough that danger might still be lurking nearby and that, though this was supposed to be their last day, caution was called for.

Wherever the booted feet were going, or whatever was their business in this wood, they were not heard from again that day.

Midway through the afternoon, a tremendous rainstorm drenched all eight. No blankets or coats could keep away heaven's downpour. Such misery had not prevailed since the day of their setting out.

Waiting was harder in some ways than danger. One had too

much unwelcome time to think. Sometimes the imagination conjured up worse unrealities than what actually happened.

What had happened, Jakob found himself wondering as he sat in the wood, shivering. How could he have almost given them away! Jakob thought he could not stand yet another hour of the wet and cold, *hearing* rather than feeling the heavy drops of rain pounding upon the top of his head, as he tried his best to shield Dieder from the worst of it.

In the midst of all the waiting and walking and uncertainty, there had yet been a haste to these weeks, an intensity such that already events and days and faces and places had hopelessly blurred in his brain. It would be years before his mind would be capable of focusing again on the individual men and women to whom they owed their lives, and unraveling the multitude of places they had been hidden.

When night finally fell, there was hardly rejoicing in the tiny Hebrew camp. It seemed too much to hope that this wandering in the wilderness of the Polish desert would not last to the duration of the same forty years as the pilgrimage of their ancient predecessors in the wilderness of Sinai.

Jakob led them safely to the edge of the wood, though by the time they reached it the darkness was extreme.

They stopped.

The moon was just rising, casting but hints of light over the landscape. It was a good thing this winter was not so severe as the last or they would all have long since been dead. As it was, they'd had only rain, not bitter cold, to overcome.

Jakob could make out forms and images, but they had not been told what the place would look like, only where to go and what to say.

He told the others to remain under cover of the trees. He would reconnoiter. He left them and moved across the open field.

He was gone twenty or thirty minutes.

Suddenly he appeared again, with the stealthy step of a cat, and motioned them to follow.

A few minutes later they were all squeezing through a narrow opening through tightly growing trees or brush. None could tell if they were entering the woods again, only that the way was very tight. In truth, as the light of day would have made clear, they were squeezing through a tall, thick hedge.

Still following Jakob, they crossed over a small wooden bridge, then continued walking up a steady incline. It was some time before any of the others realized he was now following a narrow path along the inside perimeter next to the same hedge they had squeezed through.

Even by the thin light of the rising moon, they could tell they were no longer in the woods. This was certainly no wild place. What appeared to be a sizeable and well-cared-for garden shone shadowy to their left.

The pathway left the hedge, bore into the garden area, then ended abruptly in an arbor bordered on all three remaining sides with thick shrubbery and more hedges. There appeared no way through it.

Jakob stopped.

Looking all about and probing the scratchy, leafy, solid wall of hedge with his hand, somewhere in its midst he felt a rope. He pulled it, but heard nothing.

A moment later, exactly to the left of where he stood, a portion of the wall of hedge swung aside on silent, invisible hinges.

A figure appeared in a recessed tunnel before them, holding a dim lantern, saying nothing.

Jakob motioned the rabbi forward.

"Do you have any roses?" asked the rabbi of the figure shrouded in the darkness of the tunnel.

There was but a moment's hesitation.

"No, this is not the season for blooms."

"Yes," answered the rabbi, *"but for those who love, even the petals have fragrance."*

"I see you understand the Father's way," said the voice. *"How many blossoms do you need?"*

"Eight," replied the rabbi.

"Then come, I believe we shall find some for you."

Without further words, they were admitted through a door into an earthen tunnel some fifteen or twenty meters in length. No light shone other than the small lantern carried by the large figure who now went before them.

They had crossed over the River Jordan and into the Promised Land!

They arrived at another door, then walked through it into an enclosed chamber with stone floor and walls. A stairway was visible, but they did not take it. Their guide opened another narrow door, through which a pale light shone. Immediately he extinguished his own lantern, then spoke.

"Go through this passage," he said. "It is straight but goes for some distance. At the end you will find a small room. Wait there. You will be summoned."

Jakob, in the lead again, did as he was instructed. When all eight of the wet and weary sojourners had passed through the door into the damp, narrow corridor, the door closed behind them.

Jakob led the way along the wet dirt floor, until, as promised, they reached a room at its end. There they stood, huddled in a wet, shivering circle, for perhaps five minutes.

The sound of a door opening somewhere above them sounded. They all glanced up. A tiny, thin, circular staircase in the corner was now lit by a lantern in the hand of a woman dressed in the clothes of a maid.

"Come with me," she said. "The stairs are narrow and steep, so please take care. We will be climbing more stairs, but you are safe now and need have no fear. You are among friends."

Jakob followed her, taking his young daughter in his arms, and went up the tiny corkscrew as best he could. Ulrike followed, then the others, with the rabbi last of all.

The light was sufficient to indicate they were indeed inside a house at last, and what appeared to be an enormous one. They wound around and through many passages and corridors, up two more narrow flights of stairs, through a half dozen doors, around more corners, through the oddest-shaped passageways, until at length a door opened and they found themselves suddenly in a well-lit, hospitable, wonderfully clean bedroom.

"Here is the first room for you," said their guide, turning to them with a bright smile. "The other is just across the hall. I have bread and dried fruit being brought up. Baths are being drawn for the children and you two dear mothers," she added, glancing at both of the women. "We will have dry clothes for you shortly. My name is Heidi, and if there is anything you need, each of your rooms has a bell that sounds in my room. Please, do not think twice to ring it if there is anything I have missed."

Thinking that they must have died and gone to heaven, and that the angels were now attending them, both Ulrike and Helga broke into tears and wept with abandon.

Great drops standing also in his eyes, a weary but contented Rabbi Wissen spoke to his hostess, who was dressed in a white smock that made her appear very much indeed an angel to his Jewish eyes.

"Tell me please, young lady," he said, "when will we meet our hosts? We . . . we must thank them for—"

His voice broke, but Heidi understood his heart perfectly.

"There will be plenty of time for that in the morning," she said. "You will be with us for a while. Be comfortable now. Get clean and dry and have what food and drink you want."

"Thank you—you are more kind than we can thank you for!"

"Sleep well, all of you," said Heidi. "We are happy you have come to us."

She led them to the second room, gave the still-weeping mothers instructions about clothes and the baths, then left the travelers alone.

"God be with you," she said.

"Shalom," said the rabbi.

"Shalom also to you," repeated Heidi.

⤳ 70 ⤳

A Morning in the Garden

Clouds filled with rain moved north to the Baltic through the night.

The morning dawned the perfect brilliant winter's day—crisp, bright, with a million sparkling dewdrop diamonds promising to reflect the sun's rays as soon as it was up.

Baron Heinrich von Dortmann had been out since the moment it thought of being light. He knew a spectacular sunrise was promised, and not even a war had succeeded in diminishing his appreciation for the growing, living, revealing wonders of God's creation.

He and his wife had walked a small distance into the fields and woods together, praying for the extended and ever-changing family that now dwelt with them. They had returned, and Marion had gone on to the house to help with breakfast preparations, while he had gone to the garden to await the sunrise.

It was there he met his daughter. The baron had taught her well of his ways, for she was on the same errand of Fatherhood discovery as himself.

He came upon her bent over, examining the green frond of a fresh fern that was dripping liquid jewels from the night's rain. He watched her with the same lively enthusiasm to observe growth in process as she was giving the fern.

When she turned, she evidenced no surprise at seeing him.

"Don't you simply love it after a rain, Papa?" she asked with almost a solemnity in her voice.

"I do indeed," returned the baron, also reverently.

"If raindrops are, as you have sometimes said, God's tears, then surely does a reaping of joy follow them."

"Perhaps they are tears of his joy," said the baron, smiling.

"This morning's surely are," rejoined Sabina. "Everything is so bright and clean and clear. What a gorgeous day it will be when the sun is up in the sky and making a tiny rainbow of every little pearl."

Not only did Sabina sound like her father, she had gradually taken on more and more of his countenance as well. As she had matured, a reminder of the baron's inner stature had deepened in her eyes. Her facial characteristics—skin and cheeks, lips and chin, nose and forehead—had all taken on a greater expressiveness of calm maturity. Truly she was a girl no longer, but fully a woman, and a beautiful one, radiant in the security of her Father's love.

"I am always filled with wonder that I can look upon these same plants, this fern, all the same flowers, day after day, and never grow weary of them," she mused.

"Such is *another* of the garden's many mysteries," rejoined her father. "You are but twenty-one; I am well past forty. I will be an old man before long if the hands of time do not stop! But I never tire of this place for a day. In all God's things there is unceasing revelation, unceasing creative imagination unfolding ever outward."

He stopped, crinkling his eyebrows.

"I never paused to think of that before this moment, Sabina," he said. "Might that be one of the reasons God places *growth* in what he makes, so that there is constant *newness* emerging out from within—new leaves, new skin for the lizards, new hair for us men and women, new blossoms, new fingernails!"

"Papa, sometimes you say such funny things!" laughed Sabina, the little girl emerging again in the high, bell-like tinkling of her laughter.

"But think of it! Always there is a part of nature that is dying to make room for the new—the browning fronds of the fern to give place for the tender new green unrolling from the heart of it, just as you were observing in that little fellow there. Even these rose blossoms around us over there in the rose garden," he said, gesturing widely with his hand at the plants he loved so much, "even the outside petals brown and slowly shrivel so as to open wider and reveal more of the inside. Then each blossom itself dies so that another might take its place."

"There aren't many roses blooming now," said Sabina, "in the middle of winter."

"Not many, you are right," agreed the baron, "but a few brave buds will burst through the stiff stems and icy ground, just to remind us that life still goes on inside, though our eyes cannot always see it. And if such a persistent blossom is determined to force its way out into the sun and air, not the fiercest hailstorm, not the strongest wind, not the coldest snow will prevent its doing so. It may not be a luxuriant blossom, but the strength of life will be vital within it."

"Is that why you always leave a dozen or two of the roses unpruned throughout the winter?"

The baron nodded. "You never know what story a rose might have to tell," he said. "It might require a patient and quiet listening in order to discern the subtle message it is trying to convey. That is all the more reason I like to give growing things opportunity to share their secrets, roses most of all."

Sabina thought of the yellow rose Matthew had given her, dried now and kept in a special place in her room, and what it spoke to her whenever she looked upon it. Her father was right—flowers *did* possess secrets to tell, though some of them were accompanied by their own kinds of tears.

"Even if the blooms are rare at this time of the year," the baron went on, "you know what they say about roses?"

"What, Papa?"

"That the blossoms almost don't even matter."

"Why?"

"Because, for those who love, even the petals have fragrance."

They both laughed. They had repeated this same conversation, each taking the other half of it, many times.

A silence fell as father and daughter began now to walk about the garden slowly together.

"We have some new blossoms with us in the house," said the baron at length.

"Yes, I met them last evening."

"Oh, I didn't know you had seen them."

"Heidi came for me to help the girls with the bath."

"Are they near your own age?"

"Thirteen and fifteen, I think," answered Sabina. "And there's a younger boy and girl in the other family."

"I see."

Again they walked a while along the wet pathway, breathing deeply of the cold morning air.

"Every day it is all so fresh and new," said Sabina at length.

"With new secrets of the Father's life to reveal! And everywhere today are the Father's tears—tears perhaps *not* of joy but of grief as he looks over his world," added the baron thoughtfully. "Yet even in the midst of such misery as our country has brought to the world, the Father's creativity cannot be stopped. Every leaf, every grain out in our fields in the summer, every bush and flower and tree—summer, winter, it matters not— they are all a little different today than what they were yesterday."

"Do you suppose people are like that too, a little different every day than what they were the day before?"

"An intriguing question. Hmmm . . . we must ponder that one carefully! And why should it not be so? Every day the garden is new. Every day all of creation is new! Every day, it sometimes seems, our house of retreat has new inhabitants. So why should not man himself change every day as well?"

"Little wonder then that we do not tire of growing things," said Sabina. "You have done it again, Papa! You have answered the question I did not even know was within me!"

"I was only thinking aloud to myself. Truly, I had never thought of it from quite this angle before."

"I can tell from that look in your eye that you are not altogether through pondering it yet."

"You are right, one more truth occurs to me. Not only does God continually make all things new, but he never makes the same thing over again. Imagine, Sabina, of all the roses ever to grow on the face of the earth, no blossom ever duplicates another. *Every one* uniquely its own!"

"Just like snowflakes."

"It is beyond my comprehension to contemplate. Nor does he ever *save* anything. Just look at this glorious sunrise in the sky to the east just now."

Father and daughter beheld its beauty, spreading throughout the sky above the surrounding hedges and trees of the garden.

"Orange and red and yellow, with the blue of the sky rising behind it and the golden blast of the sun preparing to peek over the horizon—"

He stopped, and they stood a moment together in silence.

"God's paintbrush is so lavish with its colors," the baron went on, "yet when another twenty minutes shall have passed, he will toss away this morning's brush and never use it again. Never! It will be gone before our guests are out of bed!"

"It does seem a shame."

"Oh no, don't you see, Sabina? In God's divine extravagant 'waste' is the glory of whatever his finger touches! Man constantly seeks to have and save and hoard. The children of Israel tried to store up the manna just as so many poor souls think to keep their security in my brother Otto's bank. But God creates a sunrise and lets it dissolve into the blue, never to make just that same sunrise again. God fashions a rose and lets it go back to the dirt whence it came, never to make that same rose again. He saves nothing, he hoards nothing. He has no pockets, no banks, no libraries even to store up his truths. His truths live—like the sunrise and the roses. Even in their death, there is life, for new roses and ferns and sunrises emerge to replace those that have passed."

"Do you mean we should not even cut the roses and try to prolong our enjoyment of them?"

"No, our Father gives us all things to enjoy. I believe it causes God delight every time one of his creatures puts a nose to the blossom of a rose, smells deeply of its perfume, and then gazes upward and outward upon the world with renewed wonder, renewed hopefulness, and new love for all things."

"There is something in the smell that seems to beckon toward a hidden place you can never quite lay a finger upon."

"Such is one of the many secrets the Creator has placed within the heart of the rose, which to touch ever sends some deep part of our being calling out after the eternal. The rose has many secrets, just as the garden has many mysteries. No, my child, it gives God pleasure when we enjoy what he has made. We may pick them and give them to one another and let them spread happiness to our hearts' content."

Sabina was silent, thinking again of the yellow rose in her room.

"If only we do not try to keep them too long?" she suggested.

"Yes, and make the thing itself the object of our love, rather than him who made it," said her father, not realizing the several depths upon which Sabina was taking in his words. "All things will pass," he went on. "Even this lovely garden, all these lovely roses, and our house itself one day will be gone. But the life they gave will live on. Thus we must wisely steward all these wonders God has allowed us to enjoy and take care that they give *life*, so that when the objects themselves are trampled under the passing feet of time, the life they have given will live on."

"I do not like to hear you speak of the garden passing away, Papa. I know it is true, but still I don't like it."

"Ah, the shortsighted idealism of youth!" chuckled the baron.

"Are you teasing me, Papa?" asked Sabina, smiling but feigning hurt.

"Perhaps I am."

"I know you are right. But I like to think that one day my own children, and theirs after them, will continue to enjoy the garden as I have."

The baron's face clouded. These were not days when he took pleasure in thinking about the future. Notwithstanding the promise of today's sunshine, a dark cloud hung over the world, and he knew this place he loved so dearly was exactly under the middle of it.

"Who can tell? Perhaps they shall," he added in a pensive voice. "But then, I would rather my grandchildren, and your grandchildren, and all those who come after us—I would rather they knew but a few of the true mysteries of the garden, than that they possessed a hundred gardens more beautiful than this. Roses and gardens are not ours to hoard or possess, or even merely to love and enjoy, as much as I dearly love and delight in them. They are given us, as are all created things, that we might be awakened to discover their secrets. The whole creation delights in secrets, but secrets whose purpose is to reveal, not hide, mysteries written into the world that we might learn of him who is the Author of secrets and Revealer of mysteries and Maker of beautiful things and Creator of all life and love in the world."

"You should have been a poet, Papa!"

The roar of laughter that exploded from the baron's mouth was utterly childlike in its merriment, and strangely incongruous with the serenity of the morning stillness. Not even the cloud over Europe could quench the inherent joy that his being took in the delight of living.

"Ah, what an extravagantly creative God is our Father! And see," said the baron, pointing, "the sun has exploded over the trees. The colors of the paintbrush have faded already."

"But he is making another right now for the people in England who are still asleep."

"And preparing a new one for us on the morrow. The manna never stops flowing from his hand."

"You see the hidden meaning in everything."

"There is meaning in every atom of the universe. I find myself wondering, too, if all these sunrises and roses and living things *must* in fact be perishable. Otherwise we would not be so wondrously capable of beholding their beauty. Perhaps in the withering of the flower and the fading of the colors of the sunrise over the clouds, we are constantly forced to look beyond their passing forms into that great Soul of all created things where dwells the Father. If they were not perishable, we should only worship their bodies, their husks, and never seek the mysteries beyond."

∽ 71 ∾
Life at *Lebenshaus*

The baron sat down in his study to prepare himself for the day.

Ever since that morning after the war had broken out, more than three years earlier, when he had sought God for direction, opportunities for ministering to the Father's children had not ceased.

Aaron's family had naturally been the first they had taken in. But quickly there had been others. Strangers had been coming to *Lebenshaus* for years; they never knew why or how. Suddenly, however, they appeared more and more regularly. Before he knew it and without having sought it, the baron was an important link in the underground rescue network, meshing Christians and Jews in a loose federation of dangerous compassion.

Within months he and Aaron had begun a series of clandestine remodeling and construction projects to ensure the safety of their guests and the integrity of the secret ministry of *Lebenshaus*. They added rooms and passageways, doubled many interior walls for soundproofing, added bathrooms, and blocked off certain whole corridors.

Making use of the latest technology, they had incorporated warning lights, bells, and other means of communication in their scheme. The baron and the doctor found it a challenge to acquire supplies while keeping their work secret—a difficulty also experienced in the purchasing of food and in the logistical difficulties inherent in a myriad of other household details as time went on—and much of it had gone at a much slower pace than they might have liked. But in the end, most necessary modifications to house and garden had been safely completed.

Perhaps the most ingenious work of all they had undertaken, under pretense of garden work, involved the installation of a hidden electrical device, buried in the ground some three centimeters below the surface just inside the lower opening in the hedge, and connected by underground wire with the house, which, when activated by the pressure of a foot, set off a bell inside. With advance warning that persons had entered the garden, the baron could go quickly downstairs into the cellar below the south parlor, and thence through the newly discovered tunnel that led outside under the southwest corner of the west wing, extending some twenty meters underground to a wooden door, there to await the new arrivals.

This door Schmidt and Hans had stumbled upon when digging up a tremendous overgrown shrub that covered a steeply contoured wall of earth along the hillside in the northwest corner of the garden.

The baron had immediately been summoned. The door was excavated, pried open, and the missing tunnel discovered. Running through the dark, moldy, damp sunken corridor, they soon found themselves swinging back rusted hinges of a heavy stone door with crowbars and hammers and entering the cellar. The baron was beside himself to find such communication between the underground portion of the house and *Der Frühlingsgarten.*

"To think," he said, "that all these years the legendary tunnel was thought to be on the north side, when actually it had been dug straight through the cellar! We had the wrong garden attached to the old stories!"

The half-rotten wooden door had been replaced and great quantities of shrubbery and hedge transplanted to hide it as effectively as before. A pull cord was installed to ring a second bell inside the cellar, where the stone door was completely outfitted with new hardware.

By the time these operations were complete, a nearly foolproof system was in place whereby only those who had been informed of all three aspects of obtaining entry were admitted to the secret life of *Lebenshaus*—the opening in the hedge, the precisely phrased password, and the hidden cord in the hedge. None but those sent through the mechanism of the network would know how to make use of all three.

As the complexity of their activity grew, the baron released most of his permanent staff. The war took all the younger men, and he took to the employment of day laborers in his fields, many of whom were women of the region who now, with husbands absent, sought whatever work they could find.

Those few faithful servants who remained, whom he trusted and whose Christian faith was sound—Heidi, Carola, Hans, Schmidt, Heiko, and a handful of others—he took into his confidence. There was a danger to them if they remained, he said. If they wanted to leave, he would understand and wish them well. All decided to remain.

Heidi—zealous and faithful Christian sister who found excitement in the adventure of it all, and whose servant's hands and heart were constantly on the lookout for ways to express themselves—had taken up quarters in the southwest corner's vacant room so as to be closer to the guests.

Not long after the war's outbreak, the baron also had a serious talk with his daughter.

"Now do you see how big is the danger?" he asked her. "Are you sure you don't want to reconsider and go to Switzerland or to join the McCallums?"

"No, Papa," she had assured him. "I want to stay. My place is with you and Mama."

In the years since, the new and even more important work of *Lebenshaus* had become a very personal ministry for Sabina. As she entered into the full dimensions of the womanhood her parents had seen emerging for some time, she was all the more aware that God had given *her* this to do as well.

The baron found himself reflecting often on his talk with his friend Dietrich Bonhoeffer, how they had each faced difficult decisions to make and had been presented with different courses to walk. Now, as he heard it, Dietrich was with the resistance and involved in an effort to overthrow the Nazi government and contact the British for peace.

He could never himself have walked such a road, the baron thought. There was no other place he would rather be serving God than exactly where he was!

What unity of Spirit he was privileged to be part of every day! His admiration grew for Jews everywhere, despite so many surface differences of religion. He could never look upon these descendants of Abraham and not sense a kinship and affinity with them deep within his being.

As he reflected on all the changes that had taken place, and the enormity of kingdom responsibilities the Father had placed within his hands, spontaneously Heinrich von Dortmann slipped to the floor beside his desk.

∾◡◠

As the head of the house prayed in the solitude of his office, his daughter, Sabina, walked briskly along the straight second-floor corridor of the west wing toward the rooms of last evening's new guests.

"*Morgen*, Fräulein von Dortmann," a short, balding man standing in an open doorway greeted her.

"*Morgen*, Herr Müller," she replied.

"Did your father complete my identity card?" he asked.

"I'm sorry, I don't know, Herr Müller," answered Sabina. "He was working on yours and several others last night, but we did have some new arrivals. You will see him at breakfast."

"Thank you, Fräulein. It is just that I must be on my way."

"I'm sure my father is well aware of your situation, Herr Müller. Excuse me."

Sabina continued on, smiling to herself. The little man asked about his papers at least three times a day. Never had she seen anyone so impatient. Where was he going to go that was safer than *Lebenshaus*? But whereas most of their guests seemed perfectly content to remain right where they were, Albert Müller, Jewish watchmaker from Dresden, was anxious to be on his way.

"*Guten Morgen,* Sabina," said an elderly lady, passing her in the hall on the way to the bathroom.

"*Morgen,* Frau Sievers."

Veering to the right, Sabina now entered the circuitous guest quarters of the east wing, which her father had extensively remodeled since she and Matthew had explored it together, to accommodate the large volume of human traffic that had become the chief function of *Lebenshaus* since the dramatically stepped-up persecution of Jews. In all the maze of corridors, people of all ages moved calmly about, moving to and from their rooms, any one of several bathrooms, or either of the two stairways by which the upper region of the house communicated with the lower. The estate von Dortmann was no longer a mere spa for the soul, as Thaddeus McCallum had phrased it, but was truly a house where near-certain death was daily exchanged for *life* by those who came to make it their temporary home.

～◦◦～

Meanwhile, in his office, the baron remained on his knees.

"Oh, Father," he prayed softly, "I have such a multitude of things to be grateful for. Thank you for this marvelous house of your provision where we can feed and care for the frightened lambs of your flock, where they can find rest for their souls. Protect this place, Father. Encircle your angels round about it with their invisible swords of fire, keeping eyes that belong to the enemy from penetrating the hedge of thorns you have built around those who call upon your name.

"Oh, God, protect all your people in this war-torn land who are trying to share life with those who suffer. I pray for Dietrich, wherever he is and whatever his business. Keep him from falling prey to the machinations and motives of those who would change the world for their own ends. Keep him pure, and let him look only to you as the object of his service.

"Whoever these dear ones are who joined us last night, I pray that you will be a Father to them, that you will reveal yourself to them in all the small ways that you make yourself known. Help us to serve and give ourselves to them. Let them feel the depth of our love and the warmth of your Spirit during their time with us. Make me especially their servant, that I might reveal to them the life and character of your Son, Jesus."

The significance of the prayer he had just heard leave his mouth came down upon the baron's consciousness, and the mood of his entreaty turned solemn. Gently he rocked back and forth on his knees, in growing weight of spirit. He knew the hour was late and the cost of true discipleship was increasingly being exacted from those who were numbered among God's men on the earth.

"Help me, Father," he continued softly after a moment. "Help me to be more your child and more a servant to those for whom you may want me to lay down my life. Give me courage to do what you set before me. Help me to trust you, Lord. Give me the grace and strength to face whatever may come with utter faith in your goodness."

He paused to take a quavery breath into his heaving lungs. Tears rolled slowly out of his eyes.

"Be my Father, Lord," he whispered, weeping quietly. "Make me more the son you would have me be. You know the vulnerable places in this weak and fearful heart of mine. I am not the man to occupy this position. Oh, Lord . . . why have you placed me here, with so many looking to me for their hope and encouragement and sustenance?

"Let me bear the burden of this terrible time for my wife and daughter, and all these others. Increase my strength where in my own eyes I seem but a child. Increase my passion to know you and my willingness to obey you. Let me serve these people . . . let me sacrifice myself for them in whatever ways you put before me. Strip away any remainders of my self, that all my being might do only what you would have of me . . . and calm my fears, my Father, as I contemplate with uncertainty the days that lie ahead. Deepen within my breast the confidence that I reside nowhere but in the palm of your hand."

His lips fell silent, and the very calm for which he had prayed came over him. He remained, breathing in and out steadily and with rising assurance coming back to him. In a few moments his tears were dry, and he rose to his feet.

He took another deep breath, then turned and left his study.

He walked straight to the remodeled dining facility on the second floor, where he expected to find their new guests.

Sabina was there ahead of him, and she proceeded to introduce him to the Wissen and Kropf families. The baron gave each person in turn a heartfelt welcome.

"But I recognize your voice, do I not, Herr Baron?" said Jakob as the two men shook hands.

"So do I," added Helga Wissen. "You are right, Jakob."

The baron laughed good-naturedly.

"You have caught me—I confess!" he said. "You all saw me last night."

"But where?" asked young Dieder Kropf. "I don't remember seeing anything, it was so dark."

Again the baron laughed.

"Where you saw me, young man," he said, "was in the tunnel when I let you in from the garden. You see, I bring all our guests into the house through the tunnel personally."

∾ 72 ∾
Clues Leading South

There was a certain diabolical cleverness to these people, thought Emil Korsch to himself.

It was not surprising to find them so successful in business and financial matters. They were shrewd and wily. He could see the danger posed and why Hitler had sworn to eradicate them.

Not that he didn't hate the swine. But it heightened the challenge of the hunt and added a certain invigorating factor of formidability that would increase the pleasing satisfaction of his final victory. A high-stakes game of chess—with death to the loser!

A most cunning stratagem indeed! The old straight-line-leading-nowhere ploy!

And he had fallen for it! Halfway across Poland, he had grabbed at every straw they carefully left for him, thinking he was getting closer all the time. He had never even stopped to reflect on the rationality of the absurd direction. What could possibly lie to the northwest? The direction had been diversionary from the outset!

It hadn't been until Bydgoszcz that he began to smell the rank odor of deception.

There suddenly the trail had diverged in two directions. One seemed still pointed northwest, it would appear toward the Baltic. The other turned sharply, toward Poznan . . . and the south.

Suddenly the truth had dawned on him. Reaching the Baltic accomplished nothing! Getting Jews out by boat through the Swedish and Danish channels was impossible. There were scattered reports of such madcap attempts, even toward Finland. But no, the only real safety for them lay south—in Switzerland!

What kind of fool did they take him for! He hadn't exactly come down with yesterday's rain! They were dealing with Emil Korsch, assistant to *Reichsführer* Himmler himself!

Switzerland was the obvious destination toward which the rabbi was bound! Only there would his sacred relics hope to find security from the Nazi clutches.

Once he'd realized the gambit they were attempting, the pieces all fit. *"Rheinsdorf,"* village of the Rhein—he'd never heard of it, but he would find it; *"Kirkhaus,"* churchhouse; *"Fürstenburg,"* village of the prince—whatever the codes meant, they smelled of religious scoundrels, and they all had a Bavarian smell!

If these were locations along the southern border network, which he was now sure of, he would uncover their whereabouts. They were clues he'd paid handsomely for. Beating wasn't the only way to get information. If he had to pay for it, he would do that too, though it wasn't as interesting.

He'd obtained a name, too. *Stegerwald.* Where to find whoever or whatever it was, he wasn't sure. There was also talk of a tunnel.

He would find the rabbi if he had to stay down here a year. If the box did get to Switzerland, they would think it safe. But he would track it even there if he had to.

He glanced out the window at the passing countryside. The train was nearly empty. The only people who traveled openly within the Reich these days were usually on some kind of official business.

He would be in München tomorrow, Salzburg the day after. He would get a car, establish contacts with the SS in the southern sector, and proceed to uncover the southern links of the underground network.

When he did, he had no doubt, the rabbi would be his!

ᴄ⃝ 73 ᴄ⃝

The Dungeon

Sabina and her mother were enjoying a few rare moments alone in the sitting room they shared between their bedrooms. They had been talking about Matthew.

"I have heard nothing in over a year, Mama," Sabina was saying, the hurt of uncertainty obvious in her voice. "There's nothing I can do. I can't write . . . what if he's forgotten?"

"He hasn't forgotten, Sabina," reassured Marion tenderly.

"But then why hasn't he made any attempt to—"

Suddenly the baron burst in. He was covered with dirt and mud and, usually sensitive to such things, appeared altogether oblivious to the fact that his boots had tracked in a dreadful mess. His eyes glowed like two tiny round suns.

An expression neither his wife nor daughter had ever seen was on his face. Immediately both were stricken with terror. He looked as if the Gestapo had just raided the place, had discovered everything, and were about to send every one of them to a concentration camp!

"Marion, Sabina . . . guess what!" he exclaimed before they had a chance to give voice to their alarm. "I have discovered the dungeon!"

"You mean—"

"That's right—old Eppie knew her legends! I only wish she were still alive. I'd have gone straight to her room, even before telling the two of you."

"But how?" exclaimed Marion.

"It was under the ground! The key was there . . . the old movable brass works . . . stones hiding it all—then the door released and gave way! Some old ancestor must have been a genius with mechanical contrivances. Who knows what other wonders there might be about the place!"

Both women sat staring at him, incredulous.

"Well, come on—why are you just sitting there like a couple of statues? I want to show it to you!"

They rose in mounting excitement and followed him.

By the time mother and daughter reached the corridor, the baron was halfway down the main staircase and out of sight. They quickened their pace to try to keep up with him. They found him waiting impatiently at the bottom. The next moment he was through the door into the south parlor and bounding down the stairs into the cellar. Again he waited, and, when Marion and Sabina reached him, he led the way into the underground corridor along the length of the house.

"As many times as I've been down here, and as much as I've investigated, there it was right in front of my nose the whole time," he said excitedly as he went. "Just imagine what uses we might be able to put the place to!"

Quickly following her mother and father, Sabina's only thought was of Matthew. *Oh, if only he could be here now to see this!*

Halfway through its length, the baron stopped in the middle of the dirt floor and crouched down to one knee.

"Look, here it is," he said. "The small brass lever behind this brick of stone is the secret to the whole thing. It's so well camouflaged that unless you knew exactly what you were looking for, you'd miss it entirely."

He reached forward and gave the metal handle a gentle pull, then stood back while his wife and daughter gazed in amazement at the result.

∽ 74 ∾

Hidden Workroom

Seven months later Heinrich von Dortmann hunched over a crude wood table in dim light. The earthy aroma was ample reminder that their activities were of an underground and clandestine nature.

Dr. Aaron Abrahams sat opposite. They were typing up false identity cards, adding stamps and photos, and personalizing information to the blanks supplied by a printer in Fürstendorf known to the Catholic priest who was their ally in such illicit projects. This week's set was for a family they hoped to pass off as Catholic refugees from Dresden, whom they were transferring to a monastery in Potsdam. The typewriter on which the doctor was now pecking out the names was not the best, but they had obtained it from a governmental office, and thus its type was of the sort not to arouse suspicion. Scattered about the table were pens and scissors and glue and other tools of their surreptitious trade.

The very afternoon of his discovery, the baron and the doctor had returned with measuring tools, string, paper, and pens, and by evening they had managed to string a makeshift light overhead by means of a long cord stretched through the underground corridors up to the small library.

Making a permanent installation of electricity became the first order of business. A few articles of furniture had then been brought down, though the way was so narrow that the table at which they sat had been constructed from within. Otherwise the room was much the same as he had found it. He hadn't disturbed the ancient table and chest on the far side, nor the aged wardrobe, in or behind or under which, for all he knew, Bismarck's treasure might be located just like Eppie had said.

A thorough archaeology of the place was intrinsic to his objective, but he wanted to wait until he could relish every moment of the intriguing task. Therefore, he placed all the articles of his present work in the portion of the room he had found empty and left the rest to await that day. Whatever the ghosts of Bismarck and the old count who wanted to get his hands on the estate might think of the proceedings, the baron did not stop to inquire. There was only one Ghost he believed in.

No one but Marion, Sabina, and the doctor knew of the place, which made all the work of getting it ready most difficult and delicate. Not even the servants had been told.

The baron immediately interpreted the discovery as an indication from the Lord that even greater precautions than those taken heretofore were necessary. He gradually began hiding important papers below the house, as well as transferring more of the supplies and material having directly to do with the business of the network.

He also began giving more regular attention to his journal in the solitude afforded by the dungeon's quiet, the only room in the house where such loneliness could now be assured. Perhaps he enjoyed the underground chamber because of Eppie's stories, perhaps because of the obvious antiquity of the place. Whatever the reason, the baron here felt more closely in touch with his own early years, with his ancestry, with the history of his country and the European continent, all of which he had been chronicling since he was a youth.

He considered it important to write, to preserve both a personal and a historical legacy, especially one day for Sabina, and for whoever else might chance to come across it—telling about his past, his and Marion's early years together, the history of the estate, and their work hiding Jews during this terrible time of persecution.

What purpose the Lord had in placing such a mixture of imperatives inside him he didn't know. But a growing sense of urgency steadily deepened upon him to permanently record, not only the events of *his* life, but also his perceptions concerning the historical struggles of his people, his modern perspective on the spiritual cataclysms of the sixteenth century, in which, since he was a schoolboy, he had taken a great interest, in addition to many observations he had made on a great variety of topics throughout his life.

In spite of the activity in the house above him, as often as he had opportunity he ventured down into the bowels of *Lebenshaus*, here to relive former epochs, both of his and many others' life-journeys, and various of the spiritual pathways he and his predecessors in the Spirit had trod.

He forced himself to find time to work diligently, setting pen to paper as often as he could steal an hour or two away from his fields and his guests. He kept his notes and writings safely concealed, where he could be sure they would not fall into any but the hands the Lord destined to receive them.

PART VI

The Mystery of Sacrifice—
1944

The House of Schmundt

The years of the war had not been spiritually serviceable for Gustav von Schmundt, heir apparent to the Schmundt estate of north Germany.

They had given him all external advantages needful for a successful climb to the high echelons of the Third Reich. He had learned to deport himself in every way like the superior specimen of humanity he considered himself. He possessed power and prestige and was moving progressively upward within the hierarchy of the SS, and in carriage and physical appearance, no German mother could have been more proud of such a son as he.

Currents of true *life*, however, flow along underground rivers through the hidden caverns of will, motive, desire, and choice. While Gustav had been maturing in worldly stature and climbing the ladder of social prominence, these subterranean tides of being had steadily dried up within him. The parched streambeds of *character* contained now but scarce a trickle, an inevitable result when the demon of self occupies the throne in that concealed kingdom of the soul.

His desires were his own, his motive to please none but himself, his will bent only toward his own satisfaction. How could it be otherwise when the multitude of choices of his existence had for years pointed in no direction but fleshward, each tiny volition further deepening the arid rut of his self-preoccupation?

Neither the strength of his motives nor the efforts of his will could achieve for him stature of the most important kind, an inner integrity of true manhood. Nor had they been sufficient to gain the one thing most important to him in all the world.

To the undiscerning eye looking on the outside, he would seem to have all that one in his position would wish for.

What he desired most, however, still eluded him.

Sabina von Dortmann was never far from his mind.

Gustav strode across the small room he occupied and gazed out. It was a dingy and unappealing part of the city. But it was Berlin, the center of the empire. The *Reichstag* was only two kilometers away. How could he hope for closer proximity to the center of the world's destiny?

So he thought, at least a year ago. Now he wasn't so sure. Nobody voiced such things. To even think aloud these days could get you shipped to Auschwitz along with the Hungarian Jews. But in the privacy of his own thoughts Gustav saw disturbing signs. Ever since the surrender of the German army in Stalingrad in the winter of 1943, the fortunes of the Third Reich had been on a downhill slide. The collapse of the Russian invasion was followed by surrender in North Africa. Last January, the Allies had landed in force at Anzio, Italy, then just two months ago in Normandy, France.

They were coming this way, that much was clear. The generals of the *Wehrmacht* could say what they wanted, but Gustav knew this war was winding down. If something wasn't done quickly, it was going to be over soon, with the Germans on the wrong side of the surrender table!

Then just two weeks ago Count Stauffenberg had attempted to assassinate Hitler.

It was all unraveling.

Gustav continued to stare out into the night.

He hadn't had many opportunities in the last four or five years to feel lonely. Had such sensations nagged at him, he would quickly have dismissed them as weak and effeminate. He had been too busy, too puffed up with the arrogance of being a feared agent of the Gestapo, too caught up in the importance of the Nazi mission. Honest introspection was no element of the Nazi creed. Humility was as hated a commodity of personhood as Jewish blood. Loneliness smacked of everything Gustav despised. His mother was lonely, and he pitied her for it. He would never submit to such an admission concerning himself.

But . . . one must be practical. His years in the Gestapo had taught him that if nothing else.

It was time to give serious thought to what would become of

him if the unthinkable *did* happen and the great and glorious Reich of Der Führer collapsed.

He was twenty-five. What would there be for him at home? His father would return from his post to the estate. There Gustav would be, a grown man, single, still under the roof of his doting, neurotic mother. It was not a prospect to arouse jubilation.

The war had changed many things, but it had not changed his passion to make Sabina von Dortmann his own.

It was time to bring her around to his way of thinking, to convince her that she could secure no better match than her neighbor and former childhood friend. He had been patient long enough. It was time to press toward a formal solidification of their engagement. Surely she would now see the advantage of taking him. He was glad she was feisty! It would make life more full of zest.

There was but one problem with the scenario as he envisioned it. Even should he marry Sabina, it still left them under the roof of one of their two fathers. If he intended to make the Dortmann estate his before he was an old man, he had to solve the problem of the presence of Sabina's father.

He despised the pious old fool. His own father felt the same way. Gustav knew the count would buy the estate out from under him if he had half the chance. Even marriage, however, wouldn't adequately remedy the problem. The baron was strong as an ox, twice as healthy, and too adroit in financial and farming matters to allow even the war to disturb his standing.

The only way to secure the estate, and to insure no interference from Sabina's father, was to get rid of the baron somehow. The estate would then fall into Sabina's hands, and thence, by marriage, into his own.

It was the only solution. And while it yet lasted, the war might be able somehow to provide him with just the raw material for such a *coup de maître*.

Such was one possible scenario.

There were others, however. Did he want to live in the country around Niedersdorf for the rest of his life? With beautiful Baroness Sabina as his wife, he could go anyplace, do anything.

He was still a young man. Opportunities would surely

abound, even after a surrender. He knew enough about history to know that defeat occasionally presented the greatest opportunities of all.

Working, sometimes directly, sometimes indirectly, for Emil Korsch had taught him a great deal about realism. He suspected, though he would not dare hint at such a thing, that Korsch himself was probably not even much of a Nazi at heart, but was only going along with the programme of national socialism out of expediency. The moment the German army had surrendered at Stalingrad, he had detected subtle changes in his superior. Korsch had begun watching events in the east with increased interest, paying keen attention to the advance of the Russian army.

Then there had been comments here and there, hints that Korsch was already making what he might call "contingency plans" in case the war didn't turn out as they had all assumed it would. The references were sufficiently veiled so that any form of treason could be denied if Gustav should take it into his head to try to turn on him. But at the same time, Korsch let it be known that he liked Gustav and would take care of him when the time came, *if* he continued to show himself loyal now.

As Gustav pondered all these things in his scheming brain, with images of Sabina and her father and Emil Korsch all vying for prominence in his mind's eye, the thought began to come whether he might not accomplish his ends with all three in a single masterstroke of cunning genius.

A smile slowly spread across his young face.

His eyes, indeed all his features and entire demeanor, had taken on such a look of steel that Sabina would not have recognized him. Though he could be said to be handsome, and in this respect was as unlike his mentor Emil Korsch as two men could likely be, the icy dispassion of countenance struck a similarly frozen chord. National socialism reduced its adherents to machines, a quality always evidenced by the loss of sparkle in the eyes. To feel compassion, sympathy, or tenderness was death to Nazism.

All Gustav was capable of feeling was a prideful determination that he *would* possess Sabina von Dortmann. But he must plan his moves with care.

Why could he not ingratiate himself with Korsch all the more with the very sort of information that would bring the proud and mighty Baron von Dortmann down from his high perch? The notion was so brilliant and well conceived he could not believe he had not thought of it before now! Korsch hated Christians and he would jump at a chance to arrest someone of the baron's stature. They had spoken of the baron years ago, but then had allowed him to drift out of the forefront of consideration.

Yes, the baron could well be the door to his future, thought Gustav. And if he could gain power over Sabina in the process, putting her in a position where she would have to marry him to save her own beautiful but haughty skin, so much the better!

The smile now widened, and in the quiet of his room, Gustav von Schmundt laughed to himself. He would put Korsch in his debt and Sabina in his power, and get rid of the baron—all at one and the same time!

He hated to stoop to it. He wouldn't exactly call it cowardly, but by any standards it was a low thing to do. Yet sometimes ruthless measures were called for, and this was such a time.

He picked up the phone to call home.

∽ 76 ∾

The Holy Box

Rabbi Heziah Wissen had ventured south against the pleas of his wife and daughters.

He had established many contacts with several other rabbis still in the country, visiting many safe houses, and making his way southward to Innsbruck, from where he had been smuggled into Zürich.

In Switzerland he had met with Jewish leaders from throughout Europe, passing along what information he possessed about the underground's work in Poland.

News of the Allied landing at Normandy reached him at Zürich. Though to do so would put his life in danger, and though Nazi death camps now operated at full capacity in a feverish attempt to rid Europe of Jews before the Allies put a stop to it, immediately he began making preparations to return to Germany. He would not leave his wife and daughters alone as the war ended.

He returned through the network to Innsbruck, thence north.

After an absence of ten months, he had now been back at *Lebenshaus* a week. It was early August 1944.

He and Baron von Dortmann found themselves alone in the library one afternoon. As if drawn by common consent, they had come together in the place that housed wisdom greater than their own.

"Worse times could be approaching, Baron," the rabbi was saying. "As the Allies draw closer, Germany's leaders may move in unpredictable ways."

"The wild beast trapped in a corner is always the most dangerous," assented Baron von Dortmann.

"Especially after the recent unsuccessful attempt on Hitler."

The baron nodded. His heart had been heavy to hear of it, not because the assassination had failed, or because it had been attempted, but merely because his beloved nation had sunk to such depths that honorable men should consider killing its leader the only solution. Perhaps his heart was heaviest of all from the news he had received that his friend Dietrich Bonhoeffer was apparently among those who felt that way.

"It may be time for you to reconsider your position, Baron," added Rabbi Wissen.

"How do you mean?"

"They will be looking for us with even greater intensity than before. You have your own family, your own safety to think about."

"What are you saying, Heziah?" said the baron, with a rising astonishment in his voice.

"That you should consider asking all of us to go elsewhere. I do not want to endanger *Lebenshaus*. The longer we are here, the greater the risk of discovery for—"

"Don't speak another word of it, Heziah!" interrupted the baron. "I do not make commitments to carry out only when it

happens to be convenient to myself. When I make a commitment, it is for life."

"I only—"

"Of course. I know exactly what you were thinking, and I am
appreciative," said Dortmann, calming and speaking in a sensitive and sympathetic tone. "But we will have no more of it. We
will take all needful precautions. Your recent travels were
dangerous enough. But for many people, to remain behind
closed walls is safest. This is your home, and home for the
others, as long as you are safe here. If that should change, then
we will pray and seek our Father's mind on the matter."

The rabbi nodded.

"You've never asked me about the contents of the box I left
you for safekeeping," said the rabbi after a lengthy pause.

"I did not need to know."

"Are you not curious?"

"I reserve my curiosities for matters of the spiritual realm that
intrigue me. I do not consider curiosity in the physical realm an
altogether edifying exercise."

"Another of your unusual traits. Nevertheless, I think it is
time I tell you."

"As you wish. But I am equally comfortable not knowing."

"The time may come when the contents of the box will put
you in far greater danger than the presence in your hidden
rooms of twenty or thirty Jews."

"It is that valuable?"

"Of inestimable value. Though it is small, it contains several
items that have tremendous historical significance for all of
Jewry. How they came from Jerusalem, after its destruction in
70 A.D., to be housed in Warsaw is a mystery lost far back many
generations in antiquity. There are rumors and legends of their
extensive travels, some involving Russia, others the Orient—
some of the legends speak of the Mediterranean and Africa. The
point is, at some time centuries ago, they did arrive, by whatever means, in Warsaw, and eventually came into my hands, as
the rabbi for that region, for safekeeping."

"I must admit I am intrigued by what you say," said the
baron.

"You have heard of the Urim and Thummim?"

"Of course. The mysterious stones from Aaron's breastplate."

"The two diamonds in the box are said to be the Urim and Thummim."

"What are they? I have never actually read a description. I had no idea they had survived!"

"In my opinion, I cannot think it likely these are truly the Urim and Thummim spoken of in the Pentateuch. No one even knows what exactly the Urim and Thummim were, but legend and tradition say that they were gems of great value whose hues and shades changed, growing lighter or darker, depending upon whether good fortunes or ill were forecast. The one, which has been said to be the Urim, is a great clear diamond of fifteen carats—priceless by any standards, but rendered all the more so by its reputation of being from Aaron's breastplate itself. The second, the Thummim, is a smaller stone, also a diamond, of some twelve carats, and of a gorgeous pale blue. Truly it is one of the most spectacular gems I have ever laid eyes upon."

"I am overwhelmed, Heziah," said the baron. "The very thought of it is astonishing."

"Also in the box," the rabbi went on, "are two ancient dreidels, as well as several minas of precious metals, two of pure gold. Two or three are said to be from the time of David and Solomon, and even to have been used by Solomon personally in the settling of many of the thorny matters brought before him. I am not sure. But there is strong evidence to suggest that the remaining stones are actually the ones used in Nehemiah's day to reestablish the tribes."

"Both also are items used to determine God's will in ancient times, if I am not mistaken."

"Exactly, Baron. Do you see why the Nazis would be anxious to get their hands on them?"

"Of course."

"Not only are they valuable in and of themselves, not to mention their historical value, but such a one as Hitler would give anything to possess objects with reported oracular and divine power, either to know the will of God, or to predict the future. I do not know whether Hitler is aware of their existence, especially so close to Berlin. But the box and its contents are known of, that much I believe. I have been sought ever since fleeing my native Poland by what I can only think is a demonic power. Wherever that box is, there could be danger."

"They are safe," reassured the baron.

"You do not want me to remove them now that you know what the box contains?"

"I cannot think of any place these Jewish treasures would be safer than where I have them."

"Preserving them is vital to our Jewish past and heritage. I hope one day to take them back to Israel when a new temple is built."

"Back to Israel?" repeated the baron.

"Someday our nation will form again in Palestine. Whether a generation from now, or a thousand generations, the land will be known as Israel once more. God has promised it."

"You would love nothing more than to see that day, I am sure," the baron said with a smile. "And to personally deliver the holy box into its archives."

"Even Jews must cherish their dreams, Baron."

A lengthy silence fell.

∽ 77 ∾
The Baron and the Rabbi

When the baron and the rabbi picked up their conversation once again, it was the latter who spoke first, and in a more personally thoughtful vein.

"I have noticed, Baron," he said, "that you here—you and your family especially, and my own wife and daughters have commented on it too—that you appear to think of God so *individually*. Your Christianity does not even seem what I would call a *religion* for you, but frankly I don't know what I would call it."

The baron smiled.

"Your perceptions are most accurate, Heziah. Our faith is *not* a mere religion to us."

"What is it then?"

"A way of life."

"Religion is a way of life for everyone, Baron, is it not? I would say the same of our Jewish faith. Does not everyone who maintains a belief consider it a way of life?"

The baron nodded thoughtfully.

"Yes, I see," he said slowly after a moment. "Yes, you are right. *Hmm* . . . how might I draw the distinction?" he mused.

A pause followed, then he smiled again.

"We had another visitor here at *Lebenshaus* several years ago, before the war—an American lad and his father. The boy asked me almost the same question—what was it about our beliefs that made them so personal, so close, so intimate in everything we did and thought."

"What did you tell him?"

"We spoke at some length about God's fatherhood. For my wife and daughter and myself, that is the key to it all. "

"God's . . . *fatherhood*. What exactly do you mean, Baron?"

"Our faith is not a religion as men commonly mean when they use that word. Rather, we are on a quest together, a lifelong journey, an adventure to discover all we can about a Father whom, it is sad to say, very few of his creatures know with intimacy."

"Go on. I am intrigued."

The baron proceeded to summarize the gist of his conversation with Matthew McCallum.

"So you see, Heziah," concluded Dortmann, "we are engaged in a life of discovery, not the following of a religion at all. Our foundational prayer, the sole objective of life for us, is to discover who God is and then to do what he would have us do—to *obey* him once we *know* him."

"Everything you've said, Baron," said the rabbi, "is nothing I would take exception to as a practicing Jew. In fact, from listening to you talk, you *could* be a Jew—and a devout one at that!"

Baron von Dortmann laughed.

"I will take that as a high honor," he said. "To be truthful, I have always considered myself a Jew—in the spiritual sense."

"I for one would not dispute your claim. There is nothing in what you have told me that precludes a Jew—even though we do not believe Jesus is the Christ as you do—from an equal participation in that fatherhood you speak of."

"It's a delight to hear you, Rabbi. God is our Father—yours as well as mine. I believe we have an elder Brother, whose name is Jesus, who came to help us know our mutual Father better. The fact that you do not consider him your elder Brother certainly does not make the Father any less your Father than he is mine."

"It is not common to hear Christians express such an equable, open-armed view of God's family."

"I happen to believe in a wider reach of the Father's embrace than most Christians," agreed the baron. "If it is a fault, I readily admit it. I am convinced that God's arms stretch to infinities of inclusion our feeble brains cannot begin to grasp. That, however, is a discussion we must reserve for another time."

Now it was the rabbi's turn to laugh. "Do I detect in your tone that your religion has its sacred taboos just as does ours, to venture too near which can prove dangerous?"

"How right you are, Heziah," laughed the baron. "There remain many widely practiced but acceptable forms of burning at the stake and excommunication that occur right within the mutual fellowship of believers!"

"I will question you no further along those lines, Baron. I can see I have stumbled unwittingly into a theological quagmire and I want to return to the practicality inherent in something you said."

"Happily."

"You spoke of knowing the Father and obeying him."

"Yes. Such is the cornerstone of my faith."

"My question then is this: Do we not possess all that is required to know God and obey him, as you say, in the Holy Scriptures?"

"I couldn't agree more, Rabbi."

"Then what is the mystery, the process of *discovery* you are so fond of speaking of? Isn't everything clearly laid out in front of us?"

"Ah yes, I see the dilemma," the baron said, nodding.

He pondered the rabbi's question.

"You, as a Jew," he finally said, "view obedience to God as obedience to the Law, would that be accurate?"

"Of course."

"That is perhaps where the true distinction between us comes in. I view it as obedience to the Father *himself.* Here we come to the heart of the *personal* element of my belief we were talking about earlier."

"You do not believe the Law to be the method by which God reveals himself?" asked the rabbi.

"I believe that the Law, the Levitical law of what we call the Old Testament, was and is a true revelation of God. But only a *partial* revelation."

"Partial?"

"Yes, a revelation of God only intended for a time, as one aspect of a progressive revelation that now enables men and women to know the Father, not as he was known in former times, but face-to-face, heart-to-heart, with a daily, ongoing, hand-in-hand intimacy."

"How is such intimacy achieved?"

"I'm afraid that question, Rabbi, lands us squarely in the middle of the difference between Christianity and Judaism. It is Jesus, whom we believe to be the Son of God, whom the Father sent to take the revelation of him to a higher level than the Law could ever achieve: to the point where personal interaction—a personal *relationship,* if you will—between each one of us and God the Father is now possible."

"So at root, then, you do believe Judaism is wrong." The rabbi's tone carried no hint of challenge. The question was purely an informational query.

"Oh, by no means!" rejoined the baron. "Forgive me if I conveyed anything of the kind."

"You believe that Jesus is the foundation that enables you to know the Father personally as you speak about."

"Indeed, that is correct."

"Then does it not follow that if I, a practicing Jewish rabbi, say that I do *not* believe that Jesus is the Son of God, you would reply that you think I am in error?"

"Perhaps, if we isolated our discussion to the question of whether Jesus is the Son of God, then yes, I might say I think you to be in error on that point. But it does not follow that I consider Judaism *wrong* as an entire system of belief. I see no profit to be gained by splitting semantical hairs. Judaism is the father of Christianity. There would be no Christianity without

Judaism. Jesus was a Jew, Paul was a Jew, the entire fabric upon which our beliefs are based is Jewish. Most of our Scriptures we share with you. I do not view Judaism as 'wrong,' only incomplete. Jesus didn't bring a *new* system of belief; he brought *completion* to Judaism."

"You continue to amaze me, Baron," chuckled the rabbi. "You positively refuse to be drawn into a confrontation over disputed points, don't you?"

"Another of my faults."

"One not shared by many of your fellow Christians."

The baron sighed his acknowledgment of the truth of Wissen's remark. "I am not fond of the word *wrong* at all," he said. "It is altogether overused by Christians. I am not trying to avoid your question. There is something more here for me than right or wrong, so to speak."

"Most seem bent on taking every dialog or discussion on spiritual or philosophical matters straight to the precise place where there is difference, desiring, it would seem, that every discussion become eventually a debate over disputed tenets," added the rabbi. "A tendency of my fellow Jewish rabbis as well. You, on the other hand, seem always on the lookout for such potential points of discussionary icebergs so that you can intentionally steer your ship clear of them."

"You have found me out," laughed the baron. "That is precisely what I try to do."

"You are an open man, Baron, for one with such strong and personal beliefs."

"Strength of belief need not make a man stubborn and cantankerous."

"It often does."

"I have always found my Father's hands to be open in gentle invitation to man, rather than stiffly forbidding, as if he were a celestial policeman barring entrance to his presence. I am constantly on the eager lookout for broad areas of harmony and unity, rather than for specific points of difference. I seek brotherhood, wherever it can be found. Few things excite me more than the discovery of brotherhood or sisterhood in another human soul."

"Do you consider me your brother then, Baron?" asked the

rabbi. His voice contained an earnestness that was not lost on the sensitive spirit of Heinrich von Dortmann.

"In the larger sense in which all men are brothers as the created beings of God, most certainly," the baron replied. "Technically, in the sense in which Christians use the term to indicate others of the Christian faith, what we call 'brothers in Christ,' I suppose not. In speaking of the spiritual bonds between us by virtue of our common God, our common spiritual heritage, certainly a brotherhood exists between us on that level. In such a sense, perhaps we are *cousins*—there is an elder Brother in my family whom I acknowledge relations with, but whom you do *not* consider your brother. However, we both acknowledge the same God as our Father. We both acknowledge Abraham and Moses and David as our spiritual ancestors and fathers in another sense of the word. So perhaps 'cousin' is as close as we can come to defining it."

"I like it . . . *Cousin* von Dortmann!" said the rabbi.

The baron laughed. "So do I, *Cousin* Wissen."

After some time, the rabbi once again returned to the point they had left a short while earlier.

"So by knowing God, you mean knowing Jesus?" he said. "And by obeying God, you mean obeying Jesus?"

"I would say that I am able to know the Father intimately because Jesus, as God's Son, teaches me about and shows me the Father," replied the baron. "He said that if we have seen him we have also seen the Father."

He paused and thought a moment.

"Then too," he went on, "I would say that I obey the Father *by* listening to and observing Jesus, obeying the Father as *he* obeyed the Father. Added to that there is obeying what *he* told us to do, because his whole mission on earth was to demonstrate the life lived in obedience to the Father. Everything Jesus said and did was reflected straight from the Father, which makes our knowing of him and our obedience to *his* instructions a knowing of and an obedience to the Father as well."

"I think I understand it as clearly as I ever have," said the rabbi. "At least you have explained it very clearly. Now I am going to have to ponder it. You present Christianity in a way that cuts through all the theologies in all the textbooks, and all the treatises in comparative religions in which we learned types think we must steep ourselves. It is very practical for you, I see that most clearly."

"Christianity is the most practical of all religions, Rabbi. Even, if I may say so without getting too close to those icebergs you spoke of, more practical than your Judaism."

◆ 78 ◆

North Again!

Emil Korsch hated to be made a fool of!

How he could ever have been tricked into following that red herring to Switzerland, he couldn't imagine.

At least it had not been a total loss. While there he had followed his München connections toward Innsbruck, which was supposed to be interlaced with Jewish and Christian connections into the surrounding mountains.

The little village of Scharnitz bore more looking into in that regard. But it would all have to wait.

Once he'd realized his fatal error, he'd sped north again. If need be he'd return to Bavaria and Austria another time.

Rabbi Wissen remained his supreme and only priority!

But as the Gestapo chief raced northward, cursing his folly for wasting a year in Bavaria and Austria, the rabbi had the whole time been right under his nose.

How could he have guessed that his earlier miscue had nearly thrown him directly into the rabbi's path? The two men had, in fact, been in Innsbruck at the same time, and one afternoon had actually come within half a kilometer of one another.

Neither could have known. Neither would ever know the irony of fate's little trick of timing.

Now Korsch was back in Poznan and was more determined than ever to find the rabbi. He knew neither the box nor its contents had surfaced. At least neither Hitler nor anyone in the high command knew of them. He had his sources, and he would have heard if something that big had been discovered.

Korsch had set discreet inquiries afoot the moment he was

back, but nothing substantive had come of them. He had contacted Schmundt the moment he was back in the north. The last communiqué from him said that Rabbi Wissen was nowhere to be found. Rumors indicated a southward flight, probably toward Switzerland.

Korsch exploded in wrathful fury upon reading the message in Schmundt's hand.

Was the fool toying with him? He had had enough of the Swiss dead end! He didn't want to hear about Switzerland! The Semite professor was somewhere much closer at hand!

Returning to the place where the trail had gone cold, Korsch reprised the series of events since he had tracked the rabbi's flight out of Warsaw.

After laying his hands on the fellow Luddoff in Wloclawek and torturing the information out of him, he had traced and followed the moves of the rabbi to Ciehocinek, then to Torun and Bydgoszcz, where they had apparently turned south to Wagrowiec and Poznan.

There the trail had forked. He had taken the wrong road toward the south.

Now here he was trying to pick up the scent, the one toward the Baltic this time, but so far without much success. He had roughed up a few people, but if anyone knew which direction the Kropf and Wissen families had taken after leaving Poznan, no one was talking.

Korsch had been thrown off track by some fellow impersonating a *Wehrmacht* officer, who he was now sure must have been a member of the underground. That man would be dead when he caught up with him! Korsch had gone to Dresden, with clues that he thought led toward München and thence to Switzerland.

Now as he paced angrily back and forth, memory of the acrid incident drifted back into his consciousness. As important as the exchange with the imposter of a captain was, it was one exchange that would never find its way into any of his reports!

If he ever got his hands on the fellow, he vowed he would utilize the most skillful means of the Gestapo to obtain what he wanted to know. They had ways of making people talk!

Thus far all Schmundt kept telling him was about clues toward Switzerland. He was sick of hearing about them!

Korsch wondered if the fellow was going to prove as valuable as he'd originally thought. He wasn't sure if his blood ran quite cold enough. Still, he had his uses and had proved a decently capable agent till now. In fact, his protégé, reports had it, was actually succeeding in making something of a name for himself in some modest-level Gestapo circles. So he continued to keep in touch with the young fellow and told him to let him know if he heard anything that *wasn't* connected with Switzerland.

Notwithstanding their joint efforts, however, the rabbi remained unfound.

ᖆ 79 ᖇ

Another Visit

Marion had not seen Ingrid von Schmundt for sixteen months.

It was thus with great surprise that her neighbor appeared one morning, full of smiles, for a visit.

"Hello, Ingrid," said Marion, hurrying downstairs the moment an anxious Heidi had located her. While her mistress went down to her guest, Heidi hastily spread the need for caution to the second floor.

Marion led her neighbor to the small parlor next to the door.

"You are perspiring, Marion. Whatever have you been doing?"

"Oh, just housework, Ingrid," answered Marion, still trying to recover from her surprise and anxiety over her friend's appearance.

"Housework indeed! What are servants for, Marion? Why would you be doing such a thing?"

"I enjoy working with my women. Surely you must have felt the effects of rationing yourself."

"My husband's and son's proper loyalties keep us very well taken care of," said Ingrid, her nose inching into the air.

"You are fortunate. But we find we enjoy the added work."

The countess laughed. "I will never get used to the ways of you and the baron! You and I used to see things the same. Sometimes I wonder if I even know you anymore. Working with your women—such notions!" exclaimed Frau Schmundt. "I tell you, Marion, that husband of yours has not been good for you. You've changed."

The uncharacteristically sharp reply that sought exit from Marion's lips in defense of her husband did not get past the back side of her teeth. She swallowed it, taking in a breath to steady herself.

I hope I've changed, she said to herself. *I would not want to be the same person at forty I was at twenty! I hope I've put some roots of growth and character and personhood down in all that time.*

But to her guest she said, "I'm sorry you feel that way, Ingrid. Heinrich has not changed me. We've grown together. He works with his men, I with my women. These are times when all people need to join together. We have no desire to be above them, so to speak. "

"But you *are* above them," objected the countess with annoyance.

"That is not how we see it."

"How else is there to see it?"

"We view servanthood as the pinnacle of being."

Countess von Schmundt threw her head back and made no attempt to disguise the disdainful tone of the laughter that erupted from her wide mouth.

"Why Marion," she said after a moment, dabbing her eyes as she tried to stop laughing. "That is one of the most ridiculous things I have ever heard!"

Marion held her tongue, compassion now replacing the earlier vexation that had fluttered briefly when she had heard her husband ridiculed.

"Servanthood indeed! Servants are servants, nothing more."

"There was one who said that the last would be first, and that the way to achieve greatness was to be the servant of all."

"Well, whoever he was, he was a fool," rejoined the countess.

Marion closed her eyes briefly, wincing in her breast to hear her Savior spoken of so virulently.

Thinking better of herself, the countess added, "Forgive me,

Marion. You probably were referring to the baron, and I did not mean to insult him." There was no remorse in her tone, only decorum. In truth, she would gladly have insulted the baron, for she despised him. She only meant that the dictates of her societal code indicated that she should not do so openly in front of the idiot's wife, whom, for sake of the past, she would yet pretend to respect.

"It was not my husband I spoke of," said Marion softly.

"It's not just working with your servants, Marion," the countess went on, trying to manufacture a tone of injury but not succeeding altogether in hiding the irritation prompting it. "You used to invite me over. When I came, we would go to your private sitting room or the *Gute Stube*, or even enjoy cake in the kitchen together. You have become so stiff and formal. The last two visits you have set me down not ten paces from the door as if you don't *want* me in your house." As she spoke, she was wondering how she could ever have imagined her son married to the daughter of such simpletons!

"I'm sorry, Ingrid," said Marion. "Such was not my intention. I only—"

"And then there was that business with the strangers I saw and your husband lying about them and saying he would invite me for another visit. I tell you, Marion, it would not be difficult for me to take offense. Whatever has been going on around here is—"

"What do you mean?" asked Marion, too quickly. Her nervousness betrayed her, and Ingrid's skillful ears noted it.

"What do I *mean*?" repeated the countess as if the question was absurd. "Why, strange visitors and your keeping me from the rest of the house, your husband's lies—my Gustav has seen strange lights about the place at night. I tell you, Marion, I'm not such an innocent as you may take me for."

"I've never taken you for an innocent, Ingrid."

"Do you deny that something's going on?"

"Nothing's going on out of the ordinary, Ingrid," replied Marion, perspiring again. "You know that *Lebenshaus* has always been open to all. Sometimes we have had guests we didn't know who came here for refreshment and to enjoy our garden. Surely you remember, Ingrid, how we feel about sharing what God has given us. I've never made any secret of it, and I spoke to you about it years ago."

"Why are you trying to prevent me from the rest of your house?" As she spoke, the countess now thought how she had resisted Gustav's request that she come here. This, however, was proving rather fun—she enjoyed seeing Marion flustered.

"I had no such intention. In fact, I believe Carola has baked some fresh cake today and I was about to go to the kitchen to ask her about it," said Marion, trying to calm her nervousness. "Why don't you come with me, and if it is finished, we'll enjoy some together."

Settling her ruffled feathers, the countess nodded her agreement, and the two women rose and left the room.

All the way down the two corridors to the kitchen, the countess looked this way and that, her eyes and ears alert for anything she might tell her son.

Marion led her into the kitchen, where, as she had said, Carola was busy knifing generous clumps of creamy chocolate frosting over several multilayered yellow cakes.

Marion proceeded to cut two slices out of the one Carola had already completed, and she and Ingrid each took a seat at one of the small tables.

"There is enough cake there to feed an army, Marion!" exclaimed Ingrid.

"We have many workers, you know."

"Not since the war," rejoined the countess. "I was told you were down to a live-in staff of·only six or eight. What about rationing?"

"We grow most of our own food. You know Heinrich's farming gifts."

"There are six large cakes there," insisted the countess.

"Day workers have dinner with us too," said Marion.

The countess took in the information and said no more, but her visage said that she was far from convinced.

Silence fell momentarily as the one woman picked at her cake and the other devoured hers.

Suddenly the door from the outer courtyard opened. Voices, although hushed, became audible before their owners were visible and preceded the sound of footfalls along the short corridor into the kitchen. There was nothing Marion could do to prevent her guest from hearing their conversation, and the whispered voices became all the more incriminating.

" . . . if we had any new roses for sale."

"He had it exactly backwards!"

"The look on the poor fellow's face told me he was only confused. I don't think he'd eaten in days."

"What did you do?"

"I let him in, and the—"

The baron's voice suddenly stopped the instant he and Schmidt came into view. A quick glance of his eyes about the room caught Marion's terrified gaze attempting to silence them. He sized up the situation in a second.

"Ah, Ingrid!" he exclaimed, face brightening in welcome. "Go ahead without me," he added, turning back to Schmidt.

But the countess was as shrewd as they, and she had well noted the nervous expressions and glances flying about the room. Something *was* going on here, she was certain of it.

Whatever it was, Gustav was sure to get to the bottom of it.

She put on what thin veneer of pleasantness one of such shallow character could manage, finished her slice of cake, gladly accepted another, visited as amiably as she could with the baron and his wife for but another minute or two, then excused herself.

She had a great deal to do, she said, and the day would get away from her if she was not careful.

On the top of her agenda was a telephone call to her son!

ॐ 80 ॐ

Suspicions

Gustav put down the phone and leaned back in his chair.

He had wondered if something was afoot at that place. He should have listened to his suspicions earlier!

His mother had done just what he'd asked. What she had just told him confirmed nothing specific—he couldn't have hoped for that—but it hinted that the baron was hiding something.

Every time he was home he took up his old secret vantage point in the woods, more to watch Sabina than anything. It always gave him a sensation of power over her to know she had no idea she was being spied upon.

At the same time, there were enough little things that went on around that place—like the Americans visiting before the war, for one—that always made him wonder if the baron was up to more than he liked to let on. He saw why his father never trusted him.

Then there was that time he'd visited two years ago, in the winter—he remembered the day well. It had been very cold. He had been out in the woods early and had seen someone wander out onto the roof balcony, followed a few minutes later by Sabina. The attention of his binoculars had all been upon her, but he had thought it curious at the time how panicked she had been to see what he assumed was a guest on the balcony alone. A look of fear had come over her face as she had glanced around hurriedly and fairly pulled the person, whoever it was, back inside.

Strange behavior, he thought, for the hostess to show when the balcony had always before been a spot they had been proud to show their visitors.

He'd scarcely given it another thought, however—until now.

There was nothing he could put his finger on. But that hardly mattered.

In these times, just the vaguest hint of a secret was enough for the Gestapo!

It was just what he had hoped for!

Now—how to put all the pieces to his little scheme together for maximum profit and benefit to himself?

Christians were so ridiculous with their secretive little ways of doing things, their words, their symbols! Well, he had outsmarted them!

He knew Emil Korsch would be intrigued. Korsch had, some years ago, been extremely interested in the baron and the goings-on around his estate, as a means of getting information on that pastor he'd had such a vendetta against. Since the Bonhoeffer fellow had been thrown into prison Korsch hadn't mentioned the name Dortmann again. He'd seemed to forget the Christian element altogether in his passion to locate that Jewish rabbi he'd been after all this time. Every communication, whether confidential memo or telephone call or personal visit, had centered around whatever information Gustav had been able to gather about the rabbi, the supposed network of which he was a part, and whatever remaining gathering of Jews might yet secretly exist in Berlin. Gustav had spent a good deal of his efforts over the last two years in the attempt to lay his hands on information concerning the whereabouts of Rabbi Wissen, while Korsch himself had been following him in the south and in Switzerland.

Perhaps, he thought, *it's time to bring Korsch back to something more tangible.* There were no more Jews left in Germany, or so Goebbels had declared over a year ago.

But the Christians—they still posed a serious threat! The Bonhoeffer fellow may have been in prison, but the implication was circulating that he and other leading Christians had been involved in the assassination plot against Hitler a few weeks ago.

What if—

Gustav's hand suddenly shot to his forehead and his eyes opened wide in disbelief!

Baron von Dortmann!

He was *known* to have connections with the Bonhoeffer traitor! It was for just such a reason that Korsch had hired him in the first place—to watch him. Then the war had taken them both off in different directions.

But—it had to be true! There could be no other explanation for the suddenly obvious string of facts.

The thought was too unbelievable! Too deliciously, perfectly, fantastically incredible!

Here it had been, all this time, right under his nose!

Gustav couldn't believe it. Everything fit! It *had* to be true!

He had uncovered what would bring Sabina's father down, what would put her very life in his hands, and information that would insure his place in Korsch's schemes for after the war.

It was such a discovery, it might even make him a hero! A medal from the Führer himself!

He would contact Korsch immediately!

No, come to think of it, he would get more information first. He would be sure of himself before he blew this little spy network sky-high!

He flew from the apartment, not even stopping to lock the door. He had to have someone he could trust for this assignment, someone with an innocent look whom they would feel sorry for and admit into their confidence.

Especially now that he knew what he was sure was their secret code! Once in a while his mother served a useful purpose for him.

All those years playing with Sabina in the garden were going to pay off at last!

∾ 81 ∾

A Stranger

In the middle of their *Abend Brot*, Heidi came into the dining room.

"There is a man at the door, Herr Baron," she said.

"The back door or the front door, Heidi?"

"The front door."

"How did he arrive?"

"There is no auto. He appears tired and I assume he came by foot."

"Did he ask about our roses?"

"*Ja*, Herr Baron, but when I told him we had none, he asked to see you personally."

"What exactly did he say?"

"He said, 'Do you have any new roses for sale?'"

"Those were his exact words?"

"Yes, Herr Baron."

"He said nothing of the petals?" asked Baron von Dortmann, a puzzled expression crossing his brow.

"When I said this was not the season for the best blooms, he merely returned me a blank look. I asked if he had anything to answer me in reply. He appeared surprised, then insisted I bring you to him."

"Insisted?"

"He said he needed help, that he was a Christian and a friend of Pastor Bonhoeffer's."

The servant's voice betrayed her uneasiness.

"I do not like his looks, Herr Baron," she added.

"I understand, Heidi," said the baron, rising slowly, thinking to himself as he set his knife down on the table. He found a vague mixture of feelings filling him, reluctance to turn away a brother, yet puzzlement and a certain discomfort with the circumstances of the situation. "I will go to him . . . but leisurely. Did you tell him we were at supper?"

"Yes, but he became quite insistent. He said that brothers must help one another at such times."

"He said nothing about what his trouble was?"

"No, sir."

"Very good, Heidi. Go quickly and tell the others. Stay away from the windows, and get all the people into the hidden chambers. I will take my time walking to the front door. Marion, alert the rest of the staff to be calm and about their business. As you go pray that God will give me wisdom and the right words to speak—Sabina, if you hear me ring the bell, take your mother quickly to her hidden closet. Otherwise, go to the *Gute Stube*. If I need you, I will come there."

The women did as the baron had instructed them.

When he was alone in the room, he moved from the table and slipped to the floor on his knees.

"O Father," he said quietly, "let me be your man, and *only* your man, in all circumstances . . . whatever befalls us. Show me what you would have me do. Put the discerning eyes of your Spirit into my heart, that I may know quickly whether this stranger is indeed one of yours."

He remained where he was two or three minutes more, then rose and slowly walked to the front door.

The man waiting for the baron wore the simplest of peasant attire and stood with hat in hand with a look on his face not of nervousness or anxiety, but, as Heidi had correctly surmised, of importunity.

"I am Heinrich von Dortmann," said the baron, shaking his hand. "I understand you asked to see me. Won't you come in?"

Without giving his name, the man followed the baron through the door and into the small parlor just to their right, glancing down the corridors in both directions, then quickly up the grand staircase.

The baron closed the door behind them, then offered the stranger a seat.

"What may I do for you?" he asked cordially.

"I understood I might seek asylum here."

"Asylum—what exactly do you mean?"

"Refuge, sanctuary—I was told you helped people."

"If I am able I will help any man," returned the baron. "How did you come by my name in this regard?"

The visitor hesitated momentarily, divulging his first hint of disquiet.

"I am a friend of Pastor Bonhoeffer's," he said. "He told me you would help me."

"But as I understand it," replied the baron, "Dietrich was arrested over a year ago and has been at Tegel Prison in Berlin ever since."

"Yes, uh—of course you are right. He told me before being arrested."

"I see," said the baron. "When did you speak with him, if I might ask? I haven't seen Dietrich in years."

"Let me think . . . it must have been two years ago or so."

"Sometime in 1942?"

"It could have been—the exact date escapes me. But he was most clear about his connections with you. He said that if ever a fellow believer was in need, Baron von Dortmann was one to reach out a helping hand."

"Perhaps you saw him when he was in Vienna in the spring of '42, at the underground pastors' conference?"

"I believe you have hit upon it exactly, Baron. That is exactly when I spoke with him. Why, were you there too?"

"Oh no, I'm no pastor. I haven't been to Austria in years. In any event, I am sorry to disappoint you, but I am not really in a position to offer you what you seek."

"My information was most specific," said the man, eying the baron carefully.

"Your . . . *information?*" said the baron.

"Yes, that since Pastor Bonhoeffer was in prison, you were now in charge of the underground Christian movement in this area."

The baron could not prevent himself from bursting out in laughter. His guest, however, continued to stare stoically at him, without registering the slightest hint of a smile.

"I'm sorry," the baron said, "but nothing could be more erroneous."

"So you will not offer me a room where I might spend a few days as one who shares your religion?" said the man, the insistency returning to his tone.

"It is not that I *will* not," replied the baron calmly. "It is simply that my family and I have other duties that demand our attention. I am very sorry. But if you are hungry, I can offer you food."

"That will not be necessary," said the man stiffly.

The baron rose, and the stranger with him.

They left the room, and the baron saw the man outside. Without further words of farewell, the stranger began walking away from the house.

The baron watched him for a few moments, then returned inside. As he strode quickly up to his office, it suddenly dawned on him that the man had never given his name.

He entered his study and walked quickly across to the window. The fellow had veered to the far western edge of the driveway and was peering about, attempting to gain a vantage point from which he might see around the side of the house and into the backyard. Then he continued his way around the circle, now snooping about the north side.

At length he paused and turned straight back toward the house, glancing up, as if drawn by his gaze, straight to the corner window where the baron stood. For a moment, though they were too far apart to see one another clearly, they seemed to look straight into each other's eyes. Then the man turned and made his way down the driveway through the trees, and finally disappeared from sight.

Another ten minutes the baron watched, then suddenly saw a car moving northward towards Niedersdorf. It had not come along the road from the south. Even from the great distance from which the baron was observing, it looked suspiciously familiar, and gave every indication of having been waiting for the strange visitor somewhere hidden from sight along the road.

He left his office and returned downstairs, where he met Marion waiting for him.

"You can tell everyone it is safe now," he said, "although we must henceforth be on our guard."

"What did he want?" Marion asked.

Her husband recounted the gist of the conversation as they walked together back to the dining room.

"Could he have been a brother, Heinrich?" asked Marion.

"Not unless I am woefully mistaken. May God forgive me if I have erred."

"You are certain, are you not? Otherwise you would never have sent him away."

"Yes, I suppose I am certain. It so goes against my grain to judge another. I'm afraid I set the man up."

"What do you mean?"

"I tricked him into exposing that he was not telling the truth."

"How?"

"I asked him several questions. He said Dietrich mentioned me in Vienna in 1942. Dietrich was in Norway, Sweden, and Switzerland in '42, but *not* Vienna. There was no underground pastors' conference that year. And despite my questions, it was clear he was used to doing most of the asking. Not since the gathering at the count's have I felt such probing persistency of interrogation. I tell you, Marion, I am all but certain I have just been in the presence of the Gestapo."

Marion caught her breath and turned pale.

"Oh, Heinrich—"

"Don't be anxious, my dear," said the baron reassuringly. "We will take all necessary care and vigilance."

The baron said no more. But from that moment on, his prayers began to take a new turn.

∽ 82 ∽

The Three Girls

Two days later, before retiring, Sabina had asked her father permission to show the rabbi's daughters the garden.

"You know the rule, my dear," her father replied. "None of our guests must be seen. Even the day workers know nothing."

"I know, Papa. I thought if we went early."

"How early?" he asked, frowning.

"However early you say."

"If you must, take them at first light. But do not be out too long. The workers begin arriving at six."

Not since Matthew's visits had Sabina enjoyed any guests more than Rabbi Wissen's daughters. She had never known girls of their character and depth. How different they were from her cousin Brigitte! A oneness of spirit had sprung up between them almost the night they had arrived, and now, more than two years later, she felt she'd known them both all her life. Though she was several years older, and in many respects they looked up to her as an older sister, they had become cherished friends as well. There was no doubt Sabina was a woman now, though the playful streak of her being would keep her delightfully childlike even at eighty.

Like her father and mother, Sabina was keenly conscious of their own relationship to these people—this chosen race—and she rejoiced at the privilege of being part of that ancient Hebrew stock. It was a humble privilege to be both Jew and Christian, and Sabina blessed both her mother and her father for the heritage given her.

She was awake even before the first light of day snuck through the window of her bedroom. She dressed quickly, put on her outdoor shoes to protect against the dampness of the morning, and then walked quickly through the corridors up to the second floor, where she awakened Ursula and Gisela.

"Papa says we may go out to the garden," she whispered, "if you would still like to."

They sprang from their beds in a flash. The wide eyes and eager expressions of the sisters was all the answer she needed.

The enthusiasm in their face at the thought of being out-of-doors again was almost more than they could contain.

She wished they could go to the balcony first, but that would be too dangerous. The roof could be seen for a great distance. There might already be workmen out somewhere in the nearby countryside. It seemed everyone was suspicious these days, thought Sabina as they made their way down through the dark corridors and out into the courtyard, which now showed the grey of early morning.

The two sisters had not been outside, and had scarcely been near a window, since the night they had arrived at *Lebenshaus*. Now in their first moments outside they relished drinking in the feel and smell of the crisp morning air. It was damp with dew, containing a refreshing chill that foretold a beautifully warm day of early September.

Knowing they had to take care to be quiet, each in her own way gave expression to the emotions inside.

Sabina threw up her arms and spun around. "Isn't it wonderful?" she said softly. Both girls watched her abandoned dance of delight, then, both in the same instant, followed Sabina's lead, shedding for the moment the heaviness of the past years' fearful hiding.

Suddenly children again, they giggled and ran about, rejoicing in the freedom of being outside.

Sabina led the way, running, down into the garden, and began showing them all her favorite spots. Indeed, it seemed every nook had its favorite features for some uniqueness all its own. Many blossoms still filled the rosebushes from their second blooming, and hundreds of additional fall flowers were now coming into the profusion of their reds, oranges, and yellows.

The time passed quickly. Soon the eastern horizon began to brighten and Sabina knew they must presently return to the house. She took them into her mother's special place.

"Sit here with me a moment before we have to go back in," she said in a hushed tone.

The three girls crowded together on the bench. Sabina said nothing more, wanting to see if they would notice the peculiarities of this particular location. A subdued quiet fell over them all.

Ursula was the first to speak.

"Look, Gisela, a fig tree."

"I thought so," said her sister, who then rose, leaving the bench. A few paces away she stooped to one knee. "And look here—it's parsley. Did you know," she added, glancing back up at Sabina, "that parsley is the bitter herb we use on the Seder plate at Passover?"

"Yes, I did know that," answered Sabina. "How about this plant . . . do you know it?"

As she spoke, Sabina now left the bench, sunk to her knees beside Gisela, and pointed to some bright orange flowers. "See what is left after the blooms are spent?" she added, reaching out and breaking off a pointed green pod. With the tips of her fingers she broke it open, and both girls exclaimed in recognition of the tiny black contents inside.

"Poppy seeds!" they both exclaimed in unison. "We use poppy seeds in our special cakes," added Ursula.

"I knew that too," said Sabina.

"Are all the plants from Palestine?" asked Ursula.

"The ones you see right here. This is my mother's garden. She wants all our Jewish guests to feel welcome!"

The three rose from their knees.

"Oh-oh, I think it is time for us to go in," said Sabina. "I see Papa coming down into the garden, and I'm certain he is looking for us."

∽✢∾

As the three young women knelt in the dewy dirt of the garden, a pair of binoculars trained themselves distantly on the scene.

Curiosity, revenge, and cunning determination strangely mingled in the mind of their owner.

What could they possibly be doing? he said to himself. *Are they burying something, digging something up, planting a new seedling? Why at such an early hour, down on hands and knees in the dirt?*

And who were those two girls he did not recognize?

He had personally seen no visitors, though this had to

confirm the conjectures of his mother and the report Karl had given him after he'd picked him up at the end of the baron's driveway three days ago.

Whatever they were up to, he must know. He had a right to know! All of this would be his one day. Whatever concerned it was his business.

He would find out!

⮞ 83 ⮜
God's Handmaidens

The three girls were greeted by the baron.

"Did you have a nice outing?" he asked.

Both Ursula and Gisela began talking at once, then stopped, looked at Sabina, and burst out laughing.

The baron smiled, but put his finger to his lips, indicating the need for restraint. Walking back up the hill, he stretched out his arms and shepherded them toward the house like a mother hen her chicks.

A sensitive man like Heinrich von Dortmann could well see that a bond had developed between his daughter and the rabbi's two girls. Not wishing to break the spell of the morning, he suggested that Sabina take the two younger girls to her rooms. He would have Carola bring breakfast to them there.

"But keep away from the window," he warned her again, "and don't use the balcony off the sitting room."

"Yes, Papa."

She led the way up to her private sitting room, and soon they were eating and talking as if they had been schoolgirls together. But the course of their dialog was not so typical of common schoolgirls. These were three of that rare breed of pure feminine character, whose fathers and mothers had well trained them in the way of the Father of them all.

"Are you betrothed, Sabina?" asked fifteen-year-old Gisela.

"No, certainly not," Sabina answered emphatically, thinking unconsciously of Gustav.

She saw her quick reply had taken the other two by surprise.

She realized that the two Jewish girls had such a vastly different cultural and religious background and heritage than she.

"I'm sorry," she said. "I suppose our traditions are very different in many ways. Are *you* betrothed?"

Gisela shook her head, but seventeen-year-old Ursula now spoke.

"I am," she said. "But I don't know what is to happen now—I may never see Joseph again."

"Your parents do not consider you young for betrothal?"

"Jewish girls are promised early for marriage. It is a most serious part of our life. We are trained in the ways of homemaking and mothering and . . . "

Her voice began to tremble.

"I don't know what will come of me now," she added. "I don't even know where Joseph is."

"Do you love this Joseph?" asked Sabina quietly.

"Love him?"

"Yes. Are the two of you in love?"

"I don't know. I don't suppose I ever thought about it."

"You're betrothed, and you have never thought about whether you're in love with him? That is much different from our customs."

"I love my parents, and I trust them. They know what is best for me."

"That is enough in the matter of marriage?" asked Sabina.

"It is enough. A Jewish girl must love her God and her parents. That love is extended to her husband only after she is married to him."

A shy smile stole over Ursula's face.

"I do feel very special things when Joseph is near me," she whispered to Sabina and Gisela. "I am most fortunate, for he is very handsome."

The girls laughed together at Ursula's joyous but embarrassed confession.

"You are old enough to marry, Sabina," said Gisela. "Is there no one your parents look to for your betrothal?"

Again Sabina thought of Gustav and the misunderstanding between their mothers. The next moment she found her mind going back through the years to that moment with Matthew when she realized how much she cared for him.

Tears filled her eyes at the happy yet bittersweet memory of their last evening together, and the romp they had enjoyed the following morning down underneath the house. The thoughts were filled with such mingled joy and anguish, knowing that she too might never see him again, just as Ursula had said of Joseph. Whenever she remembered, her heart filled so full with many emotions that her eyes overflowed as well.

"Yes," she answered at length. "There is someone I care deeply for."

"Did your parents choose him for you?"

"No," said Sabina. "That is not usually how it is done. But I think they like him almost as much as I do."

"Do tell us about him, Sabina," said Gisela.

"Oh yes—please!" added Ursula.

"What I would mainly say," said Sabina, smiling thoughtfully, "is that I feel so much *myself* with him—just like I do with the two of you. I can laugh and run and have fun and be playful, but I can also talk about serious things. We were so young when we knew each other. I was only sixteen. We had such fun!"

"When you *knew* each other—you make it sound as though you don't know him anymore."

"We haven't seen one another for five years."

"Why?" exclaimed both girls in disbelief.

"Because the war has separated us, just like it has you from Joseph, Ursula. You see, Matthew is an American, and I have no way of knowing if I will ever see him again. He has not written me a letter in three years and—"

Sabina turned away, tears flooding her eyes again and an ache suddenly filling her breast.

Each of the two Jewish girls reached out a hand to place on Sabina's arm.

After a moment, Sabina took a deep breath, sniffed, and wiped her eyes and nose.

"But I too am lucky," she said, forcing a bright smile. "Matthew is also very handsome!"

The girls all giggled with the radiant and innocent joy that only bubbles forth from the pure in heart.

❧ 84 ❧
Gustav Visits

Later that same afternoon the roar of a large automobile sounded, emerging onto the driveway of *Lebenshaus.*

From their vantage point on the first floor where they were in the midst of preparing several of the guest rooms for potential new arrivals, Marion and Heidi glanced out the window and down below to see the cause of the commotion.

The moment the driver stepped out of the car, Marion sucked in a breath of air. "Gustav!" she breathed.

It took her but another second to gather her wits.

"Heidi," she said, trying to sound calm, though her voice gave away her fear, "get all the guests into their rooms—immediately! Keep them silent. Listen for the bell in case there is need to take shelter in the hidden chambers. Make haste!"

With the words Marion flew from the room to find her daughter.

Sabina was in the guest parlor with Ulrike Kropf and the two Wissen girls. They all glanced up with astonishment the instant Marion burst through the door.

"Sabina—come with me! The rest of you, take the back stairs to your rooms immediately!"

Already Marion was leaving the room. Sabina sprang after her.

"Gustav is here, Sabina," said Marion, hastening down the hallway with Sabina doing her best to keep pace. "He drove up only a moment ago. Keep him outside. However you can, whatever you have to do, don't let him inside if you can help it! We will try to get everyone hidden."

"Where's Papa?"

"Out in the fields. I'll go for him as soon as I can."

Marion turned and ran up the library stairs to the second floor, while Sabina hastened on along the corridor and down the grand staircase. She arrived at the ground floor just as the front bell sounded.

She paused a moment or two, took a couple of deep breaths

to calm her agitation, then opened the door and stepped out, almost in the same motion, closing the door behind herself.

"Gustav," she said brightly, "how nice to see you."

"*Guten Tag*, Sabina," he said, stepping back as she exited so forcefully. "You are . . . on your way someplace?" he added with uncertainty. In truth, he was more taken aback by her friendly tone than by the peculiar way in which she had so hastily answered his ring and nearly flown out the door.

"No," she replied.

"You seem . . . out of breath."

"Do I? I have just been—uh—cleaning my room."

Gustav apparently considered a reply, thought better of it, then said, "I am home for a few days, and I wanted to visit you. May we go in and sit down?"

"Oh, Gustav, it's such a grand day—I'd rather stay outside. Would you like to walk in the garden?"

As she spoke, Sabina began wandering away from the house. Gustav followed, hardly about to refuse. Sabina hadn't treated him with such friendliness in years! Such a walk would fit in with his plans admirably—it was just why he had come!

He quickly caught up with her, and as they walked around the west wing he put his arm confidently around her shoulder.

Sabina squirmed out from under its reptilian weight and stepped away, continuing to walk but her face growing red.

Affronted, Gustav glanced toward her.

"What was that for?" he said.

"I could ask the same of you," she rejoined, not without tartness.

"Come, Sabina," he replied with a smile of bravado, "we are adults now. You don't have to be afraid of me."

"I am not afraid."

"Then why so timid?"

"Because I don't want you thinking you can be so familiar with me."

"Are you still upset over the business of the rose at my birthday?" he laughed.

"No more than with your putting your arm around me." Sabina was doing her best to keep annoyance from getting the better of her. Whatever she might say to the contrary, she knew well enough that Gustav was indeed a dangerous young man. She must watch herself.

"A rose . . . my arm—what are you so nervous about, Sabina? Do you still refuse to look realistically at the inevitability of being my wife?"

"Inevitability," repeated Sabina. She did not want to become angry. Yet she was determined to put a stop to her neighbor's profound misunderstanding. "You're the one who has to look at it realistically, Gustav. I have no intention of becoming your wife."

"*Ach*, Sabina," exclaimed Gustav, "don't be a fool. Are you so blind? Don't you see that I have become an important man?"

"That changes nothing."

"What is it—do you think you're in love with that ridiculous American? Ha, ha, ha!" Gustav roared in cocky laughter.

"You leave Matthew out of it!" she snapped.

"*Ah, meine leibe Fräulein,*" he chided with a cunning glint in his eye, "so the flames do still burn." This would make his final victory over her all the sweeter!

"If it fell into the wrong hands," he went on, "the information that you are an American sympathizer could be, uh, shall we say, very awkward for you and your family. Spies for our enemies are shot for treason, you know."

"We are not American sympathizers," said Sabina defensively, bringing her emotions gradually back under control. The mention of Matthew's name brought enough pain to subdue her spirits.

"You maintain no contacts with your American friend?"

"I have heard nothing from Matthew in three years," replied Sabina.

Gustav detected the hurt in her voice. It stabbed through his ego like a knife. But he was too proud, and too skilled in the ways of his Gestapo colleagues, to allow it to show. The mere momentary twitch of his upper lip divulged his pain at knowing the American had a home in Sabina's heart, but he was careful to say nothing to betray himself.

Almost the next instant, however, his lip curled in arrogant remembrance of his encounter with the cowardly diplomat's son at his father's villa. *What do I care*, he said to himself. *We*

will bury America, and her lover with them all! I will be the one who
will possess the vixen in the end!

"Please, Gustav," said Sabina, stopping. "I think I've had enough of a walk for today. I don't feel like going to the garden."

"But I *do*, Sabina," he replied, suddenly more Gestapo agent than friend and suitor.

"Please, Gustav—"

"In fact, I insist," he said, taking her arm and pressing her forward into motion again. "There is a certain part of your father's garden I am most anxious to see."

Realizing it was futile to refuse him, Sabina compliantly followed Gustav down the hill and under the arch. Nauseated by the very thought of his presence desecrating her father's roses, she attempted to lead him along the path that led around the western border. But Gustav was insistent about their course. As little as he knew of the garden, he seemed to know just where he wanted to go. With horror, suddenly Sabina realized they were in the middle of her father and mother's special place, where she had been that very morning with Gisela and Ursula.

It only added to her horror to see Gustav take a seat on the bench her father had built for Marion. She couldn't imagine why, but it seemed he had intended to come to this very spot!

"An interesting array of plants around us here," he said after perusing the small plot. "Unless I am mistaken, they are not native to Germany."

"My father has traveled widely and collected many different varieties." The nervousness in Sabina's voice was impossible to mask.

"Where are these particular varieties from?"

"I, uh . . . farther south, I think."

"*South?*" repeated Gustav.

"You know. Where it's warmer."

"Ah, I see," he said, nodding knowingly. He scanned around, then stood up and walked slowly about. Sabina watched, perspiring now far more than the heat of the day would account for. He seemed to be taking note of her father's small brass emblems too!

I've got to get him away from here, she thought. *No matter what has to be done to get his eyes off Papa's signs!*

She stood also, as if a new idea had suddenly occurred to her.

"Would you like to see my father's rose garden?" she asked. "It is the most special place of all for him."

Slowly Gustav glanced this way and that, trying to absorb what he saw. He had noted Sabina's agitation and knew there must be more reason for it than met the eye. He would put the pieces together later. For the present, he would not let her suspect he knew a thing.

"Yes, that would be nice," he said. "I would like to see your father's roses."

He did not even realize until later that he had forgotten to ask about the two girls he had seen. *No matter,* he thought. He had discovered what he needed to.

∾ 85 ∾

Gustav Makes a Discovery

This time as he made his way along the dirt tractor paths through the fields, Gustav was perfectly sober. He was no impressionable boy on his return from an evening listening to a Nazi recruiting diatribe. Now *he* was the highest-ranking Gestapo agent in this whole area, and he was on a secret mission that could mean—well, if he was right, it would be of huge importance!

He would know soon enough.

He struck a match and glanced down at his watch. It was two-thirty in the morning.

He threw down the flickering light, ground it into the dirt with his boot, then continued on.

Finally reaching the Dortmann estate, he who had traversed this way many times as a neighbor now began the long ascent up the hill as a spying midnight enemy.

He approached from the north, walked in the dim light of the cloud-enshrouded moon around the vegetable garden, found the east path, circled around the house, past the oak tree, arriving at length under the stone arch entryway into *Der Frühlingsgarten.*

He paused and glanced back, up across the courtyard and at the silent stone faces of the house's two adjoining wings.

How many times had he sat in the hunter's box in the woods, scanning those very walls with his binoculars for any sight of Sabina, staring sometimes for hours at her window and the balcony to catch but a momentary glimpse of her figure?

Now her window was dark. Behind it she lay in her bed sleeping. He needn't waste his time gazing at her window now and longing for her who lived behind it. Those days were past. He could put his schoolboy fantasies behind him. He was a man now. It was a man's game . . . and he was about to walk off with the prize!

It sent a strange thrill through his frame to stand here, alone in the darkness, and to realize that at last he had them all in the power of his grasp—Sabina, her proud father, the whole lot of them!

And they yet knew nothing of it.

Here he stood, in the very heart of the baron's empire, about to enter the depths of his garden itself, and up there the pompous fool slept, having no idea that his precious secret had been found out and that it was all about to come down on top of him!

He smiled at the irony of it.

He, Gustav von Schmundt, would soon possess all the power he needed to lay claim to the treasured rose garden and the entire estate von Dortmann, as well as the most prized jewel in all the region—the hand of the baron's daughter!

He cast about him a final gaze, unable to keep the feeling of triumphant inner satisfaction from widening his smile still further, then turned and, walking beneath the stone arch, plunged into the sacred precincts of Baron von Dortmann's Spring Garden.

This was no pleasure tour. Gustav knew exactly where he was going and what he was after. It wouldn't take him long to confirm what he had suspected since earlier in the afternoon.

A noise in the night suddenly arrested his step.

He stiffened, ears perking up. It sounded like it had come

from nearby, a shuffling sound followed by a thud. Now all was still again.

He stood several moments more, then hastened in the direction of the sound. Quickly becoming confused in the maze of paths, however, he lost his bearing on just where he thought he had heard it coming from.

Again he stopped. The night was silent.

It must have been an animal, perhaps a cow shuffling about, down in one of the barns.

He turned and attempted to retrace his steps and pick up his former direction.

In two or three minutes, walking through the shadowy pathways, he arrived at the place where he and Sabina had spoken together earlier.

He took out his small lantern and lit it, then began to examine the plants and the tiny brass labels beside each of them.

Crown of thorns, a reminder of our Savior, read one. *Hebrew herb garden. The sacred olive tree of Israel . . .*

It was exactly as he had thought—all the plants in this area were from Palestine!

The baron was a greater fool than he had ever imagined! To leave the incriminating words out there for anyone to see!

He sat down on the bench he had occupied earlier in the day. This was far bigger than just their being Christians and connected with the Bonhoeffer fellow.

This obsessive interest in what they called the Holy Land opened the whole scheme to plain view. The Dortmanns' interest was in Jews as well! They were probably involved with the very network Korsch was so determined to penetrate!

There could be no doubt: They were Jewish sympathizers!

Suddenly Gustav remembered the tiny brass plaque he had noticed earlier on the back of this bench itself. He hadn't wanted to look at all these clues too closely for fear of giving away to Sabina what he knew.

He jumped from the bench and turned around.

There it was, old and greening from the weather. He held his lantern down close to it, squinted in the mingled bright and darkness, and read the words: *To my dear Marion, may this small garden from the land of your people be always a reminder of the paths*

*and byways walked by our Lord himself. From your husband, Heinrich
von Dortmann.*

Gustav read the words a second time—*the land of your people
. . . your people . . . your people!*

Suddenly the thought exploded in his mind.

It wasn't merely that these people were Christians, nor that
they possessed an unhealthy interest in the land of Palestine,
nor even that they had connections with the Jewish network.

Gustav's mind reeled with the discovery!

The baron's wife was herself a Jew!

～⌒～

A few minutes later, as Gustav made his way in feverish haste
back down the northern slope of the knoll toward his own
house, a silent file of new arrivals wearily climbed the narrow
circular staircase out of the underground room at the end of the
dirt corridor, up toward the rooms that Heidi, Marion, and
Sabina had earlier prepared for them.

～ 86 ～
Somewhere in Poland

The dark corner of the tavern in a seamy section of the Polish
city of Poznan suited to perfection the purpose of their clandestine appointment. Two tall glasses of dark beer, half-
consumed, sat on the table in front of the two men.

"You said you had information so important it must be
delivered in person," said Korsch.

"For one who has been on the trail of Christians and Jews for
many years, yes, I consider it of great value." Gustav smiled
knowingly. He was young, but he had already learned the ways
of the Gestapo well.

Korsch understood his meaning.

"Don't worry, my clever friend. If you give me what I want,
you will not be forgotten."

"What exactly might you mean?"

"It is my conviction, where we happen to be in the east, that we will see Russians before Americans. I have taken steps to ensure such an occurrence will be to my advantage. If you prove loyal, I may be able to find a place for you."

His words were pregnant with more significance than either man would have admitted. The Reich was collapsing. Any but a fool could see the signs everywhere, though the facade must be kept up so that none could call you a traitor. But among the more practically minded, a desperation had begun to set in to see what might exist on the horizon with which one could line one's future pockets.

"I don't much like the idea of having to do with the Russians," said Gustav.

Now it was Korsch's turn to smile with a knowing grin. He too possessed useful information, though for the present his own lineage was best kept from the count's son.

"We may have no choice," rejoined Korsch, "if we hope to survive."

"You have contacts?"

Korsch nodded.

"High enough to keep you from prosecution if the war should go against us?"

"Yes—high enough."

"Then perhaps, for such assurances, I will give you what I have. But there is one thing more I want."

Korsch laughed. "I know, you have made no secret about it. If I get what I want, I will make sure you get the girl."

"She must not be harmed."

"I still know nothing of why you are here, or why you would think harm would come to her."

"Just give me your assurance, and agree to allow me to be part of the raid."

"What raid?"

"You will see. Give me your word."

"All right, all right," laughed Korsch. "You are a sentimental sop, Schmundt! You've wasted enough of my time with all this—what do you have to tell me?"

Gustav took a long swallow of beer from the glass in front of him, set it down with deliberation, then began.

"You were tracking the Bonhoeffer fellow for some time," said Gustav. "My first assignment from you, in addition to the Jewish problem, was to get you information on him through the neighbor of my father, Baron von Dortmann."

Korsch nodded, eyebrows gathering toward one another in deep listening intensity. "Once we had him in prison," he said, "and his underground organization shut down, that aspect of our activity was no longer necessary. I thought you understood that I wanted you exclusively working with me on the tracking of Rabbi Wissen."

"I have done as you have instructed," rejoined Gustav, "but because of the proximity of the two estates, and my interest in the baron's affairs—"

"Your interest in his daughter, don't you mean?" interrupted Korsch.

"Perhaps you are right," consented Gustav. "In any event, information indicates that the underground Christian organization is not shut down at all."

"What! And you said nothing to me?"

"I have only just learned these things," said Gustav. "I came directly to you the moment I was sure."

"Go on."

"Bonhoeffer and the baron had dealings together. The baron was a frequent visitor, as you yourself told me, at the seminary nearby. He admitted to you at my own party that he and the pastor had an ongoing relationship. When the one seminary was closed down, other illegal training centers opened not far away. But Bonhoeffer scarcely had to do with them. He was never there. You were unable to lay a hand on him. Someone had to be in charge of their operation. Bonhoeffer disappeared completely, left the country, and for more than a year has been in prison. But the underground Christian activity has not stopped in that time."

Gustav paused for effect.

"It is my conviction, Herr Korsch," he went on slowly, "that Baron von Dortmann took Bonhoeffer's place as the leader of the subversive Christian network and has been acting in that capacity all this time."

By now Emil Korsch was listening intently. He said nothing

about Gustav's revelation, trying to absorb the enormous implications. In another moment Gustav went on.

"What if the baron's estate, right there in front of us, has been a center for illegal Christian activity, replacing the seminary at Finkenwalde and deepening the cloak of secrecy even further than Bonhoeffer did? I believe such is exactly the case. Under the guise of his farming, he is bringing in Christians from all over the Reich—training them also in the subversion for which their kind are noted.

"I tell you, Herr Korsch, Baron von Dortmann is a traitor, the very kingpin of this Christian resistance movement. There is no doubt in my mind that he is still in touch somehow with Bonhoeffer and is involved in the wider underground movement."

Again Gustav paused, allowing his superior time to take in this rapid flow of information.

Korsch continued to conceal his reaction. His mind was moving rapidly now, in many directions involving money and Swiss bank accounts and a rekindling of his hatred of Christians and their scheming ways.

He recalled his conversation with the baron at the Schmundt villa. Dortmann was a strange one, he had known that immediately, with such odd and outspokenly treasonous notions about loyalty. Yes, everything the count's son said fit perfectly together.

"In short, Herr Korsch," said Gustav, "I believe Baron Heinrich von Dortmann is a spy, working for the resistance, and as such might well have been part of the recent plot to assassinate the Führer."

The twisted and greedy mind of Emil Korsch was reeling, thinking what a vast wealth this information could bring to his Swiss account.

He might well own Otto's whole bank before he was through! To implicate the banker's brother with Count Stauffenberg and the anti-Hitler plot was of monstrous import—even by innuendo, whether it was true or not!

This information would cost Otto everything, possibly even his life, and would make *him* a rich man.

He might not need to seek asylum in Russia at all! He could

live comfortably in Switzerland, or perhaps South America, for the rest of his life! He would bleed the coward dry!

One thing was certain—he would handle this arrest personally. He would take enormous pleasure in spitting in the face of the pompous Christian aristocrat Heinrich von Dortmann!

All these thoughts ran swiftly through the guileful brain of Emil Korsch in but a few seconds. As quickly as the reaction had come, however, he had stifled it and now showed no trace of emotion. It would not do to let the young fool think the information he'd brought was *too* valuable.

"There is one item more," said Gustav slowly, drawing out his words. He was not quite the fool Korsch considered him. He well knew the turbulence he had set into motion inside the other man's brain and now, in his turn, took pleasure in toying a bit, even with a man so dangerously high in Himmler's estimation as Emil Korsch.

"And what would that be?" said Korsch, trying to sound dispassionate.

"I made a little discovery in the baron's garden."

"In his *garden?*"

"Yes, just a tidbit of information that could perhaps prove useful."

Again he paused for effect.

Korsch was growing weary of the young fool's machinations, but sat patiently waiting.

Gustav told him of the plants he had seen and what they signified.

"So you see, not only are there connections with the Christian underground, but with the Jewish as well . . . "

For once in his life the facial features of Emil Korsch showed instant expression. His eyes shot wide, and his already-pale face turned sallow as a corpse.

Of course!

How could he not have thought of the connection before! All those religious idiots were alike, and they stuck together at such times. The trail of the Jewish network led directly to the home of the banker's brother, Baron Heinrich von Dortmann!

" . . . and the conclusion of the matter," added Gustav with a triumphant flourish, "is nothing less than that the baron's wife is herself a Jew! It is quite possible, *mein Herr*, that the baron's home has been acting as more than a Christian underground center, but has been part of the Jewish escape network as well, helping to move Jews either to the coast or along the routes we suspect that lead down to Switzerland. I suspect there are Jews hiding there right now, even as we speak!"

An evil light dawned over the countenance of Emil Korsch.

The most important thing about this incredible revelation was something the moron Schmundt failed to see the enormity of the significance of. By linking the Christian resistance network to the Jewish network—with the Dortmann estate sitting squarely in the center of them both—the biggest fish of all might have been snagged!

How could he have failed to make the connection before? The direction the traitors had followed since leaving Wloclawek bore in a straight line to the north of Stettin!

At last he had discovered his whereabouts!

Rabbi Wissen was with the baron!

He would nab them all—and the holy stones of divination to boot!

∽ 87 ∾

Heinrich and Marion

The hour was late. The baron and his wife had already been talking together for some time.

The mood between them was somber. The peaceful calm of life as they had known it at *Lebenshaus* had begun drawing to a close that fateful morning when they had stood with their daughter on the balcony listening to the sounds of invasion and destruction in Poland.

Five years had passed since then.

Now a new threshold was about to be crossed, perhaps an eternal one. Both were wise enough to apprehend the potential extent of the sacrifice looming before them.

They sat together on the couch in their sitting room, legs stretched up on an ottoman in front of them, the baron's arm around Marion's shoulder, Marion's head nestled comfortably between his shoulder and chest. They were of the kind who needed no constant flow of words to exchange the flow of their love. They were as content, each in the other's presence, whether silence or tumult, solitude or throng was the accompanying backdrop to their togetherness. They had spent the evening together and had, by mutual accord, quietly relived many of the paths they had trod with one another through the years.

They were in no hurry to retire.

Both were sufficiently worldly-wise in the innocence of their "childship" to realize the import of the time. The eleventh hour for the people of God in Germany was come. The clock continued its fateful clicking toward the black midnight of their destiny.

Heinrich and Marion von Dortmann—son and daughter of the most high God, the God of their mutual father Abraham and all who followed him in the royal lineage of Jesus Christ, firstborn Son of the Father—knew that they could well be sharing their last such intimate earthly moments together.

Neither had spoken for ten minutes. The entire house stood silent. The great clock on the wall opposite slowly ticked off its reminder that the passage of time is no respecter of persons.

"Gustav's visit yesterday bodes ill," the baron said at length, his tone revealing that he had been considering the implications for some time. It was Gustav's presence that had alerted them to the danger about to befall their place of retreat and safety.

"The son of our neighbors is much changed," said Marion.

"They are all changed," added the baron. "The count . . . Ingrid—this dreadful Nazi darkness has consumed even those considered respectable before the war."

Again silence fell. The clock continued to measure out its steady cadence, though neither husband nor wife was aware of its metronomic sound. The solemnity of the occasion drew its curtains down around them.

"We cannot keep our guests any longer," said the baron at length. "To do so will only endanger them."

Marion nodded her assent.

"*Lebenshaus* must always give life. When it can no longer be a *safe* house for those whom the Father sends, we must allow him to care for them otherwise."

"Are there other places?"

"Many. The rabbi and I spent most of the afternoon together discussing possibilities. Aaron worked all day downstairs on identity cards. The network toward the south is well established."

"Can people truly travel so far without discovery?"

"The rabbi was successful in both directions, moving in and out of Switzerland. He says the resistance swells daily with those eager to help Jews escape the Nazi holocaust."

"We have so many to care for, Heinrich."

"Twenty-nine at present, with the new arrivals."

"Can we hope to transport so many to other places of safety, or all the way to Switzerland?"

"Not without the Lord's help, and then only in small groups. We have three automobiles now. Some may have to walk through to Fürstensdorf, where I am confident there will be additional means of transport."

"That is eighteen kilometers."

"At night, through the forest—it could be managed. The pastor there has been at this work longer than we. He works closely with a Catholic priest who has many contacts among monasteries and convents. I have been in touch with both."

"Is that not dangerous?"

"Everything is in code."

"Oh, Heinrich, it all sounds so frightening!"

"These are perilous times. But I am convinced for them to remain here would be more dangerous."

"Do you have everything ready that they would need?"

"Nearly. I have identity cards prepared for all the twenty-nine. I think we have sufficient clothes. I am forging new car registrations so there can be no link to us here. I think we are as prepared as we can be."

The clock struck the hour. Heinrich glanced up. The hands stood at eleven o'clock. It was nearly time for them to retire to their chamber. There was yet a great deal to be done. Tomorrow would be a full day.

He pulled his wife yet closer to him in a squeezing embrace.

"We've had a good life together, Marion," he said at length. "I want you to know I've never felt anything but the deepest gratitude to our Father for the privilege of being your husband."

"Thank you," whispered Marion softly. Quiet tears rose in her eyes. "I could never have wished for a more sensitive, loving husband. You have been more good to me than I deserve."

"There are more facets to this relationship we've shared than on any well-cut diamond. That's what has made my life with you such a treasure."

"How do you mean?"

"We've been lovers in our youth, and lovers ever since. We've been husband and wife, Jew and Gentile joined in that wonderful bond of Christian brother and sister. We've been parents together. We've been privileged to minister hospitality and life to others together. In so many ways our Father has allowed us to be joined, rib to rib, heart to heart, soul to soul."

"You make it sound so poetic, like a storybook romance," said Marion with a soft laugh.

"Sometimes when I become pensive," said the baron, "I think of it exactly that way. Sometimes I fill my journal with such thoughts!"

"I hope no one ever reads it."

"Why, Marion—I was thinking of making a book out of it someday!" joked the baron.

"No—you don't mean it?" she said, halfway alarmed, stretching her head up and looking earnestly into her husband's eyes. The sparkle of fun that danced from them, even in the midst of this most terrible of earthly trials, told her again, as it had so many times before, that she could trust him—with her secrets, with her very life.

Gently she laid her head back down on his great, expansive chest.

"Besides every one of a thousand reasons that I love you," the baron added, serious once more, "you have been the best friend a man could have."

"You harbor no regrets?" she said.

"Not one."

"Not even for the pain I occasionally put you through when I could not trust you?"

"A small price to pay for the honor of sharing life with you."

"You do *me* honor by always regarding me so highly."

"I do regard you."

"I know. I finally believe you. But it remains a mystery. Even through all the ups and downs, you've never been anything but gracious and kind to me."

"It is no mystery to me. A secret, perhaps—but no mystery."

"And what *is* the secret?" said Marion softly, her lips smiling, for she well knew what he would answer.

"The secret of the rose—what else."

"Oh, Heinrich, I do love you. But I am so worried that my past is now endangering—"

"Speak no more of it, my love," interrupted the baron. "We will face the danger as we have faced life's storms—together."

"I feel so safe and protected by you," breathed Marion after a moment or two.

"Our Father will keep us in his hands."

A lengthy silence settled over them once more. Slowly Marion's head moved up and down with the movement of Heinrich's deep-breathing lungs. Nowhere in all the world did either of them feel so contented, she with her head nestled close to his chest, he with his broad arm stretched around her shoulder and waist. In all ways they had grown to be as one, but here was that oneness most deeply and richly felt.

"Do you fear death, Heinrich?" asked Marion at length, her voice barely above a whisper.

The baron sighed deeply and thought a long time before answering.

"I don't know," he said after some time. "I have always prayed to have courage when the moments of greatest confrontation against evil and darkness come."

He paused, his lungs breathing in and out slowly as he pondered the question that had been inwardly occupying more and more of his prayers as omens and portents of the future became more clear.

"Certainly I possess fears," he said. "It would be a lie to say I do not fear death. My flesh of course fears it. You cannot imagine, Marion, what a weak man I feel like inside. So many people look to me for direction and protection and help and guidance. You

and Sabina and so many others over the years—I think sometimes you all consider me as a tower of strength. But I tell you,
deep inside there are times I am just a frightened little boy,
wondering who this grown man is that people call *the baron von
Dortmann*.

"Ah yes . . . I have fears. I wonder what kind of man I will
prove to be when the moment of severest danger comes—a
moment I sense is close at hand. If I did not have you beside
me, and was not able to look into your eyes so that we might
silently say to one another, *All is well . . . we are secure in the shelter of our Father's arms*—if I could not share that with you,
Marion, I think I would crumble from the weight of my fears.

"I cannot say I do not fear death. But I do *not* fear what death
may do to us. Indeed, it can do nothing. It can only touch the
flesh, and that does not concern me. It might be able to separate us for a season. To be apart from you is the greatest injury
death could inflict. But only a brief season. Our Father will
make all things right, and sooner than we think. My belief in
that overarching truth is far stronger than the culmination of all
my temporal fears. My confidence in that right-making enables
me even to endure the thought of having to say *auf Wiedersehen*
to you—until we see each other again! Not even death would
cause me to say *good-bye*."

"Do you think we will have to part, Heinrich?"

"I know not, my love," sighed the baron. "Even if such a trial
should come, there are many who have had to endure worse
these dreadful last years."

"I know you are right."

"If it should come, our Father will keep us in his arms, even
in that."

Heinrich paused, then added, "I love you, Marion, my
Liebchen, my darling. You have been the only love of my life—I
treasure you."

"And I you, Heinrich."

Husband and wife sat several more minutes together, then
silently rose and went to bed.

The clock on the sitting room wall continued to tick. It read
seven minutes till midnight.

❧ 88 ❧
Last Night at *Lebenshaus*

Baron von Dortmann and Rabbi Wissen spent a great deal of the following day together. By mutual consent, they quietly spoke individually to all the community of their little flock throughout the afternoon, agreeing to come together that evening, after supper, as one—Christians and Jews alike—for a shared time of parting, symbolic worship, and prayer.

Once their plans had been laid, the two leaders, along with Sabina, Aaron Abrahams, and Jakob Kropf, spent several hours in the depths of the hidden regions of the house, making all necessary last-minute preparations for departure.

They gathered at eight o'clock in the library, where the baron had earlier instructed that several bookcases be moved so chairs could be brought in. It was the only room, other than the ballroom, large enough for forty—the baron's family, their most trusted servants, and all the extended family of their Jewish guests—to fit comfortably, and its interior location eliminated the necessity for caution in using lights that might have been visible from the outside. A dozen or so candles were set about the room, musty with the scent of knowledge, and their flickering in the still air was further reminder of the antiquity of what they were about to do. Several pitchers of water sat on the floor.

Baron von Dortmann and Rabbi Wissen sat quietly in front. The mood was solemn. When all had gathered and were seated, the baron rose.

"My friends," he said, "I have gathered us all together so that spiritually and symbolically we might bring to a close this portion of life we have shared. Tonight does not represent the culmination of the story for any of us. But I do sense that this particular chapter of the book is about to end.

"Indeed, it *must* end. As I have told those of you who are in my larger family, and as the rabbi has told you friends sharing our home with us, it is my conviction that we are in imminent danger of discovery. It is urgent, therefore, that you guests, you of God's people from that land where our mutual patriarchs walked, you friends whom we have grown to love as our own

. . . it is urgent that you leave us, and that we make provision for you to continue your journey where you will be safer than you henceforth can be here. We have been making and will this night and into the morrow make all needed preparations for such a journey. Communications are already going out to prepare the way, as the Scriptures remind us was the appointed role of the prophet Elijah, and to make straight the paths you will be required to walk."

He paused a moment, then continued.

"There is a heaviness of spirit in such a parting. We all have lived daily for years with the dangers inherent, for most of you because of the mere blood of the Hebrew children that flows in your veins, for the rest of us because of our decision to count ourselves among those who love the people of God.

"At the same time, perhaps there can be a sense of anticipation as well, in view of what lies ahead in the provision and plan of God. It is our hope and prayer that you will be able to retrace the pathways prepared for you by your own rabbi earlier this year, all the way to the safety of Switzerland."

An audible rustle of suppressed gasps, whispers, and sighs went through the room, for the ultimate destination toward which preparations were being made had not been divulged until this very moment.

"I want, therefore, to take these final minutes we have together to share with you, my family and friends, in the most sacred and holy observance that we as Christians experience together. It is appropriate and fitting to do so, in the manner in which our Savior similarly shared with his friends on the night before he was crucified.

"For Jews and Christians to come together in one accord at such a time as this, to mutually participate in Communion and Passover, is perhaps unprecedented. I have not heard of such a gathering in my life. But I ask you all, of both faiths, to put aside differences of doctrine and belief for this brief season, and to open yourselves this night to one another, to our common Hebrew heritage, and to our common God—Yahweh, the Lord—our Father in heaven. We are *all*, at this moment, common pilgrims in the Egypt of a dreadful exile. You who will soon leave this place will go seeking a land of peace and free-dom—truly a land of promise.

"Therefore, we invite you, Jews among us, friends whom we love, though you perhaps cannot share in the symbols of our sacrament, we yet ask you to join us in heart, to join us in prayer, and to join us in worship of our common God. We will be privileged to likewise join with you. And now . . . Rabbi, would you like to share your thoughts?"

ᏛᎥ 89 ᏛᎥ
Betrayal

As he sped along the familiar road toward Niedersdorf, which he had traversed a thousand times in his young life, the emotions surging through the heart of Gustav von Schmundt were unexpected and altogether unfamiliar.

He had personally betrayed not just a mere man, but an enemy of the Reich.

And the betrayal went far beyond that.

The man in question was his neighbor, the man he had played around as a child. For his own thirtyweight in silver, Gustav had turned in the baron, who had given life to the woman he loved. This was the man he hoped to make his father-in-law—even if, as it now appeared, the baron would become so related only posthumously.

He had done the nefarious deed willingly, by his own choice, knowing full well the implications.

He had been a Gestapo agent long enough to know what this night's mission was all about, and what would be its inevitable result. It was not a simple infraction of German law to be a Jew, to marry a Jew, to harbor Jews. There were many laws one could break. But *this* was a crime of treason punishable by only one means when Emil Korsch happened to be involved—instant death. Never did it occur to his twisted mind that he was contemplating committing the same crime himself.

Gustav had done what he had done by an act of his own will. But an unaccustomed feeling of something akin to remorse now attempted to rear its inconvenient and unsought head in what was left of his embryonic conscience.

He hardly knew what to do with the pangs that shot through his gut every minute or two as he bounced silently along in the passenger side of the front seat. He tried to stare into the night with an expressionless dispassion, trademark of the SS. But the loaded rifle sitting in his lap bore down upon his legs every minute with a grim and heavy weight.

ᴄ⹀ 90 ᴄ⹀
The Passover Seder

As Baron von Dortmann resumed his seat, Rabbi Wissen rose, and now stood before the gathering.

"I too have not been in such a setting as this, nor have I heard of one. I will no doubt be roasted myself like a Passover lamb by any of my fellow rabbis who ever hear of what we have done."

A slight ripple of laughter temporarily broke the solemnity of the occasion, though by now moisture had begun to gather in nearly every eye of the band of people who had become so intrinsically bound together.

"We celebrate the Passover in the spring, in our month of Nisan. It is our holiday of newness, of springtime, of rebirth and freedom. However, the event toward which every year's Passover points is the night before our fathers left Egypt, when the angel of death passed over their homes, so that, the next day, they might leave the land of their bondage for the land of Israel. Truly, our beloved countries of both Poland and Germany have become as bitter with the sounds of the suffering of Abraham's children as Egypt of old. There are many angels of death, sent throughout the land by a modern-day pharoah, to seek and kill God's people. We therefore celebrate the Passover now, in remembrance of that time, and in preparation for our own flight.

"When our people left Egypt with Moses, they knew not what lay before them. They knew only that they were escaping a land of death and slavery. Neither do we know what is ahead. There may well be a wilderness before us that we can see no more clearly than they when they embarked. But our God will go before us, as he went before them. And better a wilderness with God than the death camps of the Führer Pharoah."

He paused briefly and glanced over at the baron.

"I would likewise like to invite you, our Christian friends—" and now he glanced back and toward the baron's family and staff—"to join us in what we do. I see this not as a celebration of an event in the past, but, as it was for our fathers in Egypt, as a preparation for God to direct this new angel of death to pass over us as we leave here. We, therefore, invite you, Christians, our hosts, you who have provided for us and protected us and harbored us safe in our journey, to share with us in this Passover supper, this most sacred of *our* holy institutions."

"We will be honored to do so," said the baron where he sat.

Rabbi Wissen turned and walked to the side of the room to a flat table covered with a white linen tablecloth that he and the baron had prepared prior to the meeting. He pulled back the left side of it, revealing a large plate containing what looked to be an odd assortment of food. Beside it sat a basket of bread, a cup of wine, and a small bowl.

"Our own families are aware what this plate signifies, but I will explain it for our new friends," he said, gesturing with a smile toward the Dortmanns and their servants.

"This is our *Seder* plate. As centerpiece to our meal of the paschal lamb, it helps us tell the story of Passover, and we repeat this story every year as Moses taught us—teaching our children to teach their children, so that our traditions might be preserved for all time.

"The Seder plate contains five ingredients, which we have assembled on our plate tonight. *Zroa*—roasted bone, to remind us of the sacrifice our people offered to God before leaving Egypt. *Baytzah*—hard-cooked egg, a symbol of new life, and of the offerings in the temple in Jerusalem. *Maror*—horseradish root or romaine lettuce, whose bitter taste reminds us how bitter it was to be slaves in Egypt. *Horoset*—a mixture of fruit, nuts, and wine that looks like the mortar the Jewish slaves used in the making of bricks during their bondage. And *Karpas*—leafy green parsley to bring springtime to the Seder table."

Again the rabbi glanced toward the baron. "This Seder plate is all the more special," he said, "in that its ingredients have come from the garden and farm of our host. Also we have here a small bowl of salt water, which reminds us of the sea our people had to cross when they escaped from Egypt. And we always prepare a glass of wine to sit next to the plate for Elijah the prophet, whom the baron has already mentioned. Legend says that Elijah may come and visit our Seder meal and take a sip of the wine.

"Then finally, in this last basket, sits the Passover bread, hard and flat as you can see, unleavened. It is called *Matzoh*, because our people left Egypt in such a hurry that there was no time for their bread to rise."

At this point, he glanced toward the baron with a slight nod.

❧ 91 ❧

Unpleasant Thoughts

With every kilometer, the dreaded weapon in Gustav's lap grew heavier and heavier.

He had never killed.

He had seen it done—and had winced inwardly each time death came so close. He had succeeded tolerably well in masking his inner repugnance at what he was forced to witness. He even tried to convince himself that he would grow out of such squeamishness and took every beating or arrest or questioning or raid as fit opportunity to gain more practice in the hardened art of cruelty, which was the stock-in-trade of his Gestapo colleagues.

Never had Gustav met a more frigid specimen of humanity than he who sat beside him at the wheel at this moment.

Emil Korsch had killed. Gustav had seen him do so without so much as a flinch, unless it was the faint flicker of a morbid smile.

Now here they were on the way to the house where he had spent so much time as a youngster. A rifle sat in his lap, a rifle that Korsch would expect him to use.

What would he do if it came to a face-to-face showdown with Baron von Dortmann?

What would he do if it came to a choice between past loyalties and present ones? This was an aspect of the scenario he hadn't foreseen. Which did he want more—whatever future Korsch might be able to give him, or Sabina?

So many thoughts flooded the mind of Gustav von Schmundt at this moment. This was the land of his childhood. Had it really been as innocent as the memory now seemed? Had he in truth played and talked and been on such friendly terms with a man he might actually have to kill?

How could such a thing be?

Was this a terrible dream?

Kill . . . *him!*

Could he pull the trigger? Could he kill Sabina's father?

What would become of Sabina then? He knew her well enough to realize she would sooner die like an animal at Auschwitz than marry her father's murderer!

Yet Korsch would expect nothing less of him.

Not only was his *own* future on the line, perhaps too was his very life. Promotions and benefits did not brightly bode on the horizon for SS agents who balked in the line of duty, especially ones who turned soft on Jews and their sympathizers.

What had he gotten himself into, Gustav wondered.

He was beginning to recognize the landmarks of the countryside. It wouldn't be much farther now!

∽ 92 ∽

The Communion Supper

Unaware of the peril speeding toward them, the baron rose again and walked to the table beside him, folding back the right side of the linen cloth. There sat an identical basket of bread and a large cup of wine.

"We too celebrate this event you have spoken of," said the baron. "Our Lord taught his followers likewise to remember the Passover and to pass the tradition on. When he ate this same Passover feast with his friends, it was a night just such as this, a night of parting, a night when the portent of death hung in the air. He knew his time on earth was through, that his work had reached the fulfillment of its purpose. Therefore, not only was death present, but, through that death, freedom as well.

"So many of our symbols and traditions have common meaning. It is my prayer we can tonight celebrate that unity toward which the things of our Father are always pointing.

"You were taught to do this in remembrance of God's faithfulness. We have been taught to do this in remembrance of his Son. He broke bread with his followers at their last meal together. This will be our spiritual Last Supper, our Passover supper, as my cousin—" he glanced over at the rabbi with a smile—"has expressed it. As Christians we eat the same bread as you, and we drink the wine in remembrance of the blood that was shed."

He paused and looked around the room, flickering in candlelight, knowing full well the import of his words, then added: "Tonight, we will *share* the bread."

He turned back to the table, joined now by the rabbi, where together they folded back the linen cloth in the center of the table to reveal an empty bread basket identical to the two on either side.

Simultaneously the two men picked up their respective baskets, brought them together, then removed the bread from them and placed all of it together in the center basket.

The baron and the rabbi glanced up at one another as the bread mingled together. Their eyes locked for a moment—the enormous, some would say scandalous, significance of what they had just done not lost on anyone in the room. All watched in silent awe, full of the joy of incredulity; each, in his own way, sensing the presence of God's Spirit among them.

The lips of both men broke into smiles, neither able to contain the exhilaration of feeling the walls of division being shattered at such a wonderful moment.

They turned and faced their people, both still smiling broadly.

They walked slowly forward among the seated assembly of family and friends, Jews and Christians, aristocrats and peasants, Poles and Germans, and, as the two servant-hearted men they were, began individually to offer the bread to their people. The rabbi took the basket first and served its contents to each of the baron's family and servants. Then he gave it to the baron, who in his turn now served all the Jews present. There was not a dry eye in the room as, at length, each man slowly and reverently served the other.

The hush of awe that descended over the room was filled with a deeper quiet than mere lack of noise could humanly account for.

The baron now served the wine to the Christians present. When he set the goblet back onto the table in front and once again took his seat beside the rabbi, a long silence of several minutes followed.

Everyone in the room was praying.

Some lips moved in whispered words meant only for the Father. Tears flowed from others. Gradually several of the men sank to their knees and bent their faces to the floor. When at length Baron von Dortmann rose and stood, his face was wet from tears, both of rejoicing and of preparation for his own personal ordeal, which the Spirit told him lay ahead.

He walked to the other side of the room, stooped down, and picked up an empty basin and one of the towels that sat beside them, then poured water from one of the pitchers into it. The rabbi joined him and did likewise.

"There is one final aspect of the supper we Christians recall, which is perhaps the most important of all," he said. "It is the living example of sacrifice."

"It is also highly symbolic in our Jewish tradition," added the rabbi.

"We are told that only in servanthood is greatness achieved in the kingdom of heaven. There is no greater love a man can show than that he lay down his life for his friends. Rabbi—if you please," said the baron, indicating the empty chair.

Rabbi Wissen set down his basin, then took the seat.

Baron von Dortmann got down on his knees, set down his own basin, carefully removed the rabbi's shoes, then proceeded tenderly to wash his feet, gently drying them one at a time with the towel he had placed over his arm.

When he was through, the rabbi took his turn on his knees,

and likewise washed the baron's feet. Every eye was glued to the visible expression of mutual love, yet none seemed prepared for what came next.

Both men rose, then began to move through the rest of the assembly, the two together proceeding to wash the feet of the others, and not stopping until all pairs of feet were clean.

At last, the joint expressions of love, faith, commitment, remembrance, and preparation were completed. The baron and rabbi took their places in front of the others. Each prayed aloud. Then, after a few final words from them both, all rose and sang, first a single stanza of a Christian hymn, then a selection from the Psalter.

Hugs, tears, well-wishing, and good-byes followed. Thirty minutes later, not a single person had left the room.

❧ 93 ❧
Evil Approach

Still they sped along the lonely, deserted country road, toward an intersection where the destinies of many lives would converge.

They were close now—very close. Gustav knew every meter. The light of the full moon above them illuminated the familiar surroundings as if it had been noon.

The terrible moment had nearly arrived.

The rifle began to feel like a hot, searing rod, burning his right hand where it lay loosely across the chassis and grip and trigger. He could feel the sweat beginning to drench his back and armpits, though it was certainly not a warm night. His breath was coming in shorter and shorter increments.

He had to keep his calm! If Korsch even suspected what he was thinking, it would be the end of everything for him.

The car began to slow.

"How much farther?" said a voice.

Gustav continued to stare out the window.

"How much farther!" repeated Korsch angrily.

Coming suddenly to himself, Gustav jerked his head around.

"Oh . . . about a kilometer, *mein Herr,*" he answered. "You will see a clump of trees on the right. The driveway goes between them."

Korsch continued to slow, then turned off the headlights of the car. There was sufficient light to creep along, and there was likely to be a guard posted. Even though no one at the place could hope to hide from him and his troops, Korsch didn't want the cars to be seen sooner than necessary.

He wanted to wrap this thing up neatly. He already had equipment digging a large pit not far from here for disposing of the human refuse.

The three automobiles and four trucks behind him also extinguished their lights on his cue. Korsch had brought plenty of assistance. He had the feeling this was a big operation, and he wasn't about to let a single one of the vermin survive the night.

He hadn't told the milksop sentimentalist next to him any of that, of course. But the girl was a half-Jew herself. They could not let her live any more than the Hebrew mother or the resistance-leading father. If this underling of his was as sharp as he thought, why was he so blind to the obvious with respect to the girl?

There were the trees. Korsch slowed still further, then slowly turned in and began creeping up the steep, curved drive.

Gustav's lungs were laboring now, his chest feeling an increased tightening grip of fear. He *knew* before this night was over he would square off face-to-face against Sabina's father—and either have to kill him or feel a bullet from Korsch's gun in his own back.

Gustav had never believed in premonitions, but now the reality of this one had seized his entire being in a panic from which he could not hope to escape.

❧ 94 ❧

Angel of Death

Emil Korsch knew he had set his plan well.

No one would escape alive.

When they had nearly reached the crest, he stopped. He waited about two minutes. That would give the fifteen men in the last truck time to jump down, spread out and quietly encircle the house, then slowly creep up the hill. Every corner, every exit would be guarded by an armed SS trooper. Two of the men carried searchlights, which, as the cars roared up in front, they would turn on to immediately illuminate the entire back of the house. All his men had orders to shoot to kill.

Now!

Korsch thrust the engine into gear and slammed his foot down on the accelerator. With lights blaring the car screamed upward and onto the flat entryway, sending gravel flying in all directions. He careened wildly forward, braking to a stop, head-lights pinned against the front door.

It took but a few seconds for each of the other cars and the trucks to likewise skid to a stop.

Amid shouts and openings of doors and the sound of booted feet jumping to the ground and running across the gravel to their positions, within seconds the estate von Dortmann, once proud refuge to those in need, stood bathed in the glaring and ominous light of the Nazi Gestapo's eyes.

No more would *Lebenshaus* be a secure hideaway for sojourn-ers in need.

Its secrets had been revealed! The angel of death who now approached vowed that *this* firstborn Dortmann son would soon know the cost of defying his pharaoh.

Emil Korsch stopped and glanced around at the men under his command.

For a brief moment, silence again returned. All was still, heavy feet planted in readiness, rifles poised. The only move-ment was the swirling dust kicked up from the tires still dancing in the glare of the silent headlights.

Then slowly he continued his walk forward toward the door, feet crunching across the dry gravel.

He did not even try the door.

An explosion from his pistol shattered the lock and sent splinters of wood flying. He raised his foot and clubbed it into the door, sending it crashing back with a thudding echo throughout the house.

With a signal from his hand, suddenly the storm troopers behind him sprang into motion. They followed Korsch across the threshold, and within sixty seconds the entire house resounded with the pillaging sounds of violation and plunder.

It did not take long for the verdict to be announced.

From above one of the men called loudly down the stairway to Korsch.

"*Es ist leer, mein Herr!*"

The face of their leader turned ashen with disbelief.

It could not be empty! How could the fox have escaped the net!

"Have you searched every floor, every room?" he demanded. Even as he spoke, he knew it was true. Every light in the place now gave visual evidence that no one was here. The sounds he had expected to hear by now, the sounds of running and scurrying and screaming and shouting—there was none of it. Only the hollow sounds of his own men running about . . . but finding nothing.

"Yes, *mein Herr*," answered the man. "Every floor."

"Continue your search!" shouted Korsch. "They must be here somewhere. These Jew-hiders are fond of fabricating secret rooms and fake walls and secret passageways. Tear the place apart if you have to! I want them! Let me hear the sounds of guns and destruction. If they are not here, then we will leave the place in ruins in case they ever decide to come back!"

Wrath quickly replacing his shock, Korsch stormed through the now-lit corridors and to the rear courtyard, where the contingent of men still stood guard.

"You men," he shouted. "Search every barn, every building on the estate. They may be hiding. Send the fire of your machine guns through the floors and into the rafters and lofts. Take nothing for granted. Blow the buildings apart! Let me know if there are vehicles anywhere."

Immediately ten men charged off toward the outbuildings of the estate.

Already gunfire was exploding throughout the house. Windows shattered, doors were blown off their hinges, every bedroom was turned inside out. It did not take long for the secret bedrooms and hiding places of the second floor to be found.

Korsch was summoned.

His wrath turned to white fury in the discovery that they had indeed located the enemy's lair. Jewish vermin *had* been hidden here! He knew, just like he had two years ago at that place in Wloclawek, that the beds had been warm only a short time before.

In a paroxysm of blinding rage, Korsch sent a spray of gunfire around the small room in which he stood, nearly wounding one of his own men from the ricocheting lumps of lead and sending cloth and feathers and glass flying into the air.

He stormed from the room.

Where was that Schmundt traitor!

He found Gustav at the base of the stairway, still trying to take in the destruction he realized he had himself caused.

Yanking at his collar, Korsch forced him out the door.

"Look, Schmundt," he said, "if I find that you alerted the swine, that you had second thoughts in respect of the girl, you will be a dead man!"

"I swear, *mein Herr*, I am as surprised—"

"Silence, you dog!" shouted Korsch, clipping him against the side of the head. "Where might they have hidden the box?"

"What box?"

"The holy box, you imbecile. The rabbi must have been here!"

"Surely they wouldn't have left it for us—"

"They might have considered it safer to leave than to take. Now where might we look? We don't have all night!"

"The garden!" said Gustav, with sudden inspiration. "It was always the baron's favorite place on the estate!"

Within seconds Gustav was running out the back door, followed by Korsch and ten uniformed SS men.

They met three or four men running up the hill from the direction of the barns.

"There are no vehicles!" one of them said to Korsch. "All the buildings are empty."

A violent string of oaths burst from Korsch's lips. He motioned Gustav to continue where he had been going.

He led straight to the collection of plants where he had made the discovery that led to his betrayal of the baron. He stopped. Korsch and the others came up to him, carrying lanterns and weapons in readiness of arrest. Gustav glanced hurriedly around at the olive and fig and crown of thorns and other reminders of a mount called Olivet.

"He often comes here," said Gustav. "This garden is his favorite place to be alone and pray. I thought there might be a clue to his whereabouts, evidence they had buried the box here or something . . . but I see nothing."

"Bah! You are a fool!" shouted Korsch. "Where else?"

Gustav turned and ran off toward the rose garden. The heavy tramping feet followed, treading over Marion's prized plants, stomping them into the ground. Korsch stopped, then grabbed a machine gun from one of the men, and, as soon as all were out of his way, leveled every remaining reminder of the land of Palestine, which he hated. By the time he caught back up with Gustav, they were standing in the center of the rose garden.

"There is nothing here! What did you expect?" he said to Gustav. Then turning to his men, he added, "Destroy it."

Gustav led back to the house, while behind them gunfire and heavy boots proceeded to make dust and rubble out of what had been one of the most cherished and loved rose gardens in all of Germany.

Realizing by now that the baron had succeeded in mocking them all, Gustav's former pangs of conscience had gone soundly back to sleep and given way to a waking of the demon of pride, never far from the surface in most men. No longer having to face the prospect of killing the baron, anger now rose up to replace the fear he had felt earlier. In complete irrationality, he despised the baron now all the more for making him look the idiot, and by the time they reached the house he was bent with equal passion to find a clue to either his or the box's location.

With the sounds of rampaging destruction crashing and breaking, shattering and clamoring all about them, Gustav led up the stairs two at a time.

"Follow me!" he said to Korsch.

Half a minute later they were standing in the middle of the library.

It took but two or three hasty glances around to reveal that a sizeable gathering had been here, and recently. There were

chairs enough for thirty or more. Food still lay about uneaten,
two half-glasses of wine, basins of water on the floor, with two
or three towels, still damp, draped over the back of a chair. A
seven-tiered candle holder was all he recognized.

Jews had been here all right! And in large numbers!

Methodically trying to make sense of it all, Korsch grabbed
up one of the glasses, downed the contents of wine in a single
gulp, wiped his lips with the back of his hand, then went out
into the hallway in search of one of his men.

"When you are through on this floor," he said, "throw as
many of the books as you can on the floor. Get all the rest of the
men to help you. Then set fire to them."

He left the library, Gustav on his heels.

"I'm going to give you one more chance to save whatever
future you may have left with me," said Korsch, casting upon
his young protégé a steely glare. "Where might we find the
baron's private papers, his files—anything that could tell us
where to find the rabbi?"

"He has a study, an office."

"Why didn't you say so earlier?" roared Korsch. "Lead me to it!"

Gustav did so.

Korsch stormed inside, stood a moment in the middle of the
room, a calm gradually stealing over him in the midst of his
passion. The demonic nature of his sensitivities immediately
sensed the baron's presence, and he began to walk slowly about
the room, knowing that his own master, he whom the baron
called the enemy, would reveal to him what he needed to know.

"Leave me," he said quietly.

Gustav backed away and closed the door.

Finding himself suddenly alone in the house upon which he
had gazed so many times from afar, in the very corridor he had
dreamed of walking, he turned, walked quickly away from the
study, and a moment later stood, hand trembling, opening the
door to Sabina's private chamber.

Slowly he walked inside. It had not been disturbed, though the
light that shone gave evidence that it had been cursorily searched.

A mingling of a thousand sensations rose within him! Every
sight reminded him of Sabina. There was her bed! Her dresser!
Her mirror!

He breathed in deeply, smelling the faint, lingering reminders of her presence.

Making himself wild with fancies, he walked through every centimeter of the room, looking over every trinket, every object to remind him of her, then picked up her pillow and held it close to his face.

Meanwhile, four rooms away, a wicked and cunning smile spread over the rutted face of Emil Korsch.

What looked to be a hand-drawn map of some kind buried amongst some papers on the baron's desk had led him to the envelope now held up to the light.

It really was rather careless of the fool of a baron, he thought to himself, *to leave revealing papers about.* But then he'd probably left in a hurry and hadn't planned on his house being searched.

The letter had obviously not gone through the normal postal channels. But that made it none the less legible.

Korsch squinted. It was a hasty scrawl. But the name on the envelope was clear enough.

Wilhelm Stegerwald, Fürstensdorf.

The villainous grin widened. It may have taken a long time, and a wild goose chase to Switzerland with only incomplete pieces, but at last all the clues fit together.

Now he had the right name *and* the right town!

Stuffing both map and envelope into his pocket, Emil Korsch removed his pistol from its holster, emptied its contents against the baron's desk, leather chair, and through the window, then turned and ran from the room.

Their business in this place was completed!

∽ 95 ∽
Sacrifice

It was a lonely stretch of wood through which the pilgrims made their weary way.

The night had been a long one. They had walked through fields and forests too numerous to remember. Most of the children present had been asleep on their feet for hours. Jakob

Kropf carried his little Angela, and by now most of the men had one of the children in their arms. The rabbi and his family numbered also among the walkers. The danger for these would be greatest for the first twenty-four hours of their flight, the baron had told them, but after that, the journey south might perhaps be one of relative ease. Their Jewish guests, amongst themselves, had discussed and determined who would leave *Lebenshaus* by car and who by foot.

All told, seventeen had gone on foot. Each of the three cars had taken five. The vehicles had taken different routes and were bound for different safe houses, and were hopefully, by this time, many kilometers to the southwest. Those that embarked on foot through the baron's garden, into the wood, and south toward Fürstensdorf, had to try to make the distance before daybreak.

Everything had been arranged. The contact would guide the large troop into the village and to the home of Pastor Stegerwald without detection. Transport by a commercial van owned by the resistance would leave that night with preauthorized bills of lading for Innsbruck, where they would be able to stay at two safe houses for up to a week and then be taken a few at a time across the Swiss border.

The van must leave Fürstensdorf tonight. They had to reach their contact by dawn or all would be lost.

It was not until the three automobiles were safely on their way, and the walkers making last-minute arrangements, that a foreboding disquiet began to come over the baron.

He brought Marion and Sabina to him in his study and closed the door.

"You know I am not one to frequently say that the Lord has spoken to me," he said to an attentive wife and daughter. "But he may be doing so now. I cannot say for certain, but I am feeling a strong urgency that we must leave with the others."

"Leave, Heinrich . . . leave *Lebenshaus?*" said Marion.

"Yes, my dear. Perhaps it is only that we must see them safely through into the hands of the pastor. He sent a map, which Jakob has memorized. But I am yet uneasy. I planned to walk the way with them. Now, however, I feel the two of you must accompany us as well. If we have been discovered, Marion, I must get you to Switzerland."

"What about the servants?" asked Marion.

"They must go back to their own people. To remain here for any of us, for the present, is too dangerous."

The three took hands, prayed together, and then set out to make their last-minute preparations.

During the next hour, Heinrich, Marion, and Sabina went over the house, weepy but strong, saying good-bye to the place they loved so dearly. Would they be back in a day or two . . . or would they see this beloved place of life never again?

Both Sabina and the baron had business in the basement, though her father knew nothing of Sabina's errand to what they had once called the icehouse.

Heinrich locked up his dungeon workplace, where so many secrets had yet to be stored away for another season, then hid the key and returned upstairs. He would never set foot inside Eppie's legendary chamber again, though the memory of his life would live silently on within its hallowed stone walls, awaiting the hour of its second discovery.

∽∾∾

That had been only hours ago. Now, with the night nearly gone, they were already far from home.

Despite the fact that everyone was nearly too exhausted to stand, Baron von Dortmann continued to exhort his foot-dragging charges onward.

As they came out of a thin clump of birch and pine, the first grey hints of dawn showed themselves toward the east. The moon, which had guided their way all night, had set an hour before; its eerie light, to which their eyes had been accustomed, now was gradually replaced by that of the stronger sun moving upward and out of his nightly place of slumber behind the great sphere called earth.

Jakob led the way out of the cover of the trees, with the cloak of darkness slowly lifting its protecting shroud from them.

They made their way along the high bank of a slender stream. He paused every minute or two to glance about, trying to remember the directions in his sleep-starved brain. Behind him walked Baron von Dortmann, the two exchanging words as necessary.

They came to a narrow footbridge across the stream, took it, then continued straight onward through the grassy pasture that lay spread out in front of them. In the distance, the spire of the church of Fürstensdorf and some of its taller buildings could be seen in the grey haze.

They entered a small orchard, walked single file through its trees, then left along its farthest edge, moving at length out of the orchard onto a dirt road, flat and wide, which ran perpendicular to their direction, extending to their right and left in a straight line farther than they could see. Directly across from them, at an angle of some thirty degrees, a narrower dirt road came from the midst of a small but dense wood, across a small open area, then joined the wider roadway.

Their instructions were to cross the wide intersection and walk into the trees by the small road. A hundred meters into the wood, they would be met by the pastor's son, who would lead them safely into the village.

Jakob stepped out onto the dirt of the road, followed by the baron. He stopped and glanced around in all directions, then motioned the others to come.

In the distance, the sound of a car's engine came faintly into hearing.

Indistinct at first, gradually it loudened, then split into the unmistakable sound of two cars.

The baron remained where he was, his ears listening attentively, unconsciously urging the single file of nomads to greater haste. It was clear the automobiles were coming in their direction—and fast.

It might be no more than a local farmer in search of loose livestock. They must make the seconds count regardless. It would not do for this many people to be seen, and what remained of darkness was quickly vanishing.

"Come, Ursula," whispered the baron, "Ulrike . . . Heziah, my friend—we are nearly there . . . keep moving, all of you."

Two huge automobiles rounded a curve in the distance, and suddenly headlights blazed in the pale light and bore down upon them along the straight dirt road.

The band now broke into hurried flight across the narrow road and toward the wood. In the shadowy distance the solitary outline of a figure had emerged amongst the trees and now stood mutely watching as the most feared of Jewish nightmares played itself out before him. Silently the pastor's son prayed for the fugitives—men, women, and children—who were moving as quickly as they could toward him.

It was too late.

They had easily been spotted. The two powerful autos rumbled across the pitted and rutted road with the wild recklessness of a battlefield attack. Their headlights picked out the fleeing forms in front of them in all the naked exposure of their helplessness.

In the pandemonium of mingled charge and retreat, only Heinrich von Dortmann, son of God, stood unmoving and calm between the two. That courage for which he had so earnestly prayed had descended from on high, and the full measure of his sonship was about to be required of him.

Across the road ran the last of his charge. Only two hesitated.

"Heinrich . . . ?" implored Marion, though her tone revealed that she already knew the truth. Her eyes filled with tears.

Suddenly all time stood still. The sounds of racing engines and scurrying feet faded out of the ears of husband, wife, and daughter. The exchange lasted but a few seconds. Yet in after years, all of life seemed concentrated around the holy remembrance of the baron's countenance during this brief time bubble of eternal import.

"Godspeed, Marion," said Heinrich. His voice was soft, but his entire countenance radiated the quiet calm and authority of his elder Brother.

She did not argue, and slowly began backing away.

"Papa . . . come, Papa?" pled Sabina, beginning to divine the meaning of her father's firmly planted steps.

"Go, Sabina," he said, still softly. "Go with your mother."

"Not without you," she cried, bursting into tears.

"Sabina," he said, speaking quickly, more tenderly than she had ever heard him speak. "You know that for those who love, the petals have fragrance. Such is the pleasant portion of the lesson of the roses. It is not so easy to see that sometimes the fragrance of love must come from the thorns. Our Master's crown was not made from fragrant blossoms, my child."

"They will imprison you!"

"*You* will all be free."

"I want you to be free too!"

"I will be free, Sabina. For the Father's children, the *greatest* freedom comes from giving one's life for those you love. Is there any higher truth our Master has taught us? You know it is so."

"Yes, Papa," replied Sabina, tears of anguish, love, and admiration streaming freely down her face.

"Now go, my child, and may God be with you."

"Oh, Papa . . . "

"I will see you again."

"But when?"

"When he wills it to be so."

Even as he said the words, suddenly the roar of approaching immediacy sounded again in his ears. The bubble was burst. It was time to drink of the cup.

The baron turned directly into the face of the approaching cars and began walking down the middle of the dirt road straight toward them.

The two autos screamed to a skidding circular stop in front of him, sending clouds of choking dust high into the air all about. Even before the engines had sputtered to a stop, all the doors flew open, and within seconds the road was filled with uniformed SS troopers, rifles stretching across the span behind the baron to the woods, their sights poised on the sixteen figures now standing immobilized and in terror.

From the driver's side of the lead car, Emil Korsch burst out onto the dirt, pistol brandished in his hand, eyes afire in the diabolical satisfaction of at last outwitting these Jews and Christians he despised.

A silence, heavy with a multitude of fears and hidden emotions, hung a few seconds in the air, broken only as Gustav got slowly out of the other side of the car, carrying a rifle, but pointing it to the ground.

The only movement was the baron's continued steady step forward toward those who would accuse and arrest him.

After an uncertain pause, Gustav slowly walked toward Sabina and motioned her to him. She backed away toward her mother.

The sound of Korsch's voice prevented Gustav from pressing himself further.

"So, my friend, Baron von Dortmann," he said, a cunning smile across his lips, "we meet again. It seems my reports have been correct, that you are indeed one of the resistance leaders."

The baron said nothing, only stared straight into the eyes of the enemy, continuing to slowly approach him. *Lord God, our Father*, he silently prayed, *blind his eyes, and bind his power to harm your people.*

He turned to gaze behind him one last time toward his family and friends.

"Marion . . . Sabina . . . Heziah," he said, "continue with our people into the wood. Whatever happens to me, keep moving and do not turn back. Do not fear for me."

Yet a moment all was still. Even the tongue of Emil Korsch was stopped.

"Go, I say," the baron repeated. "They will not harm you or follow. None of the men will fire. Now . . . go."

Weeping now in earnest, Marion obeyed, then Sabina and the others continued toward the wood.

The baron turned his gaze back and locked his eyes upon those of Emil Korsch.

"Stop!" cried Korsch, but the word sounded hollow and uncertain.

"You may not prevent them," said the baron. "They are under my orders to go." Slowly he walked straight up to Korsch and stood in front of him. "It is me you want," he said softly.

"Stop them!" Korsch cried to his men. "Schmundt, I order you to kill this man!"

Turning in the direction of the SS troopers and Gustav, in a calm baritone of command, the baron spoke. "By the authority of Jesus Christ, I command you men to hold your fire and to allow those people to go to safety."

"Schmundt, kill this fool!" screamed Korsch.

The baron prayerfully sought the eyes of his young neighbor, who could no more raise the rifle in his hand than if it had weighed five hundred kilos.

Then he cast the penetrating gaze of his eyes again upon Emil Korsch. "Herr Korsch," he said softly, in scarcely more than a whisper, "in the name of the most high God, I command you to hold your tongue. You may arrest me, but you will seek these people no more."

Yet a second he held the eyes of the agent with his command.

Behind him, the sound of running footsteps retreated toward the wood. The baron turned and took several paces toward his wife. Marion stood, the last of the group to flee, heartsick at the terrible parting, weeping but silent.

Heinrich's eyes found hers. They still contained the sparkling smile of life! She saw his lips move in final silent farewell.

Auf Wiedersehen, Liebchen . . . I love you!

Marion's heart smote her, and in great anguish she attempted to return the words.

Heinrich smiled, then turned and again faced the Nazi agent, who stood immobile and mute.

Suddenly the moment was broken.

Korsch grabbed him rudely, threw his arms behind him to bind him, then motioned with his head toward his comrades. The troopers all came toward him, suddenly oblivious to the others, and began beating and striking their prisoner as they dragged him toward the car.

Marion could bear no more!

She turned and fled toward the wood, scarcely able to keep her feet for disconsolate weeping. Already the others were far ahead, had reached the pastor's son, and were being led off the road, into the undergrowth of the wood where they could no more be seen.

৵ 96 ৎ

Freedom

The mouth of the tunnel yawned black against the peak of the high, snow-covered mountain in front of them.

Heziah Wissen and Jakob Kropf, closer brothers now than at any moment in their sojourns of more than two and a half years together, shook the hand of the fellow who had led them up the steep sheep track into the Austrian Alps. From here they would have to continue their journey alone.

They waited until the seven women and girls, and Jakob's nine-year-old son, had caught up and had the chance to regain their breath after the steep climb. Then with his small lantern in front of him, Jakob took the lead and plunged into the abandoned railway tunnel into the heart of the mountain. He was followed by his wife and their seven-year-old daughter, Ursula and Gisela, and Marion and Sabina—Christian hosts for two years, now being cared for in turn by their Jewish friends—with Rabbi Wissen bringing up the rear just behind his wife, Helga.

How fitting for it to end in such a manner, thought the rabbi to himself, as the line ahead of him gradually disappeared into the mouth of the mountain.

The whole of the last several years had been as a long, dark tunnel for the Jews of Europe. None ever knew how long their own personal darkness would last, or whether light would ever come for them again. For most it never had, and the tunnel had ended in death.

Similar thoughts ran through the mind of each of the pilgrims slowly following the sure foot of Jakob Kropf. Each in his own way had been deepened and matured by the last three weeks together, a journey that had lasted longer than first anticipated. They had learned to depend upon one another and love one another, to pray for and trust one another. They had learned all the more the price and value of freedom—and life.

Not far at any moment from their thoughts was the price paid by the one who had made their freedom possible. He was not often spoken about, out of respect for her who it seemed likely was by now his widow. But rarely was there a waking moment when at least one of the ten was not offering up a prayer for the safety and protection of him who had proved himself their servant, even unto the making of the ultimate sacrifice one man can make for another of his kind.

Perhaps the greatest personal impact had been registered upon the two Jewish men—now walking before and behind the small troop—upon whom circumstances had forced a mantle of leadership neither had sought.

This was especially true in the case of Jakob Kropf, a man of peasant upbringing and but scant education, who suddenly found himself arm in arm with one of Europe's leading Jewish rabbis, combining his skills and practical common sense with the rabbi's spiritual wisdom. The two men had grown to love one another in a tight friendship of mutual cause and purpose, to the point where either would without hesitation give his life for the other.

Always before each of their mind's eye was the sobering example of the man who had quite literally given his life that the rest of them might escape. The memory of the baron's willing surrender had elevated in measureless ways the stature of manhood residing within the soul of both Jakob Kropf and Heziah Wissen.

The profundity of the man's Christian faith spoke louder and more forcefully to each with every passing day. The rabbi had never been able to forget the words from the baron's mouth about Christianity *completing* and bringing to *fulfillment* what the law of Judaism had only begun.

The words had struck him at the time. When combined with the growing significance of the baron's action within his memory, a deep truth began to break through upon the learned rabbi: *The baron's very life validated his conviction as to the truth of his Christian testimony.*

It was exactly as the baron had said—his faith was no mere religion to him, but a daily, practical way of *living*. When he had turned into the face of certain death, offering himself in place of wife and daughter, and in place of the rest of them, the reality and truth of his belief was suddenly authenticated more powerfully than anything he had seen come out of the Jewish law in all his years.

Sacrifice of a technical sort was intrinsic to the Jewish system. But not the willing sacrifice of one laying *himself* down for another. What the baron had done was unheard of. The rabbi had never seen anything like it in his life!

Especially in that he had been the one, the *only* innocent among them! Only *he* possessed pure Aryan blood—undefiled. A Gentile, a German of the highest order, a son and descendant of nobility.

That was the astounding factor that blew all reason and intellectual analysis out of consideration like a hot, searing, desert wind.

Everyone else a Jew, including the man's own wife and daughter! All the rest of them guilty in Nazi eyes!

Yet he—the innocent!—had stepped forward, had walked into the Nazis' hands and had let them take him, so that the rest of them—all Jews, all guilty of the Nazi crime of pedigree—might go free.

The thing was too incredible even to contemplate!

Heziah Wissen hadn't slept a wink that night in Fürstensdorf!

Suddenly everything he had heard and thought he believed, everything he had read and written and spoken about the man Jesus whom Christians called the Christ—every word had to be seen in an altogether changed light!

He had seen a man *live* the very servanthood of which Jesus spoke, to the very point of laying down his life for his friends.

He was himself alive because a man took the words of his Master, Jesus, seriously enough to *do* them, and to follow that Master's example.

Heziah had always been taught to believe that the death of Jesus had no meaning beyond that of *any* mortal man's death. After all, death came to everyone eventually. But now he had witnessed, with tears in his aged Jewish eyes, a Christian following in those same ancient footsteps of sacrifice.

Death *could* bring life. He had seen it happen!

The baron's submission corroborated that simple fact! How could he look upon what he had seen and be anything but changed for all time? If the baron then could exemplify—in a *small* earthly way, for a handful of people—the principle of a willing sacrifice giving life, then what might the death of Jesus mean to *all* of mankind . . . if what the Christians had always been saying might possibly be true: that he *was* indeed the Son of God!

How could a Jewish rabbi be thinking such thoughts?

Heziah could not deny that all of a sudden everything had to be examined anew!

Such his brain had been busily doing every waking minute ever since.

The living example of a life truly lived was more powerful than all the books in all the libraries of the world!

He had seen a change come over the countenance of Marion von Dortmann as well.

He knew that the profound truth of what her husband had done was steadily deepening in her heart. Initial grief was being replaced by the reality of how complete his love had always been.

Marion too had spent much of these three weeks recalling his words. So much now came back that they had shared through the years, every word now heavily pregnant with more solemn and eternally substantive meaning. She had always known what a unique man he was. Yet now, in his absence, that special bond they had shared pierced all the deeper into her heart, mingling both the thorns and the blossoms of the red roses they had always shared.

Especially did his words return to the inner ear of Marion's heart that death can do nothing, nor could it separate those who loved and who remained in the hands of the Father.

Her tears were gradually replaced by a quiet, even solemnly smiling expression of *knowing*. For did not something deeper than life or death abide in the quiet chambers of her heart— that greatest of all things which Saint Paul said would stand above even faith and hope in the gallery of eternity?

In the depths of her being she cherished the memory of his sparkling, radiant eyes, and the last sight of his lips calling her his "little darling," with his assurance that he would see her again.

Jakob continued to plod through the darkness, wondering if this tomblike tunnel would ever end. They had been three weeks getting here, and now it seemed the tunnel of their final darkness would last three days!

All at once, far in the distance, he thought he descried a faint glimmer.

He quickened his pace, though he could not go too fast, for the stoney ground beneath their feet was uneven.

There could be no doubt now . . . yes—the light was becoming larger. They were coming to the end of the tunnel!

Behind him he could hear some of the younger ones exclaiming for joy. The light grew, and in a minute or two they would not need his lantern.

They were running now!

There were people at the other end! Six or eight, he couldn't tell. Now it looked like a whole crowd, half a village, was gathered outside the door of the tunnel!

What were they . . . why were they all shouting and waving their arms . . . what was the commotion! They were all yelling . . . were they being warned to go back?

Jakob emerged through the mouth of the tunnel, squinting in the sunlight, shielding his eyes, amid shouts and cheers and great boisterous outpourings of happiness.

Opening his eyes after a moment, he finally found his voice.

"But what is all the excitement?"

"You have made it!" cried a man in peasant garb, running up to shake his hand. "You have arrived . . . you are safe!"

"You mean—"

"Yes—yes, my friend. You are in Switzerland!"

At the word, all the rest of his nine comrades burst into tearful exclamations. Jakob found himself in Ulrike's, then Heziah's, then Sabina's, then Ursula's, then Marion's arms, and before the handshaking and hugging celebrations were through, all ten found themselves in a huge, wide, unifying embrace, quietly weeping and praying.

"We thank you, our God," prayed Heziah, and all the others joined him in expressions of gratefulness to God.

They became aware again of the throng of villagers from the high alpine region who had come to welcome them and were clamoring in what sounded like a hundred voices all about them. Their initial astonishment now turned to bewilderment.

"But who *are* you all?" exclaimed Ulrike Kropf, laughing at the seeming absurdity of her question.

"We are Christians and Jews from the village of Rheinkirkhaus down below," answered a plump lady in peasant dress with a wide, homey smile. "We have come to take you home with us, to feed you and find you places to stay."

"But how did you know we were coming?" asked Rabbi Wissen, now stepping forward.

"News of your journey preceded you," answered the lady.

"We heard of your escape from the Gestapo. It is all through the underground. We have been waiting and praying anxiously."

"Is . . . *everything* about the incident known?" asked the rabbi with solemn expression.

"Do you mean about the one whom the Nazis captured?"

The rabbi nodded.

"Yes, we have heard the whole story. Oh, but which one of you is Frau von Dortmann?" the plump woman asked, her red cheeks bulging in a wide smile.

Marion stepped forward to her, Sabina at her side.

"There is a message for you," the lady said, taking Marion's hand. "It arrived two days ago. Ever since you left Fürstensdorf, Pastor Stegerwald spread word through his contacts to learn what happened to your husband."

As the woman spoke, notwithstanding her cheery countenance, Marion could not keep from closing her eyes. Sabina took in a deep breath of air and tried to steady herself.

"We received word two days ago—your husband is alive, Frau von Dortmann! They are holding him in prison, but he has not been sent to a concentration camp. No one knows why, but the Nazis are keeping him alive."

Renewed shouts of great joy arose.

Rabbi Wissen and Jakob Kropf found themselves on their knees, each in his own way thanking God for preserving the life of their friend.

Marion and Sabina fell into each other's arms, weeping. They remained there for several minutes, oblivious to all the merriment around them.

At last they released one another.

"He did say that sometimes the fragrance of love must come through the thorns," said Sabina. "Perhaps he was speaking of this moment."

"He said he would not say *good-bye* to me, but *auf Wiedersehen*," added her mother. "At first, I must confess, when I saw them taking him away, I did not believe him. I should have trusted him. Now I see that he was right."

"About what, Mama?" asked Sabina.

"We *will* see him again."

Already some of the villagers were leading their fellow new

arrivals down the hill toward the Swiss village, whose rooftops were visible below them, with no less triumphant fanfare than had they been members of a victorious army, as in truth they were.

Sabina and Marion gazed into one another's eyes. There both saw tears—some of joy, some of deep concern. They embraced, squeezed tightly, then turned and walked down the path toward the hope that awaited them.

WEST FARGO PUBLIC
LIBRARY

~~~

Epilogue

Still the quiet oak rocker creaked slowly back and forth.

Though the time together had been short, there were many memories. She had had *so* much to tell.

But now he grew weary with remembering. The story was long, and he was weak and tired. Recalling her words was his only pleasure, yet his deepest agony. Memory of her face was all he had to live for, yet the one thing he would fain forget.

The recollection was unfinished. But in his condition, even thoughts of happiness were fatiguing.

He lifted the small box once more to his nose and drew in another tired breath from the melancholy fragrance of the dried petals, then set it again on his lap.

He closed his eyes and leaned back in the chair.

He would remember more another time.

In a few moments he was asleep.

❧❧❧
Note on Dietrich Bonhoeffer

I recognize the danger of fictionalizing the events of any real man or woman's life. Inaccuracies of both fact and motive are able to creep in unawares in the format of a story. I found, however, in researching both the period and that region of Germany (now Poland) once known as Pomerania, that Bonhoeffer could not be kept out of the events engulfing the Dortmann estate. Not only was *Lebenshaus* so close in proximity to Finkenwalde (such was the case even before I had heard of Bonhoeffer's seminary), but the baron and the young pastor were of such like spiritual outlook and temperament that it seemed impossible they would not be friends. The further along I got in the story and research, the more I found, as described in the introduction, that Bonhoeffer himself was turning out to be the unexpected personality who—unknown even to me as the author!—was proceeding to intrude himself onto the pages at every turn. Indeed, I came to feel, and feel such more strongly than ever, that the saga of brave and committed evangelical believers in Germany during the Second World War cannot in any accurate way be told *without* the large, looming presence of Dietrich Bonhoeffer playing a pivotal role. I knew about him but scantly when undertaking this project. I find the admiration and honor I feel toward him now to be equal to what I feel toward any other single man of God. It is my conviction we all owe him a tremendous debt for his example, and I have been changed by my encounter in the spirit with this brother who gave his life rather than water down or relinquish what he knew was true. In any event, the conversations between Bonhoeffer and Baron von Dortmann are, of course, fictional, as is Bonhoeffer's visit to *Lebenshaus*. All other data—his movements, dates of his brief biography, places, quotes from his writings, dates of his books, facts about the Confessing Church, speeches and articles, etc.—is exactly factual as near as I have been able to determine. Where I have inadvertently erred, either in spirit or in fact, I humbly apologize, both to his memory and to the friends of his still alive today. My intent by including Dietrich Bonhoeffer by name in *The Eleventh Hour* is only to honor him and give him what I consider his rightful stature in the history of European evangelicalism in this century.

∽ᴄᴥ

About the Author

Californian Michael Phillips began his distinguished writing career in the 1970s. He came to widespread public attention in the early 1980s for his efforts to reacquaint the public with Victorian novelist George MacDonald. Phillips is recognized as the man most responsible for the current worldwide renaissance of interest in the once-forgotten Scotsman and one of the world's foremost experts of MacDonald. After beginning his work redacting and republishing the works of MacDonald, Phillips embarked on his own career writing fiction. Since that time he has written and cowritten 48 novels and it is primarily as a novelist that he is now known. His critically acclaimed books have been translated into eight foreign languages, have appeared on numerous best-seller lists, and have sold more than six million copies. Phillips is today considered by many as the heir apparent to the very MacDonald legacy he has worked so hard to promote in our time. Phillips is also the publisher of the magazine Leben, a periodical dedicated to bold thinking Christianity and the legacy of George MacDonald. Combining all categories that have made up his extremely diverse writing career, Dream of Freedom was Phillips' 100th published work. Phillips and his wife, Judy, make their home in Eureka, California. They also spend a great deal of time in Scotland where they are attempting to increase awareness of MacDonald's work.

Be sure to look for the second book in
The Secret of the Rose series,
A Rose Remembered.
Here is a sample from the first few pages of that book.

∽ 1 ∾
The Land

If anything could be considered timeless amid the passing of life's fleeting hours, surely it was the land.

There were spiritual considerations, of course, that possessed deeper claims to immortality. She knew that.

But on the physical plane, the earth and the fruit it brought forth out of the ground—according to the ancient parable recorded by the gospelist Saint Mark—possessed, like no other aspect of the created universe, links to eternity.

The armies of six millennia of Nebuchadnezzars and Caesars and Alexanders and Napoleons and Hitlers tramped across it, changing its borders, subduing its nations, and slaughtering its inhabitants. But never had they altered by so much as a speck its miraculous power to produce, to recreate, to regenerate itself in the midst of what chaos the men above it wrought upon one another.

Generations came and went. Tribes, clans, families, and races all rose and fell. Life passed into life, as men and women, the great as well as the obscure, returned to the earth as they came.

Yet the land abided, an enduring reality under the gaze of the heavens. Over it the inexorable march of history passed, father to son, mother to daughter, one conquering dynasty giving way to the next—while the earth remained, surviving them all.

Karin Duftblatt let her eyes wander across the countryside out the windows in every direction.

Expansive fields of slowly ripening grain, extending right and left from her gaze, were beginning now to lose the green of their youth in preparation for the deep golden brown of their old age, which would arrive with the harvest later in the year.

It was a tranquil scene, broken here and there by green pastureland or trees, and now and then an uncultivated hillside. How could it now be so peaceful where bombs and blood had such a few short years ago filled the air and covered the ground? How could the land bear such abundant fruit where so much death had once been?

Didn't the land know what holocausts, what crimes against God's creation, it had witnessed?

Oh, but she loved this land! She could not help it, though there were places farther to the north she avoided. Some memories were too painful, even after all this time.

It may not have been the most beautiful of the world's landscapes. But she would always love it, mostly for what the black soil was capable of producing from out of the God-imbued riches of its subterranean depths.

Love the land and its growing things she did, though neither did she begrudge the present focus of her activities in the city. As much as she enjoyed an occasional drive into the countryside like this, she doubted she could live here again. The city may have tended to make its inhabitants cynical and callous, but it also helped her forget the past. Her work was there as well, and because of its importance, she needed to remain in the city.

She glanced about again as she drove, breathing in deeply and then exhaling a melancholy sigh.

Conquering dictators had indeed fought over this particular segment of Eastern Europe's geography. The Huns and Franks and Magyars and Mongols had all tried to subdue it. Napoleon had stretched the reach of his domination this far early in the last century, as had their own mustached Teutonic madman in this. By many names had it been known, this Prussian, Pomeranian plain between the two great and ancient powers of Germany and Russia.

Never, however, had this land been fully its *own*.

Now it possessed borders and a name that hinted at the racial individuality of its people. No one in the world was deceived, however, into thinking that the territory to which had been affixed the name "Poland" was anything but a subject of the new power that had arisen to the east, in the same autocratic tradition of the worst of the world's ancient conquering empires.

Out of the rubble of fascism's defeat had arisen the spectre called communism, whose shadow now, sixteen years later, blanketed half of two continents. Its persecution was not so visible. No less lethal, however, were the results.

If a handful of brave souls could not by themselves prevent the silent and insidious carnage, they might at least be able to make it known to the rest of the world.

Such was the mission to which she and the man she was on her way to meet had given themselves.

Ordinarily she would have sent another of her people. It was a long drive from her home in East Berlin, halfway across Poland. But word had come that this delivery was unlike any before it, and it must be managed by as few hands as possible.

Thus she had decided to make the pickup herself and return personally to the city with the evidence they had so long sought.

The American Dreams Series

*Best-selling author Michael Phillips brings
readers an epic series of love and sacrifice leading
up to the turbulent Civil War.*

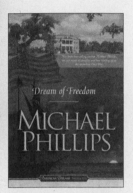

Dream of Freedom

In the midst of a nation's turmoil, a few
will stand. A few will fight. And one man
will make a decision that has the power to
change his family and the South forever.

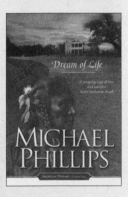

Dream of Life

Secession has begun. Loyalties and families
are divided. And every man must decide for
himself the true cost of freedom.

BOOK 3 COMING SUMMER 2007!

have you visited
tyndalefiction.com
lately?

Only there can you find:

→ books hot off the press

→ first chapter excerpts

→ inside scoops on your
favorite authors

→ author interviews

→ contests

→ fun facts

→ and much more!

Sign up for your **free** newsletter!

Visit us today at: **tyndalefiction.com**

Tyndale fiction does more than entertain.

→ *It touches the heart.*

→ *It stirs the soul.*

→ *It changes lives.*

That's why Tyndale is so committed to being first in fiction!

TYNDALE FICTION